Tremble and Burn

Anna Furtado

*Yellow Rose Books
by Regal Crest*

Copyright © 2017 by Anna Furtado

All rights reserved. No part of this publication may be reproduced, transmitted in any form or by any means, electronic or mechanical, including photocopy, recording, or any information storage and retrieval system, without permission in writing from the publisher. The characters, incidents and dialogue herein are fictional and any resemblance to actual events or persons, living or dead, is purely coincidental.

ISBN 978-1-61929-354-0

First Edition 2017

9 8 7 6 5 4 3 2 1

Cover design by AcornGraphics

Published by:

Regal Crest Enterprises

Find us on the World Wide Web at
http://www.regalcrest.biz

Published in the United States of America

Acknowledgments

Beta readers make initial drafts more coherent and readable. Thank you, Earlene and Nancy. Final readers make sure the story going to print is the best possible. Thank you, Earlene and Nat. Publishers and editors work tirelessly behind the scenes. Thank you, Cathy and Patty. Cover artist creations are like pollen to reader-bees. Thank you, Ann McMan. Finally, you, the reader, make it all worthwhile. Thank you!

Dedication

For the women and men who lived, worked, and survived, for those who gave their lives as a result of the 1906 San Francisco earthquake and fire — and for ethnic minorities, whose struggle for equality continues.

Chapter One

December 5, 1905

STEAM BILLOWED FROM around the behemoth engine and moved along the station platform in bulbous clouds. From out of the swirling white steam, Doctor Elizabeth Kellogg appeared carrying a small suitcase in one hand and a leather medical bag in the other. Relief filled her as she let realization sink in—she was finally at the end of her long journey from Baltimore. Her troubles were behind her.

Someone called her name. Directly ahead of her, standing near the station doorway, a woman in a long coat and a wide, ornate hat, its brim filled with flowers, gestured with her gloved hand. Elizabeth thought the wide sweeping motion above her head might send the hat flying, but it only flapped a little and managed to stay in place.

"Doctor Kellogg. Doctor Kellogg, over here."

Elizabeth stepped toward her. Beside the woman, a slight young man in a beautiful brocade jacket of red and gold stood perfectly still, hands wrapped in his sleeves and crossed over his chest. The woman's hat cast a shadow so wide, it darkened his face, leaving Elizabeth without benefit of reading his expression.

Elizabeth walked toward the unlikely pair. When she reached them, the woman said, "Doctor Kellogg, welcome to San Francisco. I trust your journey was pleasant?"

She wouldn't complain at the length of the journey. Her discomfort was nothing compared to living with the Sword of Damocles her brother left hanging over her head for the past year. She was here now. She'd escaped his threats and intimidations. However, she only knew this woman through Mrs. Stockton's letter, so she had no intention of expressing relief at reaching her destination.

"Pleasant enough," she said, "thank you."

"I'm Mrs. Rosemont. Mrs. Stockton wrote I would be meeting you. Please, call me Amelia." She turned toward her companion. "Quan Luck, take Doctor Kellogg's bags."

Quan Luck reached for the bags, but Elizabeth held out the valise for him.

"He can carry both your bags without any trouble, Doctor Kellogg."

"I prefer carrying my medical bag myself, Mrs. Rosemont—Amelia."

Elizabeth made eye contact with the young man. His eyes darted toward his hands as they gripped the leather handles of her case.

"Thank you, Quan Luck."

He said nothing, but she thought she detected a small smile appear across his lips. She turned her attention back to Amelia and said, "How is Mrs. Stockton doing? Is there anything I can do for her?"

"I think time and age are beginning to catch up with her. Although her body doesn't allow her to move about like she used to, her mind is still as quick as ever and her causes are still uppermost in her mind. I can't say if she'll avail herself of your experience, doctor, but if she does, she'll do it in her own time. By the way, I've already spoken to the station master. He will have your trunks delivered later this afternoon. It's all taken care of."

She gestured toward the end of the platform and a waiting carriage. "There's our transport. After you, doctor. We'll go straight to the house we have procured for you. We think it's well suited for your needs. It was owned by a doctor who recently retired to his summer home on the Peninsula. While he was here he used the San Francisco house as you will, for both living quarters and as a clinic."

As they wove their way around passengers and platform workers toward the conveyance, Elizabeth said, "Your group has been most kind in seeing to my needs. I'm eager to get settled and begin my practice."

"Oh, you'll have plenty of time for settling in, my dear. Mrs. Stockton has given strict orders we're to allow you time to become accustomed with your new home and surroundings. She insists you be able to get to know the city and enjoy the upcoming holiday. You are not to start your duties in earnest until after the New Year begins. Mine is the first of many Christmas galas taking place around the city by members of our group, and by attending some of them, you'll be able to meet us and familiarize yourself with our causes, which we already know align with some of your own aspirations."

As they approached the carriage, the driver, dressed in smart, black livery and wearing a short top hat, disembarked and helped them into the seat behind his. When Elizabeth realized Quan Luck didn't get into the seat beside the driver, she questioned her companion.

"Mrs. Rosemont, where is Quan Luck?"

"Oh, he'll ride in the back—and please, dear, call me

Amelia," she insisted again.

"All right, Amelia. Why is he not riding with your driver?"

Amelia wrinkled her nose, but managed to suppress her look of distain a fraction of a second later. "Oh, he'll be fine, dear. He's looking after your bag in the back."

The driver gave the horse the command to move out. Elizabeth turned around and peered through the small opening in the rear of the carriage. Quan Luck sat balanced on the narrow baggage platform at the back, her bag tucked firmly under his arm. The already precarious seat was made even more dangerous as they bumped over the rutted street. She saw his white knuckled grip on the edge of the platform and decided it best to keep her opinion and her irritation at the young man's treatment to herself.

When she composed herself, she turned back to Amelia and said, "How long has Quan Luck worked for you?"

"A few months. He's not in my regular employ. I use him on occasion for deliveries and such things. Actually, he works for a friend of Mrs. Stockton, a Miss Margaret Weston. She's a photographer who does portraiture out of a shop on Market Street. You'll meet her during some of our Christmas gatherings as many of us engage her to take photographs of our attendees during the celebrations. She is a dear."

Elizabeth wondered why her endearment didn't strike her as genuine. "I'll look forward to meeting her, then," Elizabeth said. And I hope she treats Quan Luck with more dignity than you afford him. She decided she didn't know Amelia Rosemont well enough to give voice to such a thought...yet.

The carriage jerked into a turn and made slow progress, vibrating over the hard-packed street. They traveled away from the bustle of the train station to the chaos of the main thoroughfare of San Francisco — Market Street, Amelia informed her.

Carts and wagons moved up and down the road with little organization to their pattern. Horses chuffed and neighed. An occasional automobile wove around the crowd. People ran hither and yon across small breaks in the traffic, holding onto hats as they dashed between vehicles, gripping parcels in their arms. Traffic thinned as they reached a wide street and turned onto it. The horse strained a little as they made their way up the incline.

"Van Ness Avenue," Amelia informed her. "Your home is right up there." She pointed up the street to the row of homes ahead of her, but Elizabeth had no idea which one would be hers.

They were jostled by an uneven piece of road and Elizabeth glanced out the back of the carriage to make sure Quan Luck hadn't fallen off. Amelia said, "Your bag will be fine back there, doctor, have no fear."

Elizabeth stared at her, wondering how long she would be able to hold her tongue.

The carriage came to a halt beside a charming gray clapboard, two-story house with a small front porch trimmed with the popular gingerbread. Elizabeth smiled. This would do nicely. "It's lovely," she said.

Amelia looked at her, pleased. "I'm glad you like it. Let's go in, shall we?"

The driver set out the weight tied to a thick rope, the anchor to slow the horse should it decide to move without being instructed to do so. Then he jumped down and jammed a chuck under the back wheel before offering a hand to his passengers for them to disembark. Quan Luck came up behind them holding Elizabeth's bag. He stared down at his feet until they moved toward the house, then he followed behind them.

When they reached the front door, Amelia opened it and turned. "That will be all, Quan Luck. You can leave the bag inside the door and return to your regular duties."

He waited for them to enter the long foyer and placed the bag inside. As he turned to go, Elizabeth said, "Thank you, Quan Luck." She lowered her voice and added, "I'm sorry you had to bear such an uncomfortable ride."

For the first time, he made eye contact with her, surprise registering in his dark eyes. In an instant, he brought his emotions back under control, showing nothing but a serious expression. His thin lips pulled from a slight smile back to a straight line, erasing his satisfaction at her acknowledgment of the treatment he had endured. He looked down at the floor, bowed, and without saying a word, stepped back out onto the porch and closed the front door without a sound.

In the hallway, oblivious to her own callousness, Amelia pointed up a long stairway. "Your living quarters are up those stairs. I'll leave you to explore that section of the house on your own. Down here," she gestured along the hallway, "you'll find an office, an examination room, and a waiting area."

They walked toward the open door and stepped into a small waiting room. Several matching chairs lined up around the room. Windows, covered in dark, heavy drapes, gave the room a formal, almost oppressive, look. She would have to see how she could make the room more comfortable, more appealing to the women who would come here to consult with her for their medical needs.

Amelia led her to the next room. Elizabeth took in the wall of glass-fronted metal cabinets, plenty of room for supplies and medicines. The room looked crisp and clean. The accompanying enclosed lower cabinets, painted white, glowed in the sunlight streaming through two tall windows. An examination table sat in the middle of the room with a small metal table for instruments beside it. Under the table, she spied the enamel bucket for refuse. The tall windows in the room were also covered in thick drapes, which had been drawn back to allow light into the room. Sheer curtains would afford privacy while letting in light and making the room seem less oppressive to already anxious patients, she noted.

"This is a well outfitted examination room. It will suit the needs of my patients well." With a small adjustment.

Once again, Amelia smiled. "We hoped it would. It was fortuitous the doctor who lived here retired when he did. He moved to a small farm outside of San Mateo down on the Peninsula. He's a good friend of Mrs. Stockton, so when she found out he would be looking for someone to buy the house, she procured it for your use. Of course, the doctor was pleased to know there would be another doctor taking his place in the district."

They walked out of the examining room and into the adjacent office. A large oak desk faced the door and took up half the room. Pushed under the desk was a padded leather chair, which looked quite comfortable. Another wall of glassed-in cabinets at eye level, this time finished in rich oak to match the desk, lined one wall. Below them, a shelf where Elizabeth imagined she could put her medical books for easy access. Beneath the ledge, enclosed cabinets with doors and drawers would serve her storage purposes. Gas lamps dotted the walls opposite the cabinets and on each side of the entry door, promising a decent amount of light for writing reports, along with the lamp sitting on the desk.

Elizabeth nodded her pleasure as she glanced around the room. "This is perfect."

When she noticed another door at the far end of the room, she asked, "And this door? Where does it lead?"

"To a small kitchen. There's a full kitchen upstairs in your living quarters, but this one," she started toward the door, "is enough to make a cup of tea or to prepare a little lunch during the day."

Elizabeth stepped into the tiny room and looked around. "Yes, it's small, but functional."

"There's also a storage closet through there. I believe Doctor Mason used it for extra medical supplies. "

Elizabeth peeked through the opening at the bare shelves. "It's perfect."

"I hope you'll find the upstairs will meet your needs also, Doctor Kellogg."

"I'm sure it will. Please, you must call me Elizabeth, Amelia."

"Well, only when we are in private or during social functions. We all fully appreciate a woman in medicine deserves the distinction of being called by her well-earned title, so in more formal settings, be assured we will address you as Doctor Kellogg."

"I appreciate your sensitivity, Amelia. So, when will I get to meet the rest of the group?"

"As you know, Mrs. Stockton has been quite unwell as of late, so she said she will send you word when she has a good day and she hopes you will be able to visit her at her home for tea. We have many Christmas parties coming up as far as the rest of us are concerned. You'll be coming?"

"Of course. I look forward to it."

"Good. Then I'll leave you to the rest of the house. Your trunks should arrive in a little while. If you need anything, please don't hesitate to let us know. I'll leave you my calling card, so you can send word if you do need anything. Otherwise, we'll be in touch."

"I'm sure it won't take me long to settle in. I'll have to order some supplies, but once I do, it will be a simple matter of waiting for them to arrive and getting them stored away. Then, I'll be ready to get started."

"I know you expressed a desire to work with the poor women and children of San Francisco. We also hope to introduce you to Theodora Barculo. She runs the Chinese School and could use your services from time to time, too. People think she does marvelous work."

In spite of the declaration, Elizabeth thought Amelia's wording didn't indicate any of her own support.

"Mrs. Stockton mentioned her in one of her letters," Elizabeth said. "She said she was a force not to be trifled with. I wondered what she meant?"

"It's true. She has a large personality. She seems stern on the outside, but they say, inside, she's very caring."

Elizabeth mused over the use of "they" while noting Amelia Rosemont didn't seem to be one of them. "Then I'll look forward to meeting her, too, and to helping out in any way I can."

"Once you're settled, you should take the time to explore the city. Market Street is teeming with shops and services. Spend some time getting acquainted. You may also want to explore the area referred to as South of the Slot, but I wouldn't recommend going down there alone." She wrinkled her nose again—the way she had when referring to Quan Luck. "If you decide to do it, let me know and I'll send one of my men to accompany you."

Elizabeth thought she wouldn't argue with Amelia. She had spent more than a year working in a clinic in the lowliest section of Baltimore ministering to the poor and downtrodden. Such an area didn't intimidate her, but this was no time to dispute the advice of a woman she'd met so recently, at least not until she had the full measure of Amelia Rosemont.

They left the office and walked toward the front entrance.

Amelia said, "I've promised Mrs. Stockton I would take excellent care of you, so please don't hesitate to let me know if there's anything you need."

"I shall," Elizabeth said, questioning whether or not she would. "Thank you so much for meeting me and providing the driver and carriage, and for Quan Luck's help, too."

Elizabeth thought she noticed the fleeting look of disdain again.

"And please thank all of the ladies for securing this wonderful house for me. Once my practice gets started, I'll be able to take over the funding of it myself."

Amelia waved her words away. "We are committed to having a woman doctor to meet the needs of our peers, and to give aid to the people, especially women, in the poor districts who need so much care. We were delighted to find you and to find your desire to serve and your philosophy so aligned with ours."

They said goodbye. Elizabeth watched Amelia descend the porch steps and return to her carriage. When she turned to look around her new home, she breathed a sigh of relief. She was here. Baltimore and her troubles were behind her. Her brother could just go to Hades. He couldn't touch her now, couldn't ruin her as he threatened to do back in Baltimore.

MAGGIE WESTON LOOKED up from the photographs she mounted as the bell above the door pinged. Quan Luck stepped inside.

"Good morning, Quan Luck. How are you today?"

"I am having a good day, miss."

"And how was your excursion with Mrs. Rosemont?"

He shrugged.

"It went that well, then?" She knew by the look on his face it didn't.

"Missy Rosemont doesn't like Chinese people. She employs me when she needs someone to do not so pleasant jobs."

Maggie's smile disappeared. "I know, Quan Luck. I'm sorry.

Why didn't you refuse when she asked you to accompany her?"

"You never know. Someday she may be able to help me with my goal. I don't want to upset her, spoil my chances. Her husband is a lawyer for the city. He went to Stanford. Some day, I might meet him, talk to him about my dream. He may be able to help me."

"It's no reason to take that woman's abuse. You should have said 'no.' What did she have you do this time?"

A wide grin broke across his face. "It was easy this time. All I had to do was accompany her to the train station and carry a bag. It wasn't even heavy. I took it to the house the Big Ladies rented on Van Ness for the new doctor. It is a nice house."

"Mrs. Rosemont actually let you step foot in the house?"

His smile faded. "Only in the front door—to put the bag inside." His eyes began to sparkle when he said, "At least she didn't make me run all the way from the train station. She let me ride on the carriage."

This surprised her. "Really?"

He chuckled. "On the luggage shelf."

Maggie scowled. "Quan Luck, it's dangerous back there."

"I know. But what was I to do? Mrs. Rosemont told me it was where I must ride."

"I can't believe her. When she's around those other Big Ladies, as you call them, she acts as if she cares about everyone in San Francisco, but an intelligent, hard-working young man like you is relegated to luggage. What's wrong with her?"

"I think she likes to be one of the Big Ladies more than she likes to help people."

Maggie stared at him, stunned. "You know, I think you're right."

"The doctor is nice," he offered.

"That's good to hear."

"Mrs. Rosemont told her she would meet you at the parties the Big Ladies have in their fine houses for Christmas."

"Why ever did she mention me?"

"The doctor asked if I work for her all the time. She told her only sometimes. She did not tell her she makes me do the most menial work only. Then, she told her I work for you in your photography shop and told her she would meet you when you come to take pictures for the Big Ladies during their parties."

"Well, I'm glad you found the new doctor to be pleasant. Did she speak to you?"

"Oh, yes, she told me she preferred to carry her doctor's bag herself rather than have me carry it. I only carried her case. She thanked me—more than once. She is most kind."

"Then it seems she'll fit right in with the ladies on Nob Hill. Well, most of them. I wonder how long it will take her to figure out Mrs. Rosemont isn't exactly one of them."

She assumed he'd had enough of their conversation about Mrs. Rosemont when he grunted, moved into the middle of the room, and asked what duties she had for him today.

"I have a stack of portraits on the counter. Will you sort them and put them into the cardboard frames and write their names on the envelopes for me?"

"Yes, miss."

"Quan Luck, when are you going to start calling me Maggie as I've asked you to?"

"I cannot, miss."

"But I want you to."

"We can compromise?"

"How so?"

She wasn't sure she would like what he would offer in this negotiation.

"I will call you Miss Maggie. So, if anyone hears me address you, they will know I still have respect for you—because I do. I respect you a great deal for how you treat me and you gave me this job at fair wages. Not like some." He nodded toward the street outside. She knew who he meant—Mrs. Rosemont.

His point was valid. If anyone came into the shop and heard him call her by her given name, they might assume impropriety. She couldn't risk Quan Luck's reputation. She cared about him too much to let it happen.

"I see your point," she said. "I'll agree to those terms." She grinned. "You're going to make a fine lawyer one day, Quan Luck."

He blushed, looking even more youthful than his seventeen years. Then, he bowed from the waist acknowledging the compliment.

Maggie said, "I have some photographs to develop. I'll be in the dark room while you sort those pictures out. If you have any questions, please knock.

"I will, Miss Maggie."

As Maggie began working on the day's photographs, she wondered about the new doctor. Quan Luck was a perceptive young man and she had no doubt his first impression was a good one. He even seemed a little taken with her. Perhaps the new doctor was someone she would come to respect, too.

AS MAGGIE FINISHED developing her final photograph and

placed it into the fixing solution, she heard raised voices from the front of the shop. She couldn't make out the words, but she knew the voice was that of a woman and the tone reflected strong disagreement. As the conversation got more and more heated, Quan Luck's voice rose in tone and volume, too—a rare occurrence for the young man.

Maggie picked up a pair of long metal tongs, pinched the photograph at the corner and agitated it in the solution to hurry the process along. When the appropriate amount of time passed, she fished the photograph from the pan and hung it on a line stretched above the container to allow it to drip dry with the others she had developed that morning, then she pulled open the darkroom door.

Light and loud voices engulfed her as she approached Quan Luck and a woman she recognized. She had taken the woman's portrait many times before, the last one a week ago. It had been among those she'd finished developing a few minutes ago but it still had to be made into the rather old fashioned *carte de visite* she requested. When Maggie entered the room, the pair stopped shouting at one another and turned toward her. The woman seethed. Quan Luck looked dismayed.

"Mrs. Jacobs, is there a problem?" Maggie said.

"There most certainly is. This young man doesn't seem to be able to give me my *cartes de visite*. They were supposed to be ready today."

She wondered if she had been mistaken about Mrs. Jacobs's order. Should it have already been put into the stack she'd asked Quan Luck to sort? She'd been so busy of late, perhaps she'd gotten the due date confused and processed it out of order. She gave him a questioning look.

"Missy Jacobs's pictures not in stack, miss. I try explain. Too early for pictures."

Maggie detested when he spoke with poor English. She knew he did it to deflect accusations of not knowing his place, of trying to be pretentious. She hated he felt the need to do such a thing. However, this was neither the time nor the circumstance to challenge him.

"Early?" Maggie questioned.

"Yes. Pictures not done until Thursday."

The woman interrupted, "Young man, today *is* Thursday. My *cartes de visite* should be ready today."

Maggie jumped in before Mrs. Jacobs went any further. "Um, no. It's actually Wednesday, Mrs. Jacobs, and I assure you your cards will be ready tomorrow after lunch."

Mrs. Jacobs gave Maggie a puzzled look. "Are you sure? I

was certain today was Thursday."

Maggie turned to Quan Luck and asked, "Did we get *The Call* this morning?"

"Yes, miss." He pulled the newspaper from under the counter and handed it to her.

The masthead read *The San Francisco Call*. The date printed below it read Wednesday, December 6, 1905. She showed it to Mrs. Jacobs, who said, "This is yesterday's paper."

"No, ma'am. It's today's *Call*. I assure you, today is Wednesday."

Confusion washed over Mrs. Jacobs's face again, but she brought her expression under control. She shrugged and said, "Then, I guess I'll be back tomorrow."

She walked across the shop, opened the door, and left without further comment.

Quan Luck nodded toward the door. "She acts the same with my father when she picks up her clothes. Sometimes she comes for laundry but she hasn't even dropped any off. My father said he thinks she should see a Chinese apothecary. He can give her herbs to clear her mind. They work. Then she might know what day it is — or at least believe me when I tell her the truth."

Maggie laughed and said, "If it's any consolation, she didn't believe me either. I imagine she'll ask several people what day today is as she makes her way down Market Street. Maybe after four or five of them give her the same answer she might start to believe it."

The incident had her wondering about Mrs. Jacobs's frame of mind and if the apothecary in Chinatown — or perhaps the new doctor — might be able to help.

December 13, 1905

ELIZABETH STACKED THE last of the supplies, which arrived the previous day, into the white enameled cabinet in the examining room. Preparations to open her practice were almost complete. A few more deliveries were yet to come, but the first wasn't due until the following week. On Thursday, she had plans to visit Mrs. Stockton, who invited her to tea. She had no plans for the rest of this day, though. Perhaps she would take the suggestion made by the ladies of Nob Hill and the surrounding area who had already dropped by to welcome her. They told her not to miss out on exploring the shops on Market Street.

Perhaps I will.

As she climbed the oak staircase to her living quarters on the second floor, gratitude filled her for the opportunity she had been given. Back in Baltimore, during her last months there, she felt desperate and wondered if she'd ever find another place to practice medicine and live her own life free from the oppression of her reactionary brother. It took time, but she extracted an ultimatum from him: leave Baltimore within a year and he would not expose her.

Her search for a place to relocate proved more difficult than she hoped but she had requirements. Finally, almost at the end of the agreed upon length of time, a chance meeting pointed her in the right direction and everything began to fall into place.

A conversation with a young progressive doctor, whose acquaintance she made when he came to visit the clinic she worked in, led to an introduction to a businessman friend of his from San Francisco. The man knew all the right people, in particular, Mrs. Stockton, a wealthy matron from an area of San Francisco called Pacific Heights. According to him, she had similar interests to Elizabeth's own about helping the downtrodden. The man made introductions by letter and soon Elizabeth and Mrs. Stockton corresponded on their own. After several weeks, Mrs. Stockton offered Elizabeth a proposal. "Come to San Francisco," the letter read. "We will be pleased to host you. We will secure a place for you to live and practice medicine among our peers. We will also see that you are funded to work among the poor women and children of our city who are in great need of the understanding and compassion of a woman doctor."

And here she was, preparing to work among the people who needed her, but first, she would take the opportunity to get acquainted with her new city.

ELIZABETH CHOSE TO walk rather than hire a carriage. How else could she fully take in her new surroundings? Delivery carts and all other manner of conveyances moved along Van Ness Avenue to and from Market Street. Elizabeth tried to stay out of their way, but the traffic proved chaotic and people, she observed, made mad dashes hither and yon in every direction between vehicles and horses where ever they could. The streets of Baltimore were busy, but traffic patterns contained a bit more order to them and thus required a little less risk to negotiate them. Elizabeth took a deep breath and plunged across an opening to the other side of the street.

When she reached Market Street, she turned toward the bustling business area. As she reached a group of shops her interest piqued and she slowed to look at their display windows. As she glanced at the millinery array, wondering why she thought she needed one more hat, she heard strains of piano music coming from the next shop and wandered toward it.

A young man sat at an upright piano. His long slender fingers flew over the keys as he sang with a smooth-sounding voice. She recognized *Somebody's Sweetheart I Want to Be*. When the musician noticed her in the doorway, he stopped playing and stood up.

"Well, hello, there, lovely lady. May I assist you to find some sheet music today?"

Elizabeth thought she detected a slight brogue. "Oh, no," she said. "I'm exploring the area and couldn't resist a peek in to see where the music came from."

"Do you play?" He gestured toward the piano.

"Some," she said. "But I haven't played in quite a while."

"You should think about taking it up again." He brushed a fingertip across his thin mustache. "Would you like to try?"

"No, thank you. I don't have the time." She stepped backwards over the threshold.

"Please," he said, "tell me why an elegant lady such as yourself is so burdened by duties she doesn't have time to indulge in the soothing sounds of piano music."

He sat down again and ran his fingers up and down the keys producing arpeggios with a flourish. "Music soothes the soul while activating the emotions," he said. "You should take it up again."

She gave him a polite smile, realizing his smooth pitch was nothing more than a way to sell his wares. He reminded her of a carnival barker, albeit, a more refined one. As she turned to leave, she saw him get up from the piano again. When she strode out into the street, she heard his footsteps behind her. She spied a photography studio next door and, afraid the music huckster might follow her, she ducked in. As she closed the door behind her, she noted the man didn't follow.

Now might be as good a time as any to make inquiries about getting some cabinet cards made to give to her new clients.

When she turned around, she registered her surprise at coming face-to-face with someone she knew.

"Quan Luck? Is that you?"

A wide grin broke across his face.

"Doctor Kellogg, welcome. I get Miss Maggie for you. She take good care."

He trundled off as Elizabeth stood taking stock of the little shop with its bundles of photographs and a display of teapots and other delicate porcelain and ceramics for sale on a table in a corner. Quan Luck must have referred to the woman Amelia Rosemont had said she would meet at her holiday party, scheduled to take place in a few days.

A few minutes later, a woman, small in stature, no more than five feet tall, entered the shop from the back room. She carried herself as if she were taller, Elizabeth noted.

The woman said, "Good day to you, Madam. Quan Luck told me someone was here. How may I help you?"

The two women locked eyes. A wordless moment of something unspoken passed between them until Elizabeth pulled herself from a swirling rush of emotion and forced herself to offer, "I'm Doctor Elizabeth Kellogg. I met your man, Quan Luck, last week when I arrived from Baltimore. I had no idea this was your shop. It was happenstance I stopped in."

Stop babbling. She took a deep breath.

When Elizabeth spoke again, Maggie began at the same time. They stopped mid-sentence again, then both women laughed, breaking the tension.

Maggie said, "I'm sorry. Let me start again. I'm Maggie Weston, portrait photographer. Quan Luck told me he met you at the train with Mrs. Rosemont. Welcome to San Francisco. May I help you with anything?"

Elizabeth's eyes crinkled. "Actually, I came in to escape from your next door neighbor—the music man. He strikes me as a bit of a rogue."

Maggie laughed. "He's all that and more. You have to be careful of that one. He thinks he can sweet talk anything in a skirt." Maggie thrust out her hand. "It's a pleasure to meet you, doctor."

"Thank you, Miss Weston. I'm pleased to meet you, too." When Elizabeth held out her hand, a frisson of pleasure surged up her arm. She paused to allow the feeling to wash over her, then, she grasped Maggie's hand firmly in her own. When she spoke again, the timbre of her voice sounded lower. "I would like to talk about having some cabinet cards made—for introductions to new patients."

"You'd like a sitting, then."

"Yes, when could you do it?"

"Any other day, I might be able to take you right away, but I have an appointment—a large family—coming in any time now. They have a passel of children, unruly ones at that. It will, I'm sure, take me the rest of the afternoon to get one or two decent exposures. I hate to ask it, but would you mind coming back tomorrow?"

"It won't be a problem. Shall I come back in the afternoon?" Elizabeth asked.

"Perfect. Perhaps around one o'clock? Would the time work well?"

"Yes, it will be fine. I'll see you then."

As Elizabeth turned to go, Maggie said, "If you're heading back to Van Ness, you'd better cross the street. Otherwise, Michael-the-Maul, as we like to call him around here, might accost you again—unless, of course, you like his type."

Elizabeth wrinkled her nose. "I assure you, his type doesn't appeal to me at all."

Maggie took one step closer and looked up into Elizabeth's pale blue eyes. "Do you have a type, doctor?"

Elizabeth cleared her throat. "I—I have a type, yes. Perhaps when I know you better, Miss Weston, I can discuss it with you."

Why in the world did she say such a thing? You must stop, Elizabeth. It's far too forward—and far too dangerous. A shudder ran through Elizabeth. She recognized it as a warning. She had to control her emotions—and her immediate attraction to Maggie Weston.

Maggie held Elizabeth's gaze. "I think I'll look forward to that discussion, Doctor Kellogg."

Elizabeth's hand trembled as she reached for the door knob to exit the shop. She never shook. She had a reputation for the steadiest hands in her medical class. Nothing fazed her. Yet, here was Maggie Weston, a perfect stranger who touched her to her core in an instant. Not good. This isn't the way it's supposed to be. Coming here was supposed to be a clean break, a new start.

She gave Maggie a weak smile, then, exited the shop.

She took Maggie's advice and crossed the street to avoid the reprobate music man and wondered what she would do about her newly-discovered attraction to Maggie Weston.

MAGGIE WATCHED FIVE fidgeting children through her view finder and struggled to keep her thoughts on the task at hand. The parents of the children sat in a corner of the room, watching silently. Maggie shook off her titillating reflections of her interaction with Doctor Kellogg. If she didn't get back to business, they'd never finish this challenging portrait.

She popped her head above her large Imperial studio camera, which sat on a wooden tripod in the middle of the room. "Children, you must sit still. It won't be long, I promise. But if you don't sit still, all of you at the same time, we'll never finish this and," she tried not to show her frustration, but she knew it seeped through, "you'll sit here until dark if need be."

The children's father cleared his throat. It was probably his attempt to register his displeasure at her threat.

Maggie tried to calm herself with a deep breath. Then an idea struck her. "Well," she said, "you know, I baked some cookies yesterday."

The children stopped fidgeting and focused on her as if realizing for the first time she inhabited the same space as they did.

She pushed on. "Yes, I did. They are upstairs in my apartment. I'll get them and you can each have one if you will all hold still while I take three pictures. Will you do that?"

The four eldest children nodded with enthusiasm. Indeed, they would cooperate for a tasty treat. The youngest was too young to understand the art of negotiation. She'd have to hope for the best with him. He continued to squirm on his older sister's lap. These children all had too much pent up energy. She had to diffuse it if they were to sit still at all—promise of a reward or not.

"All right. This is what we're going to do," Maggie said. "You are all going to get up from your seats, but you must remember your positions and go back to them when we're ready. Is everyone clear?" As one, the school-aged children chimed, "Yes, miss." Somewhere in San Francisco, a teacher could be proud of her lessons.

"We are going to play one game—a short game. When we're done, you are to return to your seats, stay perfectly still and smile. Hester, you hold onto your little brother. Don't worry about what he's doing. I'll make sure he's smiling when we take the pictures. When we're done, I'll go upstairs and get you each your treat." The children voiced their enthusiasm for the plan. Young Hester deposited her baby brother into her mother's lap, where he cuddled close and thrust his thumb into his mouth.

Maggie wondered if she'd be sorry she unleashed them from their positions to let out their pent up energy. She dragged three chairs from various places around the studio and lined them up a few feet in front of the posing couch and instructed the four remaining children to gather 'round.

Maggie walked over to the side of the room where the Victor Talking Machine sat on a small table, its large sound horn tilted at an angle above the round turntable. She removed a record from a protective paper sleeve and placed it on the flat, round disc. She wound the crank round and round as the children watched, mesmerized.

"Musical chairs, everyone. Do you know how to play?"

The children shouted their, "yes."

Their parents smiled.

The record of Enrico Caruso's *Celeste Aida* didn't fit the game, but it would have to do. The children wouldn't mind. At least she wouldn't be demanding they sit still. She wound the crank and watched the turntable speed up. Then, she set the needle onto the record with care. Caruso sang between the scratchiness of it. The children marched around the chairs. When Maggie lifted the needle, they scrambled for a seat. Hester was the first out. She looked demoralized. Maggie removed a chair and called her over, instructing her to turn the handle three times to keep the record in motion. The young girl broke into a big smile and did as instructed. Maggie placed the needle on the record and repeated the process. The youngest boy was knocked out of the game next. She called him over and he turned the crank. She continued until only the oldest boy was left and declared him winner of the game. As his prize, she allowed him a turn at the crank as his siblings had done and she played the record without stopping this time. The children listened, mesmerized by the sound emitted from the large horn.

When she told them to take their places for their portrait, the children behaved impeccably. Even the toddler sat quietly on his sister's lap. A fraction of a second before she pressed the shutter lever, Maggie said something to make them laugh, certain at least one of her photographs would please the parents.

Before storing the plates in the darkroom for developing later, she asked the family to wait as she ascended the stairs to her living quarters and returned with a small plate with seven gingersnaps on it. Each child took one treat and thanked Maggie, shyness tingeing each voice. The toddler giggled when he received his. At first, the parents declined theirs, but at Maggie's insistence, they removed the last two cookies from the plate and thanked her for her generosity and her patience with the children before the family left the shop.

Maggie flipped the sign on the studio door to indicate the business now closed and went to work in the darkroom. As she performed the familiar activities, bringing the images to life on paper as if she were a prestidigitator, her mind wandered back to earlier in the day when she met Doctor Elizabeth Kellogg and a tremor ran down Maggie's spine. A wide grin broke across Maggie's face when she thought about seeing the doctor again the next day.

Chapter Two

December 14, 1905

AT MAGGIE'S INSTRUCTION, Doctor Kellogg stood beside a table decorated with a lace table cloth, a teapot, and two porcelain cups and saucers to stage the scene for the photograph. In one hand, Elizabeth gripped a small book. Maggie insisted the book would portray an air of learned dignity, while the tea would offer an atmosphere of welcoming and comfort, things she would need when dealing with the upper echelons of the elite women of San Francisco.

"They can be quite snooty, you know," Maggie said. "They don't take well to strangers. You might find them hard nuts to crack, as the saying goes."

Doctor Kellogg's eyes crinkled at the outside edges. "How do you know so much about them, Miss Weston?"

"Mrs. Stockton's little group. They've invited me to take pictures of their group of ladies for quite some time now. You can't help but learn things about them when you've worked around them for as long as I have." While she spoke, she fiddled with her camera, adjusting, tapping, twisting.

"I see. Then, I think you might be a great help to me, Miss Weston."

Maggie looked up from her adjustments. When she made eye contact with Doctor Kellogg, she felt the heat rise in her cheeks.

"P-please, call me Maggie, Doctor Kellogg." She felt the doctor's eyes penetrating to her soul.

"Then I insist you call me Elizabeth."

"Oh, no—I couldn't."

"Yes, you could. Please, I'd like it if you did, Maggie."

"All—all right, if you insist. But I do think, if we're with the ladies, I should address you as Doctor Kellogg. Otherwise, they might think I was being too familiar. Disrespectful. Neither of us needs that, believe me. Some of them—well, maybe one in particular—still thinks, even in this day and age, people like me—from the working class—need to know our places." Maggie returned to her tinkering. "Now, turn a little toward the table and look over at the Talking Machine over there in the corner. It will give you something to focus on."

Elizabeth did as she was instructed.

"Think of something pleasant, Doc—Elizabeth."

Elizabeth's head snapped toward Maggie, her eyes widened. Maggie lifted an eyebrow, questioning her, but when Elizabeth said nothing, Maggie refocused her efforts. "Please turn your attention toward the Victor and stand perfectly still, Elizabeth."

Elizabeth turned her head back to the Talking Machine on the small table in the distance while Maggie made a final adjustment on the camera.

Without moving, Elizabeth said, "Having a Victor in a portrait studio isn't something I'd have thought to find."

"Oh, I had Quan Luck bring it down from my living quarters upstairs a few days ago to use in a portrait with a musician. We've been so busy I haven't had a chance to ask him to cart it back upstairs for me yet."

"You like music then?"

"I love music."

"What kind do you favor? Anything in particular?"

"Oh, I love opera, especially anything Mr. Caruso sings."

"Ah, I see."

Completing her setup, Maggie said, "I'm ready now, Elizabeth. Please keep looking over there and think of something pleasant."

Maggie saw a fleeting look of astonishment register again on Elizabeth's face, then she settled into a countenance of serene contentment. She looked beautiful.

Maggie wondered what thought achieved the look, but she pushed it aside and moved quickly to take the picture lest she lose her chance to photograph the expression. She asked Elizabeth to turn a little to face the camera so she could take another exposure. As she focused the camera, she observed her subject through the lens. The word "breathtaking" came to mind and when it did, Maggie felt her heart speed up. She took a deep breath, trying to calm herself.

"Think of something you'd love to do," Maggie said.

Now, it was Elizabeth's turn to raise an eyebrow, but her expression quickly settled into a cryptic smile. Maggie watched her eyes crinkle at the outside corners and snapped the image. Then, she announced they were finished.

As Maggie lifted the last plate from the camera, Elizabeth said, "Did you know Caruso was coming to San Francisco?"

Maggie looked up, stunned. "I hadn't heard, no."

"He is. In April. I already have tickets. Would you like to go with me?"

Maggie couldn't contain her excitement. To hear Caruso in person would be like a dream come true. But she didn't fit in with

San Francisco's elite. "I'm not sure. I have nothing proper to wear to such an event."

Elizabeth waved away her concern. "Don't be silly. I'm sure you have suitable clothing. We'll go through your wardrobe and find something."

Elizabeth would go through her wardrobe? She'd be quite embarrassed. Her cheeks colored again. "I don't know."

"Nonsense. If you like Caruso as much as I think you do, you shouldn't pass up such an opportunity. Please say yes and we'll work out the details closer to the time. No need to worry about it now. Will you come with me?"

"Didn't you procure two tickets with someone in mind? Someone else, I mean?"

"No." She gave Maggie an enigmatic smile again. "It must have been you I had in mind. Now, say you'll come. The performance is scheduled for the evening of April sixteenth."

Should she? It might be the only chance she'd ever get to hear Caruso in person. Better still, she'd get to hear him in the company of this fascinating—and beautiful—woman. "I-I'd love to come. I'm excited to come. Yes, I'll come with you. Thank you, Doctor Kellogg—Elizabeth."

"Good. I'm glad to have it settled. Tell me about how you turn those," she pointed toward the plates resting in the crook of Maggie's arm, "into portraits for cabinet cards. Photography has always fascinated me but I have no knowledge of how the pictures get onto paper."

"I could show you, sometime, if you'd like."

Maggie watched as the look on Elizabeth's face changed to utter delight. Was it the potential of learning the developing process which caused the look, or was it something else entirely? Maggie felt her own buzz of pleasure at the thought of Elizabeth standing beside her in her darkroom. A shiver ran down her spine again. She pushed the feeling away.

"Do you have time to return tomorrow?"

Elizabeth's delight turned to a frown. "Mrs. Stockton sent word I'm to come to tea tomorrow. From what I've been told, her good days are few, so I must go to see her. I guess we'll have to leave it for another time, but since Mrs. Stockton's group of ladies have insisted I take the time for myself before I begin seeing patients, I'll have time. It was most generous of them to give me until after the Christmas season to get settled."

"It sounds like Mrs. Stockton's doing. She's a gracious person."

"Shall we say we'll leave it for another day for you to show me how you produce your wonderful photographs?" Elizabeth asked.

"Let me know when you'd like to do it. As long as I don't have a specific appointment, I'll be happy to show you through the developing process."

"I'll look forward to it."

Elizabeth started to leave, but turned back and said, "Would you like to know what pleasant thought I had, Maggie?" She held Maggie's glance as she said it. Maggie felt her cheeks warm.

"O-only if you really want to tell me."

Elizabeth smiled. "Let's just say, I thought about a beautiful woman I recently met."

As Maggie watched Elizabeth walk down the street, away from the shop, she wrestled with her feelings of pleasure at Elizabeth's statement. Of course, the good doctor could have been referring to someone else. Yet in the innermost depths of her soul, she knew it wasn't correct. What was true was Doctor Elizabeth Kellogg called her beautiful—and made her feel the same way.

December 15, 1905

ELIZABETH SAT POISED on the edge of the tapestry covered settee opposite Mrs. Stockton. The older woman's hand shook as she brought her delicate teacup to her lips. When she set the cup back into its saucer, Elizabeth let out a quiet breath in relief at her concern Mrs. Stockton might have spilled and caused herself some embarrassment.

Their meeting lasted over an hour, surprising Elizabeth since her hostess's condition seemed so fragile. The purpose of their time together, Mrs. Stockton said, was to get to know one another better—and for her to offer her support to Elizabeth in both her office practice and in her duties attending to the needs of the poor. Mrs. Stockton's concern for the poor, especially women and children, was apparent.

"I will send you a young woman at the New Year, my dear. She is familiar with the needs of some of the families who are located South of the Slot."

"South of the Slot?"

"Oh, yes, my dear. You'll become familiar with the precincts of San Francisco soon enough. South of the Slot refers to the area south of Market Street. The slot denotes the cable car aperture in the road. Below the slot is where people need the most help. Many of the men are dockworkers or work in the warehouses or at other menial tasks. Their wives are the ones who need the care. They're also the ones who are most wary of coming into the area above Market Street.

"Violet Farrell lives and works down there. She runs the Quaker mission. She helps the women of the area as much as she can; however, she has nothing more than a basic curative knowledge for cuts and bruises. She's the one who brought to our attention the need for a doctor, preferably a woman, to help these poor souls. Many times, their husbands drink up their pay before they come home and leave them with no means to feed their children or themselves. Because of poor nutrition, their health is tenuous in many cases. Sometimes, they need the services of a midwife, but at other times, they should have the experience of someone who can educate them about the health hazards of having baby after baby. But you know most of this, we've corresponded about it and I know we are of one mind. Of course, utmost discretion is needed in the latter, but I know you know all about this, too, my dear."

"I do know all about it. It's not unlike some of my experiences in Baltimore. I assure you I will be able to gain the confidence of these women and offer my help and support. It may take a while, but it will happen."

"I appreciate your dedication and your determination, Doctor Kellogg." Mrs. Stockton reached for her cup again and winced.

"Mrs. Stockton, I hope you don't think me too forward for bringing this up, but I hope you will also let me attend to your health needs. Perhaps I can help you."

She waved away Elizabeth's remarks. "I'm an old woman with an old woman's aches and pains, dear. You will have other people more in need of your knowledge and talent."

Elizabeth knew a dismissal when she heard one. "Well, I hope if you do have need and you think I might be able to help, you'll let me know."

Mrs. Stockton took her measure, then said, "I will. I promise. That old fool who has been my doctor for years is out of touch. I'm sure you have much more modern methods and medicines than he has. But I'll let you get your feet planted firmly before I come 'round to talk about my old bones and their aches and pains."

Elizabeth gave her a reassuring smile. "As you wish, Mrs. Stockton." She drained the last of the tea from her cup and placed it on the table in front of her. "May I pour you more tea, Mrs. Stockton?"

"No thank you, doctor. I've had enough for now. I'd like to discuss one more thing with you, though."

Elizabeth eyed her with caution. She didn't like the sound of this.

"I've heard a rumor."

Now, she liked it even less.

"Let me preface this discussion by saying I have misgivings about the source of this rumor and I'm only bringing it up because I want you to be aware of it."

Well, that was a little better. "Please, go on."

"Someone in our group of ladies isn't necessarily what she seems. I fear her motives for involvement with us isn't as altruistic as the rest of the group. Unfortunately, this woman's influence and acquaintances are far flung across this city and, indeed, through some other parts of the country."

While Mrs. Stockton spoke, she held Elizabeth with a pointed gaze. "This person has come to me with a concern about a rumor for which she had no evidence or basis. I have put a stop to this rumor — at least I hope I have — and if it raises its ugly head again, there will be consequences."

"What is the nature of this rumor, Mrs. Stockton?"

"The nature of it doesn't matter, doctor." Her icy blue eyes pierced Elizabeth's and caused her heart to pound in her chest. "It also doesn't matter whether or not it's true. The only thing of consequence is your caution and discretion — and your awareness about this person having designs to ruin your reputation."

"I assure you, Mrs. Stockton, I am a model of discretion and I shall try to be as cautious as I can. Of course, it would help to know who it is I should be wary of." She kept her eyes trained on Mrs. Stockton. She had only met three people, well, four if you counted Quan Luck, but if they were speaking of a woman, he didn't count in the realm of this discussion.

It certainly wasn't Maggie Weston. Which left only one person — Amelia Rosemont.

"San Francisco is filled with a varied population. In my long years I've met many people who would not conform to what some people would term the norm. I want you to know I understand not all of us are meant for marriage and to have a man to run their lives. There were times in my own life I wished I hadn't married Mr. Stockton. He could be a boor on occasion, but he did have a talent for making money and he provided for me well. He's been dead for twenty years and they have been the happiest of my life." For the first time, Mrs. Stockton broke out in a wide grin. "In my long life, I've come to appreciate we are not all made the same. And in our differences, if we can find some measure of happiness, we should take it and accept one another along the way. But when we do, we should be conscious of the fact that some people may be looking to use our differences against us. This is where caution and discretion come in."

It was Elizabeth's turn to try to peer into this woman's soul. "I understand, Mrs. Stockton. I shall try my utmost not to let you down in any aspect of my life."

"Good. I'm glad to hear it. You are a charming and intelligent woman, Doctor Kellogg. I'm sure you'll do us proud. I trust you."

Did she? How lovely. Now if Elizabeth could only trust herself, especially around Maggie Weston.

"Now, before you go, tell me, have you managed to make any friends yet?"

"I have made one. You know her, as a matter of fact. She's the photography expert many of the ladies use at their functions."

"Miss Weston?"

"Yes, that's her. I met her quite by accident. Then, I engaged her to take my photograph for cabinet cards. I thought I should have some for the women who visit my clinic. I haven't seen the results yet, but I should have them soon."

"Miss Weston is a lovely woman. I'm glad you met her. Perhaps she can help you learn your way around San Francisco. She does more than portraits, you know. She goes out and takes photographs of the area's architecture and natural surroundings. You should ask her if you can accompany her some time. I'm sure she'd be happy to let you go along with her."

That tidbit of information filled Elizabeth with excitement. Another excuse to see Maggie Weston? She'd take it.

"Now, dear, if you don't mind, I think I've expended all the energy I have to spare this afternoon. I think I'll retire to my room to rest."

"Certainly, Mrs. Stockton. I hope I haven't pushed you beyond your limits by my visit."

"Not at all, dear. I've enjoyed it immensely. Now, be sure to ask Miss Weston to show you around the city.

She tried to contain her delight when she replied, "I certainly will."

Mixed emotions filled her as she left Mrs. Stockton's stately Pacific Heights mansion on Jackson Street. The first was dread at having any more interactions with Amelia Rosemont after discovering she might be a threat. The second was elation at Mrs. Stockton's suggestion Maggie Weston would be a good friend and companion.

December 16, 1905

THE FOLLOWING AFTERNOON, Elizabeth sat in her kitchen drinking a cup of tea and contemplating her visit with Mrs. Stockton the day before. She would be leaving to attend the

Christmas party given at the home of Amelia Rosemont in a little while. Between her initial appraisal of Amelia's treatment of Quan Luck and the insinuation and insight given to her by Mrs. Stockton, she knew it would be difficult for her to maintain a façade of propriety with Amelia tonight, but she was determined not to act otherwise.

The bright spot in the night would be Maggie Weston, who would be there to take photographs. However, Maggie would be attending to business during the party and likely wouldn't have time to socialize. Just as well, she thought. If she took Mrs. Stockton's caution to heart, and she would, she'd be sure to keep her distance from Maggie at Amelia's party.

Still, she needed to look for an opportunity to talk to Maggie, to see if she could schedule another chance to spend time with her.

The familiar thrill of attraction skittered through her.

Now she had two reasons to see her. There was the invitation to observe the developing process for the photographs Maggie took, and Mrs. Stockton's own suggestion for Maggie to show her around the city. She could look for an occasion to do so — a discreet one — one where Amelia Rosemont wouldn't have any reason to take issue with her or to allow her fodder for gossip. Or she could take care of it before the party ever began so as not to risk any reason for Amelia Rosemont to point fingers.

She finished her tea and went to her bedroom to change for Amelia's party. Then she put on her hat and coat and walked out the door to hail a carriage to take her to Market Street.

MORNING SUNLIGHT BEAMED through the shop window creating a square of light on the floor. Maggie came around the corner with her arms full of supplies.

"Quan Luck, I thought you left already. Don't you need to get home for your uncle's celebration?"

"Yes, Miss Maggie. I wanted to make sure you didn't need anything more from me before tonight."

She gazed into the young man's dark, velvet eyes, appreciating his thoughtfulness. The pink in his cheeks faded to a copper tinge. "I couldn't have moved those tables and developing pans without you. With the new arrangement, I have more room in my darkroom. I appreciate your help. I think we're done for now."

He smiled and said, "Then I will go." He moved toward the front door of the shop.

She watched his delicate fingers as he reached for the handle and said, "Don't forget, we need to leave for Mrs. Rosemont's party by four o'clock. I hope it won't interfere with your celebration too much. I wouldn't ask you to come with me on such an important day for your family, but I need help with the equipment."

From over his shoulder, he replied, "Don't worry. The celebration will go on long into the night, even after the guest of honor is fast asleep. It will not be a problem for me to come back. I will be here to help you before four o'clock."

"Thank you, Quan Luck. I'll see you then. I hope you have a good morning working with your father so you can all get to the celebration."

As he stood in the doorway, Maggie watched Quan Luck's shoulders sink. She knew he didn't enjoy working in his father's laundry. She had been there with him. The place was dark, damp, and quite steamy from vats of boiling water. His father and uncle pushed clothes around in them with large paddles, their hair tied back in long braids lying along their spines. Sweat beaded up on their foreheads. Their hands were red from handling the harsh soaps they used to wash the clothes clean. When the two older men walked, they never quite stood up straight, as if their work left them stooped into a permanent question mark.

The bell over the door to the studio jingled as Quan Luck pulled it closed. Maggie watched him cross Market Street and head back toward Chinatown. He looked so young and handsome in his rich brocade jacket, the one he wore on formal occasions instead of his plain black one. He stood tall in it at about five-foot-four. He was not yet bent with the work of his father. She sighed. She longed for this young man to achieve his dream of going to Stanford University farther down the San Francisco Peninsula. She didn't know if she would be able to honor his request to find someone to help him pursue his dream, but she would certainly try. No one deserved it more.

Her musings continued as the morning dissolved into afternoon and turned gray and dreary. When a light rain began to fall, she hoped it wouldn't last. It would make the situation more difficult. Hauling all her equipment up the hills of the city to Mrs. Rosemont's party was challenging enough without the complication of rain.

As soon as she entered the darkroom to retrieve something, she heard the bell over the door ringing. She hoped it wasn't someone wanting a portrait. She only had another thirty minutes until Quan Luck arrived and they needed to finish packing up all the cameras and other paraphernalia to make their way to Mrs. Rosemont's party. When she came around the corner to the main shop, her look of concern transformed into one of delight at the sight of her unexpected visitor—Elizabeth Kellogg.

Surprise registered on Maggie's face. "Oh, Doctor Kell—Elizabeth."

"Have I come at a bad time?" Elizabeth asked.

Maggie noted Elizabeth's clothes looked dry and felt relief the rain no longer fell. "No, not at all," she said. "I'll be leaving for Mrs. Rosemont's in a little while, but I'm waiting for Quan Luck to arrive to help me."

Maggie's heart pounded under Elizabeth's intense gaze. She cleared her throat and asked, "Has it stopped raining?"

"Yes, it has."

"What a relief." Getting the words out felt like speaking with a throat filled with spun wool. She tried again. "I was worried about the equipment in the rain."

Elizabeth kept her eyes on Maggie. "As luck would have it, I'm going also. It doesn't sound like you have a carriage."

She tried to sound casual even though her heart continued to pound. "Oh, no. We'll walk. We'll be fine. We're starting out in plenty of time but I'm glad to hear the rain's stopped."

"Well, I've hired a coach for the evening. I'd be happy to have you come with me."

She sounded so calm, so casual, and here's me, Maggie thought, with my heart running wild, pounding like some big base drum.

"I've also stopped by to ask a question of you. Actually, to make a request at the suggestion of Mrs. Stockton."

The remark pulled Maggie back to the conversation. "Request?"

"Yes. Mrs. Stockton suggested you were the ideal person to show me around San Francisco. In the New Year, I'll be moving about the city to offer medical help to those in need and to those who cannot afford to avail themselves of clinics. The ladies are funding this endeavor and I'll be working toward gaining the confidence of the women who live south of Market Street. I also may be attending to some of the children at the Chinese School for Miss Barculo when she has need. Are you familiar with her school?"

"I am." It was difficult to get the words out. Why did she find Elizabeth Kellogg so thrilling? And why did concern well up in her chest at the mention of Theodora Barculo?

Theodora was a force to be reckoned with. Maggie also suspected the woman kept a secret. Perhaps it was the way Theodora looked at her when they first met, a look which penetrated to the depths of her soul while taking in her physical aspect. She suspected she was looking for something in particular, to see if Maggie was of the same mind.

Maggie chose not to acknowledge it. She had no idea who Theodora Barculo was at the time. In the end, she was glad she hadn't participated in the exchange. She liked Theodora and admired her dedication to the Chinese community, but she felt no attraction for her. Besides, maybe it was Maggie's imagination. On second thought, she doubted it. "Yes, I know Theodora. She does wonderful work with the Chinese immigrants in the city. She's fierce in advocating for them."

"Then I'm sure she and I will become good friends. I cannot abide injustice."

Maggie felt a distressing twinge and wondered why. What did she care if Elizabeth and Theodora became friends? It was no concern of hers. Or was it? This thought made her want to take the opportunity to get to know this woman standing before her with even more urgency. "I'd be happy to show you around the city, Elizabeth. When would you like to do it?"

"As I said, I'm free until the beginning of the New Year, so I'll let you choose the day."

"Perhaps we can do it one day next week. Let me look at my diary and see which day would be best."

"Good," Elizabeth said. "There's one more thing. You promised me I could watch as you developed some photographs one of these days. I hope I'm not imposing too much by bringing it up again, but I was looking forward to it."

Maggie's heart felt as if it skipped a beat. Perhaps she didn't have anything to worry about regarding Theodora.

"I had planned to spend the entire day tomorrow working on the photographs I take tonight. The shop is closed on Sundays, so I have the whole day to devote to it. Would you like to come back then?"

A smile broke across Elizabeth's face. "I'd love to."

The conversation ended with the chiming of the shop bell as Quan Luck entered. He looked at both women and hesitated.

Elizabeth said, "Quan Luck, it's good to see you again."

Quan Luck thrust his hands into his sleeves and bowed "Doctor. I pleased for see you also."

"Quan Luck, stop," Maggie said.

Elizabeth stared at Maggie, surprised at her reprimand.

"I'm sorry Quan Luck," Maggie added, "I shouldn't have shouted."

He lifted his head a little to make brief eye contact with her and lowered his gaze again.

Maggie continued, "Quan Luck, you told me about your

encounter with Doctor Kellogg at the train station and in her house the other day. Surely you know she will not think you're trying to act above your station if you speak proper English in her presence."

When he looked up again, Maggie glared at him, willing him to accept what she said.

Elizabeth said, "Quan Luck, you have nothing to fear from me. I understand some people look down at the Chinese. Indeed, it happens everywhere in the country, I'm afraid. But I am not one of those people. Please feel free to be yourself around me." Then she added, "I hope we can be friends."

Quan Luck faced her, his demeanor completely changed. With his back straight and his head erect, he said without any hint of an accent, "Thank you, Doctor Kellogg. I hope we can be friends, too. I would like it very much."

Maggie's grin widened and she pronounced, "Better."

Quan Luck directed a question toward Maggie. "How may I help to get ready for the party?"

Maggie said, "Well, as it turns out, we have plenty of time. Doctor Kellogg has hired a carriage for the evening and has invited us, and our equipment, to accompany her." She turned to Elizabeth and, with a look of challenge on her face, she said, "I hope you'll not relegate Quan Luck to the baggage area as Mrs. Rosemont did."

Maggie noted Elizabeth's look of horror with amusement.

"Of course not. I'd never do such a thing. I was appalled when Amelia did it." She turned to Quan Luck and continued, "I'm sorry it happened, Quan Luck. I had no idea it had occurred until we were under way. If I could have, I would have put a stop to it."

Quan Luck gave her an innocent smile. "I know, doctor. I understand. You didn't know Missy Rosemont. How could you? You just arrived."

"Still, I'm sorry it happened."

"You were most cordial to me. I appreciate it."

"Well, you certainly will not ride with the baggage if I have anything to say about it, and tonight, I do have a say."

As Quan Luck bowed, Maggie said, "Since we have time, Quan Luck, I wonder if you'd do me a favor and bring the Victor upstairs to my living quarters. I've been meaning to ask you to do it for days now, but we've been too busy."

He started toward the studio as he said, "Yes, Miss Maggie."

When he was gone, Maggie said, "Perhaps after we've gone through the developing process, you'd like to stay for something to eat and to listen to Caruso."

Elizabeth's eyes crinkled at the outside edges. "I'd love to, Maggie."

"Wonderful. Now let me consult my diary to see when we might take our tour of the city."

BY THE TIME the equipment was loaded into the carriage, a light rain began falling again and Maggie felt even more grateful for not having to make the trek on foot to the mansion on the edge of Nob Hill. Quan Luck held two large bags on his lap sitting beside the driver while Maggie and Elizabeth sat in the passenger seat behind them, the large wooden Imperial camera and tripod at their feet. They began the gradual ascent up Taylor Street.

The clop of the horse's hooves against cobblestones beat a mesmerizing rhythm. Maggie's thoughts drifted to dreams of strolling arm-in-arm across Golden Gate Park with Elizabeth and her heartbeat sped up a little. The climb up the street became more inclined, tilting the carriage upward.

Still, she reveled in her thoughts with Elizabeth sitting beside her until she was jolted from her reverie when the tempo of hoof beats became erratic. The rain-slick street made it difficult for the horse to maintain its footing. The driver cracked his whip demanding more of the animal than it could manage. Maggie winced at his fierce attempts to make the animal move forward. The horse strained at the leather tracings and whinnied in protest.

Elizabeth leaned forward and said, "Stop here, driver. We'll walk the rest of the way. I'll not have you beating that animal for something over which it has no control."

Relief washed over Maggie. The man scowled at Elizabeth.

"You'll get your full fee, don't worry."

His scowl turned to surprise, then to delight. He raised his hand to the brim of his hat in acquiescence and took the coins Elizabeth held out to him.

Quan Luck jumped from the conveyance and scrambled to remove the equipment from his seating area. He unfastened one of the two large equipment bags, slung it over his shoulders, and removed a thick quilt from it. Then he took the tripod with the camera affixed to it from Maggie and Elizabeth's feet and covered it with the quilt, wrapping it securely so the camera was protected against the misty night before leaning it against the carriage. Shifting the bags, he held his hand out to Elizabeth to help her down from the carriage. He did the same for Maggie, who took a third, smaller bag from the passenger compartment.

The three then trudged up the steepest part of Taylor Street to the Rosemont home. As they made their way up the hill, they heard the carriage turn around in the street and move back down the hill, the clip-clop of the horse's hooves growing fainter as it moved back toward the flat plane of Market Street.

The mist receded as they hiked upward, Elizabeth beside Maggie and Quan Luck bringing up the rear. Maggie carried the small cloth bag.

Elizabeth gripped her ever-present doctor's bag. She turned to Quan Luck and said, "Let me relieve you of some of your burden, Quan Luck. I can carry one of those bags."

He shook his head in vigorous refusal. "No thank you, doctor."

"Are you sure? I have a free hand." She held up her hand to show him.

"I can manage."

Maggie smiled at her thoughtfulness and they carried on up the hill.

MAGGIE GRINNED AS the big house came into full view. She turned to look behind her to see how Quan Luck faired carrying her photography equipment. Quan Luck reassured her with a smile. His soft, dark eyes reminded her of velvet every time she looked into them. He was a kindhearted soul and she wished she could do more to help him. He caught up with her, without even panting from his trek up the steep San Francisco street. Hefting her own bag of supplies from one hand to the other, she turned back toward her destination, the house on the hill was grand, but it was no match for Mrs. Stockton's mansion in Pacific Heights. She wondered how Amelia Rosemont came to insert herself into the group of wealthy women who lived in much more lavish houses. Well, it was no business of hers. She should be grateful the woman invited her to take photographs of the group gathering for this Christmas celebration and for the hefty fee she'd be paid for doing it.

She paused, thankful for a chance to catch her breath. Elizabeth stopped beside her as did Quan Luck.

Maggie turned to Quan Luck and said, "It's not far now. Are you all right?"

The young man smiled and looked toward the satchel in Maggie's hand. "You want me to take your bag? I can manage." He hefted the camera to reseat it on his shoulder.

"I think you're doing quite enough, Quan Luck. I can manage this. Only a few more steps and we're there. It's lucky for us

Doctor Kellogg offered us a ride in her carriage and we were able to make it as far as we did in the rain."

As they continued toward the house, Elizabeth asked, "Does it always take this much equipment to take photographs outside the studio?"

"Not usually, but Mrs. Rosemont wants so many different types of photographs I had to bring more equipment than normal."

She glanced toward the house bedecked with pine boughs and holly. In the large front window, Maggie spied warm lights with silhouettes of the party-goers against them. Candles glowed in all the windows of the lower floors of the house. A large wreath graced the door at the top of the steps, giving it a much grander appearance than it, in fact, was.

She looked over at Quan Luck again. "Ready?"

He nodded, took in a visible breath, and followed Maggie and Elizabeth toward the stairs. Before they ascended, the large door swung open. Strains of Christmas music played on a piano wafted out the door. Then, children's voices, singing "Silent Night" surrounded them.

As they mounted the front steps, a young Chinese boy of about ten emerged and bounded toward them. His bright, black eyes beamed. His black hair shone in the lights from the house. The boy's hair was cut short, trimmed around his ears, and slicked back on his head in contrast with Quan Luck's long, single braid cascading over the back of his brocade coat.

The boy looked like a Christmas elf in his short, red jacket over a dazzling white shirt with black trousers which came to his knees. A large sprig of holly graced the wide lapel of his coat. The oversized bow at his neck and white knee socks with shiny black high button shoes completed his ensemble. When he reached Maggie, he looked up at her and said, "Miss Barculo sent me to help. She saw you from the window." He beamed and pointed to the large multi-paned window overlooking the street. Then he glanced from Quan Luck to Maggie with a look of anticipation.

Maggie took the smaller of the two bags from Quan Luck's arm and handed it to him. "What's your name, young man?"

"George Washington Moon," he said, beaming with pride.

"Well, George Washington Moon, you have quite a big name."

"I was named for the first president of the United States." His smile grew as he expressed his knowledge.

"My name is Maggie Weston and this is my friend, Doctor Kellogg. You may help my friend, Quan Luck, here, carry his burden. I can handle this one little bag on my own."

"Oh, no, Miss Weston. Miss Barculo said I was to take your

bag. She said I was to help you."

Maggie shrugged in Quan Luck's direction and let the boy take her bag.

"I am fine, Miss Maggie. Let the boy help you. After all, he must do as Miss Barculo tells him."

Quan Luck gave him a nod of encouragement. The boy flushed and turned toward the long flight of stone steps in front of him and began his rapid ascent. The trio followed.

"Silent Night" ended as they passed a large parlor. Maggie spied three rows of young children. The boys were dressed in outfits identical to the one George Washington Moon wore. The girls wore dainty crimson dresses with white collars. They, too, sported sprigs of holly pinned to their dresses. The audience clapped and murmuring voices filled the room as people moved from their seats.

George tugged at Maggie's sleeve and indicated she should follow him down the hall.

Elizabeth said, "I'll go in and greet Mrs. Rosemont. I'll tell her you're preparing for the photographs."

"Thank you," Maggie said.

George indicated their destination when they reached the next room. As Maggie stepped through the doorway, she took the bag George gripped with both hands. Quan Luck opened the tripod to secure the camera and removed the quilt, folding it with care and placing it on a chair. Then he turned his attention to the bags and began pulling out equipment. The little boy looked on with interest.

Theodora Barculo entered the room, talking and waving her hands. "Oh, Miss Weston, we're so glad you agreed to do this. It will be wonderful. Amelia wanted me to be sure to greet you. My dear, when I saw you trudging up the hill with that bag, and your poor man laden down with all your equipment, well, I had to send little George here to help you." She turned to the boy, who stood there at attention, awaiting orders.

Theodora said, "George, show—" she looked at Quan Luck, stared at his face for the first time, and registered surprise. "Quan Luck, is it you?"

Quan Luck beamed at her. "Yes, Miss Barculo." As soon as he addressed her, he directed his gaze to the floor at her feet.

Maggie scowled as she looked from him to Theodora.

Theodora said, "Why, I thought your father wanted you to work with him in the laundry, Quan Luck. What are you doing working for Miss Weston?"

Quan Luck blushed and continued staring at the wood floor.

Maggie cleared her throat and offered, "Quan Luck's father

and I came to an agreement. He allows Quan Luck to work for me as long as he continues to help him in the laundry a few mornings a week. I needed someone to help me in my photography shop and Quan Luck is a quick learner."

"I see. Well, good for you. Do you still have those big dreams, Quan Luck?"

Quan Luck's cheeks turned even redder than Maggie thought possible. She felt embarrassed for the young man. Theodora Barculo had a reputation for being compassionate in her work with Chinese women and girls, but she was noted for being hard on Chinese young men. Perhaps it was due to her run-ins with the tongs, the men who controlled Chinatown and everything in it. Some tongs were benevolent societies run by local businessmen. Some were thugs and criminals, running the opium dens and the houses of prostitution in the Chinese section of the city. Barculo had little patience for how these hoodlums treated their fellow countrymen and she equated all Chinese men to having ties to the tongs, seldom differentiating between those societies doing good and those who profited from illegal activities. She detested how the criminal tongs treated women and children in particular.

Maggie gave Quan Luck an apologetic look before hooking her arm through Theodora's. "Let's go find Mrs. Rosemont and find out what her plan is for the portrait session, shall we?"

Theodora beamed as she took in the sight of Maggie's arm on hers and led her out of the room.

AS MAGGIE AND Theodora walked down the hall, Maggie asked, "So, do you know where Mrs. Rosemont is?"

Theodora pointed down the hall in the opposite direction. "Perhaps you'll find her in her sitting room. The last I saw of her, she was walking arm in arm with Doctor Kellogg down the hall. They were having quite a *tete-a-tete*."

Maggie frowned.

A group of people emerged from the main parlor and called out to Theodora. The children were about to sing again and they wanted her with them when they did.

Theodora glanced at Maggie, an apologetic look on her face, but Maggie said, "I'll be fine. I'll go look for her myself."

Maggie thought Mrs. Rosemont might have captured Elizabeth to discuss her work with the poor women and children of the dockworkers and other poor people of San Francisco. In her opinion, Mrs. Rosemont wasn't on a par with the rest of the women in Mrs. Stockton's circle, but who was she to sit in judgement of the woman's motivations. In her experience, people always revealed their true colors in the end. If she proved to be something other than she projected, it was Mrs. Stockton's worry, not hers. Then why did Amelia Rosemont make her uneasy?

Maggie turned in the direction Theodora indicated earlier and continued down the hall. She heard voices coming from an open doorway. She was about to pop her head around it when she caught a part of the conversation. It caused her to hesitate.

"Doctor Kellogg, I've had a letter from an acquaintance in Baltimore." The voice belonged to Amelia Rosemont.

"And..." Elizabeth. Her response sounded tentative, distrustful.

"My friend seems to have met some people who said your leaving Baltimore was rapid and without explanation. They said you planned to set up a practice there, but then, almost without warning, you abandoned those plans and left."

Maggie took a step back to ensure she couldn't be seen and leaned close to the wall. She checked the hallway to see if anyone else occupied it. There was no one. Strains of children's voices and piano accompaniment drifted down the space. Everyone was in the parlor, listening to the children sing—everyone but Mrs. Rosemont and Elizabeth.

Mrs. Rosemont spoke again. "But, of course, I shouldn't pry."

"Mrs. Rosemont, I owe you a debt of gratitude for meeting me at the train and settling me into my new home. Please don't misunderstand when I say my affairs in Baltimore are in the past and I have left them all behind me. In my correspondence with Mrs. Stockton, I told her I was entertaining several options before her offer to come to San Francisco arrived. My decision was based on the opportunity to work among the city's poorest to help the women and children here."

Overcome with guilt for eavesdropping, Maggie sidestepped back down the hall on tiptoe. As she made a final retreat toward the room where she had left Quan Luck, she heard Mrs. Rosemont say, "I didn't mean to pry, Doctor Kellogg. Of course, we appreciate all you are planning to do for us here on the hill and for what you will do for the poor of this city."

Was Mrs. Rosemont sincere or merely trying to backpedal from her snooping? Maggie didn't hear Elizabeth's response as she slipped back into the parlor and picked up a second, smaller tripod Quan Luck removed from one of the bags. As she stood beside him, assembling it, she wondered what motivated Mrs. Rosemont to have the conversation she'd overheard.

AMELIA ROSEMONT'S ATTEMPT to confirm cross-country gossip rang in Elizabeth's ears as a din rose around her in the room. Amelia's failed attempts to organize her guests into some semblance of order for their first photograph wasn't working.

When Maggie took control, Elizabeth felt relief wash over her. The sooner they got this over with, the sooner she could make her excuses and remove herself from the source of her threat.

Several pictures later, Elizabeth reveled in Maggie's confident movements as she stepped out from behind her camera. "Ladies, if you could assemble yourselves with the tallest of you in the back row and the shortest in front. We'll seat some of you from the ends into a third row to get you all in the photograph once you're lined up."

This was the last of many group pictures Mrs. Rosemont had insisted on and the process moved at a snail's pace. A great deal of shuffling ensued all around Elizabeth with much chatter accompanying it. After a time, the tallest women were lined up, backs to the oak wainscoted wall. Elizabeth stood among them and tried to wipe any remaining concern from her face.

Maggie motioned to Quan Luck. "Three chairs, I think, Quan Luck."

He nodded and moved to the far side of the room to hook his arms through three ladder-backs, one through one arm and two, back-to-back, over the other arm. He positioned them in front of the women without looking up and arranged them in a neat row. He moved beside Maggie when he finished his task.

"Thank you, Quan Luck," Maggie said. "Mrs. Rosemont, Mrs. Gough, and Doctor Kellogg, please take a seat," Maggie said. Mrs. Rosemont rushed to claim the middle chair. Elizabeth took a calming breath as she sat next to Mrs. Rosemont.

"Now everyone standing, move in closer to one another."

The last two rows pulled themselves in like an accordion and settled into place. Maggie scrutinized the group before returning to her position behind the camera. She peered through the viewfinder. "Here we go. Steady now. No one move, please." As Maggie spoke, Elizabeth found herself feeling calmer. She concentrated on Maggie as she made her final adjustments on the camera.

When she picked up the small rubber bulb and wrapped her hand around it, squeezing, Elizabeth almost choked as the action caused a thought to flit through her mind—of Maggie squeezing her breast in the throes of passion. Elizabeth held her breath. It took every ounce of effort she could gather to keep from closing her eyes to relish her fantasy. Finally, she heard the soft *snick* of the camera's iris petals opening.

When they closed again, like the blinking of an eye, Maggie said, "All finished."

One of the tallest women in the back row asked, "What, so soon?" She looked to be well past middle age. "The last time I had my picture taken, it took forever. They strapped me into a metal and leather contraption. Brrr! Never want to go through that again."

Maggie smiled. "Those things are no longer necessary. It's one of the advantages of using this beauty." She patted the camera with affection. "Taking photographs has gotten much faster."

The woman smiled. "Well, I'm all for progress, then."

Some of the women tittered.

Amelia fidgeted where she sat. "My dear, is it permissible to move now?"

The edge in her voice let Maggie know she had held still quite long enough. "Yes, please, you may all move. We're quite done with this session."

Chaos and chatter filled the room again as everyone moved around the room or headed for the door to the front parlor, some people commenting about time for another round of refreshments.

Amelia moved close to Maggie. "I'd like to have you take a picture of Doctor Kellogg and I, if you would, Maggie dear."

Elizabeth heard the request. The hair rose on the back of her neck. Why on earth would Mrs. Rosemont want a picture with her? It didn't feel right.

Maggie smiled. "Of course. Let's clear the room and we'll get right to work." She frowned as she looked over at Elizabeth.

"It will only take a few minutes of your time, Doctor Kellogg."

Mrs. Rosemont shooed the remaining people out of the room, saying, "Come, now, everyone. Let's move the party back to the front parlor and let Maggie here finish up her work in peace. Everyone to the other room. Enjoy the refreshments."

While Mrs. Rosemont gestured toward the door, herding her guests into the hallway, Elizabeth whispered, "Determined, aren't you Mrs. Rosemont?"

Theodora hung back while Mrs. Rosemont escorted the last of the other women from the room. Before leaving to join the others in the hallway, she leaned in close to Elizabeth and whispered, "She's up to something."

ELIZABETH FELT FAINT. She stood, wide-eyed, looking out the doorway, waiting for Mrs. Rosemont to return. If Theodora thought something was awry and, given her recent conversation with Mrs. Rosemont, she felt it was a distinct possibility. She had no idea why Theodora would warn her, but it didn't matter. Now, all she had to do was figure out a way to get out of this.

Maggie leaned in close to Elizabeth's ear. "I heard Theodora. Don't worry. She'll think of something."

Mrs. Rosemont returned, saying, "Now, dear, where would you like us?"

Maggie gave Elizabeth a furtive shrug as she walked past her. She removed two of the ladder-back chairs from the group they used for the previous photograph. "Mrs. Rosemont, you sit here and Doctor Kellogg, please stand behind her. Steady yourself by putting your hand on the back of the chair. Good. Now, hold those positions."

She twisted knobs, adjusted the camera, even moving it from the place where it had stood for all the other pictures to give it a different angle. Then she moved it back to the original position. When she had pushed and pulled and rotated and tapped, she directed them to a focal point across the room and fiddled with the camera lens again. Once the adjustments were made, she again lifted the rubber bulb, wrapping it in her firm grip. Before she squeezed, Theodora rushed in.

"Doctor Kellogg, come. We need your assistance."

Elizabeth broke her pose. "What is it, Miss Barculo?" She picked up her medical bag from the floor and quickened her step to Theodora's side.

"It's Mrs. Evangeline. Something's happened. She's ill. Please, we need you."

As Elizabeth rushed from the room behind Theodora, she spied a grin on Maggie's face and heard an exasperated sigh escape from Mrs. Rosemont. She breathed her own sigh of relief at her reprieve. Was it concocted? Or was there a true emergency?

In the hallway, Theodora grasped Elizabeth's arm and guided her toward a small room opposite the parlor where the guests were gathered, enjoying eggnog and conversation.

A rotund woman who had not attended the photography session sat in a wing-back chair, fanning herself, her cheeks beet red, her chest heaving. Elizabeth knelt by the woman and took her hand. She was surprised to find it was warm and dry, not clammy as she assumed it would be.

"Mrs. Evangeline, I'm Doctor Kellogg. I'd like to see if I can help you. Will you allow me?"

The woman nodded. Elizabeth removed a stethoscope from

her bag and placed the earpieces in her ears, then pressed the small cone to the woman's ample chest, and listened. Theodora stood beside Mrs. Evangeline without saying a word. While Elizabeth listened, she noticed two figures standing in the doorway. One was Maggie, the other, Mrs. Rosemont. She ignored them and carried on her examination.

Elizabeth removed the stethoscope from her ears and asked, "What have you eaten tonight?"

"A couple of small cakes," Mrs. Evangeline replied between breaths.

"And to drink?"

"Oh, the delicious punch Mrs. Rosemont always serves. I can't get enough of it. It's so tasty."

Elizabeth looked toward the doorway. "If I may inquire, Mrs. Rosemont, what are the ingredients of your punch?"

Mrs. Rosemont's face reddened. "I have no idea. The people who prepare the food are the ones responsible for it. If you think something's wrong with it, I'll not use them again, I assure you. I'll not tolerate—"

Elizabeth held up a hand to stop her. "I'm sure there's nothing wrong with the punch, otherwise, we'd have a room full of people with symptoms, which we do not. Everyone seems to be enjoying it." She gestured across the hall where the party-goers continued to relish the festivities, punch glasses in hand, some sipping every now and then.

She felt Mrs. Evangeline's forehead and noted it to be a little overheated, but not enough to cause alarm. As she watched the woman, she saw her flushed skin already returning to a more normal hue.

Maggie stepped into the room holding a small crystal cut cup filled with yellow frothy liquid and handed it to Elizabeth.

Elizabeth smiled, appreciating Maggie's insight to help with her investigation. She raised the cup to her nose. The alcohol in the drink should have made her rear her head, but she didn't let on how strong the concoction was. She turned to Mrs. Evangeline and said, "How many of these did you drink?"

"Oh, I don't know dear, maybe five or six. They're such dinky little cups after all, and I was thirsty."

"I see—and how are you feeling now? Any better?"

"I'm quite a lot better. Almost back to normal, I'd say. All this fuss over nothing is unnecessary."

Elizabeth searched her bag once more and pulled out a small vile filled with white powder. "May we have one of these cups filled with water, Mrs. Rosemont?"

Mrs. Rosemont looked around. Elizabeth wondered if she

was looking for a servant to order around. Not finding anyone to do her bidding, she turned from the doorway.

"I'm going to give you some of this."

The woman's eyes widened and she looked at Theodora, who asked, "Is that really necessary, doctor?"

Elizabeth began to wonder if it had all been a ruse. "It's nothing harmful, I assure you. It's willow bark. Believe me, after the amount of punch our friend here has consumed, she's going to need it for the headache she'll have tomorrow."

Theodora smiled. Mrs. Evangeline turned red again, this time from embarrassment. The color dissipated as fast as it appeared.

Mrs. Rosemont returned with a cup of water.

Elizabeth poured some of the crystals into the cup and stirred with a small pestle. She handed the cup to Mrs. Evangeline. "Drink this down. I'm going to give you some to take home with you. When you wake up tomorrow, mix it well into about as much water as is in the cup and drink it down quickly. You may have a slight headache throughout the day tomorrow, but you should be as good as new by Monday."

Mrs. Evangeline slugged the contents of the cup as if it were more eggnog and wrinkled her nose as she pulled the cup away from her lips.

"I know it's bitter, but believe me, it will help. And please, do not drink any more punch tonight."

"I won't, doctor. Thank you. You've been most kind."

Elizabeth patted the woman's shoulder and smiled. She poured some of the white powder into a small envelope and handed it to her patient. As she set about packing up her bag, she saw Quan Luck appear at Maggie's side with the equipment bags and the camera.

He wore a big smile on his face as he said, "Miss Maggie, carriage here. The one you ordered this afternoon."

Maggie turned to Elizabeth and said, "Doctor Kellogg, may I return the favor of a ride to you?"

"Yes, Miss Weston. Thank you."

Mrs. Rosemont scowled. "But we haven't taken our photograph together."

"Perhaps another time, Mrs. Rosemont," Elizabeth said.

She knew she shouldn't have held out hope to Amelia Rosemont, but she assumed it was the only way she'd be able to escape tonight. For good measure, she added, "I'm quite tired and would like to go home now."

Mrs. Rosemont didn't look happy. "Fine. Good evening to you, then." She turned to Maggie and snapped, "When will my photographs be ready?"

"I should have them done by Tuesday afternoon, if you'd like to come by the studio then."

"Oh. I thought you'd deliver them."

"No. Patrons pick them up at my studio."

"Why can't you have Quan Luck deliver them?"

"Because he's not a delivery boy."

"He's not?"

The other three women in the room watched the interchange with interest.

"No. He's not."

Mrs. Rosemont gave Quan Luck a look of disdain. "What is he then?"

"He's my assistant—a very capable assistant, I might add, and I need him in my studio helping me, not running around the city dropping off photographs."

Mrs. Rosemont's face burned with anger. "Well, I never—" She turned on her heel and left.

Theodora shook her head and said, "Now you've done it. I doubt you'll be photographer for Mrs. Rosemont's Christmas parties ever again."

Elizabeth apologized. "This is my fault."

Theodora said, "It's that insufferable woman's fault if it's anyone's. She's not to be trusted."

"You're right," Maggie said. "And I don't care if she ever invites me back." She lowered her voice and added, "I never cared for the woman anyway."

Elizabeth turned to Mrs. Evangeline. "I hope you feel better. If you have any problems, come and see me at my clinic."

"Thank you again, doctor. I'm sure I'll be fine." She winked and looked up at Theodora, who wore an enormous grin.

Elizabeth said, "Did you two contrive this?"

Theodora's eyes twinkled. "Best not to ask such a question, Doctor Kellogg."

Elizabeth returned the smile and said, "I have no idea what question you're talking about, Miss Barculo."

THE NEW DRIVER followed a different route down the hill from the previous carriage ride. The longer ride negotiated the hills in a less treacherous manner, easier on both horse and passengers. The rain looked as if it would remain at bay for the trip.

Maggie and Elizabeth sat behind the driver in the passenger seat, Quan Luck sat up front holding onto the equipment bags.

As they neared Market Street, Maggie asked, "Do you

actually think Mrs. Rosemont had some ulterior motive for wanting a picture with you?"

"Who knows what that woman's motives are. I didn't care for her the day I met her and I like her even less today." Elizabeth crinkled her nose.

Maggie chuckled. As she thought about the conversation she overheard between Elizabeth and Mrs. Rosemont earlier, she wondered what rumor Mrs. Rosemont had heard about Elizabeth, but decided it was unwise to admit to eavesdropping. Instead she said, "A lot of people wonder about her motives for anything she does. She's wormed her way in to the circle of wealthy matrons in the city, yet she doesn't seem to subscribe to their ambitions to help the poor."

Elizabeth said, "And I'm afraid you've lost her business."

"Oh, don't worry about it. I, like you, have never liked the woman. Only I've not liked her longer."

Both women laughed.

The carriage stopped in front of the photography studio. Quan Luck climbed out and removed the camera and the bags and helped Maggie descend.

Maggie turned to Elizabeth and said, "Would you like to come in for a cup of tea?"

Elizabeth glanced at the carriage. "I'd better not. I should avail myself of the transportation since it's getting late."

Quan Luck said, "If you would like to have tea with Miss Maggie, I will escort you home afterwards." He looked down at his feet as he spoke. "I will wait in the shop until you are ready to go."

Maggie raised an eyebrow at Elizabeth to encourage her to stay.

Elizabeth held Maggie's gaze as she spoke. "It's not that I don't appreciate your offer—or yours, Quan Luck—but I am tired tonight. I had a conversation earlier with Mrs. Rosemont which was rather upsetting. I think it drained me. As much as I'd like to join you for a cup of tea, Maggie, I think I'd better go."

Maggie couldn't hide her look of disappointment, but she said, "I understand, Elizabeth. Will I see you tomorrow? We talked about developing the photographs I took tonight."

Elizabeth brightened. "Yes, I'm excited about it. What time should I be here?"

"There's preparation for the developing process you would find boring. It's not as magical as seeing an image materialize on the paper. Why don't you come around ten o'clock. I should be ready to start developing by then."

"I'll see you at ten, then. I look forward to it."

"As will I," Maggie said. She fished a coin out of her pocket to pay the driver, but Elizabeth leaned down and touched her hand. Sparks traveled up Maggie's arm causing her to inhale sharply.

"I'll take care of the carriage—and I'll see you in the morning," Elizabeth said. She re-boarded and directed the driver to her Van Ness Street address.

Maggie and Quan Luck stood in the street and watched the carriage disappear into the darkness.

Maggie said, "I'm afraid I'm not the only one who will lose Mrs. Rosemont's business, Quan Luck. You will doubtless be punished by association and she won't call upon you any longer."

He replied, "Mrs. Rosemont expects indentured servitude and pays a pittance for it with an unwilling hand. I won't miss working for her. Besides, she has proved to have no desire to help me in my quest to become a lawyer. She has never even given me the opportunity to meet her husband, so I will be happy if I never have to work for her again."

Maggie grew thoughtful. "I wish I knew what she was up to. She acted most peculiar regarding Doctor Kellogg tonight." In spite of the fact she knew Quan Luck was the most discrete person she knew, she decided not to bring up the conversation she'd overheard.

"Doctor Kellogg is a fine lady. She will be a good friend, Miss Maggie."

Would she? She most certainly wanted to be Elizabeth Kellogg's friend. No. She didn't want to be her friend at all. She wanted more.

Chapter Three

December 17, 1905

WHEN ELIZABETH ARRIVED promptly at ten o'clock the next morning, Maggie led her to the darkroom to begin her demonstration. They entered through the door separating the room from the main studio. Then they passed through a black, heavy curtain, which created an antechamber to keep all light out of the small room in case the main door was opened by accident during the developing process.

In the pitch black of the darkroom, Maggie felt Elizabeth's presence. They stood close and in the darkness, so close in fact, Maggie could feel the heat of her body and hear her soft breaths. It made her heart flutter. The air crackled between them. She took a deep breath and reached out for the ruby lantern she knew occupied the shelf beside her, explaining the red glow would allow her to see what she was doing without adverse effects on her exposures. Her match flared to life and she touched it to the lamp's wick. A small yellow flame sprung up in the lamp when she touched the match to it. When she closed the lantern's hinged door, the room took on the promised red glow. She watched Elizabeth's features, highlighted by the red light and noted Elizabeth's look of intense concentration as Maggie spoke.

As Maggie went through the process of exposing the photographic paper with the image taken at the party the previous evening, she was acutely aware of Elizabeth's body next to her. At times, Elizabeth peered over her shoulder to get a better look at what she was doing and Maggie could feel her breath close to her ear. It caused a tremor to course through her body.

When she placed the prepared paper into the developing solution, Elizabeth said, "So, you leave it in this solution until the image appears?"

"Yes, and if I've not gotten the exposure quite right for the intensity of the dark or light features, I adjust the time in the solution to bring out the details. It's tricky, though, because a little too long and it's over-developed and everything is too dark. If I move it to the next pan too soon, the image will be washed out."

She felt Elizabeth lean in closer from behind, felt the slight pressure of her body against her back. Peering over Maggie's shoulder, Elizabeth's breath tickled her ear as she spoke again. "Then what do you do?" Her voice sounded throaty to Maggie's ears.

Maggie felt her whole body quiver again and hoped her voice would be more steady than she felt when she answered. "You—you must start all over again."

"I see. And how often do you need to repeat the process?" She whispered, "Over—and over—again?"

Maggie felt her legs might give way at the sound of Elizabeth's voice. Was she reading a discrete hint into the conversation which wasn't there? She didn't think she could stand much longer if Elizabeth kept this up. "I—" She stepped sideways under pretext of needing more room rather than her true attempt to gain some self-control. She picked up a pair of long metal tongs from the bench. "I'll need to agitate the paper a little—" Her hand shook when she did so. She hoped it was too dark for Elizabeth to notice such a detail.

"May I help?" Elizabeth said.

Maggie took in a deep breath. She'd never felt like this before. Never. Her quivering didn't stop. She wasn't sure she wanted it to. "Y-yes," Maggie said.

Elizabeth placed her hand on top of Maggie's as she held the photograph in the tool. The picture appeared as a dim image, then darkened.

"You're shaking." Elizabeth whispered. "Should we stop?"

Stop? Did she mean stop the developing process? Or the narrative? It didn't matter. In spite of the weakness Maggie felt, she knew she didn't want either to stop. "No," she said. "We must continue."

Out of the corner of her eye, she spied a smile appear on Elizabeth's lips.

Together, they moved the paper back and forth in the solution. The image turned darker still in places. They continued moving the paper back and forth with a gentle motion. Elizabeth pressed against Maggie's side again, holding her hand with a feather-light touch as they agitated the paper.

Maggie suspected some of the trembling wasn't hers alone. Was Elizabeth quaking, too?

Back and forth…back and forth…the paper moved through the liquid. Maggie's breathing sped up, felt rougher. Back and forth…back and forth. Elizabeth leaned close to her ear again. Her breathing sounded as rough as Maggie felt her own to be.

The sound plunged deep into her core and made her feel things she'd never felt before. Made her think thoughts she'd never experienced before. It would be so easy to turn and kiss

Elizabeth Kellogg on her full lips.

Maggie tightened her muscles, locking her knees in place. It intensified the feeling between her legs. She tried to relax. It was time to remove the photograph, but she wasn't able to do any more than feel Elizabeth's hand, her own ragged breaths and the ache, deep and low in her body.

It took every ounce of willpower she could muster to speak. "Out. It's done. We must take it out."

Elizabeth sprang back, removing her hand as she went. "I—I'm sorry," she said. "Did I ruin it? Did I ruin everything?"

Maggie held the paper suspended above the developing pan and took a deep breath. Solution trickled from one corner into the pan. "No. Not ruined," Maggie squeaked. "Perhaps a little darker than necessary. We'll see how it looks when we're done."

Elizabeth's next words sounded strained to Maggie's ears. "Perhaps I should go. I—I'm distracting you from your work."

"No," Maggie said. She knew her voice was too loud, too forceful, but she didn't want Elizabeth to go. She wanted her to stay—forever. She wanted her to wrap her arms around her and kiss her. "You can't leave anyway. If you open the curtain, everything might be ruined."

It wasn't true. The door would prevent it, but she had to keep Elizabeth from leaving. "Please. Stay. You wanted to see the process. It isn't done yet." Please, don't go.

A long pause. In the red glow, Maggie saw Elizabeth take in a deep breath, then, she said, "No, I won't go. I want to see this through."

Maggie wondered if she was talking about the developing process or what happened between them—because something surely had transpired.

Another shiver enveloped Maggie's torso and skittered down to the place between her legs. She recognized the strong pull toward this woman. She had to have her. The thought surprised her.

Elizabeth broke through her reaction. "What do we do next?"

Good question. What *was* she to do next? Nothing. There was nothing to be done with these feelings. If she acted on them, she risked losing Elizabeth's friendship—this new and blossoming friendship—forever. She couldn't risk it. She'd have to get these emotions under control.

She cleared her throat, uncertain she would be able to speak without doing so. She repeated the words she knew well, the ones she had been taught by her mentor, the ones she repeated to Quan Luck when she showed him the process months ago. "Next, it goes into the rinse to wash off the developing solution before we put it into the fixing solution. Fixing it stops the process and stabilizes the photograph. She agitated the photograph in the water bath, then, plunged it into the third pan for the final step.

Elizabeth stood beside her, leaving a small space between them. Maggie could still feel her. "What happens after this step?"

"We pull it out."

Elizabeth gave a weak groan. Maggie turned to look at her in the dim red light of the room and noted a pained look on Elizabeth's face. Perhaps she hadn't recovered from whatever had taken place between them.

"Are you all right, Elizabeth?"

Elizabeth's voice sounded tight, tense. "I'm fine." But her face looked constricted, her voice rough.

Maggie took her hand. "Are you sure?" She could feel the tension in Elizabeth's body. She envisioned moving closer, claiming her lips glowing red in the light.

"Yes."

She held Elizabeth's gaze.

"Why did you cry out, then?"

Elizabeth bit her bottom lip. "I—I'm not sure."

"All right," she whispered.

Maggie turned back toward the photograph in the pan. She picked up the tongs and drew it out of the fixing solution. They stood together, watching the liquid drip back into the pan.

Maggie reached up and clipped the photograph to a cord strung above the pan to allow it to dry. "We're finished. We can let light in now."

Indeed, if they let too much light into their lives, would they be happy with what Maggie suspected was blossoming between them? A thrill ran down Maggie's spine. She opened the black curtain, pinning it back onto a hook, then, she opened the darkroom door, finding herself almost blinded by the light.

ELIZABETH SAT WITH her teacup and saucer cradled delicately in her hands. As she raised the cup to her lips, she stole a look at Maggie, who sat opposite her in her apartment above the photography studio.

She'd hesitated when Maggie proffered an invitation for lunch again. Her trembling body warned her against her threatened lack of self-control. Yet she'd followed Maggie up the stairs to her living quarters, pushing the alarm bells in her head away. She couldn't help it. She wasn't ready to end her day with this beautiful, petite woman. She couldn't let go. Not yet.

Maggie's dark hair framed her face. The sun beamed in through the parlor window behind her, causing her hair to shimmer like a halo around her head. What was she going to do about these feelings for Maggie Weston? She couldn't allow them. She couldn't risk exposing Maggie to the kind of trouble she'd already seen. She couldn't allow a relationship like the one she had with Irene back in Baltimore. If she did, and it ended the same way — she couldn't bear hurting Maggie that way.

In addition, there was the problem of Amelia Rosemont and her rumors...or suspicions...or whatever you could call them. She mustn't give the woman any cause for speculation about the reports she may have heard from Baltimore — even though they may be true.

Glancing at Maggie over her porcelain cup, Elizabeth had to admit her feelings for Irene were more lust than anything else. She enjoyed their little trysts, but she knew it wasn't love. Too bad one day her carelessness and her brother's untimely return to their parent's home caused her the distress of being caught — almost in the act itself. However, what she felt for Maggie was so far removed from what she felt — or didn't feel — for Irene. Even at this stage in their relationship, Elizabeth recognized her feelings for Maggie as so much more. The feelings were deeper, more intimate, and much, much stronger.

It was the precise reason why she couldn't act on them — why she must never again act the way she had earlier, during Maggie's demonstration of the developing method. She shouldn't even be here now, thinking of kissing those luscious lips, watching as Maggie's bosom rose and fell, as she sat returning Elizabeth's probing stare.

Elizabeth returned her cup and saucer to the table with a delicate clink. "I should go."

"Why? We haven't even had lunch yet."

"I've taken up enough of your time."

"No. You haven't. It's Sunday. I have nothing on my schedule for today." Then she added, "I reserved the whole day for you."

Elizabeth thought she detected an air of pleading in her voice. She cared for Maggie so much. Opposing emotions tore at her. She should never have come. How was she supposed to resist this woman's charm, her beauty, her invitation?

"Since you put it that way, I'll stay." So much for resolve.

Maggie's lips formed a wide grin.

"The meat pie is almost ready. I hope you don't mind simple food."

"I love simple food. I love simple, uncomplicated things." This, however, was not simple. It was the epitome of complicated. She thought about running for the door again.

"I'll go check on the pie. Don't run away."

No, she wouldn't go. Instead, she sat listening to the sounds of Maggie moving about in her small kitchen, dishes tinkling, serving spoon scraping on tin. Fighting off the urge to go into the kitchen and do something they both might regret.

As Maggie emerged with two plates, each holding a generous portion of pie crust oozing with pieces of meat and vegetables in a creamy yellow sauce, Elizabeth saw Maggie teeter as if she'd had too much to drink. As she watched her try to regain her balance, she felt the jarring movement of the chair beneath her. Her cup clattered in the saucer on the table. What was happening? Panic rose within her.

She looked up at Maggie, wide-eyed. "Is it—"

"Earthquake," Maggie whispered. She put the plates down on the table and grasped the back of the chair.

The two women continued to stare at each other. The tremor lessened. Then it stopped.

Maggie pulled out the chair, plopped down onto it and blew out a relieved breath.

Elizabeth had one hand on her chest. The other, she thrust out to grab Maggie's across the table. Maggie took it and squeezed. Her hand felt like ice.

Maggie studied Elizabeth's face. "You're pale. The first one is always the hardest. I thought I was going to die when I experienced my first. I'd just arrived in San Francisco from Boston. I had been here for only a few days. Mr. Partridge, the man who owned the shop before me had to calm me down. I was near hysteria."

Maggie's hand warmed. Elizabeth's still felt cold.

"And after the first?"

"It gets better. Although I never get used to them, but at least I know they'll stop. That first one? I thought it was never going to stop."

Maggie glimpsed at their hands clasped in a tight grip, their fingers intertwined. "Your hand is cold."

"Shock, I think," Elizabeth said. "At least that's my medical opinion. It will dissipate. I'll recover." She tried to pull her hand away.

Maggie gripped her tighter. She placed her other hand over it and rubbed Elizabeth's fingers.

Elizabeth felt the warmth return. She felt an accompanying pleasant tingle.

Maggie rose from her seat and walked around the table. "Give me your other hand."

No, Elizabeth's mind screeched. She held out her other hand.

Maggie took it between both hers and rubbed slowly.

No. No. No, Elizabeth's mind insisted. Do not allow her to do this.

Elizabeth squirmed on the chair, grinding her pulsing parts into the wooden seat, willing her reaction to Maggie's touch to stop. She failed miserably, but her hand warmed — as did her face, her whole body.

Maggie leaned in and asked, "Feel better?"

"Yes." Her voice croaked, so she said no more.

"Good." Maggie kissed her on the cheek.

Elizabeth's blush burned with even more intensity. "I should go."

"You said that already — and we agreed you would stay. Lunch is getting cold." She gestured toward the table.

"All right," Elizabeth said. She picked up her fork.

Maggie took her seat. They ate their first bites in silence. After a while, Maggie said, "How do you like it?"

"It's one of my favorites. How did you know?"

"I have a feeling we have a great deal in common. This is one of my favorites, too, *Doctor Kellogg*."

A tremor of pleasure ran through Elizabeth at the playful use of her title. At least eating lunch would serve as a distraction.

She watched Maggie bring her fork, with a chunk of potato suspended from the tines, to her lips. A drop of sauce clung to her lip and she captured it with the tip of her tongue. She held Elizabeth with her gaze as she chewed, closed her eyes and hummed her pleasure.

Not the kind of distraction Elizabeth hoped for. She looked down at her own plate, stabbed a small piece of meat and pushed it through the gravy. If she kept her head down, she'd be fine. She stabbed at a piece of carrot, adding it to the meat. Again, she ran the fork through the sauce.

"Elizabeth, I thought you liked pot pie. I could make you something else."

Elizabeth's head popped up. Involuntary muscle movement, she identified. "No. I mean, yes. I love pot pie. I'm sorry. I was just — distracted."

Maggie put her fork down and pushed her plate away. With her elbows on the table and her intertwined fingers under her chin, she said, "And what has you so distracted, Elizabeth?"

Did Maggie bat her eyes at her? She could not be allowed to give her such lingering looks, either. Elizabeth wouldn't be able to take it.

No. She had not given her that kind of a look. She could not. Elizabeth returned to dragging the bits on her fork through the sauce on her plate again.

"Elizabeth?"

"Nothing. I assure you, Maggie, it's nothing. Maybe I have too much time on my hands. I'm used to working day and night with patients and these past two weeks have given me too much time to...think. Too many memories to recall. Then, there was the tremor we just experienced." The one in the earth and the one within me. "Forgive me. I didn't mean to appear ungrateful. Let's enjoy our lunch."

Maggie stared at her and waited.

"I—I don't know what else to say," Elizabeth added. She scooped up the food which had fallen from her fork and shoved it in her mouth. "Good," she said around the mouthful. "Very enjoyable."

Having made her pronouncement, she returned to studying the contents of her plate.

"Will you tell me sometime?"

Elizabeth looked up at her again. "Tell you? Tell you what?"

Maggie hesitated before answering. "About your memories. About your thoughts."

No. She would not. She could never tell Maggie about Irene or her brother or her reason for leaving Baltimore. Most especially, she could not tell Maggie how she felt about her. Yet, as she gazed into Maggie's eyes, she felt as if her memories and feelings could so easily be drawn from her. It made her feel out of control. Frightened. Nervous. She never felt nervous. She was always as steady as a boulder and in control—the hallmark of being a good doctor.

Maggie undermined her ability to maintain her stability. Maggie, with her shimmering dark hair, her upturned nose and her inviting pink lips. Maggie made her feel like she'd never felt before—not with Irene, not with anybody. What was she going to do about this?

Still, she couldn't resist the look of anticipation in Maggie's eyes. Could she refuse her anything? Probably not. She couldn't refuse, but perhaps she could postpone.

"Maybe someday," Elizabeth said. The spot on her cheek where Maggie kissed her burned. She raised her fingers to touch the spot and noticed Maggie's smile.

December 19, 1905

TWO DAYS LATER, when Elizabeth opened the front door, Maggie held out a basket covered with a thick cloth and said, "I thought I'd supply lunch."

She looked so beautiful standing there, basket raised, cheeks rosy from the cold morning air and her walk up Van Ness Avenue.

"Oh, thank you, Maggie. I was fretting over what we would do because I've been so busy stocking my medical supplies I didn't have time to think about lunch."

"Well, now you don't have to worry about it."

Elizabeth took the basket from her and placed it on the hall table. She gestured Maggie down the hall. "Please come in. I'm so glad you're here. Let me show you around."

They ambled from the waiting area to the examination room, Elizabeth revealing her various plans for the areas as they went. After they entered Elizabeth's office, a shiver ran down Elizabeth's back as she watched Maggie caress the dark oak desk with a delicate hand.

Thoughts formed, unbidden. Elizabeth struggled to banish them from her mind without success. She clenched her thighs against her feelings. As she observed Maggie repeat the stroking action on the matching long bookcase against the wall, she couldn't stop her juices from flowing—downward—to the place she envisioned Maggie touching her. Her mouth felt impossibly dry. A thought flittered through her mind about all the moisture in her body now pooling in one place. Maggie's words sounded from a distance as she watched Maggie's hand, moving back and forth across the wood.

Maggie lifted her hand off the bookshelf and her words broke through. "Elizabeth, are you all right?"

"I—I'm sorry, what did you say? I'm afraid I was distracted for a moment."

Maggie fixed her with a look. "I said these shelves are wonderful. Look at all your books. It's good to have so much storage for them, isn't it?"

"It—It is." She needed to pull herself together. She couldn't keep falling into Maggie's movements with thoughts of—well, never mind. What she thought, she most certainly should not be thinking.

"And what's through that door?" Maggie asked, pointing.

"A small kitchen. I can have tea and a little lunch in there if I have a break from seeing patients during the day." She took a deep breath and felt her equilibrium return. "There's also storage beyond the kitchen. It's where I put extra medical supplies. It's a splendid set up."

"And your living quarters are upstairs?"

"Yes." She wanted to show Maggie upstairs, but fear gripped

her. She and Maggie, alone upstairs? Where her bedroom was? No. You will not follow that particular line of thought, Elizabeth.

"Shall we go up?" Maggie asked.

They would have to go upstairs, lest Maggie suspect something. Elizabeth drew in a calming breath.

"Yes," Elizabeth said.

As they passed the hall table again, Maggie scooped up the basket and followed Elizabeth up the stairs. When they reached the upper floor, Elizabeth began a narration of the layout to keep other thoughts at bay.

"It was so good of Mrs. Stockton to make sure I had a place to accommodate patients as well as a place to live. This house is perfect. I'm looking forward to the first of the year when I begin seeing patients again."

She pointed out the kitchen, which was larger than Maggie's and contained a small pantry. Maggie poked her head into the room and admired the size. They went into the parlor, where Maggie appreciated the view of Van Ness Avenue from their vantage point.

"Didn't you tell me a doctor lived and worked here before? This doesn't seem like décor a man would choose."

"No. I didn't think so either. I suspect the ladies had something to do with furnishing this part of the house."

Elizabeth pointed toward an interior wall of the parlor and remarked, trying to sound as casual as she could, "The bedroom is over there," then, she turned and waxed on about the entertaining view of the activity on the street below, hoping Maggie didn't notice her deflection. She was certain of one thing. She could not bring Maggie into her bedroom. It would be too dangerous. She battled for control of her feelings as it was. From the moment she opened the front door to Maggie, her magnetism pulled at Elizabeth. The desire to take Maggie in her arms and kiss her, raged through her mind.

No. The bedroom was no place for them. Much too risky.

Either Maggie didn't notice her omission of the bedroom from the house tour or she chose not to bring it up. Instead, she indicated the basket over her arm and said, "Shall we leave the food here or take it with us?"

The cloudy, cold day left Elizabeth concerned about rain. "Let's leave it. We can come back this way and decide what to do about lunch when we return." She took the basket from Maggie and dropped it on a shelf in the pantry.

As they descended the stairs, Maggie said, "It's cold out now, but if it warms later, we could take our picnic over to Golden Gate Park. Have you been?"

Elizabeth hadn't.

"It would be an opportunity to include it in the tour of the city. We could find a place to sit and eat there, perhaps near the Conservatory of Flowers. It's beautiful there."

"It sounds wonderful, but let's see how the day goes. If we don't get to the park today, we can save it for another day," Elizabeth said. She couldn't help her attempt to ensure they would see each other again soon. When Maggie smiled at the suggestion, Elizabeth knew it was the right thing to say.

Maggie said, "Let's strike out South of the Slot first. You said Mrs. Stockton and the other ladies hoped you'd be able to attend to the women and children there. I must warn you, their needs are great. I believe you wanted to try to meet up with Miss Farrell. True?"

"Violet Farrell, yes. Mrs. Stockton said she'd be able to help—or rather I'd be able to help her. She's the one who broached the subject of a physician to help the women who came to her mission. It's one of the reasons I accepted the position here. I was doing similar work in Baltimore."

Maggie said, "I admire your selflessness, doctor. It's a noble endeavor. I think Miss Farrell will be happy to have your help."

"Then, shall we?" Elizabeth held out her elbow for Maggie. She took it without hesitation. Elizabeth picked up her doctor's bag from the hall table and the two women headed down Van Ness toward the Quaker Mission.

AS MAGGIE SAUNTERED down the wide avenue with Elizabeth by her side, she felt a thrill of happiness. She loved spending time with Elizabeth Kellogg. She'd have to think of more reasons to do so. It occurred to her the trip to Golden Gate Park might be best postponed so they could already have another outing planned.

Elizabeth said, "I'm so pleased we could do this while I still have the time, but you had to leave your studio today. Did you close for the day?"

"No. As you know, I had nothing in my diary for today when I checked last week. It was easy to leave the day free. Quan Luck is at the shop for any patrons who come by to pick up their photographs. It should be quiet though."

"I'm curious. How did Quan Luck come to be in your employ?"

"I met him while he was still at the Chinese School—another place we should visit, although you are already acquainted with Theodora Barculo." She chuckled to herself thinking about the incident at the Rosemont party and Theodora's dramatic plan to rescue Elizabeth from Mrs. Rosemont's clutches. "Anyway, I spent some time in conversation and was impressed by Quan Luck and his aspirations. He wants to be a lawyer. His dream is to attend Stanford University and to work for the rights of the Chinese citizens of the city."

"What an impressive young man."

"He is. Now if I could only figure out a way to introduce him to the right people for him to gain a sponsor to begin studies at Stanford. I had hoped Mrs. Rosemont would be the pathway for him, but I didn't know her well enough when I recommended Quan Luck to her. She was no help. She never will be. As a matter of fact, after her Christmas party, I doubt she'll even ask for him again. I'm afraid we've tarnished his reputation. He tells me it doesn't matter and, in all honesty, I hope he never works for her again. She behaves quite badly toward him. She's insufferable."

Maggie's passionate evaluation forced a giggle from Elizabeth.

She said, "I admire Quan Luck's ambitions. If there's anything I can do to help, please let me know. I'm sorry I don't know of anyone who might be of help since I'm so new to San Francisco."

"Well, you never know. One day, you might find yourself talking to the right person and you could help Quan Luck realize his dream."

"Wouldn't that be nice?" Elizabeth said.

They turned toward their destination, the Quaker Mission run by Violet Farrell near Mission Street on Ninth. As they approached the plain, flat-front, two-story building, a group of children dashed through the front door and into the street, almost running into them. Elizabeth frowned and hopped back out of the way. One stopped long enough to mutter an apology to Elizabeth. As he scurried away toward his more ill-mannered friends, he called over his shoulder, "Sorry, Miss Maggie."

Maggie laughed at the children's antics all the harder when Elizabeth raised an eyebrow at her. "He knows you?"

"They hold classes here during the week. If they didn't, the children who come wouldn't get any education at all. They also feed them a solid lunch. Once a week, they hold meetings with the mothers to educate them on nutrition and hygiene and to learn about any particular needs they have for their individual families."

"We did something similar in our clinic in Baltimore. When the women and children had medical needs, they would come to see my colleague and me. Of course, sometimes the work was more social work than medicine. I think it may be the case here, too, from what Mrs. Stockton has told me."

"I'm sure Violet, Miss Farrell, will be happy to tell you what she needs. She's small in stature, but she can be forceful. She's a lot like Theodora Bucalo in that respect, although has a much more gentle personality."

"How so?"

They hesitated to allow a large horse-drawn wagon move past them in the street, then continued their trek.

As they stood in front of the Mission, Maggie continued, "As you already know, Theodora has quite a presence. She's not to be trifled with, in particular, when it comes to her Chinese students and those she rescues from terrible circumstances like being held against their will as slaves and prostitutes. You've seen her. She takes charge. She fills a room with her presence. No one can ignore her when she wants something for those she champions."

"And Miss Farrell?"

"Violet Farrell is the complete opposite, or so it appears on the surface. She's far from self-imposing. As a matter of fact, I'd describe her as self-effacing. It might be her Quaker nature, I'm not sure, but being a Quaker embodies in her a strong sense of righteousness for those subjected to injustices. The work she does with the women and children who live south of Market Street is commendable. She's tireless. In the end, she can be as unwavering as Theodora is, but she goes about it in a wholly different manner. Some people are put off by Theodora and her brusque demands on behalf of those she defends, but people acquiesce to Violet's gentle determination with much more ease."

"No doubt her approach is what made Mrs. Stockton pursue a physician to work with Miss Farrell."

Maggie smiled. "That's what I understand. Shall we go in?"

Elizabeth didn't move. "You still didn't tell me how the young man who almost knocked me over knew your name."

"In due time, doctor. All in due time."

Maggie opened the door and motioned Elizabeth in. Beyond the walls, painted cheerful colors of green and yellow pastels, strains of piano music rode on the ether from a room down the hall.

"Violet holds music sessions once a week for the women to have a brief respite from their lives of drudgery and toil," Maggie said.

"A wonderful idea but I'm surprised they come."

"I think it was difficult at first, but once a few started coming, the rest followed when they heard about the program. Now the sessions are well attended. Michael has played for them a few times."

Elizabeth raised her eyebrows. "Michael-the-Maul?"

Maggie nodded.

"I'm surprised someone like Violet Farrell would let him anywhere near these women."

"Oh, I believe she gave him strict instructions on how to comport himself. As I said, she has a quiet way, but she's extremely forceful about how the people who come here should be treated. Michael's a rogue, but he has a good heart underneath his slick veneer."

The music stopped. They could hear quiet conversation and gentle laughter coming from music room.

As they waited for people to emerge, Elizabeth asked, "You still haven't told me how you know so much about this place and Miss Farrell?"

"I come when I can to help Violet. I set up for meetings and, sometimes, I help the children with their reading. Not as often as I'd like, but when I can spare a morning or an afternoon. Violet is appreciative of any time I can devote here."

A group of about a dozen women poured out of the room down the hall. Behind them, a petite woman in a simple gray dress shook hands with an older man. They heard him say he couldn't linger. He had an appointment. He hurried away, nodding to those in the hall without speaking.

The woman in the gray dress approached Maggie and Elizabeth.

Maggie said, "Miss Farrell I'd like to introduce you to Doctor Elizabeth Kellogg."

Violet's face brightened as she looked up at Elizabeth. "Doctor Kellogg, I can't tell you how pleased I am to meet you. Mrs. Stockton told me you'd arrived, but she said you weren't to come to the Mission until after the New Year."

Maggie volunteered, "Well, we're taking a tour of the city to acquaint Doctor Kellogg with various places she'll need to be familiar with. We can't stay long, but I wanted to make sure she knew where the Mission was and had a chance to meet you."

"I see," Violet said. She looked back and forth between them. "Do you have time for me to show you around?"

Elizabeth raised an eyebrow at Maggie, "Would you mind? I'd love a quick tour. If it doesn't fit with the plans you've made, I'll understand. I want you to be the one to decide what today's schedule is."

"I think we can take a few minutes for you to look around, Doctor Kellogg. Why don't you two go ahead?" She looked at Violet and said, "I'll put the room back in order from the recital."

Violet said, "Thank you, Maggie, it would be a great help. Come with me, doctor."

Maggie watched Violet take charge in her quiet, yet commanding, way. She heard her explain to Elizabeth about the plight of the poor in San Francisco as they walked into the children's classroom. She knew what she'd say. She'd heard her give her speech to countless people when they visited the Mission.

Women of the dock workers and warehousemen all needed the same things: to be sheltered from the abuse of their often drunken husbands, to have proper nourishment for themselves and their children, to be given opportunities to improve themselves and their community, to have more than a rudimentary education for their children, and last of all, she would add the reason Elizabeth was here in San Francisco, to provide medical assistance and support to the women and their children.

By the time Maggie had moved the chairs and made the room ready for its next use, Elizabeth and Violet returned.

Maggie asked, "How was the tour? Did you get a good feel for the work here?"

"It was insightful. Miss Farrell has this place so well organized and is doing such good work. I'm looking forward to working with her."

Violet flushed at the praise, but said nothing.

Elizabeth turned to Violet. "Perhaps you and I should meet before the end of the year to talk about a schedule and specific information I'll need to know about the service I can render."

"Wonderful," Violet said. "Come any time, Doctor Kellogg, I will make time to sit down with you whenever you have time to visit." She turned to Maggie and added, "Thank you for bringing Doctor Kellogg along, Maggie, and thank you for putting the room back together for me. I appreciate it."

Their goodbyes said, Maggie guided Elizabeth toward the front door of the Mission house and out onto the street. They headed back up Ninth to Market and Maggie gave Elizabeth a commentary on the shops and businesses along the street. This one was good for prices, but that one carried inferior goods. Another shopkeeper was always willing to find something no one else had, but the man who ran the store next door was a dour man who didn't seem to want to cater to women at all. They looked in a few windows, even visited some of the shops. Maggie felt elated to have Elizabeth's company.

After strolling for more than an hour, they emerged from one of the shops. Maggie glanced skyward and said, "It looks like a storm is rolling in. We'd better head back to your place so we don't become victims of those ominous looking things." She pointed toward the San Francisco Bay and some threatening dark clouds.

Elizabeth nodded and they set off toward Van Ness Avenue at a brisk pace, trying to outrun the storm.

THE RAIN FELL in intermittent drops, pelting them as they walked the last several blocks to Elizabeth's house. They breathed a sigh of relief as they ascended the front steps and Elizabeth opened the door, happy they had made it to shelter before the storm hit with its full force.

A short time later, Elizabeth stared out the second story parlor window and watched rivulets of water trickle down the window panes. In the grayness below, nothing moved on Van Ness. She was certain everyone sought shelter as the tempest raged. Soon the new electric street lights would glisten on the wet street below, washing away some of the gloom, but it wouldn't wash away the problem Elizabeth wrestled with — what would she do about Maggie if the storm continued into the night?

Maggie appeared at her side with two cups of tea and handed one to Elizabeth. "What are you divining as you stare out this window into the storm?"

Elizabeth blew out her breath. "I'm trying to figure out how to get you home."

Maggie turned to look up at her now. "You'd put me out in this weather?"

"No, of course not. I thought you'd like to go home. If it continues on—"

"I'll have to stay the night."

"Yes."

"Is there a problem?"

Problem? Oh, yes, there most certainly was a problem.

"No. Well, it's just that I only have one...sleeping room." She looked down at her hands. Those steady, skilled hands of a physician, which never shook, unless she was in Maggie's presence.

Maggie stood on tiptoe and leaned into Elizabeth's ear, whispering, "It won't be a problem."

Elizabeth's head snapped back. Her voice squeaked as she said, "Won't it?"

"No. It won't. I saw a perfectly adequate Chesterfield in your office downstairs."

Of course. Why hadn't she thought of that? The couch. In her office. Far, far away downstairs. Elizabeth breathed a sigh of relief. Her tremors lessened. "I'll get some linens and sleep down there."

Maggie looked indignant. "You most certainly will not. *I'll* sleep down there, but only if I need to do so. The storm might be over soon and I'll be able to return home."

Elizabeth glanced out the window. This storm wouldn't pass with any speed. "I doubt this will end in a couple of hours. Besides, it wouldn't be safe for you to walk home in the dark. No. You'll stay here—in my sleeping quarters. I'll sleep on the Chesterfield."

Maggie still didn't look pleased. "Do you fit?"

"Fit? What do you mean?"

"On the Chesterfield. Do you fit? It's small. A two-seater."

Elizabeth hadn't thought of that. "I'll make do."

"That's silly. You're what? Six feet tall?"

"I am not. I'm a mere five and a half feet. I'll fit."

"Your sofa is no more than four and a half feet at the most. My five foot frame will be much better suited. You can stay in your own bed, which must be extra-long to accommodate your vast height." Maggie's eyes twinkled, matching her teasing words.

Elizabeth contemplated how to win this disagreement. Finally, an idea struck her. "Come with me." She leapt around Maggie and headed out of the parlor.

"Wait. Slow down. Those long legs are no match for me," Maggie taunted.

MAGGIE SMIRKED. "I told you."

Elizabeth looked uncomfortable lying on the Chesterfield. Her neck rested on one round arm while her feet rested against the one opposite arm forcing her to bend her knees. Her long black skirt hugged her thighs, outlining them.

Maggie suppressed an urge to caress them. Elizabeth would never make it through the night that way.

"My turn."

"No."

"Yes. It's my turn. You'll see I'm right. Oh, wait. That's why you don't want to get up. You don't want to admit you're wrong, do you?"

"I—"

"Now I understand, Doctor Kellogg. You don't want to accept it. Get up."

Elizabeth sighed. As she sat up, her skirt shifted, revealing sumptuous calves covered by black stockings before she shoved the fabric back toward the floor. She said nothing, but got up and gestured to the sofa.

Maggie sat, then reclined. She settled her neck on the arm as Elizabeth had done. When she stretched out her legs, her feet barely touched the other arm. She crossed her arms over her torso and turned to Elizabeth. A smile broke across her face.

Elizabeth eyed her, looking as if she were trying to figure out what conjuring trick Maggie used to pull this off.

"I'm sleeping here. I fit. You, Doctor Kellogg, do not. End of discussion."

Maggie watched Elizabeth as her facial expression changed from confusion to delight. "Maybe this," she gestured toward Maggie in the recumbent position, "was my intention all along, Miss Weston."

When Elizabeth walked out of the room, Maggie sprang up from the Chesterfield and ran after her.

IN THE MIDDLE of the night, Maggie bolted upright on the Chesterfield when a loud clap of thunder rattled the walls of the house. The storm raged on, fierce and without respite. From the small window behind the sofa, lightning lit up the alley on the side of the house and flashed into the room. The flash was so bright, it reached a wooden crate sitting in the far corner of the room and illuminated the books inside. Perhaps they awaited Elizabeth's attention. Another wild crack of thunder sounded like it opened a hole in the roof of the house to the sky. A thought for Elizabeth's safety propelled her onto her feet.

She stood in her sleeveless chemise and drawers, her dress, corset and petticoat lay neatly over the back of a wooden chair. The cold air swirled around her, causing her to shiver. She pulled the rumpled blanket from the Chesterfield and wrapped it around her, putting a layer of warmth between her body and the icy dampness, before heading out into the hallway.

Another flash of lightning, visible through the transom window over the front door lit up the face of the grandfather clock in the hall. Two-ten in the morning. As she crept up the stairs to the second floor, another loud crash of thunder shook the house. The wind wailed. Would she find Elizabeth sleeping peacefully as the tumult erupted outside? Or was she awake and fretful?

As she approached the parlor, she saw Elizabeth's silhouetted form standing at the window. On silent bare feet, she approached, as the storm pummeled the outside of the house.

Elizabeth seemed unsurprised to find Maggie standing beside her. She kept her gaze out the window as she asked, "Did the storm wake you, too?"

Maggie admired how elegant Elizabeth looked in her floor-length dressing gown. When she glanced at her feet, she envied her supple-looking leather house shoes. "I came to see if you were all right. This storm is so fierce."

Elizabeth kept her gaze on the squall outside. "When the house started shaking, I thought we were having another earthquake. I soon realized it wasn't true, but I was wide awake by then. I couldn't get back to sleep, so I thought I might as well get up and check to see what was happening outside. I'm sorry the storm disturbed your sleep."

Maggie stepped closer, grasping the blanket around her neck, exposing her underthings, shaking.

Elizabeth turned toward Maggie. Her eyes widened but the surprised look vanished as fast as it appeared and she said, "You're cold." She pointed to Maggie's bare feet. "Your feet." Elizabeth reached for her and pulled her into an embrace. "You shouldn't have gotten out of bed."

Maggie smiled into her soft dressing gown. "I wasn't in bed. I was on your Chesterfield. I'm the one who fit, remember?"

Elizabeth chuckled. Without another word, she guided Maggie toward the settee in the middle of the room. The two sat. Maggie curled her legs up under her, covering her feet with the blanket. Elizabeth kept her arm around her. They watched the storm rage. Maggie thought it reflected her own emotions, powerful and demanding, the drive to kiss Elizabeth strong, almost uncontrollable. Like the raw power of the storm, pummeling everything outside, another raged inside Maggie's body. She held her breath against it, hoping the feelings would subside. They didn't. She knew Elizabeth felt something, too, but she also knew she fought against those feelings—knew if she attempted to express her own, Elizabeth might bolt. She couldn't risk never seeing her again.

As the struggle churned within her, Maggie finally said, "You don't have to be afraid of me, Elizabeth."

"It's not you I fear, Maggie, never you." She drew Maggie in closer.

Maggie rested her head on Elizabeth's shoulder and felt a slight tremor from her as she did.

Elizabeth whispered, "It's me I fear."

Chapter Four

December 20, 1905

ELIZABETH WATCHED MAGGIE as she sat opposite her at the kitchen table eating breakfast, wondering if she should broach the subject of their time spent together in the middle of the night. After some time, the storm had calmed, the wind died down, the rain turned to a light mist. By the time she and Maggie parted company, Maggie returning to the sofa in the office downstairs, Elizabeth felt calmer.

Best not to even bring it up, she surmised. What would she say anyway? That she wanted to pick her up and carry her to her bed as the storm churned outside the window? That the sight of her in a chemise and frilly drawers had made her want to rip them from her body and ravage her in the middle of the night? These thoughts threatened to rob her of the tranquility she woke with this morning. Good thing they met in the kitchen fully dressed.

"I'll give you a penny."

Elizabeth glanced over at Maggie. "What?"

"I'll give you a penny for them. Your thoughts."

"No. You wouldn't. These thoughts are not for disclosure."

Elizabeth raised her eyebrows at the sight of Maggie's blush. Had Maggie divined her musings?

A knock on the door downstairs gave Elizabeth cause to breathe a sigh of relief. She scurried down to the first level, hoping by the time she returned Maggie would have forgotten their conversation.

As she opened the door, crisp fresh air buoyed her. A teenaged boy smiled up at her and held out a white envelope with tiny, meticulous writing on it — her name, she noted.

"From Mrs. Stockton," the lad said.

"Please wait." She went to the hall table and removed a coin from a small glass dish. She gave it to him in exchange for the envelope. He tipped his cap and bounded down the porch stairs without another word.

She opened the envelope before returning to Maggie. Inside, a printed invitation announced Mrs. Stockton's annual Christmas Gala to be held on Saturday, December 23, 1905 beginning at six o'clock. It surprised Elizabeth to think Mrs. Stockton would have the energy for such an affair.

A handwritten note followed the printed portion of the invitation. The script was the same small, precise writing as was on the face of the envelope. It read:

```
Doctor Kellogg,

I hope you will be able to attend. I am looking
forward to seeing you again. Please bring a guest
of your choosing.

Sarah S.
```

When Elizabeth returned to the kitchen table, invitation in hand, Maggie gave her a questioning look. "Good news, I hope," she said.

"Very good news, I think. It's an invitation to Mrs. Stockton's gala this Saturday."

"I've heard it's quite an occasion," Maggie said.

Her remark surprised Elizabeth. "You've never been?"

"No. I'm afraid Mrs. Stockton is of an age where she doesn't think of having photographs taken of her affair. I've never been asked."

Elizabeth looked at the invitation again. "It says here, I may bring a guest of my choosing."

Maggie stared, wide-eyed.

"Come with me."

"I—I couldn't. I don't have the proper clothes for such an event."

"Well, then, it looks like we need to go back to the shops to get you something to wear."

"Elizabeth, my shop and photographs do well, but I could never afford a dress for this kind of party. Mrs. Stanton and her friends are way out of my depth. I could never—"

"Yes, you could. Allow me. We'll go as soon as we've finished breakfast."

"No. You—I—can't allow it. It will be far too expensive."

Elizabeth penetrated Maggie with a look. "I can afford it."

"You can?"

Elizabeth nodded.

"How does a physician who volunteers her time helping the poor have money to buy someone like me a fancy dress gown?"

Elizabeth thought about how to frame her answer. How would she tell her about coming to an agreement with her brother? Best to explain it in simple terms. There was no need to elaborate on why. If she stuck to the how, she could explain her ability to buy Maggie a fine dress without revealing other details.

"I am about to tell you something," Elizabeth said. "When I do, I want you to listen and not ask me any questions."

MAGGIE KEPT SILENT as Elizabeth spoke in quiet tones. "My grandfather was a prominent banker in Baltimore. My father followed in his footsteps and increased the family fortune. My brother and I never wanted for anything. My mother was the greater influence in my life. She always had a soft spot for the poor and the downtrodden. Perhaps it's because she came from people of lesser means than my father did. Although she influenced me to be aware of those less fortunate and to try to help them, she didn't have the same influence on my brother. My father wasn't a greedy man, but, for reasons I shall never understand, my brother became one.

"I had a wonderful relationship with both my parents. When I told my father I wanted to become a doctor, he tried to dissuade me. But when he saw I was serious, he allowed me to attend Women's Medical College of Baltimore, and even encouraged me. When it became apparent I might not choose to marry, he made sure I would always have a place to live by willing me our family home in Baltimore. To make sure my brother was given his share of his estate, he left him our fine summer home on Chesapeake Bay. My father died several months before I graduated from medical school."

Maggie stretched out her hand to Elizabeth. "I'm so sorry."

When Elizabeth gave her a warning look, Maggie pressed her lips together and waited for her to continue. She didn't remove her hand and Elizabeth didn't pull away.

"I was saddened at his passing, but I know he was proud of my pursuits.

"My brother was jealous of my relationship with my father, always was. I don't know why. He always tried to intimidate his way around me. Father taught me to stand up to him, though, so he seldom got his way.

"When I agreed to leave Baltimore, my brother thought he could assume ownership of the family home. I would not allow it. If I was leaving, he was welcome to the house, but not without buying it from me, as would any other interested party."

Maggie said, "I'll bet he wasn't happy, was he?"

"No he was not. But he did it. In addition, he agreed to—let's call it a parting gift to his dear sister. By the time I left for San Francisco, quite a large amount of money was deposited in my account. So you see, I have a sizable reserve and I can afford to buy you a dress for Mrs. Stockton's Christmas gala."

For a fleeting moment, Maggie thought about her own circumstances in Boston when she was younger and how she was forced to flee the city, working her way across the country until she found a position as a photographer's assistant here in San Francisco. Did similar circumstances force Elizabeth to come here? Or did she truly make a decision because the thought of a new start in a different city excited her? It sounded like she had a comfortable life back in Baltimore. She worked in a clinic tending to people with needs similar to those she'd be working with in San Francisco. Why leave? She had told her she could ask no questions. She tried to leave her concern behind, but she couldn't help but be worried Elizabeth would need her savings to support herself. "You need your money to live—here." She waved her hand around the room.

"I do not."

"You don't?" It was a question, she acknowledged, but one which didn't seem to transgress.

"My agreement with the ladies of San Francisco is separate from my transactions with my brother. In contracting through Mrs. Stockton, we agreed they would provide the house where I could offer my medical services to them, and I would see to the needs of the less fortunate in their names as part of our agreement. Women of means will pay me a fee for my medical services, which in turn will pay for my daily living expenses. So, you see, money is not an issue."

Maggie contemplated the information. Finally, she said, "I know you said no questions, but I have just one."

"One *more* question?"

Maggie thought she might not allow it, but Elizabeth nodded, looking as if it would take a pry bar to get her to answer. She knew it was a rude question, but she felt compelled to ask it anyway. "Are you quite wealthy, then?"

Would Elizabeth throw her out for making such an inquiry? Maggie registered surprise when laughter burst from Elizabeth. She said, "I suppose I am."

"Then, yes, you may buy me a suitable dress so I may accompany you to the gala, but not because you're wealthy, only because you can afford it."

"There's a difference?"

"Certainly. I wouldn't presume to allow someone to buy me a dress because they had money. I'd feel like a bought woman, someone of immoral repute." She hoped Elizabeth noted her teasing tone. "But a friend who has the means to help a friend without bringing hardship upon herself, it's an entirely different story, isn't it? So, my answer is yes."

Elizabeth eyed her. "You'll allow me to buy you a dress?"

"Of course. You can afford it."

Another laugh from Elizabeth made Maggie's heart soar.

"And you'll go to the gala with me?"

"Well, I will need somewhere to show off my fine new dress. Won't I?"

"Wonderful. Let's go visit the shops."

ONCE QUAN LUCK arrived to take care of the photography studio for Maggie, she and Elizabeth made their way to one of the dress shops on Market Street.

They found the perfect dress—a nearly finished smooth silk with brocade accents containing the iridescent colors of peacock feathers. Someone ordered it, the shopkeeper said, and failed to make payment on it. So the dressmaker hung it in the shop hoping someone would admire it and want to own it.

Maggie loved the feel of it, so cool and smooth. The golden accent threads sparkled in a beam of bright sunlight as she modeled the frock. A thrill skittered through her when she saw how Elizabeth's eyes lit up when she stepped from behind the dressing screen.

"Do you like it?" Maggie asked, blushing under Elizabeth's gaze.

"Very much so."

Something in Elizabeth's voice made Maggie feel as if she could easily become that woman of immoral repute she mentioned earlier in the day—but for no one other than Elizabeth. "I'm glad," she whispered.

Where had this shyness come from? Perhaps it was the way Elizabeth licked her lips when she looked at her. It made a tremor, which started in her chest, make a hasty descent to the spot between her legs. A vision appeared of Elizabeth touching her there, where the vibrations she felt made it difficult to stand still. Her cheeks flared again. She knew they must be the color of beet juice.

The dressmaker stepped between them, clearing her throat. She addressed Maggie. "Will madam take the dress? It would need a little alteration but I can have it ready by Saturday morning."

Maggie agreed, and as they dashed across Market Street toward Maggie's shop, the distraction of Elizabeth's rather titillating look stayed with her, making her body tingle. When they reached the shop, Maggie saw Quan Luck assisting a customer. Something about his demeanor told her he might need her assistance.

"I'd better get back to work. It looks as though Quan Luck may need help. Thank you for the exquisite dress, Elizabeth."

She opened the shop door and hesitated before going inside.

"I'm glad you liked it. It was a happy coincidence someone reneged on purchasing it. Shall I call for you on Saturday? I'll hire a carriage and we can ride to the gala together."

"It sounds wonderful, Elizabeth. Yes, thank you!"

As she stepped into the shop and engaged Quan Luck and his customer, she kept her eyes on the street and watched Elizabeth until she disappeared out of sight.

WHEN ELIZABETH LEFT Maggie at her shop door, she crossed Market Street to head for home. She glanced back at the shop and noticed Michael standing in the doorway of the music store, watching her. She thought about Maggie's evaluation of Michael as a rogue with a good heart.

She wondered if she were no better than Michael-the-Maul, chasing beautiful women like a child chases butterflies in the park. She had drooled over Maggie in that beautiful dress, wanted to take her in her arms and kiss her firmly on the lips, draw her to her, press breast against breast, body against body. However, Michael would pursue any attractive woman. Women in general were not in danger of being caught in her net. It wasn't her way. She couldn't help the strong feelings she had for Maggie. She knew it. She felt these things for her and her alone. No. She was no Michael.

Maggie looked stunning in the beautiful gown. How was she going to get through Mrs. Stockton's party with Maggie beside her in that dress? How would she be able to escape the ever-probing eye of Amelia Rosemont? Surely, she'd see the way she looked at Maggie. She'd realize the rumors she'd heard were true. What was Elizabeth to do then? It would be bad enough to have her own reputation sullied by the likes of Amelia Rosemont, but what of Maggie? She couldn't risk it. Somehow, she'd have to get out of going to the gala at the Stockton Mansion.

If she could manage to bow out gracefully, Maggie could attend on her own. She'd still send the carriage for her with her regrets. She'd say she was ill and Maggie should attend anyway. She'd explain to Mrs. Stockton later—perhaps not a complete explanation, but she could allude to Amelia's "rumors" without detail. She could inform Mrs. Stockton of the conversation Amelia had with her at her party, say it unnerved her enough to make her want to avoid her for the moment. Mrs. Stockton would understand. She could trust her, couldn't she?

By the time she reached Van Ness and made the turn toward home, she had talked herself out of the ridiculous scheme. Maggie would never go to the party without her. If she pursued the idea, she wouldn't be surprised if, on the night of the gala, Maggie didn't have the carriage driver pull up in front of Elizabeth's house and demand to know what was going on. She also couldn't disappoint Mrs. Stockton. The one person responsible for freeing her from the shackles put on her in Baltimore, allowing her to start this new life doing what she loved, far from the reach and influence of her imperious brother.

But was it true? Was she truly free of him? Or would he follow her for the rest of her life spreading innuendo, causing doubt about her scruples and her integrity? She had moved out of the shadow of the man who thought he could dominate and intimidate her. She couldn't let his influence move across the country with her. She needed to stop allowing him to control her decisions.

A block from home, she made up her mind and resolved to attend Mrs. Stockton's gala with Maggie as her guest, Amelia Rosemont be damned. It was her life. She'd do as she pleased. Of course, she wouldn't allow the likes of Amelia Rosemont to see her propensity toward women by ogling Maggie at the party. She'd control herself and act as if she'd done Maggie a favor by inviting her to a grand affair she'd never had occasion to attend. She resolved she could do it. She'd have to—for Maggie's sake as well as her own.

She entered the front door of her house and visions of Maggie in the stunning gown rose up in her mind's eye again. Could she exercise enough self-control when it came to Maggie Weston?

December 23, 1905

THE SOUND OF the horse's hooves echoed through the night as the carriage moved up the street toward Mrs. Stockton's mansion.

Elizabeth leaned toward Maggie and said, "You look lovely tonight."

"Thank you," Maggie whispered.

When the mansion came into view, both women drew in a sharp breath at the sight. The house was lit up with lanterns hung from beams and trees. Pine boughs reached across the front of the house on three levels with large wreaths strung every few feet. Giant, red taffeta bows accented each one. The interior of the house shone with the light of candles burning in every window.

The driver stopped at the end of a long line of carriages to wait his turn to pull up to the large front doors of the mansion. While they waited, the two women watched people dressed in finery leave their vehicles and climb the stone steps to the party. Excitement filled the air as their conversations surrounded them.

When their carriage reached the front of the line, the driver helped Elizabeth and Maggie disembark so they could join those ascending the steps into the warm glow above.

Maggie leaned in toward Elizabeth and said, "The decorations are more beautiful than I imagined."

"Yes, it's stunning, isn't it? It's an absolute transformation from when I was here last time."

Inside, shimmering candles and sparkling decorations filled every surface, captivating them. Elizabeth watched as Maggie took it all in. Her eyes twinkled in the candle light. She took Elizabeth's breath away.

An attendant stepped up behind them and offered to take their coats. As Elizabeth shrugged hers off, she looked into Maggie's eyes and saw her look change from one of wonder to hunger. Pleasure ran through Elizabeth, recognizing Maggie's response to her in her glistening gold gown.

"You look stunning, Doctor Kellogg."

Elizabeth blushed. "Thank you, Miss Weston," she whispered. "I love your hair. Are those tiny pearls you've woven into it?"

"They are the only jewelry I own. They were my mother's. It's all I have of her."

Elizabeth watched tears well up in Maggie's eyes. She felt helpless against the rest of her unspoken story. She wanted to draw Maggie into a comforting embrace. Instead, she reached out a hand to touch the delicate beads in Maggie's hair. As she did, she saw movement out of the corner of her eye. Mrs. Rosemont. She drew her hand back and gave Maggie an apologetic look.

"Perhaps you'll tell me about your mother one day."

Maggie brushed away a tear. "I'd like to, Eliz—Doctor Kellogg."

A few people walked through the foyer toward the main hall, all strangers to Elizabeth. She put her hand on Maggie's forearm and smiled to encourage her.

"Shall we go in?"

Maggie pulled herself up to her full height, reaching slightly above Elizabeth's shoulder. Elizabeth felt a rush of affection for this woman. No one would understand it. How could they, even she couldn't comprehend it. She gazed into Maggie's eyes and saw her own tenderness reflected back at her.

Maggie pursed her lips, smiled and said, "I'm ready, Doctor Kellogg. Let's celebrate this grand Christmas with Mrs. Stockton, shall we?"

Chapter Five

December 25, 1905

ELIZABETH'S BREATH CAUGHT at the sight of Maggie when she entered the Palace Hotel dining room. Maggie's eyes widened at the opulent sight of the dining area décor, causing Elizabeth to smile. Maggie looked stunning in her peacock feather-colored dress—the one she'd worn to the gala. Once again, she wore the tiny pearls in her hair.

"You should have warned me, Elizabeth."

"About what?"

"That I would be shocked at the sight of this place. I'd always heard it was grand—" she looked up at the iridescent glass domed ceiling above her head and followed the lines of the marble columns around the outer edge of the room " — but I never imagined it would look like this." When she looked back at Elizabeth, her eyes sparkled like the crystals in the overhead chandeliers.

"Before you came in, I spoke to the head waiter and he told me carriages used to roll up right inside the hotel to let passengers disembark where the garden court is now. It must have been quite a sight with horses and carriages entering and leaving the hotel. Can you imagine?"

Maggie wrinkled her nose and said, "Must have had quite an odor."

Elizabeth and Maggie snickered softly.

The head waiter greeted them and escorted them to their dining table. Soon, they awaited the arrival of the first course of their meal.

Time suspended. Noises receded. The Palace Hotel dining room felt dreamlike. A thought whisked across Elizabeth's mind. *If we could remain here, in this moment, for the rest of our lives, it would be heaven.*

The thought vanished at the sound of Maggie's voice. "You've become quiet, Elizabeth. What are you thinking?"

She hesitated, trying to let her thoughts congeal into something which wouldn't frighten Maggie off. "Two things," she said. "The first is how enchanted this place is with its fine décor and its beautiful holiday decorations. I'm glad you could join me today. The second is—" she reached into her pocket and pulled out a small box " — this."

She slid the box across the table toward Maggie and watched as her eyes widened. She looked up at Elizabeth without making any movement to pick it up.

Elizabeth nodded toward the box and said, "It's for you, Maggie. Open it."

Maggie's look changed from surprise to a tempest, her brown eyes deepening to become the storm.

"Elizabeth, I can't ever repay you for this fine lunch. You can't give me a gift in addition to this." She lowered her head, staring at the fine golden fork in her hand. "I feel so awkward. I didn't get you anything."

Panic overtook Elizabeth. It was too much. She'd overstepped. With one small gesture, she'd ruined everything. The noise around them intensified. The magic dissipated, leaving behind nothing but a puff of acrid smoke.

"Maggie, I didn't mean—"

"I know you mean well. It's just, I don't know. I'd like to reciprocate, but I don't have the same means. The photography shop is adequate for my needs, but it can't compare to, well, to your apparent resources. The carriages, the dress, now this." She pointed toward the box as if it were a dead rodent.

"You don't ever need to feel you must reciprocate, Maggie. I enjoy your company. I like being able to buy you gifts and provide carriages rather than see you walk the city with your equipment."

"Quan Luck carries the equipment."

"That's not the point."

"What is the point, Elizabeth?"

"The point is...." What was the point? She had no idea. She did these things because she wanted to be close to Maggie, to spend time with her, to make her happy. Unfortunately, today she succeeded in doing the opposite. What should she do now? How could she make it right?

Maggie stared at her, waiting for her to finish her explanation.

She drew in a deep breath. It was time to put everything on the table. If it was the end of their friendship, she needed to accept it wasn't meant to be. She would need to pick up the pieces and move on. She'd done it before. She could do it again, even if her feelings were so much deeper than they'd been in times past.

She started again. "The point is I've never meant to make you feel inadequate, Maggie. I hoped my gestures gave you pleasure. I never thought they would offend you. Perhaps I shouldn't have done them, but know they were done from the heart and without intent to embarrass you. Now I see my motives may have been more for my own pleasure than yours. It does give me so much pleasure to see you happy. It was my only motivation, Maggie. Please accept my apology. I'm so sorry," she sobbed.

THE MORE ELIZABETH spoke the more horrible Maggie felt. She cared a lot for Elizabeth and never meant to make her so distressed. Now, as she watched her dab her eyes with her napkin, Maggie knew she had to do something. However, she had no idea what she should do. She stretched her hand across the table and turned it palm up, waiting for Elizabeth to take it.

Elizabeth stared past her, trying to compose herself, taking gulps of air and blowing them back out through tightened lips. Finally, she looked down at Maggie's extended hand and back up at her.

"It's an olive branch, Elizabeth. Please take it."

Elizabeth looked down at her hand again, then plunged her own into Maggie's grasp. "Please don't send me away. I couldn't bear it," she whispered.

Maggie grasped her hand tighter. "This has nothing to do with sending you away, Elizabeth. It's about me wanting to have control over my own life. It's not your fault. You are nothing but kind and generous. This is my problem and I'm the one who should apologize."

When Elizabeth opened her mouth to speak, Maggie held up her free hand to stop her. "It's a long story, I'm afraid, and one I'm not comfortable sharing in a public place. If you're done with your meal, as I am, I think we should leave and I will explain it to you at home."

Elizabeth gave her a weak smile. "All right—yes, I'm quite done with my meal, too. Let's go back to your living quarters and you tell me all about it. If it helps us to remain close, I want to hear your story."

When Maggie let go of her hand, Elizabeth picked up the box from the table and put it back into her pocket.

Maggie winced and said, "Just one thing. Once I tell you what I have to say, it may be you who will send me away."

THEY SAT ON the small settee, close together, in Maggie's living quarters while Maggie explained one of the hardest times of her life. She was fifteen when she sat at her mother's side, clutching her frail hand as she took her last difficult breaths.

"Tuberculosis," Maggie said. "And I almost came undone

with the pain of losing her."

Elizabeth grasped Maggie's hand with her own. She wanted to take her in her arms to offer comfort, but Maggie looked so brittle, she decided it was the most she should do.

"After the funeral, as I climbed out of the dark chasm of grief, I realized I had nowhere to go. We had no family in Boston. Mother's people were all in Ireland. She had few friends in Boston because she worked most of her waking hours trying to keep a roof over our heads and food on the table. She didn't have much time for socializing. She did it so I could get an education. She felt it was important, so I went to school every day and studied hard."

She gave Elizabeth a weak smile and squeezed her hand.

"But those days were done. Soon, I'd have nowhere to live. In a week, I'd have to pay the rent or move out of the little apartment in Southie."

Maggie recognized Elizabeth's confusion when she furrowed her brow.

"Southie is what South Boston is called, like South of the Slot in San Francisco. All poor people must live in the southern areas of cities, I guess."

When Elizabeth nodded, encouraging her to continue, she said, "I was soon to turn sixteen. I knew I'd have to leave school and find a job immediately. With the wages a sixteen year old could earn, I'd have to leave our home, too."

Tears welled up in Elizabeth's eyes as she listened to Maggie. She whispered, "I'm so sorry you had to go through such an experience."

"That's not even the worst of it," Maggie said.

She blew out her breath trying to get up the courage for the rest of her tale.

"I went to work in a boarding house for meager wages and a place to live. The work was difficult. The landlady was a tyrant. I felt trapped and knew my mother would have been disappointed in how my life turned out.

"One day, a man came to visit his friend who was staying at the boarding house and saw me there. He and his wife knew my mother. He took me aside and asked about her. When I told him of my circumstances, he didn't say much, but he looked distressed. It was nice to hear his words of sympathy, but I knew I'd never see him again.

"I didn't know the landlady lurked around the corner during our conversation. I was given the dirtiest of jobs after he left. I didn't think I could feel any more gloomy than I already did, but after that day, I found out there were depths even lower than the ones I'd reached."

Elizabeth murmured, "Oh, Maggie."

Maggie smiled at Elizabeth through glistening eyes. "I was saved, though. At least for a while. Mr. O'Malley went home and told his wife about my mother and me. Two days later, they were both back, insisting I would come to live with them. Mr. O'Malley had a photography shop in Boston. If I was willing, he said, I could work for him in his shop and learn to be a photographer. He said many women were taking up the trade these days and did quite well at it. The O'Malleys were kind people. I was so relieved and grateful. When I left that day, I'm afraid I gave the landlady a bit of a smug look. Maybe it's why everything turned out as it did—later on, I mean."

"What happened?"

"Mr. O'Malley taught me everything he knew about photography. His equipment was out-of-date and his attitude, old-fashioned, but he was kind-hearted. The O'Malleys kept telling me they needed to find me a nice young man to take care of me. I tried to tell them I didn't want a nice young man, nor did I want someone to take care of me. I was happy learning photography and hoped to have a shop of my own someday."

"And you achieved your dream."

"Yes, I did. But before that happened, something else—something quite awful happened."

Maggie took a deep breath to collect herself, knowing the final part of the story was the most difficult.

"The O'Malleys introduced me to a young man named Harry Ryan. He was a few years older than me and quite industrious. He studied to be an engineer. The O'Malleys were thrilled to have found such a match. He courted me for about a year. I had no interest in him. I told him so. He voiced disappointment, but told me he would be a good provider and I might learn to care for him as he cared for me. I continued to voice my desire not to marry. He came to see me less and less. I thought we were finished and I would never see him again.

"One winter evening, when I was walking home from the photography shop, he came up from behind me and took me by the arm. I insisted he let me go. He refused. He claimed he had something to show me. I protested as he dragged me into the warehouse district, into a deserted alley there. He said he would prove to me what a good mate he could be. He said he'd show me what I was missing. He tried to lift my skirts. I fought him off. He pushed me against some crates. When he started to unbutton his pants, something in me came undone and a strength I didn't know I had burst through me. I lifted my feet onto his stomach and strained against him with all my might. With one final kick, he flew across the alley, stumbled, and slammed into the stone steps of a warehouse back door. I took off running, but when I looked back, he still lay there, unmoving. I ran back to him even though I was afraid he would leap up and seize me, but he didn't move. Blood seeped from a wound near the back of his head. His body rested at an odd angle. He didn't make a sound."

Elizabeth could no longer hold back. She reached out and put her arm around Maggie. She didn't resist. Her final words had an eerie calm about them.

"I killed him."

ELIZABETH FELT THE horror of Maggie's experience creep into her chest as she spoke. When she pronounced Harry Ryan dead, Elizabeth said, "You don't know for sure, Maggie. A blow to the head could have left him unconscious. After a time, he might have revived." She hoped for Maggie's sake it was true. "He could have gotten up and walked away. How do you know it didn't happen?"

"I—I don't. When I saw him lying there, unmoving, I ran from the alley. I ran all the way home. Fortunately, the O'Malleys had a dinner engagement. It's the reason I walked home alone in the first place. On ordinary days, Mr. O'Malley and I walked home together, but he left the shop early because of his plans with his wife.

"When I reached home, I had one thought. I had to flee. I packed up my clothes and my prized possession, a Kodak box camera. I saved every penny I could for months, so I couldn't leave it behind. Besides, Mr. O'Malley thought the camera useless because it took two-and-a-half-inch pictures. What he didn't realize was the small size made it easy to take everywhere. I'd bought it a few weeks before and had only taken a few photographs, so I put it in my carpetbag with my clothes and bought a train ticket to Chicago—as far as I could go and still have a few dollars to my name."

"You were very brave," Elizabeth said, knowing she'd thought about abandoning Baltimore right after her brother's confrontation. She gave up the idea, though. She wasn't bold enough to leave until she secured employment somewhere else.

Maggie appeared calmer, now. Elizabeth thought it best to keep her talking. Maybe she could pull more pleasant memories from her. "How did you come to San Francisco?"

"When I arrived in Chicago, I found a photography shop run by a woman. She hired me to develop her photographs for her.

She detested that part of the process, preferring to make the images and work with people. In light of what I had done—"

"What you *thought* you'd done."

Maggie repeated Elizabeth's statement, trying it out. "Anyway, I was glad to stay in her darkroom out of the public eye. She let me stay with her and her husband and wouldn't allow me to pay for my board. She was an extremely perceptive woman. I think she knew I was running from something or someone, but she never pried.

"Once I put aside a little money, enough to pay for train fare west with a little left over, I wanted to put even more miles between me and Boston. I told her I was leaving. She said she wasn't surprised. She came with me to the train station. As I started to board the train, she thrust something into my hand, an envelope. She told me not to open it until after the train left the station. I did as she asked and outside of the city limits, I opened the packet and found fifty dollars inside. Imagine! I had only worked for her for a few months and she gave me such a gift. I was so shocked—and grateful."

Elizabeth said, "I find people can be quite kind sometimes." And harsh at others. It made her think of Harry Ryan—and she wondered if, in fact, he was truly dead.

MAGGIE LEANED IN closer to Elizabeth. She felt so comforted by her presence. She dreaded the moment Elizabeth would announce it was time for her to leave.

Elizabeth said, "May I ask you a question?"

"Of course. You can ask me anything."

"Did you ever wonder why you didn't want to marry Harry? Why you couldn't love him?"

"I thought he wasn't the right person. I thought perhaps someone would come along one day, and I'd fall in love."

"A man?"

Maggie moved away from Elizabeth to get a better look at her face.

"What do you mean?"

"Are you expecting to fall head over heels for the right man?"

"I guess. Maybe. No. Not really." I think I'm falling for you, though, Elizabeth Kellogg, but I don't dare give voice to this feeling.

"Have you ever considered you might be a woman who is attracted to another woman? Some do, you know."

Maggie's eyes widened. Could Elizabeth read her thoughts?

"I—I'm not sure. I never felt the way I thought I should about any man."

"What way do you think you should feel? If you found the right person, of course?"

Maggie blew out her breath. "I—I suppose I would want to spend all my time with the person. I never wanted to be with Harry at all. I cringed when he would show up to dinner. Mr. O'Malley often invited him."

"Have you ever felt you wanted to spend time with someone? More time than was possible?"

"Only recently." Maggie looked down at her hands, resting in her lap. When she looked back up at Elizabeth, she said, "Sometimes—no often—more than often, I think I might be falling for...you."

THE EMOTIONS FLOWING through Elizabeth at Maggie's declaration were impossible for her to sort out. She felt elated, anxious, cautious, helpless, confused and buoyant. She wanted to cry. She wanted to laugh. She wanted to kiss Maggie fully on the lips as she longed to do for weeks now. But she didn't want to frighten her and she didn't want to lead her down a path she would not want to go.

When she felt she couldn't go on without some contact, she took Maggie's hands in hers. They were cold. "Your hands are freezing."

Maggie tried to pull them away.

Elizabeth stopped her. "Don't. Let me warm them." She enfolded them in her own and rubbed with a soothing circular motion. She felt the warmth return. It gave her time to think about what she should do next. She decided the anxiousness she felt came from concern for Maggie—concern they would end up the same way she and Irene had—discovered, ostracized, banished. She couldn't put Maggie through that. She'd already been through so much and she was still honest with Elizabeth about it all.

Elizabeth decided she must be forthright with Maggie.

"It seems you are not the only one harboring secrets, Maggie. I have a story to tell also."

Maggie surprised her by pulling her much-warmer hands away and leaning close again. She put her head on Elizabeth's shoulder. "I'm ready. Tell me your story."

Elizabeth began her confession by saying her brother never liked her. "We were always in competition. He followed in my father's footsteps and became a financier. My father was good at it. My brother was not nearly as talented. When I became a doctor, he asked me why I couldn't just become a wife and settle down, doing what I was born to do, servicing my husband and having children."

Maggie pushed away from Elizabeth and stared. "That's horrid. What did you say?"

She drew Maggie back to her, feeling comforted by the contact, as she said, "I called him a pig and walked away."

Maggie giggled.

"I lived with my father in his house while I attended medical school. My mother died several years earlier. When my father died, he left the house to me. I would never be wealthy, but I'd never want for a roof over my head or anything I needed. He knew I wanted to work with the poor and my stipend would be meager so he made provision for an adequate income in a small trust.

"My brother lived in his own house with his wife. He inherited my father's business and proceeded to ruin it. Fortunately, his house was a wedding present from my father and was paid for or he might have lost it, too. God help us, if that would have happened. He might have wanted to move in with me.

"I knew from an early age I never wanted to marry. I also realized my attraction to women when I reached my secondary school years. I met a woman while I was in medical school. Irene was her name. We liked each other a great deal. We were young and impulsive. After many months of pretending we were nothing but friends, we ended up in bed together."

She glanced at Maggie and noticed her breathing had deepened and her cheeks reddened, but she said nothing, so Elizabeth continued. "As I said, I liked Irene, but I think I liked how I felt when I touched her—and when she touched me—even more. We often spent nights at my house with trysts in my bedroom. It lasted well after I graduated from medical school and was working at the women's clinic in Baltimore.

"I had no idea my brother had a key to my house. Apparently, he brought his mistress there for his own rendezvous when I was working. On a day when I should have been at the clinic, Irene and I, young and impetuous as we were, decided to stay at home and...play." Elizabeth's cheeks turned crimson.

"We didn't hear him come in. He burst through my bedroom door and found Irene and I in an embarrassing state of undress. Fortunately, we still had our undergarments on, but we were in bed together. Unfortunately, my brother stared at us from the doorway. However, to my advantage, his paramour stood beside him with a look of utter shock on her face."

"What happened next?"

"My brother said, 'I'll be downstairs,' and left, dragging his mistress behind him. Irene and I dressed and she left the house by a back door. When I got to the parlor, my brother sat alone on a large sofa with a smug look on his face. He began to berate me, told me I was unnatural and told me I was condemned to hell. My response was simple, 'As are you, brother, and more so, for I have been unfaithful to no one, but *you* have betrayed a wife.'"

"What did he do then?"

"He blanched. I knew I had him as much as he had me. Afterwards, we sat and came to an agreement. We would give each other a year. I would find employment far from Baltimore. I would also allow him to purchase my house once he sold his. In addition, he would put an extra amount into my account for my travels and to live on after I left.

"Finding a new position to suit me took more time than I imagined it would. My time was running out when I met a young lawyer who knew Mrs. Stockton. He put us in touch with each other. After several exchanges, Mrs. Stockton and I came to the agreement about which you already know. It worked out even better than I expected because my home here is provided for me and my practice with the upper echelons of the matrons of San Francisco is ready-made and gives me time to devote to the poor women South of the Slot, as you refer to it."

"What happened to Irene?"

Elizabeth realized this was the crux of the story. It was time to bring it full circle from Baltimore back to their current circumstances. "Irene found it difficult to recover from her embarrassment. She came from a well-known family and fear of exposure filled her with dread. She thought my brother might unmask her. I'm not even sure he knew who she was and our agreement included never revealing anything of what happened. I saw Irene once after the incident. When I tried to see her again, she refused to receive me. I resorted to sending her notes. They were returned, unopened. A few months later, I read about her marriage in the *Baltimore Sun*. It took me weeks to recover from my shock at the news. Not so much because I felt the loss of someone I cared about, but because I felt marriage was so completely opposite of what Irene wanted for her life. I hope she found contentment in her decision, but I suppose I'll never know."

Maggie asked, "What about you? How did you feel about her decision?"

"For a long time, I blamed myself for putting Irene through

such a travesty. When I heard she'd married, I finally put my guilt aside. She made her decision. If she found happiness in it, then I was happy for her. If anyone should have felt remorse over the trouble he caused, it should have been my brother, but he's a donkey's behind and only looks out for himself and his own gratifications. So I had to put it aside, too.

"When I arrived in San Francisco, I determined I would spend the rest of my life without companionship. Then, I met you."

Maggie's face shone as she smiled up at Elizabeth.

Elizabeth said, "Now, I have one grave concern."

The look on Maggie's face changed to apprehension.

Elizabeth plunged onward. "Can I risk putting someone I feel so much more deeply for than I ever felt for Irene at risk of exposure? I am afraid, Maggie, so afraid—for you, for us."

Maggie looked at her, facial expression turning into an innocent, beguiling, look again as she said, "What are you afraid of?"

Elizabeth sighed. "So many things: discovery, hurting you, being alone again after finding you now. How can I act on what I feel—what I think you feel, too—with the risks so high either way? If we embrace how we feel, we risk exposure. If we don't, we risk loneliness and misery."

Maggie sat up and faced her, a look of determination on her face. "This isn't for you to decide alone, Elizabeth. I am part of this. I have some say."

She was right, of course, she did have a say. Elizabeth could try to shield her, but in the end, she had every right to decide to be a part of Elizabeth's life and let Elizabeth be a part of hers, as friends...or something more.

The twinkle in Maggie's eyes returned. Elizabeth loved seeing them sparkle.

Maggie said, "Besides, I have a huge advantage over you or Irene."

Wariness crept through Elizabeth. "What's that?"

"No one but me has a key to this place."

"Not even Quan Luck?"

Maggie guffawed. "Especially Quan Luck. I trust him, but my life is my own. No one will walk in on *us*, I assure you."

MAGGIE KNEW SHE'D be undone by Elizabeth's kiss, but she didn't care. She leaned in and pressed her lips into Elizabeth's. Warmth spread throughout her body and settled between her legs. For a brief moment, she wondered what

Elizabeth and Irene did on those dark nights in Baltimore. Then thoughts of what she'd like to do with Elizabeth swirled in her mind. She reached for Elizabeth's cheek and ran her finger down her soft skin until she reached the corner of her mouth. As she touched their lips, engaged in the kiss, a jolt of desire plunged through her body. She moaned and pressed closer to Elizabeth, deepening the kiss.

Elizabeth pulled away, leaving Maggie with an overwhelming sense of loss.

It took a moment to catch her breath.

"Are you sure you want to do this, Maggie? You must be sure."

Maggie found it difficult to speak. She couldn't manage more than a breathy, "yes," before pulling Elizabeth back into an embrace, and crushing her lips again.

Elizabeth moved Maggie into a reclining position, her head against a small pillow on the settee. Maggie's eyes still glistened, but she gave Elizabeth a questioning look.

Elizabeth said, "If at any time you don't feel comfortable and want me to stop, say so. Please, you must, Maggie."

Maggie searched Elizabeth's face, then nodded.

Elizabeth knelt beside the sofa, cupped Maggie's face and kissed her again. Maggie felt as if she'd float off the couch. Elizabeth ran two fingers over her cheek, followed her jaw line to her neck, switched to using her index finger to trail over the fabric of her dress along the space between Maggie's breasts. Maggie shivered. Her chest heaved in response. She mewed like a newborn kitten. If she thought she had come undone with Elizabeth's kiss, she had no words for what she felt when Elizabeth cupped her breast for an instant before she broke the contact.

Elizabeth studied Maggie as she took deep, gulping breaths, and asked, "Are you all right?"

Through her labored breathing, Maggie managed, "I—I never knew I could feel this. It's—you're intoxicating."

A wide grin broke across Elizabeth's lips before she claimed Maggie's mouth once more, only breaking from the kiss to move down her exposed neck. Maggie closed her eyes and moaned again, pulling Elizabeth closer.

Maggie moved her hand to Elizabeth's side, beside her breast, and began stroking, visions of touching her, peeling away the fabric covering her body, loomed in her mind. She widened her caresses until she felt the start of the soft, round shape above her corset.

As she moved closer, she trembled in anticipation, but

Elizabeth's hand clamped over hers, stopping her.

Maggie's eyes flew open. Had she done something wrong?

Elizabeth's blue eyes were dark, almost teal in the moonlight. She said softly, "If you continue to touch me like that, I can't be responsible for what happens next and I'm afraid we would be moving too fast. As much as I'd like to take this further, Maggie—" she choked out the next words, "—I think we must stop."

All the air rushed from Maggie's lungs. "Have I done s-something wrong?"

Elizabeth's look softened. She touched Maggie's hair, pushing it up off her forehead. "No, my sweet Maggie, you have done nothing wrong. You're perfect. I'm concerned you'll do something you may regret later. If we take our time and you have time to process these feelings, it will be better if we decide later to take what is between us another step."

Maggie sat up, feeling shy and muddled, she said, "You are not rejecting me?"

"Oh, Maggie, no. Never. I am concerned about rushing you. I want to give you time to be sure this is what you want. As for me, I can barely control myself for wanting to kiss you—touch you. I've dreamed about you, Maggie. I long for you. But I don't want to rush you into anything."

Maggie smiled as she pulled Elizabeth to her and kissed her softly. Then she said, "Thank you, Elizabeth. You are so kind. I'm not sure I need the time you propose, but I'll take your offer under advisement. She glanced out the window. "It's late. You have no carriage tonight. You must stay."

"I cannot."

"It wasn't a suggestion. It was an order."

Elizabeth pushed away from Maggie. "An order? Since when do you think you can order me around, Maggie Weston?" Her smile gave the teasing away.

"Oh, I don't know, perhaps since you gave me a kiss making my toes curl in my shoes." Maggie laughed.

Elizabeth joined her but stopped abruptly, saying, "No. I cannot. You only have this settee for me to sleep on. It's smaller than my Chesterfield. I'd roll off the first time I tried to turn over."

Maggie stared. "I have a bed and unlike you, I'm not afraid to have you in it."

"No."

"Why?"

"Think of the conversation we've been having. Sharing your bed would be imprudent. Remember when you stayed at my house during the storm? I told you then I knew I had nothing to fear from you, it's my own ability to control myself around you I question."

She caressed Maggie's cheek again, pulling away quickly.

"'Tis a bed for two," Maggie whispered.

Elizabeth tilted her head, questioning.

"It belonged to the couple who owned the photography shop. This was their living quarters. Being married, they had a bed for two."

"I can't."

"You can. You said you didn't want to rush things. I agree. However, it doesn't mean I can stand for you to run off into the night all alone. I'd be sick with worry. No, you must stay. You won't sleep on the settee as it's entirely unsuitable. Instead, we will use my bed and we will use it for one purpose—for sleeping. You," she jabbed her finger toward Elizabeth, "will lie beside me and use your will power, which kept me from touching you a little while ago, to stay on your side of the mattress, and you will sleep. When we awake in the morning, you will get up, get dressed, give me a proper kiss goodbye and be off to your house on Van Ness to finish getting ready for patients at the first of the year."

Elizabeth tried to stifle her smile, but the thought still haunted her—how was she going to sleep with Maggie lying right there, beside her. The longing she knew would be there would keep her from getting any rest. She blew out her breath, frustration rising.

"Yes, Maggie," she said in surrender.

December 26, 1905

ELIZABETH SPENT THE wee hours of the morning trying to lie still, suppressing groans of frustration. Visions of turning on her side to run her hand along the nightgown Maggie wore until she found the small breast she felt earlier in the evening haunted her. It got worse when the images changed to running her hand underneath the material to cup flesh until she felt Maggie's nipple harden beneath her palm.

Elizabeth squeezed her eyes shut and pressed her legs together. Her effort to control her fantasies only caused the throbbing to increase. She tried to distract herself by thinking about her list of supplies at the clinic, mentally checking off those she'd received and reviewing anticipated deliveries.

Her thoughts wandered from supply cabinets to her office,

giving rise to memories of the night of the storm and Maggie's stay. These only served to conjure up more visions of Maggie in various states of undress, Maggie in her bed, Maggie removing Elizabeth's clothing and touching her where she longed to be touched. This time, she found it difficult to stifle a whimper.

Her eyes widened in alarm when Maggie moaned, turned toward her, and flung her arm across Elizabeth's chest. The soft exposed skin of her upper arm pressed into Elizabeth's left breast through her chemise. When Elizabeth tried to change positions, Maggie's arm only served to stimulate the already sensitive flesh. Her nipple pebbled against Maggie's arm. Her distress rose still higher.

In desperation, she thought about moving her right hand down her abdomen and relieving the tension between her legs, but she couldn't risk it. She knew how she'd react to the stimulation. She'd writhe until she peaked and the tension broke. Maggie would surely awaken. No. It wasn't an option. Instead, she battled her thoughts for another hour hoping the feeling would dissipate.

When the first light of dawn broke through the curtains in Maggie's bedroom, Elizabeth sent up a prayer of thanks for an excuse to get out of bed. Shortly afterward, Maggie woke, refreshed. As Elizabeth watched her bustle around the kitchen full of energy, preparing a simple breakfast, she felt the weight of her own exhaustion.

While they sipped their tea, Maggie inquired if Elizabeth slept well. She answered by rote, saying she had. Maggie gave her a strange look. Elizabeth suspected she knew she was lying. No doubt the dark circles she must have under her eyes told a different story. Lucky for her they didn't tell the whole tale.

As a doctor, she often took stock of her own well-being and this morning was no different. She had a mild throbbing in her head and a matching faint pulsing sensation in her nether regions. If she could just make it home, she'd spend the morning taking care of the throbbing followed by a long nap. However, first, she had another item to take care of. She reached into the pocket of her dress and fingered the little box.

"Maggie, in light of our...encounter last evening...and our discussion, I hope you will reconsider this." She pulled out the box and placed it on the table between them.

Maggie stared at it, then looked up at Elizabeth, her eyes full of questions.

"I would like to give you this gift. Consider it a token of our willingness to explore our relationship and an expression of my deep...admiration."

She decided against saying any more. She didn't want to make another error.

Maggie reached for the box without smiling. Elizabeth felt a lump rise in her throat. Maggie opened the box to reveal the delicate pearl ring. When she looked up at Elizabeth, she had tears in her eyes. Elizabeth gave her a weak smile, hoping acceptance floated among those tears.

"It's beautiful," Maggie murmured.

"As are you. It's fitting."

Maggie's cheeks turned crimson.

Elizabeth added, "I thought it would go nicely with your mother's pearls. I hope you don't think me too presumptuous. I'm sorry this," she gestured toward the box, "upset you yesterday. It was never my intention."

"I don't know why I reacted as I did. I'm sorry, too, Elizabeth. I guess I felt such deep feelings for you and I didn't know if you felt as I did, so it tore me apart. Then, I thought about my past and my secret and it made me feel we could never grow closer because of it. My reaction was uncalled for. I hope you can forgive me."

"There's nothing to forgive."

Maggie looked down at her hands. "There is a possibility I might be a murderer."

"Somehow, I doubt it."

"How can you say that?"

"A young woman, spurning the advances of a young man, who runs away from her home and, I would imagine, leaves an easy trail in her wake, would have been caught up with long before she reached San Francisco. I have a feeling you have nothing to worry about." She wasn't so sure, but a least she hoped she could assuage Maggie's fears.

Maggie blew out a breath and said, "I hope you're right."

"Now, don't keep me in suspense any longer. Will you accept my gift?"

Maggie rose from her seat and stood before Elizabeth. "It's beautiful and thoughtful. I accept."

Elizabeth smiled up at Maggie. "Thank you."

"And I have a gift for you."

"You do? I thought you said—"

"Close your eyes."

Elizabeth did as instructed and waited. When Maggie's lips touched hers, she thought the thrill running through her body would propel her off the chair, sending her and Maggie to the floor. The pulsing between her legs started up again. How much of this could she endure? Maggie pressed her lips more firmly against Elizabeth's, sending another lightning bolt through Elizabeth's body.

They must stop. If they didn't, Elizabeth wasn't sure she could maintain control. She tried to end the kiss as gently as she could. When she broke away, she pulled Maggie into an embrace. Both women held on and tried to catch their breath.

When Elizabeth recovered enough to speak, she said, "What a wonderful gift, Maggie. Thank you."

"You're quite welcome, doctor."

"Speaking of doctoring, I must leave. I have matters to attend to today and I'm sure you have your own work to do, too."

"Quan Luck will be here shortly and I have some supplies he'll need to fetch for me, so, yes, unfortunately, duty beckons."

"Will you come for dinner tonight?" Elizabeth asked.

Maggie blushed. "Yes, I will come."

"Good. I'll see you then."

As Elizabeth strode up Van Ness Avenue with a wide grin on her face, the joy she felt put an extra spring in her step. A short distance from the house, she slowed, the smile disappearing as she spied a carriage parked in front. A woman descended the front steps. As Elizabeth approached, her heart sank when she recognized her—Amelia Rosemont.

ELIZABETH FORCED A smile to her lips. She hoped it would cover her dismay at finding Amelia at her doorstep.

"Amelia, good morning. Are you feeling ill?"

Amelia raked Elizabeth from head to hem and didn't bother to hide a look of displeasure.

"No, doctor, I'm not ill. Coming home from Christmas rather late, aren't you?"

"Not at all, Amelia, I felt the need for an early walk this morning and since I hadn't had a chance to put away the dress I wore yesterday, I put it on to go out for my breath of fresh air before beginning my day." Her lie caused her heart to pound in her chest. Trying to sound bright and cheery, she added, "Isn't it wonderful the rain stayed away for the holiday?"

Amelia stared, but said nothing.

Don't engage her, Elizabeth thought. She hopes you are guilty or nervous enough to offer more excuses in the midst of her silence. You'll dig yourself a deeper hole if you say anything more in answer to her question. Change the subject. Turn the tables. Make her answer for being here so early.

"Well, if you are not ill, may I ask what brings you to my doorstep so early on the morning after Christmas? If it wasn't for my need to walk off the cobwebs this morning, I would still be asleep." *Have the decency to feel a little guilty, Amelia. You might have woken me up.*

Amelia looked sheepish.

"I—er—wanted to see if you needed anything, since your settling-in period is coming to a close."

Elizabeth beamed with her first genuine smile since seeing Amelia. *Her tactic had worked.*

"My, you are industrious, coming to check on me while the morning is so young. I do have a few more days to get ready to begin my practice and I have a great deal scheduled, so if you'll excuse me, with my walk finished, I need to get back to work."

"Is there anything I can help you with, doctor?"

"No, everything is under control. I have a few final details I need to attend to, but I'll be fine."

"Perhaps we could have tea. Tomorrow?"

"No. I'm sorry Amelia. I have an appointment tomorrow. I won't be able to join you."

"An appointment?"

"Yes." *All right, Amelia. I'll offer you this little tidbit if it will get you to go away.* "I'm meeting with Violet Farrell to make final arrangement for working at the Mission. We'll be meeting the entire day, I'm afraid." *And to be sure you don't pursue this pretentious tea business...* "These next few days remaining in the year will be somewhat hectic for me, I'm afraid. Lots of last minute items I need to take care of to be ready to start my duties in the New Year. I hope you understand."

She didn't wait for Amelia's response. Instead, she brushed past her and ascended the stairs to her front door. She heard the carriage drive off as she crossed the threshold. It took every ounce of self-control she could muster to close the door without slamming it. She pressed her back against it, as if preventing Amelia's re-entry into her day, and breathed a sigh of relief.

"That went well," she whispered, but a ripple of fear ran through her. She knew she had to be careful. Amelia Rosemont was dangerous.

REVIVED FROM HER nap, Elizabeth spent the day stewing over Amelia's motives for showing up on her doorstep so early in the morning. Try as she might, she couldn't come up with a way to get Amelia out of her life. If she could be relegated to a casual familiarity instead of pursuing this odd relationship, Elizabeth wouldn't have to worry about her spying or meddling in her affairs. Frustration kept her from concentrating on the last project she needed to complete to be ready to open her clinic. She cursed Amelia Rosemont several times using words which would have shocked the roughest mariners in Baltimore.

By the time she answered the door at the end of the day, fatigue left her drained and she was numb with worry. She had to protect Maggie.

"Maggie, come in. I've put some stew on for us for dinner. I was busy most of the day, so I hope it will do for our meal."

Maggie smiled. "It will be fine, Elizabeth."

Elizabeth led the way up to her living quarters. The savory aroma of dinner met them as they ascended the stairs.

Maggie leaned over the stew Elizabeth prepared and took a long draw of the aroma. "This smells wonderful. I didn't know you had culinary skills."

Elizabeth hummed in response, distracted by whether or not to tell Maggie about Amelia and her concerns.

Maggie turned from the pot on the stove and faced her. "You seem distracted, Elizabeth. Is something wrong?"

Elizabeth pursed her lips together. If she told Maggie her suspicions about Amelia—of her trying to find something to tarnish her reputation—and by association, taking Maggie with her, Maggie might think her foolish. She felt so weary. She wanted to fall into Maggie's arms for comfort. But if she did, she'd have to explain and she wasn't sure she could. After all, these were mere suspicions. All she had to go on were Amelia's probing questions and a feeling in the pit of her stomach every time she encountered the woman.

Maggie reached out to touch Elizabeth's face. When she drew back, shock and disappointment tinged Maggie's. Elizabeth's shoulders slumped and guilt at rebuffing Maggie flooded through her.

"Elizabeth, what is it?"

Elizabeth stared past Maggie at the pot on the stove. She could send Maggie away, ending any risk of harm to her reputation, but how could she live without this woman in her life now that she'd found her? If she thought losing Irene was difficult, she knew losing Maggie would be so much more devastating. In an instant, she knew she couldn't do it. The remaining alternative was to tell Maggie, and if Maggie chose to distance herself from her because of it, at least she wouldn't have to worry about her imaginings. What if she sent her away without explanation? What if she allowed her some part in deciding what to do about this threat? What if she could contribute an idea to solve the problem of Amelia Rosemont? No, she couldn't live with suppositions. She needed to be honest with Maggie and allow her to decide for herself. "We need to talk."

Wariness suffused Maggie's voice when she said, "About?"

"Mostly about Amelia, but also about us."

Elizabeth couldn't bear it when tears welled up in Maggie's eyes. She pulled her into her arms and hung onto her, wondering if it was the last time she would do so. She drew in a deep breath and started with the thought uppermost in her mind.

"I'm worried, that's all. When I arrived home this morning, I found Amelia Rosemont on my doorstep."

Maggie looked up into Elizabeth's eyes, her forehead wrinkled, her eyes full of questions.

"What was she doing here so early in the morning? Was she ill?"

"I asked her, but she insisted she was fine."

"Then what did she want?"

"She said she wanted to see if I needed anything. She said it was because my time of adjustment was coming to a close and I'd be opening the clinic soon."

Maggie continued holding Elizabeth's gaze.

"But you don't believe it for a moment, do you?"

"No, I don't."

"You don't trust her."

Elizabeth shook her head.

Maggie's next words sounded as if she were thinking out loud. "And you think she's searching for ways to ruin your reputation."

Elizabeth nodded.

Maggie bit her lip.

"She seems to turn up at the most inopportune times. I don't know what to do about it." Elizabeth hated how whiny her voice sounded. One word came to mind—pathetic. She couldn't bear it. She choked down a lump in her throat.

Maggie pulled herself up to her full five-foot height. "We need to stop her."

"I'm not sure we can. She has Mrs. Stockton's ear."

"Mrs. Stockton keeps her own counsel. Just because Mrs. Rosemont appears to have her ear, doesn't mean she has her trust."

"Mrs. Stockton did indicate she knew Amelia's motives were different from the rest of her group when I met with her."

"Let me tell you about a perception Quan Luck shared with me about Mrs. Rosemont. He said she likes being one of Mrs. Stockton's 'ladies' more than she likes helping people."

"Quan Luck is an insightful young man."

"I agree. Mrs. Rosemont's treatment of him has been

disgusting. I'll be glad if she doesn't hire him again. I feel awful for ever having put him in contact with her. Her husband graduated from Stanford. I was hoping his association with the Rosemonts would give him an advantage to finding his way to the University. He wants to study there so badly. But of course, Mrs. Rosemont would do nothing to help. She thinks all Chinese people are stupid and illiterate."

"But she knows Theodora. She knows about the Chinese School. How could she think such a thing?" Elizabeth's voice oozed distaste.

"It's easier to look down on people than to look up to them."

"That's very profound, Maggie."

Maggie gave her a weak smile and said, "I have a confession."

"Oh?"

"When we were at Mrs. Rosemont's party, I looked for you. I had a few minutes and wanted to spend more time getting acquainted. Someone told me you had disappeared down the hall. When I headed in that direction, I—I overheard part of your conversation with Mrs. Rosemont. I didn't mean to eavesdrop, honestly, but I did hear some of your discussion. I recognized her underhanded ways at work. I should have warned you then, but I didn't know you well, so I thought it prudent to keep silent. I'm sorry."

"It doesn't matter. If you heard what she said, you know her suspicions came from gossip about what happened in Baltimore. The rumors were about Irene and I, although, thankfully, it doesn't sound like Irene was identified. The information might have originated from my brother. He always was a bit of a scandalmonger. It's a way of getting attention. I can't believe he and I came from the same parents. But I'm certain of one thing. Amelia has no proof of anything she heard, so she's fishing for evidence to support her theories.

"I'm afraid this brings us to a junction where we must make a decision." A look of distress crossed Elizabeth's face. "Perhaps we shouldn't see each other anymore."

Elizabeth's pain deepened as she watched Maggie's eyes tear again. When her bottom lip trembled, Elizabeth felt her heart would tear in two.

Maggie's voice shook as she whispered, "Is that what you want, Elizabeth?"

Elizabeth drew her back into an embrace. "No. I do not."

In a stronger voice, Maggie said, "Then we must find a way to fight Amelia Rosemont. She has no right to interfere in either of our lives. There's a way to stop her, we just haven't found it yet."

"I hope you're right, Maggie."

"Could you talk to Mrs. Stockton? Do you think she'd do something? You said Mrs. Stockton told you she knew Mrs. Rosemont's motives were different from the rest of her group."

Elizabeth paused in thought. "Oddly, she even hinted she might understand feelings between women. However, I'm not sure she could do anything to help. I'll have to think about how I might approach her about all this, if at all."

"Well, in a few days, I think you're going to get busy with your clinic, anyway. Maybe it won't be a problem." Maggie looked disappointed when she added, "Maybe we won't have as much time to spend together either."

"I'm not sure, Maggie. We'll have to see. You might be right about Mrs. Rosemont not having as much opportunity to snoop around, though. And I, for one, will make sure we can still spend time together."

Maggie grinned. "I'm glad. Now, let's have your wonderful stew and you tell me what you did today and your plans for tomorrow."

"I don't have much to tell. Today, I stored away the last of my medical supplies and re-arranged my examining room for the third time." They both laughed.

"Tomorrow, Miss Farrell and I will discuss plans for a day clinic at the mission to start in less than a week. I can't believe the time has come. I'm looking forward to getting back to work. I—"

Maggie interrupted her with a kiss.

Chapter Six

December 27, 1905

BEFORE ELIZABETH LEFT for the Quaker Mission in the morning, she penned a letter to a friend in Boston. The young woman became a Pinkerton agent when she lived in Baltimore. Elizabeth met her while she worked at the clinic in the city when the Pinkerton woman investigated the tragic murder of a young woman. She'd moved to Boston for a promotion within the agency only a few months before Elizabeth left. If anyone could get to the bottom of what happened to Harry Ryan, Edna Remington could. A few blocks before reaching Miss Farrell's, Elizabeth slipped her letter into the post box and continued on to her meeting.

Now, Elizabeth sat opposite Violet as she explained the needs of the women who lived South of the Slot. They weren't much different from those of the poor women of Baltimore. They decided Elizabeth would start by establishing a clinic at the mission one day a week, expanding her time as more women came.

Elizabeth asked, "How are your lessons going? I know you said you give classes on nutrition and hygiene. Those are important topics for these women."

"Attendance is growing. We started with two or three people last year, but we usually have ten or twelve people come for the sessions now."

"The same thing happened in Baltimore. At first, the women were reluctant because they thought the classes would be more formal and require them to leave their children, which was impossible, of course. However, when they found out they could bring them to class, they were more willing to attend."

"It's true. We had the same experience. And on those occasions when I have someone to assist me, they take the children to another room and play games with them, so the mothers get a respite and the games they play teach them about hygiene, too."

"And your volunteers, do they come on a regular basis?"

"Most come when they have a little free time. Some know when my classes are, so they'll try to come for those in order to give the women a break from the children, but it doesn't always work out. It doesn't matter. I've gotten pretty well at keeping everyone's attention in the midst of the chaos of children running around and infants squawking."

At first glance, anyone would think Violet timid and fragile. Elizabeth formed a different picture of her, though, for Violet Farrell was neither. She would stand up for these women against the adversity they faced with absolute determination. Elizabeth's appreciation deepened as she realized how total Violet's dedication was.

The bubble of sentiment dissipated when Violet spoke again. "Of course, your Miss Weston comes as much as she can. She's taken photographs of the children at their play and lessons. I have some of them hanging in my office. They are simply charming. She does such beautiful work."

Elizabeth hesitated to respond with too much enthusiasm. She didn't want to expose her feelings for Maggie inadvertently. "I've not seen much of her work. I'd like to look at them some time."

"Speaking of Maggie, if you require some assistance when you see patients, I thought I could ask Maggie to help out on a more regular scheduled basis—on the days you're here."

Elizabeth's heart skipped a beat, delighting in the idea. But would Maggie have the time? Would she have the inclination? "I'm not sure she could leave her shop during the time I would be here, Miss Farrell. Granted, it would only be one afternoon a week, to start, still. She has a business to run." *There, that should make me seem unenthusiastic about Maggie.*

"Well, she has offered to do more to help out, and since you already know each other, it should allow you to work well together from the start. You are friends, yes?"

Was it a trap? Perhaps not. Violet didn't seem like the tricking sort. That would be more like something Amelia might do. "Yes, Maggie and I are friends." Trying not to sound too eager, she added, "Shall I pose the question to her?"

Violet looked years younger when she smiled.

January 3, 1906

MAGGIE STOOD WITH Elizabeth looking around the tiny, dimly lit room inside the Quaker Mission. "I'm sorry I couldn't be here to help when you set up, but you did a wonderful job," Maggie said.

Elizabeth looked over the room with a critical eye. "It's so stark. I wish I could make it feel more welcoming, but this will have to do. Violet offered this table and the two chairs, but it's all she had. I found a mat in the storeroom to turn the table into an examination table should I need it. I'll have to find something to give me decent light in here since there's no window." Elizabeth sighed. "It will have to do for now."

"The Quakers believe in simplicity. You won't find too many extra items lying around. They only acquire what they need. Basics, nothing more. I'm surprised you found the mat."

"Well, I'm glad I did. It wouldn't do to ask anyone to lie down on a bare wooden table if I need to perform an examination. I'll have to buy a pillow and some sheets. I need a small table to put my bag and instruments on, too."

"There's a dry goods shop on Mission Street where you might find something. Do you want to take a walk down there now? They'll have the bed sheets you want. I'm not sure they'll have a table, though. There is an inexpensive furniture store in the same area. They might have something."

Elizabeth gestured Maggie out the door. "Let's go then. Is there somewhere in the area we could find something to eat?"

"Possibly."

On the way out, they found Violet in her office and told her they were leaving. Stepping out into the cold, damp winter air, they found Quan Luck running toward them.

When he met up with them he sounded out of breath, his words, urgent. "I am glad I found you. Miss Barculo sent me to find you and give you a message. She will go with the police tonight to a place in Chinatown where young girls are kept for prostitution. The police will take the girls from the house.

"Doctor Kellogg, she would like you to accompany her in case the girls need medical care. She would like you to meet her at five o'clock at the police station on Kearny Street. From there, you and Miss Barculo will go with the police to Chinatown to save the girls. I am sworn to secrecy. I cannot speak of this, only to you. The girls will be in much danger if the men who keep them in bondage find out about this plan. But Miss Barculo wants me to come back with your answer as soon as I found you."

Before Elizabeth could answer, Maggie spoke up. "Quan Luck, this sounds like a dangerous undertaking. I know Miss Barculo has been involved in this sort of thing before, but, must she involve Eliz—er—I mean, Doctor Kellogg?"

"Miss Barculo has saved many young women and girls from the clutches of men who try to use them. I surmise her desire to involve Doctor Kellogg is because she knows something about the situation and thinks her services will be needed." He turned to

Elizabeth and pleaded, "Please, doctor, what is your answer. I must hurry back. Miss Barculo is waiting for me."

"Tell her I will be there. If she thinks she'll need a doctor, the situation must be dire."

Quan Luck bowed, then turned and ran off down the street toward Market again.

Maggie said, "Elizabeth, you can't do this. It's too dangerous. The tongs are a vicious group. They're involved in all kinds of corruption and illegal doings in Chinatown. Please reconsider. I don't want anything to happen to you."

Elizabeth put a hand on Maggie's shoulder. "Maggie, I'm a doctor. I must go. Besides, Mrs. Stockton asked me to be of service to Theodora whenever she needed. This isn't a request to which I can say no. You must understand."

Elizabeth watched as a spectrum of emotion rolled across Maggie's face. "Fine. Then I'm coming with you."

"Maggie, I don't think—"

Maggie held up her hand, her face determined. She took a step closer to Elizabeth, standing toe to toe with her. She looked up into her eyes and said, "I'm going with you, whether you like it or not."

"But Theodora—"

"I don't care about Theodora Barculo."

"It has to be kept a secret."

"I'm not going to tell anyone."

"The police might not want—"

"It doesn't matter. I'm going. You think I want to find out something happened to you by reading the newspaper in the morning? I assure you I do not. I am coming with you."

She cares, Elizabeth thought. She cares a great deal. Otherwise, she wouldn't have this reaction. However, if I'm in danger, she will be, too. How am I to handle this? When we arrive at the police station, they might not allow her to go. I don't think anyone will be able to prevent her and if she tries to follow on her own, she'll be in even more danger than if she's with us.

"All right Maggie, if you insist on doing this, we'll go together."

AT FIVE O'CLOCK, Elizabeth and Maggie marched into the Kearny Street police station. As they entered, Maggie steeled herself against Theodora's displeasure, but it never came. She didn't even seem the least bit surprised to see Maggie. As a matter of fact, she said, "I'm glad you're here. My informant tells me three young girls arrived by ship a few days ago. I'm hoping they're being allowed to rest so they will look healthy for the auction. If not...well, suffice to say it's why you're here, Elizabeth."

Elizabeth said, "Auction? What kind of auction?"

"They've announced one for St. Louis Alley tomorrow. They sell them. Depending on who buys them, they either become servants or worse. If we don't get them out tonight, these girls could be prostitutes by tomorrow night.

"When the police remove them, they will be frightened and distressed. They will distrust the men who rescue them. They will be happy to see us and a good, motherly hug for each of them will go a long way to cure their anxiety and chase away their fear."

Maggie nodded. Not only would she be with Elizabeth during this dangerous task, she'd also be of some use to the operation. "We'll do our best to comfort the poor souls," Maggie said.

Elizabeth said, "It doesn't seem as if you think the girls have been harmed."

"I'm hopeful," Theodora said. "It's a pattern they follow to ensure the highest prices at the slave market. Let them rest and get some decent food into them beforehand. So, in general, they do not harm them before the auction. Once they are sold, though, they are subjected to terrible abuse. This is why it's imperative we rescue them tonight. Still, you never know. If the men involved in caring for them take a fancy to them, anything can happen."

Maggie noticed the stalwart Theodora shiver at the thought.

A young man dressed in street clothes approached and greeted Theodora. She introduced him as police Sergeant Hannigan. He gave them strict instructions.

They were to stay well away from the area of the police activity. They were to be silent, no matter what happened. The police would use as much stealth as possible to release the girls, and bring them to them. Theodora could take over, then, and the police would escort them back to the Chinese School. Finally, Sergeant Hannigan informed them he would meet them on the front steps of the station with the rest of his men in a few minutes and they would set off from there.

It sounded simple enough. Then, why are my knees knocking together, Maggie wondered? She looked over at Elizabeth and saw her face wracked with concern. Theodora looked relaxed. Of course, she'd done all this before — many times.

The group left the police station and headed into the heart of Chinatown in silence. Sergeant Hannigan and another policeman in street clothes led the way.

Theodora told Elizabeth and Maggie they weren't in uniform so as not to unnerve the girls even further, causing them to think they were being taken to jail. Two uniformed men brought up the rear, lugging a long wooden ladder.

A chill ran through Maggie's body in spite of her long woolen coat. Did the cool night air penetrate to her skin making her cold—or was it the dread coming from within?

As they trudged on, people on the street gave the unusual group odd looks and a wide berth. After several blocks, they turned into a narrow alley and Hannigan halted them at the mouth of the passageway. Fortunately, no one was around.

They stood watching the uniformed men raise the ladder to the second story window. Theodora spoke in low tones, addressing Hannigan. "You must say you are there to rescue them—make sure they understand you." She put a hand on the young policeman's forearm and said, "Speak slowly and clearly. I know you speak Cantonese, but your brogue sometimes makes it impossible to understand some words."

Hannigan blushed. "Yes, Miss Barculo," he said, as if he were one of her students. "I've been practicing."

She smiled at him. "I'm sure you'll do fine. We've been successful before, haven't we?"

He nodded. His schoolboy expression changed to an air of authority. "You must stay here. Do not approach, no matter what happens. I must have your promise, Miss Barculo." He looked at Elizabeth and Maggie. "You all must promise not to come any closer."

Maggie nodded vigorously.

Elizabeth said, "We will stay right here, I assure you."

"Miss Barculo? I'll not move until I have your word."

Maggie wondered what breach Theodora had been involved in to make him sound so adamant.

Theodora waved him away. "Yes, yes, I promise."

He gave her a stern look before he walked toward the other men standing at the base of the ladder. When he reached them, the uniformed police melted into the shadows across the alley. Sergeant Hannigan climbed the ladder with stealth while the other man held it steady.

Maggie held her breath. When he reached the window, she noticed it had a small gap at the bottom, perhaps to let some air into a small, stifling room. Hannigan gripped the bottom of the window and forced it open slowly. The faint sound of scraping wood could be heard echoing down the alley. When he had the window up, he stuck his head in and said something quietly. From a distance, Maggie didn't think she'd understand, even if he spoke English.

A cry came from the window — surprise and dismay.

Hannigan spoke again, his words sounded choppy, halting. Maggie recognized the sing-song cadence she'd heard in Chinatown.

Theodora whispered, "Good. You're doing well, Sergeant. Tell them one more time. Slowly."

Hannigan spoke again, softer now and gestured for the occupants to approach the window. No one appeared. Maggie held her breath. Hannigan gestured more vigorously and whispered two words in rapid succession.

Finally, a young girl poked her head out the window. Theodora took a step forward. Elizabeth put her hand out to stop her and shook her head. When the girl looked down the alley and saw them, she sat on the window sill and swung her legs out.

Hannigan helped her get her footing. By the time they reached the bottom, another girl was already half way down the ladder, but she stopped and called up to the room. Someone stood in the window, crying, calling out. It looked like a young child.

"She's afraid to get on the ladder," Theodora murmured. She tried to step forward again, but Elizabeth was ready.

"Please, Theodora. Stay here."

Theodora's shoulders slumped.

Hannigan said something to the girl on the ladder. She began her descent again. She barely stepped off the ladder when Hannigan scrambled back up. When he reached the top, he said something in the girl's language.

She hesitated. Then, her head emerged from the window. Bracing himself with his knees on a rung of the ladder, Hannigan thrust his hands out and plucked the girl from the window. She secured herself by wrapping her legs around his hips and locking her arms around his neck. He started back down the ladder now using his freed hands to help him move quickly.

When he reached the bottom, the other policeman in street clothes guided the two older girls toward the women. Hannigan carried the younger girl, still clinging to him. As soon as they stepped off toward the women, the uniformed men emerged from the shadows and removed the ladder.

When they reached the group, Elizabeth and Maggie each had one of the two older girls in an embrace. Hannigan handed the younger one to Theodora. She shook in Theodora's arms. The group moved off, the men carrying the ladder back toward the station. Hannigan removed his jacket and wrapped it around the youngest girl. The other two looked just as cold in thin dresses and tiny fabric shoes. Elizabeth and Maggie removed their coats at the same time and swathed the older girls in them.

As the second man in street clothes approached, Hannigan said, "You can go back to the station now. I'll escort the ladies to Miss Barculo's." He clapped him on the shoulder. "Good work tonight."

The man nodded and strode in the direction from which they had come.

The group moved away from the alley. By now, the streets were less crowded and they were able to move without drawing attention.

As they walked, Theodora spoke to the girls. Hannigan translated.

"She's assuring the girls we're friends and we're here to help them. She's telling them about her school and how they'll have the opportunity to get an education and can start a new life here."

Maggie listened as Theodora spoke in a lilting cadence.

Several blocks away, they entered the Chinese School by a side door. The youngest girl was calmer and allowed Theodora to put her down so she could walk on her own. Theodora handed Hannigan his jacket, offering her thanks. He said goodnight and took his leave.

Theodora asked if Elizabeth and Maggie would stay. She wanted to make sure the girls didn't need a doctor, but it might be better if she talked to them alone. She invited them to have some tea, if they didn't mind tending to it themselves, and pointed them toward the kitchen. When they agreed, Theodora excused herself to settle the girls in for the night.

About an hour later, Theodora joined them at a small kitchen table and poured herself a cup of tea. "On days like this, I almost wish I were a drinking woman," she said.

THEY SAT DRINKING their tea as Theodora explained what she learned from the children. The two older girls were sisters. Their parents were farmers in a poor region on the outskirts of Guangdong.

"Some men came to their village and said they would help any families who wanted to send their daughters to Gold Mountain."

Maggie said, "Isn't that what the Chinese call America?"

"Yes, it is. These men said they would ensure the girls got a good education and they would find them rich husbands. These men make a habit of duping poor and gullible people out of their daughters to sell them into indentured servitude or they enslave them in a life of prostitution.

"The girls, Mei and Xai, are twins, making them even more enticing to the men, who could advertise their services together. They're thirteen years old. Su-Lin is nine, although she looks more like six or seven."

"Her small stature is probably due to poor nutrition," Elizabeth said.

"I'm sure you're right, doctor."

"Did anyone harm them?"

"No, it seems they were fortunate. The men who took them were too busy drinking, gambling and indulging in opium while they crossed the ocean. The opium may be what saved them. I imagine the men spent most of their time in a stupor. However, they also forgot about them because they said they hardly had anything to eat on the journey."

"How awful for them," Maggie said.

"Once they arrived, they were put in the room where we found them. A different set of people looked after them, then. They brought them lots of good food and let them bathe. The girls heard some of their new caretakers talk about a "market" in St. Louis Alley. They had no idea what it was. I'm sure they were given decent food and allowed to clean themselves up in preparation for what takes place there."

"What's it like?" Elizabeth asked.

Maggie chimed in. "I've heard it's an awful place."

"It can be," Theodora said. "It's where the tongs hold their slave auctions."

Elizabeth looked horrified as she asked, "Don't the police do anything about it?"

"The tongs are too powerful—and San Francisco is fraught with corrupt politicians from the Mayor on down."

Maggie said, "I heard the tongs put a price on your head, Theodora."

"It's true. But I'll not let a bunch of evil blowhards do despicable things with young girls, including treat them like animals, because of it." Theodora's face reddened as she spoke.

Elizabeth shuddered at the thought. "These tongs are terrible people, then?"

"Actually, two types of tongs exist, doctor—the criminals and the members of the more respectable benevolent societies. Benevolent societies, such as the Chinese Six Companies and others who are members of a Joss—" She looked at Elizabeth. "A Joss is a temple in honor of the ancestors. They are the complete opposite—although the gangster element is sometimes a part of those, too. It's complicated. But groups like the Six Companies do good works, much the same as Miss Farrell does at her mission."

"And what you do here," Maggie said.

Theodora smiled. "Thank you, Maggie. I try to do what I can for these children."

Elizabeth asked, "So how does one tell a good tong from a bad one?"

"'By their work ye shall know them,' doctor. The Chinese Six Companies, one of the larger tongs, opened the Tung Wah Dispensary to care for the health and welfare of the people of Chinatown a few years back. This all came about because city government betrayed this portion of the population by failing to open the hospital they promised. If it wasn't for the Chinese Six Companies, we might not have curtailed the plague."

"I heard about the plague in Chinatown. I thought it was a fiction," Elizabeth said.

"No. It was quite real. Thank goodness they got it under control," Theodora said. "We did a good job of cleaning up the rats and beating back the disease, but we have other scourges in Chinatown still to be addressed. The gambling houses and opium dens, as well as the brothels, are rampant."

"But tonight, at least, three little girls have been saved from a life of exploitation," Elizabeth said.

Theodora nodded.

"And they were treated well so they'd give a better impression in this slave auction?" Elizabeth shuddered at the thought of such a horrible concept.

"Yes. The girls had three days of good meals and were left alone, so they got plenty of rest. No doubt the ordeal they went through when Sergeant Hannigan appeared at their window left them exhausted tonight, though. They were already asleep before I left them. They understand they're safe now. Tomorrow, I'll get them some clothes and integrate them into the school."

"I'm glad everything worked out, Theodora."

"Thank you for being willing to come to their aid, doctor."

"It's the least I could do. After all, you rescued me at Mrs. Rosemont's party."

Theodora's laugh echoed through the room. "Yes, we did a good job, there, didn't we? Evangeline is such a good sport. Although, I must say, she'd already helped herself to a little too much of that punch."

"So it was a ruse?"

"Not so much a ruse as a little innocent play-acting on an already established theme."

"Well, you pulled it off well. You must thank Mrs. Evangeline for me."

"I will. And speaking of thanks, thank you for coming with us tonight. I never know what condition we'll find these poor children in."

She looked at Maggie and said, "Thank you, too. I'm sorry if I spoiled your plans for the evening." She raised her eyebrows at her.

Maggie waved off Theodora's implication. "We were at the mission looking at Elizabeth's new examination room when your message arrived. I needed to get back to the shop and Doctor Kellogg had an errand to run before we were to meet you. I'm happy we could help."

Elizabeth noticed Maggie fidgeted with intertwined fingers on her lap as she spoke and knew she tried to avoid Theodora's inference. She said, "I'm glad everything worked out for the children and you've no need of me. I think it's time we left. It's getting late."

"Yes, I'm sorry to keep you. I've put my man on alert. He'll take you both home, if you don't mind riding in our service wagon. He's waiting outside."

When Theodora introduced Maggie and Elizabeth to Joseph, an older, well spoken, Chinese man, they greeted him and climbed aboard.

As they drove off, he said, "Miss Barculo said you lived on Van Ness, doctor, but she didn't tell me where you needed to be delivered, Miss Weston."

Without missing a beat, Elizabeth offered, "We'll both need to be dropped at my home, Joseph. It's so late, Miss Weston will stay the night with me."

MAGGIE SAT IN Elizabeth's parlor, gazing out the second floor window into the night. When Elizabeth entered the room, she held out a nightgown and a long silk ribbon to Maggie.

"It's a little short on me, so if you tie it up with the ribbon, it might be the right length for you."

Maggie looked up at her, excited and nervous about this change in Elizabeth.

"You surprised me when you told Joseph I'd be staying with you tonight."

Elizabeth smiled. "I didn't think you'd mind. I hope it didn't unnerve you."

Maggie took the garment from her and looked down at it. "No. It's just—I'm—well, I'm not sure what I'm doing here, Elizabeth."

"It's late. You're staying with me because it was easier. I'm sure Joseph is an upstanding man, but this way, you didn't have to ride with him alone at such a late hour."

Maggie probed Elizabeth looking for any hidden meaning of her words. Should she take them at face value—or assume they meant something more? She concluded it was never wise to assume anything and rose from her seat, heading toward the landing in the hall.

"Where are you going?" Elizabeth called.

Maggie turned to face her. "I'm going to your office."

"Why?"

"To sleep."

"But...I thought you would sleep here." She gestured toward the wall behind her, which Maggie knew was her bedroom.

Maggie retraced her steps and stood before Elizabeth. "Why?"

Elizabeth's cheeks flushed. She took in a deep breath before she murmured, "I'm not sure. Being in such a dangerous position tonight unnerved me, I suppose. Please stay with me. Just lie beside me. I want you close. I...*need* you close."

Maggie raked her eyes over Elizabeth's face, trying to discern the meaning of the invitation. Should she presume it had no hidden meaning, or should she read more into it? A shiver skittered down her spine.

What did she hope was Elizabeth's meaning? To lie together like schoolgirls—or something else entirely? If it was something else, was she ready?

WHEN ELIZABETH CAME into the room dressed in her nightgown, her hair taken down, she found Maggie sitting at the foot of the bed, also dressed for sleep. The pins were out of her hair and the chestnut strands lay across her shoulders. Maggie looked up at her, a forlorn look on her face, but Elizabeth thought she looked beautiful.

Elizabeth gave her a sympathetic smile. "Are you all right, Maggie?"

"I didn't know which side was yours."

"It doesn't matter. Please. Choose whichever side you'd like."

Maggie got up and moved to the right side of the bed.

Elizabeth pursed her lips.

When Maggie saw her reaction, she said, "Oh, you wanted this side." She registered surprise when Elizabeth laughed.

"I'm teasing you," Elizabeth said, her eyes dancing.

"I'm sorry. I didn't—"

Elizabeth's look softened. Maggie looked so fragile. "Maggie, it's all right. Would you rather not sleep here? If you want to go to my office—"

"No. I'm fine. I seem to be a little nervous tonight. I don't know why."

Elizabeth had her suspicions. Maggie wasn't ready for anything beyond kissing. She would honor those feelings.

Maggie fingered the ribbon at her waist. Her next statement startled Elizabeth when she whispered, "I'm afraid I don't know what to do." Her eyes darted back to the ribbon in her hand.

"Oh, Maggie."

Elizabeth moved toward her and pulled her into an embrace. She shouldn't have done it. When she felt the warmth of Maggie's body against hers, the softness of her breasts protected only by the cotton nightgowns they wore, she could barely speak. She steeled herself against her own arousal and spoke in Maggie's ear. "First of all, we don't need to *do* anything. I would never force you to do something you aren't ready for."

Maggie caught her eye. "That's just it. I think—I think I might be ready, Elizabeth. But I don't know what to do. You've been...with someone before. I've never—"

Elizabeth drew her in closer. "I assure you, when the time is right, you'll know exactly what to do."

Maggie spoke into Elizabeth's shoulder. "But, we don't have...the right...parts."

It started as a low chortle in Elizabeth's throat. By the time her laughed reached a crescendo, Elizabeth crushed Maggie into her chest, not caring about controlling her feelings any longer. In that moment, she knew she was in love with Maggie Weston. When she gained control again, she spoke with tenderness. "I assure you, Maggie, you have all the right parts...for me."

She felt Maggie shudder as she pressed into Elizabeth.

MAGGIE LAY IN Elizabeth's bed, bathed in moonlight. Her body hummed excitement and dread. She thrust her uncertainty away and moved close to Elizabeth, their bodies barely touching.

Elizabeth didn't move.

Maggie plucked up her courage and whispered, "Tonight, I would like to learn what it means to be a woman in your arms." The throbbing between her legs increased at her declaration.

Elizabeth turned toward Maggie and pushed herself up on her elbow. "You must be sure." She touched her hair, moving a strand from her cheek.

"I am sure of nothing, Elizabeth, except these confusing

feelings doing battle within me. They are wonderful and exciting, yet they make me feel dread and uncertainty."

Elizabeth made a move to speak. Maggie reached up and silenced her with a finger to her lips.

"I feel such aching tenderness toward you, Elizabeth. I want to be with you every waking moment. No, that's wrong. Not every waking moment. Every moment, even when we sleep." A timid smile appeared across Maggie's face. "Do you feel something like this for me?"

Elizabeth looked as if she might cry. Maggie couldn't bear it. "Tell me what you feel, Elizabeth. I must know."

Elizabeth pulled Maggie into an embrace, her head resting on her bosom. Maggie felt Elizabeth's chest rising and falling in ragged breaths under her cheek. Had she made a mistake in being so bold?

When Elizabeth spoke, her voice contained a tremor. "The day I walked into your shop to escape Michael-the-Maul, when you walked into the room, I thought my heart would stop beating and I'd faint. I thought you were so beautiful. My feelings from the first went deeper than any I've ever felt. But it wasn't until a little while ago, when we talked about 'parts,' I realized how much I care about you, Maggie. I think it's safe to say we are of like mind — no — we are of like heart in our feelings. I'm thrilled when I'm near you and want to spend all my time with you. So much so, I'm not sure how I will be able to be away from you when my practice begins to grow and more women come to see me at the mission. You, too, have your business. We'll be apart much more."

Maggie pressed into Elizabeth's embrace. "We'll endure the small separations, then, because we'll take our feelings for one another with us when we go and we will rejoice in them when we meet again at the end of each separation."

Elizabeth kissed the top of Maggie's head. Maggie moved to meet her lips. When they kissed, a bolt shot through Maggie's body and came to rest between her legs where it burst into a hot, pulsing need.

Her voice sounded ragged to her own ears when she said, "Tell me how two women express their feelings for one another."

"I don't think that's a good idea."

Maggie looked into Elizabeth's eyes. "Why not?"

"If I tell you, it might make it difficult for me to...control myself. I...cannot."

Once again, Maggie silenced Elizabeth with a finger to her lips. "I want to...learn."

Elizabeth held Maggie's gaze. She could see the battle going on within Elizabeth and thought it better to let her fight it until a conclusion. Seconds dragged out and Maggie wondered if Elizabeth would ever speak. Finally, Elizabeth's eyes softened and she spoke.

"I will do this under one condition, Maggie."

"What condition?"

"If you feel overwhelmed with this…information, at any time, you must tell me to stop. Will you agree?"

Maggie nodded and cuddled up closer to Elizabeth like a small child about to be told a bedtime story.

Elizabeth drew in an uneven breath. "You already know some of what women who care for one another do, Maggie. We've kissed many times."

"I enjoy it very much."

"As do I," Elizabeth whispered.

"Then there's the touching. I love to touch your hair and your cheek and your neck. There was one time when I—" She drew in another ragged breath. "When I—" and another breath.

Maggie looked up at her. "When you touched me here?" She cupped her own breast.

Elizabeth let out a strangled, "Yes."

The sound of Elizabeth's ragged reply sent another jolt through Maggie. "What else?"

"Well, sometimes, we like to embrace, our full bodies pressed together completely, as we kiss."

"We've never done that."

"No. We never have. I never want to make you uncomfortable. I don't want to presume anything."

"Perhaps it's what I needed, Elizabeth. I have already been in a great deal of discomfort when we kiss, wanting something more, not knowing what it was."

"Then, perhaps we will embrace each other with more firmness the next time we kiss." Maggie heard Elizabeth draw in a sharp breath and found herself matching her with one of her own. When she recovered, Maggie said, "Is there…more?"

"Yes."

"Tell me."

"I'm not sure we should continue. As a doctor, I'm familiar with the female anatomy. However, we are not discussing something clinical here. This is rather different. It could become rather…uncomfortable."

"Why?"

"It may bring up…feelings…you don't wish to act on, Maggie. It will be difficult to continue to lie here and not…do more. Please, let's not do this. I'm already finding it impossible not to want—"

Maggie watched her, trying to discern if Elizabeth felt what she did.

Her body buzzed as if with a thousand bees. Her need set her pulse throbbing. She wanted more of Elizabeth, but she didn't know how.

She moved even closer. She had to know. She had to have the benefit of Elizabeth's experience. How else could she know if she was ready...for more? How else could she know what to do? "Please, Elizabeth. Tell me. I want to learn."

THE STRUGGLE WITHIN Elizabeth to help Maggie left her feeling weak. Her whole body burned. The desire to take Maggie into her arms and ravage her was too strong, but how could she refuse? She had to get control over her emotions. Maggie was too precious. She meant too much to Elizabeth to allow herself to lose control. She took a deep shuddering breath and whispered, "All right."

"Beyond touching face, neck, shoulders...breasts, there is more." She needed another gulping breath before she could continue. "Caressing other places—"

The thought of touching Maggie in those "other places" made breathing even more difficult. How could she explain without thinking of carrying out these actions with Maggie?

She drew in another deep breath. She must. Maggie waited for her to continue. She'd try to be more...clinical.

"When a woman's skin is touched in the manner of which I'm speaking, it becomes particularly...sensitive. It causes a response from deeper within the body."

"What kind of response?" Maggie looked up at Elizabeth, a look of wonder on her face.

Elizabeth noticed how her chest rose and fell, her cheeks flushed. She tried not to think about the tiny nibs of her nipples, protruding through the fabric of soft nightgown. She knew her own were as tight and hard. A stream of wetness trickled down her thighs. Oh, no. How would she ever survive this lesson?

Clinical. Keep it clinical. She steeled herself to continue.

"A woman's breasts get softer, they may blush. The nipples get hard." Like ours already are. "They respond to various types of touch."

"Like what kind of touch? Fingers? Palms?"

"Yes," Elizabeth choked. "Sometimes other...touches." She found it difficult to swallow the saliva welling up in her mouth.

"Other?"

"Yes. Other. Lips. Kissing. Licking. Sucking."

"Oh!"

Oh, indeed. She didn't know how she could continue now.

"Is that all they do?"

Elizabeth quavered. "No. There's more," she squeaked.

"I'm...learning so much. Please continue."

Was Maggie this curious? Or was she enjoying being titillated?

"Um...they sometimes move downward. The navel can be a place of...stimulation."

"Oh?" The word came out more of a breathless sigh.

"Yes. And then, there are what we might call the *right* parts."

"There's more than one?"

"Yes. Men only think penetration is important. However, parts outside that area are much more important to a woman and, from what I've heard, men seem to know nothing about them."

This was good. Talking about it this way calmed her own reactions. This approach might help. "Folds exist around the vagina. Then, there's the organ of pleasure for women." Her mouth filled with saliva again. She gulped it down. She had gone off the clinical track and was back to feeling things she couldn't allow herself to feel. This approach wasn't such a good idea.

Maggie broke through her battling thoughts. "How does one experience pleasure with this organ?"

Was Maggie serious? She'd have to suspend this conversation. Elizabeth bit down on her bottom lip—hard.

"Elizabeth, you're a doctor. Besides, you're...experienced. Please, go on."

Elizabeth realized she clutched the blanket on the bed in her free hand so tightly, it made her hand cramp. She forced herself to let go. "Uh...sometimes...these areas are stroked. They help a woman become...receptive."

"Receptive?"

"Yes."

"But we don't have the parts."

Elizabeth gave Maggie a penetrating look.

"There are other ways."

"What ways?"

"Fingers, thighs...reproductions."

Maggie's eyes widened, the whites glowing in the darkness. So, she had shocked her. Good. Maybe she could end this.

"Some women enjoy them."

Maggie's eyes blazed bright blue. She lifted off Elizabeth's chest, hovering above her, her hair cascading down to rest on

Elizabeth's shoulder. Elizabeth marveled at her innocence, her beauty.

Maggie asked, "What do you like, Elizabeth? Fingers? Thighs? Reproductions?"

Elizabeth felt a torrent flow against her thighs now. "Mostly...fingers." She could barely get the words out. "Sometimes...the other...things."

She found it difficult to catch her breath.

Maggie's pupils opened. Her eyes darken.

Was it lack of light? Or arousal?

Maggie lay down. Crossed her legs. Kept them tight.

Maggie was ready physically. But was her mind and soul?

Her voice sounded strained when she said, "We should go to sleep."

"Yes," Elizabeth said, but at this pronouncement, she knew, for her, it would be another sleepless night.

Chapter Seven

January 4, 1906

ELIZABETH DOZED OFF as the sky turned from charcoal to pewter, but it was far from a restful sleep. She awoke to find Amelia Rosemont standing at the foot of her bed and sat up with a jolt. Maggie still slept beside her.

"What are you doing here?" Elizabeth demanded.

Amelia looked over at Maggie, pointed a bony finger at her and said, "I want her out. Now."

She stomped to Maggie's side of the bed, slid her arms under her, and lifted her up. Maggie remained stiff, stretched out along Amelia's arms.

A flood of panic erupted as she watched Amelia walk toward the exit with Maggie in tow. She had to turn sideways to negotiate the doorway. Maggie's weight didn't seem to bother her or slow her movements at all.

Fear engulfed Elizabeth. She flung back the covers and ran after her as she entered the hallway. "What are you doing?"

"Go back to bed," Amelia ordered. Elizabeth did as she was told, trying to guess why she complied when she should have stopped the intrusion. When Amelia returned, she slipped in beside Elizabeth.

"Where's Maggie?" Her desperation rang in her ears.

"She's gone home where she belongs. Now close your eyes."

Under some strange spell, Elizabeth did as she was told.

"I know how to pleasure a woman, doctor. Shall I show you?"

Elizabeth took in a sharp breath and woke up. Confusion swirled around her like a dark cloud. The sky had turned dove gray. She looked at the space beside her on the bed, expecting to find it empty. Maggie slept there with a peaceful smile on her face. As Elizabeth stared, a range of emotions washing over her, Maggie turned over and let out a sigh, but continued on in serene slumber.

Elizabeth scrubbed at her face reassuring herself what she had experienced was a dream. A very bad dream.

She spent the next few minutes going over the vision in her mind, looking for any hidden clues. She found nothing new. The warning she already identified time and time again when she encountered Amelia persisted.

Maggie stirred, stretched like a contented cat, and said, "Good morning, Elizabeth."

When she smiled, Elizabeth's heart melted. She hated to rush Maggie out, but the dream weighed heavily on her and she worried they'd open the front door and run right into Amelia.

"I hesitate to rush you, but I think it might be best—before the streets fill with prying eyes."

Maggie studied her before answering. "You're right. I should go."

Later, as they stood by the front door, Maggie leaned into Elizabeth and kissed her on the mouth. Elizabeth moaned. Maggie deepened the kiss, parting her lips slightly. Elizabeth's heart beat faster, reminding her about telling Maggie she'd know what to do when the time was right. Apparently, she discovered something new this morning. Elizabeth ran her tongue along Maggie's lower lip. Now it was Maggie's turn to moan.

It would be so easy to drag her back upstairs, back into her bed, and do what she envisioned last night, but she couldn't take the risk. She could already hear movement on the street outside as the city came to life. Maggie had to leave. She broke the kiss, panting, feeling as if a chasm opened up between them.

Maggie asked, "Will I see you tonight?"

Elizabeth hesitated as concern swirled around her. "I—I'm—"

"Come for dinner. Please?"

The cloud lifted and left Elizabeth with a feeling of want, no, need, for Maggie. "I'll come."

Maggie put her hand on the door knob.

"Wait!" Elizabeth put her hand over Maggie's. "Let me look outside. I have to be sure."

Maggie frowned. "Sure of what?"

"Sure there's no one...lurking outside."

January 6, 1906

WHEN MAGGIE OPENED the door to her living quarters on Saturday evening, Elizabeth was flush with excitement. She held two tickets out to Maggie and said, "I locked the shop door behind me."

"Good. The evening is ours, then." She plucked the tickets from Elizabeth's hand and examined them.

"Caruso!" Maggie squealed.

But her delight changed to suspicion as she said, "I thought you already had these tickets. You invited me weeks ago."

"I reserved them soon after I arrived in San Francisco. They just had them printed. I received them by messenger this afternoon. I couldn't wait to show you."

Maggie brightened again and pulled Elizabeth into a tight hug. A warm sensation rippled through her body as she did so.

"I'm glad I could make you happy." Elizabeth beamed.

"It will be exquisite. Can I wear my dress from Mrs. Stockton's party? Is it appropriate?"

"I think it would be perfect for the occasion. You look splendid in it." Elizabeth wiggled her eyebrows. "I look forward to seeing it on you again."

Maggie blushed and motioned Elizabeth to sit at the table, already set with dinner. Tonight, she determined, would be different.

Last night, Elizabeth came for dinner and left so quickly, Maggie didn't have time to think. She spent the night feeling lonely and abandoned, though she knew the responsibility for Elizabeth's flight was hers alone.

On Thursday night, it had been almost impossible not to ask Elizabeth to make love to her. She knew Elizabeth was near crazed with wanting to do so, but she still doubted her ability to offer Elizabeth a worthy partner because of her inexperience.

In the wee hours of Friday night, alone in her own bed, Maggie asked herself what she was waiting for. As she thought about the details of what Elizabeth told her—what two people with *their* parts could do—she recognized the possibilities, if she could only get beyond her concern about her inexperience. The alternative would be to remain unskilled for the rest of her life and relegate them both to a life of exasperation and irritability.

"You know what you want, Maggie. Elizabeth Kellogg," she shouted into the empty darkness. "And she wants you. It's up to you to make sure you get what you both want before she loses interest because of your reluctance."

Having reached her conclusion, Maggie drifted off to sleep for a while. When she awoke again, the loneliness was gone, replaced by resolve.

Now, with the evening before them and a free day tomorrow, Elizabeth stood in front of her, looking at her as if she were the most beautiful woman in the world. It was time, but first, their meal waited. She handed the tickets back to Elizabeth, saying, "You keep them. I'd be afraid I'd misplace them."

Elizabeth laughed. "If you insist."

They sat and ate the simple stew Maggie served. "This is delicious, Maggie. I admire your cooking skills."

"We each have our talents. I admire your skill with patients. You are so kind to the ones who come to Miss Farrell's Mission. You treat them the same as the high society ladies. It's commendable."

"I believe everyone deserves the same deference. Those women can't help their lot in life. They are all doing the best they can with what they've been given. For that, they all deserve our respect. It has little to do with skill."

Maggie nodded as she cleaned up the last bit of gravy from her bowl. When she looked into Elizabeth's eyes, she added, "Oh, but I look forward to learning what other skills you have."

Elizabeth choked.

Maggie jumped up from her seat and rapped on Elizabeth's back between her shoulder blades as she coughed and sputtered and Maggie repeated her apologies. They ended up laughing so hard they had to hold on to their sides.

Finally, Maggie choked out, "Really, Elizabeth, I'm so sorry."

Elizabeth stopped laughing and said, "I hope you're not."

Maggie gave her a curious look.

"I hope you're not sorry. I hope you meant what you said."

Maggie blushed. "I did." Then she whispered, "I do."

Elizabeth stood up, knocking into the table in her haste. The dishes clattered and the silverware clinked. She ignored it and pulled Maggie into a tight embrace. Maggie sank into her, knowing in a few hours everything would be different between them.

When they broke from the hug, Maggie scooped up the serving dish and stored it in the kitchen while Elizabeth rinsed the dishes and left them in the sink. Maggie grabbed her by the hand and pulled her toward her bedroom. When they reached the foot of the bed, Maggie said, "Stay with me tonight, but not like all the other nights we've spent together."

Elizabeth's emerald green eyes sparkled. "Are you sure?"

Maggie nodded.

"You must be absolutely certain, Maggie."

"My doubts are gone. I've ached for you, Elizabeth. I...must have you."

Elizabeth blew out her breath as she pulled Maggie into her, crushing her into her chest. "My darling, Maggie," she whispered.

Maggie smiled into her shoulder. "You've waited long enough."

She felt Elizabeth's protest before it could escape her lips. She put her finger to them to stop her from saying anything and added, "So have I."

Her heart nearly burst when she saw the tears well up in Elizabeth's eyes.

As Maggie touched her lips to Elizabeth's, a tear escaped, streaking both their cheeks. Maggie pulled away and swiped her thumb down its path on Elizabeth's face. Elizabeth repeated the gesture on Maggie's. Maggie smiled and held out her hand. "Come to bed."

ELIZABETH WATCHED MAGGIE as she slept, feeling an overwhelming sense of awe. Maggie was beautiful in their lovemaking and proved herself a quick study. At first, they were driven by the intensity of the passion they had struggled to keep in check for so long. Elizabeth thought she might burst into flames with the fervor coursing through her. The second time, Elizabeth moved more slowly, letting Maggie feel the sensual pleasure for a long time before she brought her to her peak. Now, Maggie slept the sleep of a satisfied woman.

She smiled at the thought and reached out to stroke Maggie's shoulder. She knew she should let Maggie sleep, but she couldn't help herself. She needed the contact.

Maggie's eyes fluttered open. "You're awake."

"And you were not. I'm sorry. I needed to touch you. You look so beautiful in the moonlight."

Maggie's smile filled her eyes. "As do you." She reached up and ran her finger across Elizabeth's lips. "I want to kiss you."

Elizabeth bent to her and their lips met. Passion flared. Elizabeth pinned Maggie to the mattress, but Maggie pushed her away, "Oh, no you don't, *doctor*. This is my time."

Elizabeth marveled at the strength of the diminutive Maggie. She immobilized her, covering her with kisses, mimicking Elizabeth's actions with her earlier. She followed a path between her breasts, stopping to attend to each one before moving down her stomach and delighted in Elizabeth's groans of pleasure. When she reached Elizabeth's mound and buried her lips in it, a jolt pierced Elizabeth's nether regions and she let out a gasp.

"May I?" Maggie said.

Elizabeth needed no explanation. She nodded.

Maggie caressed her with her hand.

Elizabeth moaned and pressed into her, her breathing ragged.

Maggie moved back up to meet Elizabeth's lips without moving her hand. She ended the kiss and watched the flush bloom on Elizabeth's face as she entered her.

Elizabeth cried out. Her eyelids slammed shut.

Maggie used her thumb to caress her hard nub. Elizabeth clamped down on her finger.

Elizabeth's eyes flew open. She vibrated with pleasure throughout her core. Never—never had she felt like this.

"Maggie!"

Maggie stroked.

"Oh, Maggie!"

Maggie continued.

Elizabeth pulled Maggie to her.

Maggie watched, a look of awe on her face, as Elizabeth rose to her peak and her body trembled. Release came with a final cry into Maggie's chest.

MAGGIE'S WORDS DIDN'T match the adoring look on her face as she caressed Elizabeth's forearm. "What are we going to do? I can't bear to be apart from you, not now. How are we going to survive?"

Elizabeth shook her head. "We need to be careful, Maggie. We can't risk Amelia, or anyone else, getting any inkling of our feelings for one another."

"I know." Maggie stopped stroking Elizabeth's arm and drew closer. "I find I cannot bear the thought of being away from you."

Elizabeth leaned in. "I understand."

Their lips met.

Maggie's breathing became uneven.

Maggie felt Elizabeth open her lips, inviting her in.

Maggie accepted the offer. Moisture pooled between her legs. She cried out as she pulled away. Her chest heaved.

Elizabeth mirrored her actions. Her voice sounded strained as she said, "We can alternate where we stay. You can come to me one night and I'll come to you another. We must return to our own places early, so as not to be seen. I wish it could be otherwise, but I can't see a way. I'll make some discrete inquiries to see if I can put a carriage on retainer."

Maggie said, "I'll ask Quan Luck. He will know someone who can be trusted."

Elizabeth stared at Maggie. "Is that wise?"

"Trust me, Elizabeth, Quan Luck is both resourceful and discrete. I assure you we can trust him completely."

"If you're sure... Yes, we'll be fine." She wasn't so sure. "We'll make certain it works."

"I will hate it. I will hate to see you leave my bed at dawn."

"I'll feel the same way."

"I hate the thought of your leaving now."

Elizabeth glanced out the bedroom window. "I must. It looks as if rain is coming. I should go before it starts."

Maggie brightened with a new idea. "It's Sunday. You could stay. Leave in the morning."

Elizabeth hesitated, trying to resist the pull of Maggie's invitation. She found it impossible. She crushed Maggie to her chest.

Maggie smiled. Elizabeth would stay.

Chapter Eight

February 13, 1906

WHILE ELIZABETH SAT in her office waiting for her last patient to get dressed after her examination, she mused on how well her arrangement with Maggie was working. Each night, after they closed up their businesses, one would board the waiting carriage and ride to the other's home to spend the evening and stay overnight. Each morning, either Maggie or Elizabeth found the carriage waiting in front of the building to take her home.

Quan Luck, Maggie had assured her, reacted as if she were asking him to deliver a photograph to someone down the street. When she told him what she required, including the request for a driver with the utmost discretion, it had taken him one day to find and retain Mr. Crane.

As instructed, the patient opened Elizabeth's office door a crack before leaving the examination room, letting Elizabeth know the room was free. She crossed through the empty room and opened the door to the parlor. Several people waited to see her. One surprised her—Amelia Rosemont. The hat she wore failed to hide strands of hair which were uncharacteristically disheveled, sticking out in disarray from under it. Her jacket was buttoned one button off. She looked as if she might cry. Elizabeth noted dark circles underlining Amelia's eyes. She nodded in her direction in acknowledgement and struggled to get her furrowed brow under control. She smiled at the group of waiting women and tried to sound cheerful as she asked, "Who's next?"

Three heads turned and indicated Amelia.

"Please come in, Mrs. Rosemont."

Amelia followed her into the room. When she asked Amelia to sit on the examination table, Amelia complied without speaking.

"How are you, Amelia?"

"Not well. I know I look a fright. I don't know what to do."

"Tell me what you're experiencing."

"Headaches. Terrible ones." She rubbed her forehead.

Elizabeth brought a light near her eyes, observing how they responded.

"How long have you had these headaches?"

"They started a few weeks ago. They're getting worse. I don't know what to do about them. I have to take to my bed in the middle of the day. They are so debilitating sometimes."

As Elizabeth felt for Amelia's pulse at her wrist, holding it with a delicate touch between her thumb and fingers, she watched the second hand ticking around the large clock face on a shelf behind Amelia.

"Your pulse seems fine—a good sign. Has anything changed to cause these headaches? Have you altered what you eat? Places you frequent?"

Amelia shook her head.

"Any new circumstances in the past few months giving you cause to worry or become anxious?"

Amelia looked down at the wrist Elizabeth held moments before. "No. Nothing," she whispered.

Elizabeth cocked her head. Why do I not believe you, Amelia?

She knew she'd have to word her doubts carefully. "Sometimes...things may be bothering a person and they don't even realize it. Try to be attentive to what you are doing when these headaches start. It may help us figure out the cause."

Amelia looked into Elizabeth's eyes and pulled herself to her full sitting height. "I might know what's causing them, doctor, but I assure you nothing's to be done about it and I have no desire to discuss it. I merely want something for the pain."

Elizabeth ran through the list of potential causes for Amelia not to be forthcoming. Did her husband abuse her? Did she have other health issues, perhaps problems with the female anatomy, about which women were often reluctant to talk?

She'd start there. "How is your health otherwise, Amelia?"

"I'm fine," Amelia snapped, "as healthy as a draft horse."

"It's good to hear. And your home life? How is it? Do you and Mr. Rosemont...get along well?"

Elizabeth watched as Amelia's eyes turned from their normal chestnut color to a deeper brown as she glared, chewing on her cheek as if debating an answer. Perhaps Elizabeth hit a nerve.

Amelia said, "My husband and I have an agreement. I don't meddle in his affairs and he doesn't interfere in mine. We live in comfortable companionship whenever our paths cross, but we have different...interests in life."

Well, if Amelia was to be believed, there weren't any problems at home, in spite of having a non-traditional marriage. Yet she had to wonder what the separate interests were that the Rosemonts pursued. Did they each engage in dalliances outside their marriage? If so, there were other concerns, like disease and, for Amelia, unwanted pregnancy.

"This may not be an appropriate question, Amelia, but you'll please indulge me. Do you need protection from unwelcome pregnancy?"

"No, doctor! I assure you I do not need anything of the sort. I'm fine. All I have are these troublesome headaches. I thought you might be able to give me something for this pain in my head so I don't have to go to a pharmacy." She added in a whisper, "I'd rather not discuss my personal affairs with a stranger."

At least Amelia showed some fire now, instead of the withdrawn, somber behavior she first exhibited.

"All right, Amelia, we'll leave it at that. I do have something I can give you, but let me ask one more question. How are you sleeping?"

Amelia looked down at her wrist again. "Not well," she whispered.

"Well, I'll assume this problem with sleep is related to the one you do not wish to discuss and say if the headaches and the problems sleeping do not go away in about a week, you should come back to see me again. You might want to think about discussing what the root of the problem is. It may be the only way to find an effective treatment."

Catching Elizabeth's eye, Amelia said, "I'm not sure that's possible, doctor."

"Then, we'll hope the medicine I give you will remove the symptoms, at least."

After Elizabeth returned to the examination room with a small white envelope of pills for Amelia, she gave her instructions for taking them.

As Amelia started toward the door to exit the examination room, she turned back, her face flushed, and she said, "doctor, would you like to have dinner tomorrow night? We could dine at the Fairmont. Or the Hotel Majestic is lovely."

Elizabeth wasn't sure she could manage sitting through an entire dinner with Amelia. What would they talk about? Rumors she might have heard about Elizabeth's indiscretions with a woman in Baltimore? Impossible. Especially dinner tomorrow night. She and Maggie already had plans. She was to arrive as usual by carriage at six o'clock and Maggie would have dinner ready, then they planned to spend a romantic evening to celebrate Valentine's Day. Elizabeth already purchased one of the special decorated cards sold in some shops these days. She smiled when she thought of the sentiment she wrote inside the card last night.

No. Tomorrow was out of the question. "I'm sorry, Amelia. It's not possible."

Amelia deflated. "You have another engagement."

"I'm afraid I do. Perhaps some other time." She didn't mean it. She hoped she'd never have to fulfill the promise. All she wanted was to get Amelia out of her clinic before she asked any more questions.

"Yes, maybe another time. You'll let me know?"

"I'll let you know if I anticipate having some time, yes, but you know how busy I am. It might not be possible for a while."

Amelia wore a forlorn look again. "Yes...well, have a grand time with your...companion."

"Companions, actually, it's more of a professional gathering."

She didn't know why she said it, perhaps to prevent Amelia from jumping to any conclusions. It was untruthful, but she didn't care. It would be better for Amelia to think she had an obligation with a group of colleagues than an engagement with...someone else.

"I wasn't aware there was a gathering of the medical profession, doctor. Is it at one of the hotels?"

"It's more of a private gathering." She needed to put a stop to this. "Amelia, I must attend to my other patients." Thank goodness others waited to see her. If they didn't she'd be hard pressed for an excuse to get rid of Amelia.

Amelia paused for another beat before she said, "Yes, of course, doctor. I'll let you get back to work."

When Amelia closed the door to the examining room behind her, Elizabeth drew in a deep breath for the first time since Amelia's problematic invitation.

February 14, 1906

"WHAT DO YOU think she was up to?" Maggie asked. They were talking about Amelia.

"I have no idea. Probing, I suspect. Looking for information to use against me, perhaps? I don't know—and I don't want to talk about Amelia Rosemont. I want to enjoy our evening—the two of us, by ourselves. No ghosts."

"A fine suggestion. Amelia Rosemont, begone!" Maggie waved her hand around the room like a magician. They laughed at Maggie's silliness. Then, Elizabeth drew her card from her dress pocket and held it out to Maggie.

"For you...my love."

Maggie's hand flew to her throat. "A card. How charming." She examined the front, saying, "It's beautiful." Before she opened it to read the sentiment inside, she asked, "Did you mean it?"

"Mean what? You haven't even read what I wrote yet."

"Did you mean what you said?"

Elizabeth's brow furrowed. "I said it was for you."

Maggie stepped closer to Elizabeth. As they stood toe-to-toe, Maggie said, "Not that. What you said after."

"I said, 'for you, my—'" Elizabeth's eyes widened in realization. "—love." Her eyes filled with tears. "I mean it, Maggie, with all my heart. I hope you don't think me too forward."

Maggie pulled Elizabeth to her. "Oh, Elizabeth, my dear, sweet, Elizabeth." She held her at arms-length, looked into her eyes and said, "I love you, too. I've wanted to say it for days now, but I was afraid I'd scare you off if I did."

Elizabeth pulled her back into an embrace. "Maggie, I do love you so. I love you with all my heart. Never have I felt this way before."

"Nor have I, Elizabeth."

Elizabeth kissed Maggie's hair and whispered to her, "If you'll open your card, you'll see I said as much there."

Maggie looked up at her with adoration, "Kiss me, first. Then, I'll read it."

When they kissed, Maggie felt as if the room trembled beneath her feet, until she realized it was her own body reacting to Elizabeth's kiss.

Later in the evening, as they lay in Maggie's bed, caressing each other's skin, reveling in the afterglow of their love-making, Elizabeth said, "I know I said I didn't want to talk about Amelia, but I find I'm worried about her. When she was in my clinic, she looked terrible. It appeared as if she couldn't take care of herself. Her clothes and hair were untidy. It's odd for a woman like her, to whom outward appearance is so important. Until yesterday's visit, she's always looked so meticulous."

"What's wrong with her?"

"I shouldn't be talking about her condition. Normally, I wouldn't, but I'm disturbed by what I see, and we do know her socially."

"Elizabeth, I consider it part of my relationship with you to support you in your work. Whether you share something with me about a patient or an acquaintance, you can be sure I will never speak of it to anyone but you."

Elizabeth gave Maggie a smile of gratitude.

"She's suffering from headaches and difficulty sleeping at night. She had dark circles under her eyes, most likely as a result of her other symptoms. I gave her some medicine to help with the pain, which will, hopefully, allow her to get some rest, but it was so unnerving to see her. I don't like the woman. I don't trust her, but she is undergoing genuine suffering."

"Perhaps her conscience has finally broken through and she's feeling remorse for her treatment of people like Quan Luck and others like him."

"Maybe. She wouldn't talk about what was bothering her. She also said something else, which leads me to believe she and her husband are not, shall we say, living as husband and wife. However, when I pressed her further, she dismissed me, refusing to talk about it."

They lay without speaking for a while, until Elizabeth began stroking Maggie's breast with light touches and kissing the curve where her throat met her collar bone.

Maggie thought she'd burst into flames with the love and want welling up inside her. Between deep, rasping breaths, Maggie said, "What an exquisite Valentine's day, my love."

"I have more to give you, my sweet. The night is still young and I still have the gift of pleasure to give you."

Maggie moved Elizabeth's hand from her breast, guiding down her smooth stomach until their fingers touched hair. Elizabeth growled at the invitation. Maggie responded with a river of juices flowing between her legs and she lifted her head to meet Elizabeth's mouth.

February 28, 1906

ELIZABETH SAT BESIDE Alanna Magee while the woman wept softly. Alanna displayed a sweet spirit in spite of deformities. She bore the effects of poor childhood nutrition and hard labor.

When she composed herself a little more, she spoke between sniffles. "Me father hated his life as a farmer. He spent more time in the local pub than his field. Crops went bad 'cause he refused to tend to them. Me mother had her own troubles. She had a bad fall right after I was weaned and she was crippled from it, so me brothers and sisters had to fend for themselves from the time they were young, but they were far too young to know how to care for a babe properly. Food was scarce. I remember hunger most of the time. Me legs—" she pointed to her bowed limbs "—went like this.

"I didn't know it affected other parts. Not till last year when I got with child." Tears fell in rivulets down her cheeks as she spoke. "Last year, I lost me wee one. The midwife said me womb is twisted 'cause the bones are like me legs. The babe couldn't get out. Me labor lasted for days. I would've died if she hadn't gone in and pulled him out. By then it was too late. He died." Her head sank into her hands and she sobbed.

She wiped her nose on a dingy handkerchief and continued. "Padraic—that's me husband— and I, we wanted children. He's pressin' me to try again. He's a good man, but he doesn't understand the babe's dying wasn't some accident of fate. He doesn't want to face the fact of it happenin' over and over again 'cause of me innards." She placed her hand over her stomach as if it could heal her.

"I don't know what to do. Losin' me babe devastated me. I don't think I could go through it again. I'm afraid of the pain and I'm afraid of dyin'."

Elizabeth placed her hand on Alanna's forearm. "You shouldn't have to. No man should dictate the choices a woman makes when it comes to her own body, even more so, a woman in your circumstances."

"I felt so useless after I lost me child, especially after the midwife told me it would happen again and again. Do you think it will?"

"I'd have to examine you to confirm if it's true or not, Alanna, but we can do that later."

Alanna nodded. "I was brokenhearted to realize I'll never be a mother. When I tried to talk to Padraic about it, he wouldn't listen and went off to the pub, just like me father. Now he doesn't want to hear it—and he's pushing me to try again. I'm not sure if it's wantin' another child or wantin'...you know. We haven't...for a while. Since the babe."

Elizabeth nodded.

"The midwife said she could give me some herbs to keep me from gettin' with child again. Some women who live on Irish Hill told me to come and see you. They said you could help me with something better than midwifery and herbs. I'm hopin' you can. I've been puttin' Padraic off for so long, I'm afraid I'm going to lose him."

Elizabeth gave Alanna a weak smile. She couldn't offer much advice until she examined her. "Will you allow me to examine you? I'll need you to undress most of the way. If you're wearing a corset, you'll have to remove it."

"I can't wear one of them things," Alanna said. "I don't know how anyone does, but with these legs and hips, I can't abide it."

"I'm not sure why we suffer them, either. In your case, I

understand how it would be uncomfortable for you, but for us here today, it makes it easier."

Elizabeth got up from her seat and walked over to a small, glass front cabinet. When she returned, she handed Alanna a plain cotton frock with no form to it. "Take everything off and put this on. I want to be able to access your entire body to give you an accurate assessment to give you the best medical advice I can offer. I'm going to leave the room for a few minutes. Lock the door behind me and get undressed. When you're ready, unlock the door and lie down on the table."

Elizabeth pointed to the plain wooden table covered by a thin pad to serve as an examination bed.

Alanna licked her lips, then, nodded.

Elizabeth recognized her nervousness. Any woman would be nervous. She gave her a look of encouragement and left. Out in the hall, she heard the soft *snick* of the lock behind her. When she returned a few minutes later, Alanna sat on the edge of the table with her arms wrapped around her, trying to contain her awkwardness. Elizabeth was familiar with the posture.

"This won't take long, Alanna. Try to relax. I know it's difficult."

Fifteen minutes later, Elizabeth sat opposite Alanna, now dressed again; and said, "The midwife is correct. The way your pelvis is shaped, I'm surprised they could even get the baby out at all. That you are alive is a miracle, Alanna. You should not get pregnant again."

Alanna began to weep. Elizabeth took her hand and said, "I'm sorry, Alanna, but you already knew this."

Alanna nodded.

"What we need to do is keep this from happening while helping you keep your husband. From what you've told me, though, I'm not sure he would go along with the solution I have to your problem." She reached beside her into her doctor's bag and pulled out a small metal box. When she opened it, Alanna leaned in to look inside.

"What is it?"

"It's a contraceptive device."

"Oh. Padraic won't have anythin' to do with that. He says it makes him feel less of a man."

"This is not for Padraic, Alanna. This is for you."

She explained how to use the cervical cap, including how to insert and remove the device. Then she asked if she had any other questions.

Alanna said, "After some time passes, what do I tell him when he asks why I'm not with child?"

Elizabeth looked her in the eye and said, "You may tell him your past experience with childbirth, where you almost lost your own life, may have damaged your internal organs to such a point you no longer may be able to conceive."

Alanna looked skeptical, then, a grin broke out across her face.

"If he doesn't like that answer, tell him his part may not be up to the job."

Now, she giggled like a schoolgirl.

Elizabeth delighted in having a part in making her laugh.

As she watched Alanna walk down the hall toward the front door of the Mission, happy she was able to relieve some of the woman's burden, Violet came up behind her.

"Were you able to help her, doctor?"

"I think I may have been able to offer her a solution. We can hope for the best in this case, Miss Farrell."

"Hope for the best and trust in God," Violet said.

And the contraceptive I just gave her.

"You're building quite a reputation with the women South of the Slot, doctor. I've heard them talking when they come for the music sessions. They all adore you. Better still, they trust you."

"Their trust is important," Elizabeth said. "I'm honored to have it."

Violet stepped around Elizabeth, and headed toward her office. As she walked away, she called over her shoulder, "I'm glad you're here, doctor."

"Thank you, Miss Farrell. I'm glad to be here, too."

Satisfaction filled her as she hurried to tidy the examination room and pack up her bag.

If she had been pleased with Violet Farrell's compliment earlier, thoughts of Maggie thrilled her even more. Maggie would have come to the mission with her, but today she had an appointment with the upper echelons of San Francisco society to photograph a group in town for a meeting. Maggie was due at Elizabeth's house in about an hour, so she wanted to hurry home and prepare a quick supper for them both.

She walked down the hall to leave and heard Violet through her closed office door, talking in muffled tones with a visitor. She liked Violet. However, since she was busy with someone, it meant she wouldn't have to stop to tell her she was leaving—and she wouldn't have to wipe the silly grin off her face at thoughts of seeing Maggie again soon.

March 4, 1906

SUNDAY DAWNED BRIGHT and warm. Maggie sat on the settee by the window overlooking Van Ness Avenue, trying to read *The House of Mirth*. She wasn't successful because Elizabeth sat nearby in a wingback chair, focused on an article in the *Journal of the American Medical Association* and Maggie couldn't keep her eyes off her. Elizabeth's sandy-colored hair glowed in the sunlight. The look of intensity she wore as she concentrated on her reading, held Maggie spellbound.

Elizabeth must have sensed being watched, because she looked up at Maggie and smiled. "How is your story?"

"Fascinating." Yet it couldn't keep her interest, not with Elizabeth sitting there, looking so beautiful. "I'll bet much more interesting than yours." She wrinkled her nose at the thought of the technical composition.

Elizabeth laughed. "I'll have you know I find these articles extremely interesting and informative."

"I'm glad to hear it."

To Maggie's ears, Elizabeth sounded indignant when she said, "I must stay informed on all the newest techniques and proposed theories, you know. How else am I to offer the best medical care to my patients? If I didn't read these articles, my practice would remain stagnant and my patients would suffer."

"Elizabeth, I was joking."

"Oh."

She looked so defenseless when she felt she had to justify herself. The formidable Doctor Kellogg definitely had her more vulnerable side, and Maggie was coming to realize few people ever saw it. She felt her heart bursting with affection for Elizabeth. Warmth turned to fire. Maggie put her book down and rose from her seat. As she approached Elizabeth, she saw surprise, then passion flare in Elizabeth's eyes. The intensity of it made it difficult for Maggie to swallow.

Maggie held out her hand, and without saying a word, Elizabeth grasped it. She felt a spark jump from her fingers to Elizabeth's. Elizabeth stood and led her to the bedroom. When they reached the bed, Elizabeth thrust Maggie backwards.

Maggie could have resisted. Instead, she toppled back, letting her weight carry her to the mattress, laughing, feeling the lightness of delight at being loved and desired.

Later in the afternoon, they sat in the same positions they left earlier, reading again.

Elizabeth said, "You should move in."

Maggie looked up, her eyes full of concern. "What about Mrs. Rosemont?"

"I haven't seen Amelia for weeks now. The last time was when she came to consult with me about her headaches. I presume, since she didn't return, she's feeling better. It's possible I'm not the focus of her obsession these days. She may have moved on to someone else...someone who is the subject of more interesting gossip, perhaps."

"I'd love to live with you, Elizabeth, but I think you should think this through. If we set up housekeeping together, we'll be inviting idle talk on the part of Mrs. Stockton's friends, should they find out. I don't want to jeopardize your standing in this community."

"And I don't want to see you have to walk out the door in the wee hours of the morning. Mr. Crane has proved to be a loyal and discrete man, but I still hate it when you have to leave and board his carriage."

"I feel the same way about you, but if I lived here, I'd have to do the same thing. I'll need to go to the shop every morning, Elizabeth."

Elizabeth puckered her lips. Maggie suspected she was formulating her next argument. "Most of all, I think I detest Amelia Rosemont dictating our lives for us."

"And, yet, we must. Let's keep our current arrangement. Although I'd like nothing better than to live here with you, unless something changes, I don't think it's wise."

Maggie observed Elizabeth as she mulled over the conversation, then, said, "You're right, I suppose. I should thank you for being the voice of reason."

How long she could maintain such level-headedness, Maggie wasn't sure.

March 23, 1906

ANOTHER TWO WEEKS passed before, Amelia returned.

Elizabeth finished her examination and took a step back. "I'm a little concerned, Amelia. This is the third time you've come to see me in a little over a week. Last time, you thought something was wrong with your eyes."

"They watered so much, I couldn't see." Amelia whined.

"Yes, I know, but, other than a little watering, there was no sign of redness to indicate irritation. And the soothing drops I gave you cleared up the issue, so it may have indicated sensitivity to something in the air. The time before, it was trembling and pain in your legs."

Amelia looked down at her hands, fingers twisting in her lap. "You said you could find nothing wrong."

"I could find nothing wrong physically. I don't discount the symptoms you felt. Your first visit, over a month ago, was for headaches. Have any of those symptoms returned?"

"No. I've only felt the pains and feeling as if my heart is going to burst from my chest." She rubbed her chest with the tips of her fingers. Her blouse and jacket lay beside her on the examining table, her chemise and corset, the only coverings on her upper body.

"I've listened to your heart. It's strong with regular beats. Your pulse is normal, and you have good color."

As she spoke, she pulled a wooden case out of the drawer in the cabinet beside her. She opened it and extended a long metal scale.

Amelia shrank back. "What's that?"

Elizabeth gave her a reassuring smile. "It's an instrument to measure blood pressure. It's something perfected recently. This is the newest model. I'll put this cuff around your arm and inflate it. You may find the compression a little uncomfortable, but I assure you, it won't take long. I'll listen to the pressure sounds while the cuff deflates and I'll be able to tell if your blood is pumping through your body at normal pressure."

"What are all those tubes?"

"They are the connections between the instrument and the force exerted in this cuff. Don't be concerned, Amelia, it won't take but a minute. It's important to know if your blood pressure is normal because of the symptoms you've described."

Amelia still looked wary when she said, "All right, doctor, if you think it's necessary."

When Elizabeth pumped the cuff to apply pressure to her arm, Amelia let out a little whimper and closed her eyes, but she said nothing. Elizabeth watched Amelia's chest rise and fall as she took deep gulping breaths.

"Try to relax and breathe normally, Amelia."

Amelia's breathing calmed. She kept her eyes closed. She looked vulnerable sitting in her state of half-undress.

Elizabeth inserted the ends of her stethoscope into her ears, then placed the other end on Amelia's arm and listened. When she removed the cuff, she said, "the pressure is a little high, but it could be because it's your first time experiencing the instrument. If you're anxious, it can affect the reading. We should monitor it for a while to see if this is the cause of the pains in your chest."

Amelia seemed to brighten a little. "Joseph says it's nothing but nervous exhaustion and I should stay at home and rest more."

"Neurasthenia is an elusive problem. We don't know what causes it and I'm not sure we know the best way of dealing with it. Commonly, rest and a reduction in activity is the current treatment. Perhaps you could try curbing your activities, Amelia. I'm sorry I can't offer you better advice."

So, at least Amelia interacted with her husband.

"But you still want me to come to you regularly, correct, doctor?"

Elizabeth couldn't read the look Amelia gave her. It struck her as odd. Best to ignore it, she decided.

"Yes. Come to see me once a week. Make sure you have your driver bring you as you shouldn't exhaust yourself with walking. We'll see how you are next week. I'll leave you to get dressed now."

"You don't have to go…Elizabeth."

Elizabeth turned from the drawer where she replaced the blood pressure monitor and frowned at Amelia. What a strange comment.

The smile left Amelia's face. "I'll get dressed and go, then, shall I?"

"Yes."

Elizabeth walked to the door to her office. "If you have any questions, knock on my office door after you're dressed."

She slipped into the office and closed the door behind her. What was Amelia playing at? Was she trying to bait her to test the rumors she might have heard from back East even in her current state of poor health?

She'd known Amelia Rosemont for several months. The more she learned of her, the more she questioned her motives. She made a mental note, once again. The woman was not to be trusted.

Elizabeth blew out a sigh of frustration when Amelia knocked on her door a few minutes later. She didn't have any questions about her health, she said. Instead, she wanted to chat as if she had arrived for a social visit.

"How is your work with Miss Farrell's group going, doctor?"

She prattled on. Elizabeth tried to think of a way to shoo Amelia out, but there were no other patients waiting, and she didn't want to appear rude, especially when she didn't know what Amelia was up to. However, Maggie was due at any moment and she didn't think it was wise to have Amelia there when she arrived. An uncomfortable feeling gnawed at Elizabeth. She had to get her out of here.

Finally, Amelia gave her a reason to withdraw.

"I know you're busy, doctor. So I should—"

"—go, yes. I have the examination room to tidy up and a new article on women's health I must read, so, if you'll excuse me, Amelia. Make sure you rest as much as possible during the next few weeks." The cure, she hoped, would keep Amelia out of her hair, except for the scheduled office visits. "Will you see yourself out?"

The smile left Amelia's face. Elizabeth detected a slight edge to her voice when she said, "I'm perfectly capable, doctor."

When the door closed behind Amelia, Elizabeth exhaled. She hoped when Amelia Rosemont returned next week, she'd have a large group in her waiting area so she'd have an excuse not to linger. How long could she keep dismissing this woman before she got herself into difficulty she couldn't escape?

WHEN MAGGIE ARRIVED for dinner, she thought it odd when Elizabeth stepped outside the front door to look up and down the street.

"Whatever are you doing?" Maggie peeked around the door jamb, uncertain what she was looking for.

Elizabeth stepped into the hall and closed the door. "I'm making sure Amelia Rosemont has gone home."

"Oh, dear, was she here?"

"Yes, she left a while ago. I was so afraid you'd run into her."

"No need to worry. I didn't see her." Maggie kissed her on the cheek.

Elizabeth drew the bolt across the door and said, "I'm glad to hear it. Let's go upstairs."

They prepared dinner together and, as they sat and ate, Elizabeth said, "That woman is up to something. She had the temerity to invite me to stay while she got dressed."

"Dressed?" Maggie registered surprise. "It seems she's always up to something."

"Yes, she's been to see me several times over the past few weeks with various complaints. I could find nothing seriously wrong, but she still looks awful. In her past visits, the ailments didn't require her to undress. Today, she said she had pains in her chest. I needed to listen to her heart, so I had her remove her blouse and loosen her corset. When we were done, I told her she could get dressed. Before I could get my instruments put away, she suggested I stay."

Maggie struggled to suppress a smile. "Am I to assume it's not your usual procedure while tending patients?

"No! I would never stand around ogling a patient while they dressed. Most women are embarrassed to be undressed in the presence of someone not intimate with them, even doctors. It's considered unprofessional to stay in the room while someone re-robes. Most people can't wait for the doctor to leave the room to put themselves back together."

"So, what do you think she was up to?"

"I—I'm concerned about the rumors she thinks she's heard. I think she may be baiting me to find out if they are true."

"How terrible. It's shameful. It's—"

"Underhanded? Yes, an apt description of our Mrs. Rosemont."

"What are you going to do?"

"What can I do? She's not brought up the rumors again. I'm not sure she has even had any information from back East in the first place. For all I know, she threw out the first volley to get a reaction. I'm afraid she caught me so unaware I may have blanched and from then on, she's used her suspicions to harass me."

"Do you think Mrs. Stockton could help? You said she was sympathetic."

"I'm not sure I want to trouble Mrs. Stockton with this, Maggie. She's been so kind to me and she's not well."

Maggie pursed her lips as if trying to work out a puzzle. It would be so easy to meet them in a kiss. When the now familiar thrill skittered through Elizabeth's body, she couldn't resist. She pulled her close and pressed her lips to Maggie's, feeling comfort in their softness.

"Stay with me tonight."

Maggie heard the plea in Elizabeth's voice. Filled with reluctance, she answered, "I'm so sorry, Elizabeth. I can't. Quan Luck is coming at first light tomorrow. I'm expecting a delivery then. I've already told Mr. Crane."

Elizabeth's face reflected her disappointment. As she fought to get her emotions under control, Maggie watched a veil fall across her face. "I—I understand. We must take care of business. It's important if we're to remain the independent women we are." She gave Maggie a weak smile, then pulled herself to her full height and said, "We'll just have to plan our next meeting, then."

Maggie laughed, glad to realize Elizabeth recovered. "Why don't you come for dinner tomorrow? I have something to show you."

Elizabeth perked up. "Is it a surprise? Tell me."

Maggie debated whether or not to wait until the following day to reveal the prize. However, when she thought about

Elizabeth's stressful afternoon with Mrs. Rosemont and her disappointment at her refusal to stay the night, she decided to give her something to look forward to and said, "I've got a new Caruso record."

Elizabeth clapped her hands together. "Oh, lovely. Where did you get it?"

"Michael-the-Maul."

Elizabeth frowned. Her voice sounded half an octave lower when she asked, "He didn't bother you, did he?"

"I assure you, Michael and I have a definite understanding about our association. He stopped trying to pull any of his enticement tricks on me a long time ago. He knows I love Caruso, though. He also knows I have a Talking Machine, since I bought it from his store, so he's always on the alert for records for me. He brought it by the shop this morning."

"How nice." Elizabeth looked delighted. "I'll look forward to listening to it with you."

Maggie speculated they'd look forward to so much more than listening to a new Caruso recording—and less about trying to figure out what Amelia Rosemont was up to.

Chapter Nine

March 25, 1906

SUNDAY HELD THE promise of springtime as Elizabeth and Maggie strolled the pathways in Golden Gate Park. They stopped to observe men and a few women as they rode bicycles past their vantage point near the Conservatory of Flowers—the grand confection-like structure in the park.

They had toured the stunning white wood and glass building, taking in the fountains and early blooms in the entryway and Palm Room under the vast glass dome. Maggie pointed out the Orchid House and they headed for it to take in the exotic plants. Their perfect Sunday was marked by a continuation of unseasonably warm and pleasant weather.

Now, they sat on a stone bench on the grounds of the Conservatory, watching the crowd and nibbling on the lunch Elizabeth brought in a basket covered with a bright gingham cloth.

"I enjoyed your new Caruso record so much," Elizabeth said. Then, she leaned in close to Maggie's ear and whispered, "...and...afterwards."

Maggie shivered and said, "I—I did, too. Enjoy the record, I mean." Her cheeks turned crimson and she added, "Well, afterwards, also."

Elizabeth's eyes danced with pleasure at her reaction. "I'm looking forward to this evening, as well."

Maggie slapped her on the forearm and whispered, "Elizabeth, please. Not here."

Elizabeth rolled her eyes in mock annoyance, "Oh, all right. I'll change the subject. I've been thinking I need to venture into the neighborhood near the docks. My patients at the Quaker Mission tell me some women there need the help of a medical doctor, but do not venture out because of various circumstances. Two of them mentioned one person, in particular. I'd like to visit her."

"You shouldn't go alone."

"I thought as much. Do you think you could go with me?"

"Let me look at my diary when we get back to the shop and we can see when I'll be free. I have several appointments this week, but I'm sure we can fit it into the schedule."

Elizabeth smiled her appreciation and marveled at how dear Maggie had grown to her.

"Do you think Quan Luck would go with us or perhaps find us someone to escort us?" Elizabeth asked.

"It might not be a bad idea. Let's see if he can recommend someone."

They strolled through the park after finishing their lunch and hired a carriage to return them to Maggie's photography studio. They climbed the stairs to Maggie's flat, glad they didn't have to end their day with their exit from the park.

April 2, 1906

MAGGIE REVELED IN the luxury of waking up with Elizabeth by her side. Even though it was well past dawn, she didn't need to return home. Maggie stretched her arms over her head and turned to face Elizabeth. Her head rested on their shared pillow, sandy hair lay tousled around her face. This delightful actuality was due to their plan to visit Irish Hill today. Quan Luck would meet them downstairs in a few hours, after he finished helping his father and uncle at their laundry in Chinatown.

Quan Luck had assured them he would be the best person to accompany them on their venture today. Maggie wasn't so sure. People down by the Iron Works and the gas house were territorial and might not appreciate the young man's presence in their domain. Dutchman's Flat, Scotch Hill, Irish Hill, the names all indicated the populace of each of those sections of the city.

Elizabeth stirred. When she opened her eyes, she met Maggie's with a smile. "How nice to greet you so late in the morning, Maggie."

"I thought the same thing when I woke up a few minutes ago. We'd better get moving, though. I have some equipment to round up before Quan Luck gets here."

"Why don't you get dressed and go. I'll make breakfast."

Maggie giggled. "Making tea and putting a plate of muffins on the table doesn't constitute cooking, doctor."

Elizabeth's eyes lit up with her smile. "Never mind. Breakfast will be ready when you're done, cooking or not." She raised herself on her elbow and kissed Maggie on the lips. The good morning kiss turned to something more passionate in an instant.

Maggie pulled away with a cry, flustered. "Elizabeth Kellogg, don't you tempt me. I've got work to do."

Elizabeth tried to stifle her smile by clamping her lips together. Then she winked and said, "Yes, Maggie, darling."

Maggie blushed and swung her legs over the side of the bed. "You're hopeless."

"Hopelessly in love."

A smile broke across Maggie's face. She turned back to Elizabeth and gave her another sizzling kiss, causing Elizabeth to squirm and press into her. When Maggie broke it off, she said, "Think about that while you *cook* breakfast. I'll be back in a little while."

She left Elizabeth panting while an ache lingered deep within.

THEY LOOKED AN odd trio walking down Seventh Street toward Irish Hill, Elizabeth in her professional-looking suit, toting her doctor's bag, Maggie in her stylish dress and maroon hat, carrying a small, wooden box camera, and Quan Luck, today dressed in an understated, black *tangzhuang*, the loose black jacket with wide sleeves and high collar worn by most men every day in Chinatown. His long braid bounced on his back as he followed the two women, carrying Maggie's bag of photography accessories.

Elizabeth turned to him and said, "Is your bag too heavy for you, Quan Luck?"

"No, doctor. It's fine. Not heavy at all."

Elizabeth stopped. He halted a few steps behind her.

"Then walk with us, Quan Luck. I don't like to see you trailing behind like some kind of pet. We are no better than you."

Quan Luck gave her a look she couldn't decipher. Did he find it repugnant to walk beside them or did he think he was unworthy as she suggested?

"What's wrong? Don't you want to walk with us?"

Maggie intervened. "Elizabeth, I don't think it's wise given the area we're walking in. On Market Street, people might ignore the three of us walking together because it's such a busy, crowded area and people are distracted with their own business, but here...well, let's say the closer we get to the clannish hills we're heading for, a young Chinese man walking beside the two of us might be frowned upon. Someone could think he doesn't know his place."

Elizabeth looked from Maggie to Quan Luck. "I detest this. I am no better than Quan Luck. He should be able to walk as our equals."

"I feel the same way, but it may not be safe, especially for

Quan Luck. It will draw less attention if he walks behind us."

"Is he not here to protect us? Or are we to defend him? Because I will, if necessary."

Quan Luck said, "I am fine, doctor. I will protect you if anyone threatens. I am trained in ancient fighting skills called, *wushu*. These men who live on Irish Hill and nearby cannot defeat me. I assure you, you are both safe."

Elizabeth didn't know if she could believe him, but he spoke with enough authority, she decided to trust him.

"Well, let's hope it doesn't come to that, shall we?"

Quan Luck and Maggie both nodded.

Elizabeth sighed and said, "I want you to understand I do not condone you walking behind us like this, although I accept it might not be a good idea to show you are equal to us in this neighborhood."

Quan Luck smiled. "Sometimes caution is greater than insistence on the appearance of equality. I appreciate what is in your heart. Because of it, I do not mind walking a few steps behind you."

A supply wagon moved up the street toward them, the horses hooves beating a muffled clomp on the hard-packed earth. Maggie encouraged them to keep moving. As the wagon reached them, the driver scowled. Elizabeth wanted to glower back, but thought it better to follow Quan Luck's example and rise above the situation. The wagon moved on. Elizabeth looked over her shoulder and glared at the driver's back.

Maggie watched her reaction. "Did giving him a look make you feel better?" she asked.

"A great deal better."

Maggie shook her head while trying to suppress a chuckle and the three of them continued down the street. When they reached the edge of Irish Hill, Elizabeth said, "Alanna said Mrs. Quinn lives on the corner of 19th and Pennsylvania." She pointed down the road. "I'm surprised it's all bungalows and cottages here. I expected tenements, like in Baltimore."

Maggie indicated a run-down little house, more of a shack, on the next corner. "Is it there?"

"I'll find out."

"If it's the place you're looking for, Quan Luck and I will walk a little farther while you go in. It looks like we can get a view of the shoreline below from up here. I'd like to take a few photographs."

As Elizabeth approached the dilapidated bungalow, a woman opened the door. When she saw Elizabeth approaching, she slammed it shut.

Elizabeth walked up to the entrance and rapped loudly. "Mrs. Quinn? I'm Doctor Kellogg. Alanna Magee thought you might need my assistance. Please, open the door. I'd like to talk to you."

Silence followed. Elizabeth debated whether or not to leave.

After a few beats, the door opened a crack. All Elizabeth could see was a blue eye in shadows and fingers clinging to the edge of the door. The woman's grip exerted enough force to make them turn white. From inside, a muffled voice, heavy with an Irish brogue, said, "Alanna Magee should mind her own business. I don't need doctorin'." The woman coughed, then winced. The woman lost her grip on the door as she coughed again. The door opened a little wider and Elizabeth saw the woman had a deep red bruise on her cheek and a dark ring, edged with green and yellow around her eye.

A fresh bruise to the cheek, an old bruise to the eye, Elizabeth evaluated as if she were standing in her clinic with a patient. She pointed to the woman's face. "That looks to me like it could use some *doctorin'*."

"No." The woman started to close the door.

Elizabeth put out her hand to stop it. It didn't take much. Mrs. Quinn was weak.

"Please, Mrs. Quinn, let me help you. Are you hurt anywhere else?"

The woman tried to stifle a cough. When she could no longer hold it in, she opened the door and stumbled toward a chair, falling into it.

As Elizabeth entered the room, she took note of her surroundings. The furniture was sparse. It was dark and dank. And it was dirty with clothes strewn everywhere and dishes piled in a sink on the far wall. An overturned chair leaned against another wall. Several broken dishes lay on the floor a short distance away. It looked as if there had been a brawl.

Elizabeth put her bag on the table and knelt beside Mrs. Quinn as she held on to her left side and tried to recover from another coughing fit.

"Would you like a drink of water?"

Mrs. Quinn nodded and waved toward a sink behind her.

Elizabeth found the cleanest cup she could in a stack of dirty dishes and rinsed it before filling it. When she held the cup out to Mrs. Quinn, she took it, gulped half of it down, then pushed it onto the table.

"You shouldn't be here," she rasped. "If my husband comes back there'll be hell to pay...for both of us." Her anger was surrounded by an edge of fear.

"Did he do this to you?"

She nodded and grimaced.

Elizabeth weighed her next words carefully. "You don't have to stay here," she said. "You could go to the Quaker Mission. Miss Farrell will find you a place to stay."

"And then what? Wait for him to come after me and drag me back to all this...finery?" The anger in her voice turned to sarcasm. "I'm his wife. I'm here to do his biddin'," she spat. "He thinks he's God-almighty and I'm a slave."

She broke down, holding her side, trying to control her sobs. When she recovered, she said, "If I leave, how am I supposed to take care of myself? I won't be a floozie, givin' myself away to men to make a living. May as well stay here. It's all I am to himself, anyway."

If this woman had cowered instead of rising to her full height and sounding angry while she spoke, Elizabeth might not have pushed. But the fire in this woman's eyes at her mistreatment from the hands of a man who should be her protector, made Elizabeth realize she should try a little harder.

"Violet—Miss Farrell from the Quaker Mission—has helped women like you before. She has places she can avail you of—safe places. Your husband would never find you. Those people who take women like you in have means, and they will find you a job. Believe me, work is available to make a living which doesn't require you to compromise your morals. Let us help you."

Mrs. Quinn deflated before her eyes. Perhaps it was the thought of someone caring, offering her options, or perhaps she couldn't sustain the anger and sense of injustice over her lot any longer. It took too much out of her.

Elizabeth continued, "However, I'm more concerned for your immediate welfare. I suspect you might have a broken rib, which could be dangerous. Will you let me examine you?"

Mrs. Quinn didn't answer right away.

"I don't want to take me clothes off."

"You don't have to undress. I'll examine you through your clothes. May I?"

The woman gave her one small nod.

Elizabeth extended her hands and placed her palms on her sides. "I'm going to press a little. Let me know if it hurts." She knew the woman was favoring her left side. She started on the right. "Does this hurt?"

"No. Not really."

She moved her fingers up a little. "How about now?"

"No."

She repeated the action a few more times with the same

result. "Now the other side."

Mrs. Quinn drew in a breath in anticipation. It caused her to cough again.

Elizabeth waited.

"What's your given name?"

"Bridget."

"All right, Bridget, if anything I do hurts too much, tell me and I'll stop." She pressed lightly on her lower rib cage. "All right?" she asked.

"Yes. It hurts worse up more."

"I'll approach slowly."

She moved her hand and repeated the process.

Bridget winced.

"Once more." She applied pressure until Bridget cried out.

Elizabeth removed her hand. "I'm sorry it hurt so much. It was necessary to find out where the injury was. Can you take in a deep breath?"

"I can, but it makes me cough sometimes."

Elizabeth pulled her stethoscope out of her bag and listened to Bridget's lungs.

"Your lungs are clear. You may have a cracked rib at worse case, or it could be a bad bruise. Either way, you need to rest. No over-exertion."

Bridget let out a bitter chuckle. "If I don't get this place cleaned up before me husband comes home from the iron works tonight, I'll see his fist again. So, tell me how I'm supposed to do my chores and keep from exertin' meself."

Elizabeth gave it some thought, then suggested, "I have two friends with me. They would help. We could get this place back in order in a short time."

"No. I can't let—"

"Yes, you can, Bridget. You must. For your own safety. I'll wrap your ribs so they are supported. It won't hurt so much if you cough. Leave them wrapped for a few days, then come and see me at Miss Farrell's Mission. In the meantime, let us help you clean up. And think about my suggestions. You don't need to stay here."

"He's promised not to do it again."

"Yes, they usually do."

"He's an honorable man."

Elizabeth sighed. It was doubtful she would talk Bridget Quinn into leaving her husband. The woman didn't realize how much her life was in danger.

IT TOOK ELIZABETH some time to get Bridget to allow her to wrap her ribs. When she finished, she wanted to give Bridget privacy while she put her clothes back on so she stepped over to the window and peered through the dingy gossamer curtain.

Maggie and Quan Luck stood in the little weed choked front yard, talking. She turned back to Bridget, now fully clothed, and said, "My friends are here. If you'll allow me, I'll invite them in to help put your home back in order."

"It's such a mess," Bridget said. "I don't know."

Elizabeth stepped toward Bridget and said, "Bridget, you can't do this alone. You've got bruised ribs at best, and perhaps a cracked one. You need to rest. We'll do this for you. My friends won't care what it looks like in here. They'll want to help."

When Bridget nodded, Elizabeth walked outside and explained the situation. Both Maggie and Quan Luck offered their help and the three entered the little house. Elizabeth saw Maggie's eyes widen when she took in the state of the shack, but she recovered quickly and she and Quan Luck set about helping Elizabeth to restore order.

Maggie plunged her arms up to her elbows into a sink full of water and began washing dirty dishes. Quan Luck found a broom and swept up broken bits of plates and debris from the floor. Elizabeth gathered pieces of clothing strewn around the room and folded and stacked them on a shelf. She gathered up other items which looked as if they had been misplaced, or thrown, or knocked over in a fight and found places for them, too. In short order, the place still looked dank and worn, but order had been restored.

Elizabeth and Bridget had another quiet conversation regarding her proposal to leave her abusive husband. Again, she refused. When the trio said their goodbyes, they made for the front door. Quan Luck opened it—and they came face-to-face with the biggest, meanest-looking man Elizabeth had ever seen.

THE MAN FILLED the doorway. As he looked down at Quan Luck, he growled, "What are you doing in my house, Chinaman?"

Quan Luck took a step back. Maggie stepped around him, pulling herself up to her full height, hands on hips. "He's here with me. Leave him alone," she snarled.

"And what're *you* doing here, *aul wagon*?"

Maggie's face turned beet red. "I'll have you know I understand the double meaning of what you said, Mr. Quinn, so watch your mouth."

"It means yer a formidable little thing. Now get outta me

way." He took a step.

She matched him.

"And…it means an unpleasant woman."

His eyes widened. He stepped around her, ignoring her. When he started forward, Elizabeth met him. Taller than Maggie by a few inches, she still only came to his chest. She gave him a challenging look and said, "Mr. Quinn, we are here to help your wife, who is in a great deal of pain because of you."

Maggie glanced back at Mrs. Quinn and saw a look of horror on her face. Clearly, she was terrified of her husband.

Elizabeth continued, "Beating your wife does not endear her to you, Mr. Quinn. You should be ashamed. You make three of her. Does it make you feel more of a man when you hit her? Because it does nothing of the sort. It makes you quite small."

Maggie wondered if she should intervene, but she decided to wait when she saw the man's face fall at Elizabeth's reprimand.

"If you touch her again, Mr. Quinn, I'll have Sergeant Hannigan from the police force come down here to arrest you."

He looked like a little boy whose toy had been taken away for some small transgression. Relief flooded Maggie. She suspected they might escape this awful situation without harm after all.

Elizabeth said, "You may come in, Mr. Quinn, but you must promise to behave yourself."

His lip quivered. Elizabeth stepped aside. Maggie and Quan Luck backed away, giving him a wide berth and a line of sight to his flinching wife.

"You see what you've done, Mr. Quinn? A woman you should be cherishing is now afraid of you. Is that what you call a marriage?"

He looked at his wife. "I said I was sorry."

"I know," she whispered.

He took a step across the threshold. Again, Elizabeth stepped in front of him.

"Mr. Quinn, my name is Doctor Kellogg. I am a medical doctor. Your wife may have broken ribs. Make sure she doesn't exert herself for the next few weeks. Do you understand?"

He pulled his eyes away from his wife. "Broken ribs?"

"Yes. Broken ribs. If a broken rib dislocates, it can puncture a lung. It can kill. Is that what you want, Mr. Quinn? Do you want Bridget to die?"

"N-No."

"Then you'd better make sure she rests. No heavy lifting. No hard work. And make sure no harm comes to her. Do I make myself clear?"

His eyes darted back to his wife. "Yes," he murmured.

"Good. Now, a polite person would thank my friends and I for cleaning up the mess I'm sure you had a hand in making. We are not housemaids, Mr. Quinn. We cleaned up out of kindness to your wife. Your thanks would not be remiss. An apology for your slurs both to Quan Luck and Miss Weston wouldn't be out of place, either."

Maggie saw a flash of anger in his eyes. It died as quickly as it ignited. As he looked down at the floor, he muttered his thanks and an apology.

Elizabeth said, "We'll take our leave, Mr. Quinn. Remember what I said. Take good care of your wife. Make her a cup of tea when we leave—and an apology to her, too, might be in order. I'm not so sure you meant the last one you made to her. This time, make sure it's sincere."

She didn't wait for an answer. She turned and motioned to her companions and they left through the still-open door. Outside, Maggie blew out her breath. "What a challenge."

Quan Luck said, "But I learned something today."

"What's that Quan Luck?" Maggie asked.

"Both you and Doctor Kellogg are much more intimidating that a six foot Irish man with a bad temper. I will make every effort never to get on your bad side. I think even *wushu* would be no match for you two."

Chapter Ten

April 7, 1906

AS ELIZABETH ESCORTED Amelia into the examination room, her mind struggled to compartmentalize all the symptoms the woman displayed. Her dress hung on her and her facial bones protruded, giving her a gaunt look. For a woman in her late thirties, only a few years older than Elizabeth, she gave the appearance of someone approaching Mrs. Stockton's age. A few months ago, when she met her at the train station, Amelia stood tall and dignified, possibly a little haughty, and she looked vibrant and healthy. Now, her shoulders slumped, she looked beaten down. When she walked toward Elizabeth from the waiting room, she noted her faltering steps.

She brought out the blood pressure instrument. Amelia remained stoic as the cuff expanded. Elizabeth pressed her stethoscope to the inside of her extended elbow and listened as the cuff deflated. Blood pressure low, Elizabeth observed. Breathing shallow. As Elizabeth removed the cuff, Amelia reached up and started scratching her arm. A normal reaction to the constriction of the cuff moments before; however, as Amelia kept scratching, red welts formed, then cracks, and blood.

"Amelia, stop scratching."

Elizabeth laid her hand over Amelia's to stop her.

Amelia looked at her like she'd just discovered her presence in the room.

"Look at your arm. You've drawn blood."

She looked down at the tiny droplets seeping from the wounds and stared.

Amelia's foot jiggled until her whole leg shook with the movement.

Worry erupted within Elizabeth as she began compiling a list of all the symptoms together.

"What other problems are you having? Any nausea?"

Amelia nodded.

"Difficulty sleeping?"

Another nod.

"Amelia, look at me."

Amelia met Elizabeth's look with vacant eyes—eyes with pinpoint pupils.

Elizabeth stepped over to the large window behind her and drew the heavy drapes across it, shutting out the daylight. When she returned, she looked into Amelia's eyes again. Instead of seeing the normal dilation of someone whose eyes were now in subdued lighting, she saw the same pinpoints as in the bright light. Her pupils were no more than tiny dots. Amelia was drugged.

"Amelia." Elizabeth put her hand on Amelia's wrist. It was cold to the touch. "What are you taking?"

Amelia moved her gaze to Elizabeth's hand. Her speech slurred as she spoke. "I—I can't bear the pain. It hurts too much. The laudanum takes it away. But it doesn't last, you see. So, I must take it again." She wiggled her foot as she spoke.

"What hurts, Amelia? If you're in pain, tell me. I may be able to help without the use of laudanum. It's addictive and from what I see, I suspect you may be dependent on it already. You need help."

Amelia looked up at her. She still took quick, shallow breaths, another symptom of the laudanum. "The pain isn't in my body, doctor, it's in my soul. I am wounded to my depths."

"Can you talk to me about it? I'd be happy to listen."

"No. You would not be happy. I told you before, it's not for discussion."

"You're saying this is a matter of the heart?"

Amelia looked down at her hands and whispered, "She comprehends at last."

Elizabeth frowned. "If you won't discuss it with me, then, consider talking to someone else. I recommend you see a colleague of mine, Doctor Henry Gibbons. He's the Dean of women's medicine at Cooper Medical College. He's an excellent listener and he's familiar with dependency on opioids."

"I don't want to talk to anyone else. You, Elizabeth, you could help me."

"I don't think so, Amelia. I can't do anything if you won't tell me what's driving you to this."

Amelia stared at her. Elizabeth wondered if she could see her or if the laudanum had sent her to another realm. After a few seconds, Amelia said, "Come and stay with me. Move into my house. If you were there, you could help me stop using the laudanum."

Elizabeth took a step back. "I'm afraid not, Amelia. You need a specialist's help. Besides, why would I leave my home here? There's no need. With proper treatment from the right person—"

Amelia slid off the table and teetered before her. When Elizabeth put out her hand to steady her, Amelia shrugged her off. "I need to go." She staggered toward the door.

"Amelia, wait. You need help."

Amelia turned and glared. A spark of flame ignited in her eyes. "Just not you, though. Correct?"

Elizabeth's brow pulled together in bewilderment. What was going on with this woman? Was it all a part of her trying to entrap her into revealing her attraction to women — or was it something else entirely?

"Your silence speaks volumes, doctor." She turned on her heel, swayed a little, and stumbled out the door.

AS MAGGIE SAT listening to Elizabeth's account of Amelia's visit, she couldn't help but think Amelia's insistence Elizabeth move in with her was the strangest part of the whole story.

"Do you still think she's up to something? Looking for information about how you might feel about women?" Maggie asked.

"To tell the truth, Maggie, I have no idea what's going on with her. It might be she's so disoriented from the laudanum she has no idea what she's saying. All I know is she's harboring a secret which appears to be eating her up inside. It seems to be the driving force behind all of her behaviors, but she won't talk to me. She won't talk to anyone, apparently. And when she stomped off, all I could think was, 'I may never see her again.'"

"I guess you could go to her house to check on her." Maggie wasn't sure she thought her suggestion was a good idea, but recognizing Elizabeth's concern for Amelia's welfare, she thought she would present it as an option.

"I don't know. I'm so uncertain about how to handle any of it."

Maggie got up from the table and started removing their dinner dishes. "You'll know if you should do something when the time comes. I'm sure of it."

"I suppose."

Maggie could tell Elizabeth still mulled over the situation, chewing on it until there was nothing left but tasteless pulp. She had to find a distraction for her.

"I can think of one distraction," she muttered. "But I don't think you're in a receptive state." She sighed in resignation.

"Did you say something," Elizabeth called from the other room.

"I said...I should show you the photographs I took when we went to Irish Hill. I had some time to develop them." Maybe she could distract Elizabeth with them.

Elizabeth stood behind her. "That's nice." She wrapped her arms around Maggie's waist.

Maggie turned around in her embrace and kissed her.

Elizabeth said, "Let me finish cleaning up, then you can show me your work."

Maggie put her arms around Elizabeth. "And afterwards?"

"After we look at the photographs, I think we'll want to go to bed. Don't you?"

"Most definitely." She kissed her again.

When Elizabeth's lips parted, Maggie thrust her tongue inside. The kiss deepened. When she pulled away, she had to calm her gasping before she could speak. "Or maybe we could skip the part about the photographs. Tomorrow's Sunday—plenty of time to show them to you then."

Elizabeth's mouth twitched as she tried to suppress a smile.

So, distraction number one would work after all.

April 12, 1906

ELIZABETH BROUGHT MAGGIE a cup of tea and sat on the sofa in her living room above the clinic.

As she accepted the cup, Maggie asked, "How was your appointment with Doctor Gibbons today?"

"It went well. He made some recommendations to try to get Amelia to come and see him. I'm not sure any of them will work. I don't even know if I'll ever see her again. But at least I have his suggestions."

After sipping her own tea, Elizabeth said, "He had the most complimentary things to say about my practice. He said he's heard a great deal about the work I'm doing both with the wealthy ladies and the women at the Quaker Mission."

"How wonderful. You must be pleased."

"I am. He also said he has three women who are in training to be physicians at the college. One, in particular, has voiced a desire to spend time with me at the clinic and at the Mission. We've arranged for her to spend time observing."

"Are you excited?"

"Yes, I'm happy to contribute to these women's training and delighted to know someone else wants to care for this segment of society. There's only one problem."

"What's that?"

"She's starting next Wednesday."

Maggie tilted her head. "Why is it a problem?"

"She'll be at my clinic bright and early in the morning."

"You always start bright and early. I don't understand."

She put her cup down and took Maggie's hand. "We need to get to the Mission early, which means she'll arrive at my clinic at dawn. I can't stay overnight the night before."

"Oh, Elizabeth, please don't worry. As much as I love having you stay, and love staying here with you, we both have our businesses to run. I understand. I've had to make sure I was at the shop to receive my order not too long ago. It will be fine. It's one night."

"I know. But it's the night of...Caruso."

"Oh."

"I'll have to drop you off and come straight home so I can be here in the morning. I'm not sure what time my trainee will arrive."

Maggie looked disappointed, but she said, "It's all right."

"I know we've had this discussion before, but I wish you'd reconsider it. Move in with me. If you were living with me, you could remain upstairs until we left for the Mission before you go to work."

"And what if I have to be at the shop early? I'd be stuck in your apartment until you left and might miss it."

"Maybe Quan—"

"No, Elizabeth, this isn't Quan Luck's problem. It's ours."

"I could stay if I ask Mr. Crane to come earlier."

"If you get up any earlier to come home, we may as well not go to bed at all. This isn't going to work. No. You come home after Caruso. It will be fine. We'll be able to discuss the performance on the way home and the next evening—" Maggie got a strange look on her face.

"What's wrong, Maggie?"

"Your new trainee. She isn't coming every day, is she?"

Elizabeth laughed. "No. She'll come once a week and spend time with me at the Mission and it's only for a few weeks. I'll tell her to meet me at the clinic after the first day and eliminate any need to alter our arrangement."

"Then the problem is solved." Maggie put her cup down and pulled Elizabeth to her. As they kissed, Maggie pushed Elizabeth back against the seat and pressed her body to her. She thrust her tongue into Elizabeth's mouth. Elizabeth, unable to control her arousal, pressed her hips into Maggie's. When the kiss ended, both women panted breathlessly.

Elizabeth sat up. "How unexpected," she said, patting her disheveled hair into place.

Maggie gave her an impish grin. "I wanted to make sure you

still cared for me."

Elizabeth looked mystified. "Of course I care. I care deeply. Why would you doubt it?"

"Amelia Rosemont asks you to move in with her. Trainees coming to your house in the wee hours of the morning. I got concerned."

"You have nothing to worry about, I assure you. Amelia has a problem. She's confused and disoriented. She didn't know what she was saying, let alone figure out the lack of logic in her misguided plan. And the trainee is a professional, as am I. You are the one I care about. No one else. I love you, Maggie. Don't ever doubt it."

"Oh, I think I know it now."

Elizabeth looked askance. "How do you know?"

"Your kiss. Believe me. Your kisses tell me...everything."

Elizabeth pulled her into another embrace. "Then you'll know this isn't a lie either." They kissed again until hands roamed and juices flowed.

Maggie pulled away, saying, "I see the truth of it now, doctor. Take me to your bed and I'll explain *my* truth to you."

A slow smile broke across Elizabeth's lips.

Chapter Eleven

April 17, 1906

MAGGIE STRODE AMID a crush of people, all moving toward the Grand Opera House. Excitement filled the air, thrilling Maggie at the thought of being able to attend this grand affair. Enrico Caruso in person. She couldn't believe it.

As she walked up the steps toward the entrance, she saw Elizabeth coming toward her. Her eyes widened. Elizabeth looked stunning. She wore a beautiful dress Maggie hadn't seen before. It opened at the neck with beautiful beading and embroidery. The coat she wore matched the dress, with cascading embroidered flowers and dots of glimmering beads at the edges. The subtle pink fabric and decorations shimmered in the lamps on the wall of the portico.

The crowd melted away. Elizabeth held her gaze as she came closer. A sparkle lit up her eyes. When she reached Maggie, she leaned in and whispered, "You look beautiful tonight, Maggie."

Maggie's eyes gleamed at the compliment. She had to overcome the lump in her throat to speak. "And you look more beautiful. Your dress is exquisite. You've been holding out on me."

Elizabeth's smile sent a tingle through her body.

"I wanted to surprise you. I'm glad you like it. Are you ready for the performance? Everyone inside is talking about it. The excitement is palpable."

Maggie nodded and raked over Elizabeth's appearance one more time. As she did, she saw her look elicited a shiver from Elizabeth. She put her arm through Maggie's. Maggie felt a frisson of delight run through her at the contact. She pressed into Elizabeth's side and managed to murmur, "I'm ready."

Elizabeth looked into her eyes and said, "As am I."

Were they talking about the performance—or something else entirely? Maggie tried to calm her breathing. Tonight was proving to be more exciting than she imagined.

EVERY TIME CARUSO sang, Elizabeth gazed at Maggie, who looked as if she would rise out of her chair in ecstasy at hearing him sing in person. Elizabeth found it difficult to contain a grin at seeing Maggie so enthralled. Making Maggie happy delighted her.

At intermission, Elizabeth guided Maggie out to the main foyer, encouraging her to listen in on people's conversations as they commented on the performance. "You'll hear some interesting observations," she assured her.

Maggie laughed and said, "I'd better not hear anything negative or I might be inclined to comment back."

Elizabeth tried to stifle her own chuckle. How she loved this woman's fire.

As Elizabeth and Maggie stood together in the press of the crowd now filling the foyer, Elizabeth heard Maggie say, "Oh-oh."

"What's wrong?"

But as she looked in the direction of Maggie's gaze, she saw the problem—Amelia Rosemont—and she headed straight for them.

AS AMELIA APPROACHED them, Elizabeth noted she looked as bad as when she last saw her at her clinic. Dark circles still underlined her eyes. Her walk gave her an unsteady appearance. Her floor-length black dress hung on her gaunt frame.

When she reached them, Elizabeth took charge of the situation. "Amelia, how nice to see you."

"Elizabeth." Amelia dismissed her and looked down at Maggie with contempt. "Miss Weston. I wasn't aware you were an opera aficionado."

"I love Caruso. To be able to hear him in person is like a dream come true. I am so happy to be here."

Relief washed over Elizabeth. Maggie's enthusiasm wasn't influenced by Amelia's apparent disdain.

"Well, I'm sure a man as great as Enrico Caruso would leave someone such as yourself quite star-struck, but I've seen these types of performances so many times I'm quite bored with them." She waved her gloved hand brushing off Maggie's eagerness.

Elizabeth watched a frown appear across Maggie's face and hoped Maggie wouldn't react to Amelia's rudeness.

"I've listened to his recordings for several years and I still find his pieces invigorating. I'm sorry Mr. Caruso has lost his luster for you, Mrs. Rosemont."

The plastered-on smile Amelia wore disintegrated into a scowl. "There's no accounting for taste then, is there."

She turned and staggered back into the crowd in the direction from which she came earlier.

Maggie watched her go with puckered lips. When she disappeared, she said, "That was...unpleasant. What do you suppose has gotten into her?"

Elizabeth sighed. "First of all, her appearance tells me she's still not dealing with her problems. Taking that into account, I'd say her personality is affected to the point she now lacks any social grace at all."

"She does look awful. How can she even come out in public looking like she does? Why doesn't she do something to remedy her situation?"

Elizabeth felt the hopelessness of someone who wanted to help, but wasn't allowed. "I'm not sure, Maggie. She's suppressing something using a dangerous solution to cover her pain. Since she won't talk to me about it, I hope she'll realize she needs to find help from someone else. I pray she seeks treatment before something dreadful happens."

Elizabeth stared into the crowd where they watched Amelia disappear earlier, wondering if she would get help in time. The bell signaled the end of intermission. She plunged her arm through Maggie's, drawing her near for comfort. "You've become my rock, you know."

Maggie smiled up at her. "Then take your rock back to hear more of Mr. Caruso, because he hasn't lost a bit of his luster for me."

"You handled her beautifully."

Maggie squeezed her hand. "I know."

WHEN MAGGIE TOLD Elizabeth it wouldn't matter if they couldn't spend the night together after the opera, she believed it to be true. Now, she felt forsaken. How she wished Elizabeth had been able to stay instead of returning to her own house.

It would have been nice to be able to talk about the performance, the people, the excitement. Perhaps Elizabeth even needed to talk more about what happened at intermission.

Amelia's focus on Maggie was odd. She didn't pay attention to Elizabeth at all. Maggie wondered about her behavior or if either of them would ever know what was going on with her.

When they left the opera house, Mr. Crane was waiting. Maggie said she could walk home, but Elizabeth wouldn't hear of it. They rode through the darkened streets, leaving the crowds surrounding the performance hall until they turned onto Market Street. They said goodnight with a demur hug in the carriage and Maggie walked to her door. Elizabeth waved and Maggie noted the look of sadness at her departure. She watched the carriage disappear back down Market Street toward Van Ness. Once the darkness swallowed them up, Maggie entered her building.

Now she lay in the blackness of the room, thinking of Caruso's voice, of the eagerness of the audience, of Elizabeth's surreptitious reach for her hand in the dark, of her stroking it with her thumb as the performance continued. How she wished Elizabeth were here now, caressing her. Her hand went to her breast, imagining Elizabeth beside her, touching her, whispering to her, pressing soft lips against hers long into the night.

She moaned and rolled on her side, willing tomorrow to come. Tomorrow, when Elizabeth would inform her student to meet her at the Mission in coming days. Tomorrow, when she would appear at her door and stay the night so they could do all the things to each other she imagined now. Tomorrow, when she longed to tremble and burn at Elizabeth's touch again.

Chapter Twelve

April 18, 1906

AS ELIZABETH ROLLED out of bed, she hurled an insult across the room as if it were responsible for the lethargy she felt. When she spent the night with Maggie, waking up at five o'clock in the morning was never a problem. She always slept well with Maggie by her side. Today, she felt out of sorts.

Maggie looked so striking as she approached the steps of the opera house the night before. She wore her dress from the Christmas party. The strands of pearls in her hair under the lamplight glistened, reminding her of dew on morning grass. She had to restrain herself not to take her in her arms and kiss her right there outside the entrance. However, leaving her at her door after the performance was pure torture.

This morning, a different type of torture plagued her. Her eyes felt as if they were filled with grit. She blinked several times against the gray dawn, feeling an unexpected wave of nausea. The room tipped and whirled. Was it her poor night's sleep or—

She sat back on the bed. It shook beneath her. As she stared at the floor, trying to get control, she watched the boards rise and fall like waves. Fear gripped her. Realization dawned.

Earthquake!

She felt paralyzed amid the bed, indeed all the furniture in the room, rattling and roiling. The floor rippled beneath her feet again, moving outward like rings in a pond. The atmosphere crackled and the building popped. Terror filled her. She forced herself to stand. The shaking propelled her back onto the bed from the awful movement.

Calm down. You've got to get downstairs.

She took a deep breath and attempted to get up again. When she stood upright, the movement stopped. Everything went quiet. She took a tentative step, and the movement began again. She stumbled to the chair where her clothes lay. As the house rocked and bits of plaster fell from the ceiling, she hurried to get dressed.

The shaking lessened. She looked around the room. If she fled, what would she take? Her coat and her doctor's bag were by the door in the hall downstairs. It's all I need.

Thoughts of Maggie loomed. Oh, dear, Maggie. Are you all right?

By the time she reached the stairs, the tremors stopped. She waited on the landing for a moment, not wanting to be thrust down the steps if the shaking started again. The unnerving quiet surrounded her, broken by an occasional creaking sound. Then, the shouting began. First one or two voices, a woman's scream. More followed. She ran down the stairs, grabbed her coat and bag on the way, and thrust open the front door.

Out on Van Ness Avenue, people appeared on porches and in the street. When she saw a woman staggering in the street, holding on to her bleeding head, she forced herself into action. As she descended the outside steps, she met a young, wide-eyed woman ascending.

"Doctor Kellogg?"

"Yes."

"I'm Josephine Holtz. I'm a student at Cooper Medical College."

Elizabeth nodded. "Are you hurt?"

"No, I'm fine. A little stunned, is all. I had to dodge bricks from chimneys. Fortunately, none touched me."

"I'm glad you're all right. Follow me, Miss Holtz. Your period of observation starts immediately."

They ran down the steps together. Elizabeth searched for the woman with the wound on her head.

Josephine ran beside her. "My friends call me Jo."

Elizabeth stopped in the street. She couldn't see the woman. Crowds of milling people formed up and down the street.

"Well, Jo, I have a feeling you're about to get quite an education. Are you up to it?"

Jo pulled herself up to her full height. "Yes, doctor, I am."

Elizabeth saw the woman emerge from a group too dazed to notice her condition. The woman still held her head. Blood dripped from between her fingers. She stopped and swayed.

Jo took off running toward her and caught her before she collapsed. Elizabeth came up beside them and they put the woman's arms over their shoulders and dragged her to the steps of Elizabeth's house. When they sat her down, Elizabeth opened her bag and went to work. The gash was deep, but not deadly. As she blotted and patched, concern for Maggie filled her with dread. Why had she not stayed with her after the performance last night? They'd be together now and to Hades with meeting this medical student.

Jo leaned over Elizabeth's shoulder. "Is there anything I can do, doctor?"

"In my bag—there's some iodine. Get it out for me, will you?"

Jo found what she was looking for and handed it to Elizabeth. As she poured the tincture over the wound, the dazed women came alive and squealed.

Then, someone yelled, "Fire!"

MAGGIE'S EYES POPPED open. Was she dreaming? Having a nightmare? She couldn't remember, but her heart was racing and she had the feeling of impending doom. She threw off her covers and got dressed with haste. Her thoughts churned. Did something happen to Elizabeth? Or was she experiencing some strange disorientation because of a poor night's sleep and frustration at not having Elizabeth by her side? Perhaps Elizabeth was right. Maybe she should move in with her. What did it matter what people thought?

The shaking started as she donned her shoes. She thought it was all part of her own disorientation from her abrupt awakening. Then she realized it was an earthquake. A big one.

The floor shook beneath her feet. When it continued, panic rose in her chest. Rumbling echoed in her ears. She saw the walls buckle and crack and a large piece of plaster fall from a corner of the ceiling. She needed to get downstairs, get out of the building. She hurried out of her flat down into the shop below.

The trembling stopped by the time she got to the bottom of the stairs. She looked around. Glass from broken frames on display lay on the floor of the shop. Her scheduling diary lay open on the floor instead of on the counter. One of the hand painted tea pots on display lay smashed to bits on the floor. She thought to stop and clean up the mess. Then, the tremors started again. Creaks and bangs from the structure around her drove her outside.

The air smelled strange. Rubble filled the street. The building next door was nothing but a heap of stone. Michael! Michael lived above the shop in an apartment similar to hers. A few people stood in the street looking around. Finally, someone ran up to her and asked her if anyone lived in Michael's building. She nodded.

The man shook his head and said, "I don't know how anyone could have survived." A policeman joined him. They stood, listening, waiting to hear any moans. She didn't think they heard any because, when they started to move debris, they did so with no real urgency. She should have been able to hear the noise of men moving rubble a few feet away. Instead, a peculiar quiet filled the space around her. She felt like crying, but no tears came.

Michael, quite possibly, was dead. She needed to do something, anything, to quell the fear and sadness taking up residence in her chest. Elizabeth's face appeared in her mind's eye. Elizabeth would be frantic. She had to go to her, make sure she was unharmed. If something happened to her, she didn't know how she would go on.

Her knees threatened to give out. She felt herself falling, knew she would hit the ground. However, before she made contact, she felt arms grab onto her, preventing her fall. When she turned to see who had saved her, she looked into dark, velvet eyes.

Quan Luck guided her back into the shop and pulled a stool upright before suggesting she take a seat. Maggie smiled her thanks and said, "I'm so glad you're all right."

"I am fine, Miss Maggie. Don't worry about me." She thought he looked sad.

"Why did you come? You should be with your family."

"I wanted to make sure you were unharmed. My family no longer requires my help."

"What do you mean?"

"My father, my uncle, all of my family are dead. My father sent me on an early-morning errand for him. If he hadn't, I'd be dead, too." His eyes glistened.

"Oh, Quan Luck, I'm so sorry."

"Let us not speak of it. Sorrow is for another day. Now, we must live. Survive. Be grateful we are alive."

His courage buoyed her.

Another small temblor crackled through the building. Quan Luck eyed the buckled wall behind them. "I think we need to leave this building, Miss Maggie. It isn't safe."

"I need to go to Elizabeth. She isn't used to earthquakes. She'll be terrified."

Quan Luck nodded. "I thought as much. It's why I came. I will take you. We will go together."

Maggie reached for his hand. "Thank you, Quan Luck. You will be part of my family now."

Tears pooled in the dark eyes. One cascaded over his cheek. He squeezed Maggie's hand and let go.

Maggie got up and walked over to the disheveled counter. When she thought to flee from her flat, she grabbed a few necessities and threw them into a small bag. She picked up the bag and put one more item in it—her small box camera. She turned to Quan Luck and said, "Let's go find Elizabeth."

Outside the shop, the sky lit up with the full light of day. A thought crossed her mind. The sunrise would be beautiful this morning, yet it brought no joy, no excitement.

Something was wrong. Slow realization blossomed. The sun

rose in the east, behind her building. The orange glow she saw now was in the direction of Union Square, a more northern direction. She frowned, trying to puzzle it out, but her thought processes weren't quite up to working out the problem. Before she could unravel the mystery, she felt Quan Luck stiffen with tension beside her.

"Miss Maggie, we must get out of here." He pointed. "A fire has started in Union Square."

A MAN APPROACHED at a jog as Elizabeth finished bandaging the woman's head. "Cornelia, is that you? Oh, no. What happened?"

Cornelia turned to him. "I'm fine. It's a small bump on the head."

Elizabeth said, "She'll be fine. She should rest a little, though."

"Rest?" He gave her an incredulous look. "No one in this city will get any rest today. Buildings have come down, but even worse, fires are raging. Look." He pointed toward the downtown area. Smoke and flames already engulfed the structures in the distance. The sky, which had lightened while Elizabeth tended to Cornelia's injury, now darkened as if dusk was upon them. Soot and ash swirled in the sky.

"You'd best get out," he told them. "People are already fleeing." He looked at Elizabeth and asked, "Is this your house?"

She nodded.

"Be glad it's still standing. You should gather your belongings and get out. Fire is coming this way. There's no telling if this house will be standing in an hour or two. We've already lost ours. Come on, Cornelia, we've got to get out of here."

Cornelia stood. He wrapped his arm around her waist and guided her down Turk Street, away from the approaching fire, as an aftershock struck. Elizabeth watched as they halted, trying to regain their balance. When the movement under their feet stopped, they walked on.

Elizabeth thought of Maggie as she hung onto a lamp post against the movement until it subsided. If the fire raged through the downtown area, was Maggie safe? It took every ounce of self-control not to run toward the photography shop. Should she go to her or would it be better to wait here in the hope Maggie showed up soon, unharmed? She blew out her breath, frustrated by indecision.

An automobile approached and stopped beside them. A man jumped out and ran over. "Miss Holtz, are you all right?"

"I'm fine Mr. Taylor. What are you doing here?"

"Doctor Gibbons sent me to find you. He said you were working with a Doctor Kellogg."

Jo made introductions. "Doctor Kellogg, this is Mr. Taylor. He's a medical student at Cooper with me."

Taylor thrust his hand toward Elizabeth. It gave her a moment of solace to feel his firm grasp.

"We've set up an emergency clinic at Doctor Gibbons's residence on Octavia St., Doctor Kellogg. He's put the word out about his availability to help those in need. He wanted me to extend an invitation for you to come and join him there. He's also requested Miss Holtz come with me to help."

"You haven't been downtown at all, have you?" Elizabeth asked.

"You can't get downtown. One of my colleagues tried earlier. The police stopped him on the other side of Octavia before Market. Fires are burning throughout the district. Buildings have collapsed."

Panic rose in Elizabeth. "Tell Doctor Gibbons I'll join him shortly. There's something I must do first."

As Taylor and Holtz climbed into his automobile, Elizabeth gathered up her bag and darted down Van Ness Avenue. When she approached Market Street, she could see fire blazing a few blocks away. She'd best turn toward Market Street now, but when she tried, other fires and more devastation blocked her way. Her panic turned to absolute terror. Desperate to get to Maggie, she circled back up Van Ness toward home, determined to find another route to Maggie's shop.

If something happened to Maggie, she'd never be able to cope. Could a cruel God take Maggie from her when she'd just found her? If Maggie was hurt—or worse—she would regret not spending the night with her so she could tend to her injuries. Or they could have died in each other's embrace. The thought of being without the love of her life brought unbearable pain. Tears streamed down Elizabeth's face, eventually, turning to sobs. Engulfed with emotion, paralysis threatened. She couldn't allow these dark thoughts to stall her progress. She had to find a way to get to Maggie.

A crowd of people flooded the street, everyone fleeing away from the destruction. She tried to determine another way into Maggie's neighborhood to no avail. Every street she tried was blocked by mounds of fallen buildings or fire.

She turned back to her own street after another attempt failed. Her shoulders slumped, her head down, she was close to abandoning her efforts.

Her wandering disoriented her for a moment. She didn't know where she was. She stopped to take stock. As she stood in the middle of the street, people streaming around her toward Nob Hill in the distance, two people parted the crowd walking in the opposite direction.

Was it Quan Luck? Maggie? Was it her? She ran toward them. When Maggie sped up in her direction, Quan Luck quickened his step and followed.

They met in the middle of the street.

Maggie threw herself into Elizabeth's arms. "I'm so glad you're all right. I was so worried," Maggie sobbed.

"I was so frightened. I thought I'd lost you," Elizabeth said. She hung on to Maggie in desperation.

"Everything's gone. All I have left is a change of clothes and one camera." She pulled away from Elizabeth and beckoned Quan Luck closer. He carried a small bundle in his arms with Maggie's camera balanced on top.

Elizabeth pulled Quan Luck into her embrace now, his pack between them. He stiffened, then went limp and he, too, wept. When she let him go, he handed the bundle to Maggie and wiped his eyes with the sleeve of his jacket. "I'm sorry," he said.

"Quan Luck has lost his entire family. I'm his family now."

Elizabeth looked at Quan Luck and said, "*We're* your family now."

More tears streamed down his cheeks. "I should not show so much emotion. I apologize."

Elizabeth said, "Please don't be sorry. These are terrible times, Quan Luck. We are all having difficulty coping. I was overcome with fear something had happened to Maggie. When I heard there was a fire, I—" Now, Elizabeth wept. When she pulled herself together, she said, "I'm glad you're safe, Quan Luck."

Tears welled up in his eyes. "My father and my uncle are dead. They were crushed by the floors above the laundry. I hadn't arrived to help them yet. My father sent me on an errand. Neighbors tried to get them out, but the building started on fire. There was nothing we could do. When I realized the situation, all I thought of was Miss Maggie."

"I'm so sorry," Elizabeth said. "Thank you for taking care of her."

She pulled them both in to another hug. This time, Quan Luck didn't resist.

"My house is safe for the moment. Doctor Gibbons from Cooper Medical College has asked me to join him. He's set up a clinic on Octavia Street. You are both welcome to stay at my house. I'm going to help Doctor Gibbons."

"No," Maggie said. "I don't want to be separated from you, Elizabeth. I'm going with you. I'm sure I can be of some help."

Elizabeth smiled. She didn't want to be separated either. "I'd rather have you by my side, also. I'm sure Dr. Gibbons will take all the help he can get."

She turned to Quan Luck. "The offer is still yours. You are welcome to stay at my home." When Quan Luck looked grief stricken, she added, "If you'd rather not be alone, you're welcome to come with us. I'm sure we can put you to work, too."

He bowed his head. "I might not be welcomed."

"Anyone who doesn't welcome your willing hands should get a stern reproach, I assure you. Come with us. I'm sure there will be plenty of work to do. It'll keep your mind occupied, so you don't have to think about...other things."

Quan Luck pinched his lips together in an obvious attempt not to cry again. He nodded and whispered, "Thank you, doctor."

He took the bundle back from Maggie and gave her a tentative smile.

Elizabeth gazed at the sky. The sun hung high above them, hazy from the smoke. Elizabeth grasped Maggie's hand and took in her first deep breath since the first tremors occurred hours before. Then, the trio moved off toward Octavia Street into the unknown.

TWO BLOCKS FROM Dr. Gibbons's residence, they saw an elderly woman staggering in the street. As they approached, Elizabeth looked for signs of injury. She could see nothing obvious. Then, Maggie shouted, "Mrs. Jacobs, is that you?"

The woman looked up, "Wha—who are you?"

Quan Luck hung back and let Maggie and Elizabeth handle the situation.

Elizabeth asked, "You know this woman, Maggie?"

"Yes, it's Mrs. Jacobs. I've taken her photograph. Mrs. Jacobs are you all right? What happened?"

"I—I don't know. There was an earthquake. Did you know?"

Maggie nodded.

"It wouldn't stop. I was so frightened. I ran out of my house. Now, I can't find my way back."

Elizabeth took the woman's hand. "Are you injured, Mrs. Jacobs?"

She gave Elizabeth a look of confusion. "Injured? No, I don't think so. I can't find my house, though. Do you know where I live?"

Elizabeth looked to Maggie.

"I think she lives somewhere around Lafayette Park, but I'm not sure which street." She looked at Mrs. Jacobs and asked, "What's the name of your street? We can help you find it."

"I don't know the name. I don't know where I live. I don't know. I can't find. I—I—"

"It's all right, Mrs. Jacobs," Elizabeth crooned. "We're going to find it with you. Perhaps if we walk this way." She indicated the direction from which they had seen Mrs. Jacobs walking.

Mrs. Jacobs muttered something unintelligible. Maggie prompted her to walk with them, Elizabeth on one side, Maggie on the other. Quan Luck walked a few paces behind. Mrs. Jacobs noticed him. She leaned in toward Maggie and whispered, "There's a man following us. Should we scream?"

Maggie shook her head. The last thing they needed was to raise a false alarm and bring more trouble to poor Quan Luck's door. "No. Please don't scream, Mrs. Jacobs. It's Quan Luck. You know him. He gave you the *cartes de visite* you ordered when you came to my shop before Christmas, do you remember?"

Mrs. Jacobs looked at her blankly. "No, but if he's all right, I won't scream."

"Screaming will not be necessary. I assure you, he's a friend."

As they walked another block, a young man ran toward them, waving frantically. As he got closer, they heard him call, "Grandmother. I've been looking all over for you."

When they met up with him, he said, "Grandmother, I was so frantic. After the quake, I came to your house to see if you were all right and Mr. Drake told me he couldn't find you. We've been searching all over the area."

Mrs. Jacobs blinked a few times. "Walter? Whatever are you doing here?"

"I'm checking on you. Why did you wander off? Mr. Drake was frantic when I arrived. You mustn't stray away."

Mrs. Jacobs pulled herself to her full height and said, "What would you have me do? Stay put and let the house fall on my head?"

Maggie decided to intervene to prevent an argument. "My name is Maggie Weston, sir. Mrs. Jacobs procures her *cartes de visite* from me. We found her unable to find her way back home after she fled from the shaking. We weren't sure where she lived, so I'm glad you found us."

She introduced Elizabeth. Quan Luck had taken up a position about a half a block away, so Maggie assumed he'd rather not be introduced. Elizabeth asked, "Do you mind my asking, who is Mr. Drake?"

"He's Grandmother's butler. He's been with her for years. He watches over her like a hawk, but she gave him the slip this morning." He turned to his grandmother. "Didn't you old girl?"

Mrs. Jacobs stared straight ahead.

Elizabeth didn't control her look of disdain at the young man for his disrespectful comment to his grandmother.

"Well, he'll be happy to have you back home safe and sound. Thank you so much for trying to get her home."

"Mr. Jacobs is it?" Elizabeth asked.

He nodded.

"I'd suggest you have Mr. Drake take your Grandmother to the Cooper Medical College when the city gets back to normal. Your grandmother's memory problems might be treatable."

"Oh, I'm sure it's just old age. She'll be fine."

Elizabeth gave him a penetrating look. "So, if it were possible to give Mrs. Jacobs a better life with a better memory for a few more years, you'd be opposed to it?"

"I—no. I assure you we'd try to help her all we could."

"Then I suggest you take my advice. Take your grandmother to see the doctors there. I hear they do wonders with cases like hers. You might be surprised at how vital she can become again." She decided to challenge him. "Unless you'd rather not give her such a chance."

"No. I mean, yes. I'll see she gets there. I'll tell Drake to make it so. Thank you, doctor." He tipped his hat. "Come on, Grandmother, let's get you home."

Quan Luck joined them as they retraced their steps.

Maggie said, "You thought he might want the old girl to stay as she was, didn't you?"

"Well, I wondered."

"And now."

"I think he's a young man who doesn't understand his aging grandmother. He seemed taken aback at my challenge. I'm hopeful he'll make sure she consults with the doctors at Cooper. They may not be able to help, but sometimes, all it takes is an adjustment in nutritional requirements. I've read about it in the *Journal of Medicine*."

"Your dull medical magazine."

"My most informative medical magazine."

"And dull."

Elizabeth chuckled, glad for Maggie's teasing. "I'll agree. Sometimes it can be a little dull."

Chapter Thirteen

WHEN THE GROUP arrived at the makeshift clinic in Doctor Gibbons's home, Elizabeth rolled up her sleeves and went to work. Victims of the devastation made their way out of the fire area and were directed to Dr. Gibbons for care. Maggie was pressed into service cutting sheets and linens for bandages. Quan Luck, introduced to Mr. Taylor by Jo Holtz, went with Taylor, armed with a list of supplies Doctor Gibbons requested from Cooper College. Fire victims, those with cuts and bruises, and some with broken bones continued to arrive throughout the day.

Upon Quan Luck's return, Elizabeth happened upon him in the foyer of Doctor Gibbons's home. He flushed with excitement. "Doctor, I have had my first ride in a real automobile. It was exhilarating. Imagine, no horses. Although Mr. Taylor says horsepower is in the engine. We were to the college and back so quickly. If I ever become a lawyer and can save enough money, I am going to own my own automobile."

Elizabeth laughed at his enthusiasm. Now Quan Luck had two dreams. She hoped he could achieve both of them. Their conversation ended when Maggie approached and asked Quan Luck to help her organize supplies. As he trotted off with Maggie, the front door opened and a man entered, staggering toward Elizabeth. His face was blackened with soot. His hands, burned crimson and raw. She looked into his despair-filled eyes. "Come with me," she said and he lurched beside her toward the room set up for treatment.

By late afternoon they got word the military had begun dynamiting to create a firebreak. The man who brought the news had a gash in his leg, obtained as he tried to pull supplies from his store. The dynamiting was blocks away, "...but the damn fools are sending burning embers up into the sky to be taken by the wind. I watched it rain down on our block and everything ignited in a manner of minutes. It's madness."

As Elizabeth stitched the man's wound, she asked, "Is there anything left along Market Street?"

His head slumped. "Not much. What didn't crumble in the quake has been devoured by the fire and it's moving throughout the city with a vengeance."

Elizabeth finished her stitching, covered his wound with a bandage and sent him on his way. Then, she steeled herself for the long night ahead.

Later, when she had a few minutes break, as she tried to bring some order back to the room in which she was working, Quan Luck appeared at the door with a large man slung over his shoulder. The man was so large compared to Quan Luck's slight stature, his feet dragged on the floor as Quan Luck hauled him along. Elizabeth ran to help. They got him onto her make-shift table. When she looked at Quan Luck, his beautiful brocade jacket was covered in blood. The pattern matched the blood stain on the chest of the man on the table.

Quan Luck said, "Before he passed out, he said they are shooting people. Anyone suspected of looting. The police and the military have lost their minds, apparently. He said it was ordered by the mayor. He told me he wasn't looting. He was trying to save his goods from his own shop."

Quan Luck's face glowed red. Was it exertion from carrying this mountain of a man, or frustration and anger at what was happening in their city? Elizabeth couldn't tell. Maybe it's both, she concluded, as her own anger rose at the craziness of it all.

She went to work tearing off the man's shirt and saw the hole in his chest. When she took his pulse, it was thready. The man was dying and Elizabeth could do nothing to prevent it. In a few minutes, he was gone.

She looked at Quan Luck, who stared at the man, unseeing. "Quan Luck, could you please find some other men to carry him away?" Quan Luck looked at her with vacant eyes. He nodded and left the room without a word. He returned with several men, all of them looked as if they had been wrestling on the ground, the result of rescue work, she suspected.

"Could you take him to the cellar? I believe Doctor Gibbons has set up a morgue down there." The men took up the task without speaking and left with the man in tow.

"Quan Luck," Elizabeth said, "you should see if you can find something else to wear. I'm sorry. Your jacket is ruined."

Tears sprang up in Quan Luck's eyes.

"Do you want me to help you find something?"

"No, doctor. I'll take care of it."

Elizabeth felt so exhausted, her bones ached. She needed to take advantage of this respite. She should lie down, rest for a few minutes. Instead, she cleaned up and went in search of Maggie.

MAGGIE CONTINUED TO tear bandages into strips and bundle them into rolls as Elizabeth sat opposite her. They carried on quiet conversation for a while, but when Elizabeth stopped, mid-sentence, Maggie looked up to find she had fallen asleep holding up her head with her palm, her elbow resting on the table.

Maggie got up and came around the table and kissed the top of Elizabeth's head. When she stirred, Maggie said, "Find a place to lie down. You're exhausted."

"You must be tired, too, yet you persist here."

"Elizabeth, all I'm doing is preparing bandages. You have been on your feet dealing with physical distress and high emotions since early this morning. It's been hours since you've had a break. There must be someplace in this house you can lie down and have a few minutes rest. Do I need to go with you and make sure you do it?"

Elizabeth looked like a child ordered to bed before she was ready. "No. I'll do as you suggest." She yawned, pulled herself up from her seat slowly, and left Maggie to her bundles.

A few minutes later, Maggie flinched at a loud voice coming from an adjacent room. Concerned the noise would waken Elizabeth, she jumped up and raced into the room next door.

Quan Luck stood opposite a young man she had met earlier. He arrived from Cooper College with a box of supplies. His name was Ford or Forbes, something similar. Maggie couldn't remember which. Her brain was muddled. Perhaps it was time for her to find a place to rest, too. The young man stopped his caterwauling when Maggie appeared.

Maggie sounded indignant as she said, "Sir, what are you going on about? Some people in this house have been working with patients since this morning and have only now gotten a chance to rest. Have some consideration."

The man had the decency to look contrite. "S-sorry, Miss Weston. I—I only—I just—"

Maggie raised an eyebrow.

He stopped trying to explain.

She turned to Quan Luck, "Do you know what his problem is?" She gestured toward the other man.

Quan Luck looked down at the floor.

"Quan Luck?"

"Mr. Forrest accuses me of stealing this shirt."

"What?" Maggie glowered at the young man. "Why would you do such a thing?"

"He—he didn't have it on earlier. I thought—"

Maggie couldn't contain her anger. "Mr. Forrest, this man today has lost two people in his immediate family to this terrible destruction. Yet, once he found out there was nothing more he could do for his father and his uncle, he came to my rescue, helping me flee the danger. As soon as we came here with Doctor Kellogg, he set straight to work, helping in any way he could. An hour ago, a man arrived with a gunshot wound to his chest. Quan Luck carried the man to Doctor Kellogg while he bled all over Quan Luck's clothes, but this man," she pointed to Quan Luck and continued, "had no compunction about it. Instead, his attention remained on getting the man help. He died a short time after, in spite of Quan Luck's efforts and Doctor Kellogg's ministrations. Do you not think Quan Luck deserved to change from his blood-soaked jacket into something else after all he's been through today?"

Forrest looked chastised.

"Did you actually think he stole the shirt he's wearing?"

Forrest mumbled something. Maggie thought she heard the pejorative *Chinaman* under the man's breath.

She slammed her fists onto her hips. "Mr. Forrest, Quan Luck is a better man than you could ever hope to be. Leave him alone, do you hear me?"

Forrest's face contorted with anger. He stomped past Maggie toward the doorway. As he past her, she held up her hand to stop him.

"Not that you deserve further explanation, sir, but for your information, Doctor Gibbons himself gave Quan Luck his own shirt to wear. I suggest you take Doctor Gibbons for your teacher if you want to learn compassion."

Forrest scowled at her and stormed off.

No sooner had he disappeared, when Elizabeth appeared in the doorway.

"OH ELIZABETH, I'M so sorry. Did that horrible man wake you?"

"Man? Oh, you mean the yelling? No. I was already awake. Couldn't sleep, actually. Too tired, I think. The army just came. They heard about our clinic. They dropped off cots for us to use. They're setting them up in the front parlor for us. What was the shouting about?"

Maggie debated whether or not to tell Elizabeth about Forrest, but she decided it would serve no purpose to withhold the information and Elizabeth should be warned, especially if the young man stayed around.

"Mr. Forrest accused Quan Luck of stealing from Doctor Gibbons."

"You jest."

"I assure you, I do not."

"You set him straight, I presume?"

"I did more. I boxed his ears with my words. Hopefully, it knocked some sense into him, although I have serious doubts about the possibility."

"I'll keep my eye on him," Elizabeth said.

"*If* he stays."

Elizabeth sighed. "It's true. We don't need his kind of behavior around here. Not ever, but especially not now. It might be best if he decides to go back to Cooper. I'll suggest it to Doctor Gibbons."

Jo Holtz came into the room, carrying a tray. "Doctor Gibbons insists everyone should drink this. It's his own concoction of herbs and spices in milk. He says it's quite healthy and will keep everyone's energy up."

Maggie took a glass filled with a muddy brown liquid and sniffed it. It smelled of cinnamon and basil. "It's not one of those tonics filled with patent medicines, is it?"

Jo laughed. "No. Doctor Gibbons is a strong proponent of natural remedies. He abhors those snake-oil products. I assure you this won't hurt you and it may make you all feel a little better."

Elizabeth picked up a glass from the tray and saluted the women with it. "Cheers, then."

When Jo left, Elizabeth said, "I asked the young man setting up the cots if we could have a couple of them placed in here to use for volunteers to rest. He'll be in as soon as he finishes in the parlor. He thinks he can fit about fifteen bunks in there. He's also going to bring in a couple of the more comfortable chairs from the front of the house so we can use them to rest, too."

A short time later, Maggie sat on one of the chair arms. Elizabeth slumped in the seat with her head against Maggie's side. Maggie didn't dare move. Elizabeth had finally fallen asleep.

Outside in the distance, she could hear the explosions reverberating as the military tried to stop the advancing fire.

April 19, 1906

IN THE EARLY morning, an officer from the Presidio arrived with a soldier in tow who burned his hand as he lit sticks of dynamite. While Elizabeth tended to him, applying salve and wrapping his hand in one of the strips of bedding Maggie had prepared, his commander looked on.

Elizabeth inquired about the fire.

"I'm afraid it's still out of control. Most of the hydrants aren't working, but they've found a few cisterns. Even so efforts are failing. I heard they lost the Hopkins Mansion on Nob Hill earlier today. The financial district has burned itself out, but the fire is moving west toward Van Ness."

Elizabeth's eyes widened.

"Oh, dear. Do you have someone on Van Ness."

"My house is on Van Ness." She sighed. "Well, at least everything—everyone—of value is safe."

"I'm glad to hear it."

"Do you know about Violet Farrell? She runs the Quaker Mission on Ninth Street."

"A great deal south of The Slot is gone. I'm not sure about Miss Farrell. The fire's moving toward the Mission District. We were working down there, but the fire pushed us back to Market Street. Then Mr. Mason, here, had his accident. He refused to get help on his own. When I saw the state of his hand, I decided I needed to make sure he got help."

"An excellent decision. Are there many injuries...deaths?"

The commander hesitated. "Some...not many."

Elizabeth didn't believe him. Between the collapsed buildings and the raging fire, the death toll had to be greater than he let on. Time would tell. All she could do was attend to the victims who showed up on Doctor Gibbons's doorstep.

She inquired about Maggie's building. He said many buildings were demolished along Market, but he wasn't sure about hers. All Elizabeth knew was Maggie was lucky to have escaped with her life. They had heard Chinatown was decimated. Poor Quan Luck—no family and no home. The thought made Elizabeth shiver. She shook off the feeling as she tied the bandage around the soldier's hand.

She turned to the commander and said, "I suppose it won't do much good to tell you he shouldn't use his hand."

His shoulders slumped ever so slightly. For the first time, Elizabeth noticed how young the man looked—and how tired.

"I'll try, but I'm not sure it will be possible in these times."

The soldier climbed off the table on which he sat. He stood erect, looking determined. "I'm fine, sir. I'll be able to do whatever you need."

Elizabeth met the commander's eyes. "He may need to favor his hand for a few days. Please don't fault him for it. A burn is nasty, painful."

"I understand, doctor. Thank you."

The two men left, passing Maggie as she entered the room.

"Jo and I prepared breakfast. I want you in the dining room."
"But I need—"
"Now, Elizabeth. If it gets busy later, I know you. You won't take the time to eat the rest of the day. Go." She pointed toward the door.

Elizabeth sighed and stepped toward her. "Yes, Mother."

Maggie said, "I should hope not."

As tired as Elizabeth was from a poor couple of hours of sleep in a chair, the thrill ran through her, surprising her. A slow smile broke across her face. "No, I suppose not."

Maggie threaded her arm through Elizabeth's. "Let's go have breakfast, shall we?"

Elizabeth whispered in her ear, "Yes, my love."

"Better," Maggie said. "Much better."

MAGGIE'S PREDICTION PROVED right. A steady stream of patients continued all day. Elizabeth never stopped to eat again. Doctor Gibbons attended to people in one room, Elizabeth in another. People who came fell into one of two categories; physical injuries or mental trauma. They patched broken bones, sewed up gashes, bandaged wounds and burns. When someone without physical injury showed up on their doorstep, dazed by their experiences or shaking with terror, they did their best to offer comfort. Several told horrific stories of trying to save victims and belongings or fleeing the fires with nothing but the clothes on their backs. The acrid smell of the devastation hung in the air and from the clothes of those who sought treatment.

In the early evening, Maggie decided she needed to get out of the house and she retraced the path they had followed for the three blocks toward Elizabeth's house to see if it was still standing. A block before Van Ness, the thick, pungent smoke stopped her.

She met a man hurrying up the street and asked him if he knew how far the fire had come. He told her the military had come to his door and told him to flee. The fire was approaching Van Ness and they were about to start dynamiting the homes along it. She turned around and ran back to tell Elizabeth.

"I suppose there's nothing we can do," Elizabeth said without emotion.

Maggie lifted her eyebrows. "You might not have a home or a clinic when they're done."

Elizabeth's eyes softened as she said, "You've already lost yours. Many people have. It's more important you're safe. I'm glad you're with me. When I didn't know where you were, I was frantic. I was never so happy as when I saw you and Quan Luck coming down the street yesterday morning. That's what's most important. Not a place to live or clothes to wear or even my medical books and instruments. Those can all be replaced. You—you and Quan Luck—are irreplaceable. I'm glad you're both here."

Maggie noticed the dark circles under Elizabeth's eyes. There was one person waiting for care at the front of the house when she returned and his injuries were minor.

"Elizabeth, why don't you go lie down? You didn't have what I'd call a restful night last night and you only got two hours sleep."

"There's another patient."

"Let Doctor Gibbons take care of him. Please, you need to rest. Doctor Gibbons made sure he got a nice nap this afternoon. He's fine."

"Come with me."

"I'll come with you to make sure you lie down. Then, I'm leaving you alone."

Elizabeth wiggled her eyebrows.

Maggie laughed. "No. You are incorrigible, Doctor Kellogg. You need to rest." Maggie leaned in close and said, "Besides, this place has no privacy and you know it."

Elizabeth's sigh echoed through the room.

A few minutes later, Maggie left Elizabeth on a cot in the little storage room. Elizabeth was asleep before she left, proof of just how exhausted she was. Maggie headed for the front parlor to make sure the man who waited there had been attended to. If he had not, she intended to make sure Doctor Gibbons knew he was there.

The man no longer waited, but the room wasn't empty. Doctor Gibbons stood looking out the window. When Maggie entered, he greeted her.

"Do we have any patients left, doctor?"

"The last one just left. A minor injury. He simply needed a bandage. We have a respite, at least for a little while, it seems." He turned toward her and gave her a weary smile.

"How are you fairing, Miss Weston?"

"Please, doctor, call me Maggie. I'm doing fine. I was able to sneak in a nap earlier." She looked into his kindly eyes. "Elizabeth is not so fine, though. I'm concerned about her. She hasn't rested for longer than a few minutes at a time. When I finally got her to lie down, she fell asleep immediately. I'd like her to be able to stay down for a few hours. Otherwise, I'm afraid she'll collapse from exhaustion."

"Things were quiet last evening for us. Didn't she get to rest then?"

"Not well. She slept in a chair. And we did have some patients. She didn't want to wake you."

"Oh, dear, she must take care. We need her."

Maggie nodded, happy to hear Doctor Gibbons acknowledge Elizabeth's need for rest. The two turned their attention out the window, to the sound of explosions, and the sight of incendiaries going off like fireworks, causing smoke to billow over the rooftops several blocks away. Red hot cinders swirled amid the smoke.

"If it comes any closer," Gibbons said, "we may have to move. We can always go to the hospital, but being closer to the devastation has been a great help to those in need."

A huge explosion sounded nearby. Maggie cringed. The pair watched as chunks of burning debris flew into the sky a short distance away, falling onto roofs. Flames erupted where they fell in a matter of seconds.

"Do you think we should go now, doctor?"

Silence filled the space between them. Maggie watched him chew on his lower lip. "I think we'll wait until we're told we must go. If nothing else, Doctor Kellogg will be able to get a little more rest."

He turned away from the window and said, "I'll be in my study. If anyone should come in needing treatment, come and get me." He looked at her with grave concern. "You should try to rest if you can. Take advantage of this lull."

After Doctor Gibbons left, she continued gazing out onto the street. As she did, an apparition materialized from the smoke. Three men appeared out of the billowing cloud of dust and smoke lingering at the end of the block. Tiny wisps followed them, clinging to their jackets and trouser legs as they approached. They had bandanas tied over their mouths and noses. They looked fit as they strode toward the house, leading Maggie to believe they didn't require medical help.

She opened the front door to greet them. They all wore red ribbons on their jacket lapels. She wondered what they signified.

One young man said, "Is this Doctor Gibbons's place? We're from Stanford University. We've come to offer our services."

Before Maggie could invite them in, another huge explosion sounded behind them, causing them to duck where they stood. A few blocks away, fire reigned down again.

One of the men looked over his shoulder and said, "I'm no engineer, but it would seem to me those chaps blowing up buildings to try to stop the fire are going about it all wrong."

Maggie said, "You'd better come in, gentlemen, although I'm not sure how long we'll be safe here."

MAGGIE STAYED WITH the men in Doctor Gibbons's study long enough to hear them explain they were law students at Stanford and had come to San Francisco with the Reverend Charles Gardner to help in relief efforts. When she excused herself from their company, much to Maggie's dismay, she met Elizabeth coming down the hall. Her nap lasted no more than thirty minutes.

When Maggie encouraged her to return to the storage room to rest, she said, "How can anyone sleep through that awful din? No. I'm awake now. I may as well stay up."

Doctor Gibbons and the young men emerged from his study and he introduced them to Elizabeth. Doctor Gibbons instructed the men to go to the kitchen and make themselves at home while they awaited the next battery of patients he knew would come.

When the young men left and Doctor Gibbons returned to his study, Elizabeth turned to Maggie and said, "Where's Quan Luck?"

"Earlier today he heard the Chinese have bivouacked at the Presidio. He was going to try to make his way there to seek out the rest of his family. I assume he was successful in finding his cousins since he hasn't returned. With the curfew in place, I'm sure the earliest he'll be back is tomorrow. Why do you ask?"

"It's nothing. I have an idea. It's not important. It can wait until he returns."

Maggie and Elizabeth spent the next hour or so getting acquainted with the Stanford students. They had come with Reverend Gardner, the head of Memorial Church at the university.

"He set up a relief station on Twenty-fifth and Guerrero," one of the men explained. "We're calling it Camp Stanford. Some of us elected to strike out into other areas to see if we could help out in any way. When we reached this area, someone informed us about Doctor Gibbons's clinic and we decided to see if we could offer our services."

Another of the men said, "Doctor Gibbons told us we're welcome to stay."

A blast punctuated his statement. They all cringed.

When she recovered, Elizabeth said, "I'm sure we'll be able to use your help, gentlemen. I have a feeling it's going to get busier around here."

A few minutes later, they heard shouting outside and

someone pummeled their front door. When Maggie opened it, several injured people stumbled into the parlor.

April 20, 1906

ELIZABETH MUDDLED ON through the night into the next morning, tending a steady stream of injured and sick people as if in a trance. At times, she found it difficult to lift her arms to use her stethoscope or an instrument. Fortunately, most of the injuries were minor. One of the law students, Tom Spear, trained in basic first aid, was a big help applying bandages and splints. However, the patients didn't stop coming and Elizabeth still hadn't gotten more than a few hours' sleep in intervals measured in minutes rather than hours.

Every time she encountered Maggie, she noted the worried look on her face. Her concerned glances caused Elizabeth more uneasiness than any worry she had about her own well-being. More people arrived seeking help. She pushed on.

Maggie looked in on her when she finished attending to a man with a deep laceration. From the look on her face, Elizabeth knew something was wrong.

"I think you'd better come outside."

"Maggie, I can't. The patients—"

"Elizabeth, please. Come outside."

Whatever it was, Maggie thought it was important. Maybe someone's injured and can't negotiate the steps into the house.

She put down the implement she was cleaning and followed her.

Out on the front steps, they found a man dressed in an impeccable dark brown suit. He didn't look injured.

Maggie said, "Doctor Kellogg, this is Mr. Rosemont."

Elizabeth raised an eyebrow at Maggie, who said, "Yes, Mr. Rosemont is Amelia's husband. I'll go back inside. Call me if you need me."

When they were alone, Elizabeth plastered a smile on her face she didn't feel and asked, "How can I help you, Mr. Rosemont?"

He looked distressed. "I'm here because my wife, Amelia, wishes to speak to you."

"Mr. Rosemont, as you can imagine, we're very busy here. We have a room full of injured people I must attend to. I don't have time to go to your home—"

He held up his hand. "Don't worry, doctor, we no longer

have a home to go to."

Elizabeth softened. "Oh. I'm so sorry."

He said, "You don't have to go anywhere. Amelia is in the carriage." He pointed to the street. In the driver's seat, a man sat, staring straight ahead. Inside the carriage, Elizabeth noticed the outline of a dark form.

"Is she ill?"

"I'm afraid so, doctor, but I don't think it's something you can fix."

Elizabeth cocked her head and he continued, "I'm taking her to Belmont, to Doctor Alden Gardner's Sanitarium. Doctor Gardner has assured me he can treat Amelia's problems. It's been difficult since the earthquake. She's not been able to get her…medicine."

Relief washed over her on hearing Amelia would finally get help.

"She's wracked with night terrors and painful afflictions. We've been sleeping in one of the camps provided by the army, but people are frightened of her condition. Two nights ago, she tried to kill herself. Someone recommended Dr. Gardner. I telegraphed him. He said he would accept her into his hospital—he insisted we should come as soon as possible."

"I'm sorry to hear this, Mr. Rosemont. You're doing the right thing. She needs help. I suggested it weeks ago, but she wouldn't listen. You should get her to Dr. Gardner before she's successful in harming herself."

"She put up a terrible fuss. Her tantrum was so bad they banished us from the camp. They didn't know I'd already made arrangements to leave. But now she says she won't go without talking to you first."

Elizabeth glanced at the carriage, trying to decide if it was wise.

"Please, Doctor Kellogg, talk to her. She won't leave San Francisco until she gets to talk to you. I'll wait here."

She debated for a few more seconds before agreeing. She left Mr. Rosemont on the steps and headed for the carriage.

WHEN ELIZABETH REACHED the carriage, she found Amelia slumped over in a stupor. Better than finding her ranting and writhing in pain, she thought. She opened the carriage door and climbed in, calling Amelia's name as she sat down beside her.

She looked worse than the last time she saw her, if it were possible, with sallow skin and sunken eyes. Amelia didn't stir. She called her name again. This time Amelia revived. Elizabeth stared into vacant eyes, wondering if Amelia would even recognize her.

"You came." Amelia's voice sounded like gravel in a sieve.

"I'm here, Amelia. You must let your husband help you. Go to Belmont and let them treat you. You can be well again."

"I don't care if I'm well or not. I don't care if I live or die."

"Don't say that."

"Why not?"

Elizabeth's eyes widened at Amelia's moment of fierceness.

Amelia stared at her a while before she said, "You don't have any idea, do you?"

Confusion rose up in Elizabeth. "Idea about what?"

"No, you don't have the slightest inkling. Perhaps you're too distracted by your little no-account photographer."

"Maggie? Amelia, why would you refer to her in such a manner?"

"Because she's the reason we're in this dilemma in the first place."

"Amelia, you're going to have to be more direct. I don't know what you're talking about."

"I've seen you. I know about your arrangement with Crane, know you stay with her and she stays with you. I...imagine...what you two are doing together."

A feeling of dread rose in Elizabeth's chest. Had Mr. Crane compromised them? Amelia was not so far gone she couldn't cause them a lot of trouble.

"Mr. Crane should never have—"

"Oh, don't worry. Crane is the epitome of discretion. He wouldn't admit to anything. Believe me, I tried. When he wasn't forthcoming, I had you followed. But I already knew. It hurt me, Elizabeth. It wounded me deeply—you and that trollop."

"Amelia, please!"

She sneered at Elizabeth. "You couldn't see it, could you?"

More confusion racked Elizabeth. "See what? You're not making any sense. Maggie is my friend."

"She's more than your friend and we both know it." Amelia looked into her eyes. "I wanted to be more than your friend, but you couldn't see it."

Panic filled her. Amelia wanted—no, she couldn't even imagine. Amelia? No, it wasn't possible.

As if reading her thoughts, Amelia said, "You can't even conceive of it, can you?"

Elizabeth stared at her hands. She wanted to wring them, twist them with the worry she felt—for herself, for Maggie, even for Amelia.

"At Christmas, all I wanted was a picture of us together so I could put it next to my bed. You wouldn't even allow me a picture."

Amelia rested her head against the seat back and closed her eyes.

"Mrs. Evangeline needed me."

Amelia's laugh held no joy. "And we all knew it was a ruse, didn't we?"

"I didn't. Not at the time."

Everything was beginning to come into focus now. All those times Amelia pressed her, questioned her. It wasn't about entrapping her to besmirch her reputation. All she was trying to do was to get her to admit her attraction to women so she could open the door to Amelia's advances.

"I'm sorry if I hurt you. I never meant to cause you pain."

"Yes. The pain. In the beginning, it was so great I thought I'd die from it. So I began taking the laudanum. It dulls the pain, you know. But it doesn't last and once I began taking it, I needed more and more."

Tears spilled down her cheeks. "I begged you to come and stay with me, Elizabeth. Do you know how much your refusal wounded me? You said no to me, yet you said yes to Maggie Weston."

"Amelia, Maggie and I are friends, nothing more. I told you."

"Have the decency not to lie to me, Elizabeth. I cared for you. I...wanted you with me." She slumped back onto the seat, spent.

Elizabeth tried to imagine how much Amelia's confession had taken out of her. She sat, eyes closed, unmoving. Elizabeth wondered if she fell asleep. It was time to extricate herself—to end the encounter. "I can't," was all Elizabeth could manage.

"I know," Amelia whispered. "Nor can I. I can't do this anymore. Tell Richard to come and take me away. I'll overcome this or I'll die trying. I know now it's what I must do."

Her pronouncement encouraged Elizabeth. She exited the carriage. Before she closed the door, she said, "I wish you well, Amelia. I hope Doctor Gardner can restore you to health."

Amelia stared straight ahead, still slumped in her seat. She raised her hand, all skin and bones, and dismissed Elizabeth with a wave.

Elizabeth didn't stop to speak to Mr. Rosemont. When she entered the Gibbons house again, she spoke to no one. Instead, she went straight to the little work room where she knew she'd find Maggie.

MAGGIE LOOKED UP from unpacking a box of supplies when the door opened. When she saw Elizabeth's face, she sprang up from her seat.

Elizabeth stumbled toward her.

Maggie flung her arms open and Elizabeth fell into them. She shuddered in Maggie's embrace.

"What happened?" Maggie asked.

"I can't—not here."

Maggie shifted Elizabeth away at arms' length and looked into her eyes. "You look like you need a bit of fresh air. Do you have the energy to go for a short walk?"

"I can manage it."

On their way out, they met Jo in the parlor. Dr. Gibbons had thinned out the crowd and Jo was applying a bandage to a cut on a woman's arm. It didn't seem serious to Maggie, so she said, "We need some air. We'll be back in a few minutes."

Jo nodded and after Maggie checked to make sure the Rosemonts were gone, they walked out the door.

Maggie was grateful for the unseasonable warmth of the late afternoon air since they hadn't brought their wraps. About a block up the street, they found a two foot stone wall surrounding a front yard and sat down. Elizabeth revealed her conversation with Amelia Rosemont.

Maggie tried to control her astonishment. "I can't believe it."

"I know. All this time, I thought she wanted to discredit me and instead, she wanted me in her bed."

"She knew about us. How? Is Mr. Crane not to be trusted?"

"No. She admitted trying to get information from him, but she insisted he refused to divulge anything. I think she may have been spying on us for quite some time. All the subterfuge and speculation helped tear her apart. It's what drove her to the laudanum."

"The fact that you wouldn't yield to her sly advances didn't help either, did it?" Maggie shook her head. "I feel sorry for her."

"As do I."

"Do you think this Doctor Gardner can help her? Make her well again?"

"Perhaps. For now, I'm just grateful she'll be away from here."

"Do you suppose she'll be a problem for you—for us—when she returns?"

"I don't know. I guess we'll find out if she does. We can only hope Amelia is wise enough to know if she exposes us, she runs the risk of exposing her own motives. Until such time, I'm going to put it out of my mind. She's gone and I'm relieved. I've been waiting for another boot to drop. Now, it's over. I told her I wished her well. It's all I could do."

Elizabeth hung her head.

"You're tired. You need to rest. Maybe we should go back to your house for a few hours."

"I don't think that's a good idea. We don't even know if I still have a house. We haven't heard the dynamiting in hours, but it doesn't mean they didn't already raze my home."

"I could go check."

"No." She reached out for Maggie's hand. "I don't want you to leave." She leaned in to Maggie's side. "Please, Maggie, I can't bear to be parted from you right now."

"Maybe you could try to lie down when we get back to Doctor Gibbons's place."

"Maybe."

WHEN MAGGIE AND Elizabeth parted company in the halls of the Gibbons' house, Maggie assumed Elizabeth was bound for one of the cots and a nap. She found Jo in the kitchen with Mr. Taylor, making dinner. She joined in the preparation and, about an hour later, she found Elizabeth in the hall where she left her talking to Tom Spear. She wasn't sure who she should reprimand first. She decided to start with Elizabeth.

"Elizabeth, I thought you were going to take a nap. You need to rest."

Tom tripped over his words, apologizing to both women. Elizabeth came to his rescue.

"Maggie, Mr. Spear isn't responsible for keeping me from resting. I intercepted him, not the other way around."

"What was so important it kept you from going to rest for a while?" Maggie regretted her sharp tone, caused more by desperation than anger. Her voice softened as she said, "This may be your only opportunity for who-knows-how long."

Elizabeth changed the subject. "I've been discussing Quan Luck's situation with Mr. Spear. He's promised to discuss it with the president of the law school, who will be visiting Camp Stanford in the next day or two. This could be the break Quan Luck needs. I wish he would return soon. I want to make sure he speaks to Mr. Spear. He may get a chance to speak to the president himself. I don't want him to lose this opportunity."

Maggie agreed. She took Elizabeth by the arm and dragged her into the storeroom. When they got there, Maggie shut the door and pushed Elizabeth into it. Elizabeth looked alarmed until Maggie leaned in and kissed her with passion. When Maggie broke it off, Elizabeth asked between panting breaths, "What was that for?"

"For being so kind. For giving up your much-needed rest to advocate for Quan Luck and his dream. I love you for it."

Elizabeth broke into a wide grin.

"I wish we were home. In my home. *Our* home." Elizabeth leaned in close to Maggie's ear before continuing, "I'd take you to bed right this minute. Maybe I will anyway."

"You will not." Her response had been too loud. As if repeating it softer could recall her words so no one could overhear them, she said it again.

Elizabeth's eyes sparkled in the dim light of the room. "No, I guess it wouldn't be wise. She leaned in and lowered her voice again, "But, know one thing. I want to...very much."

A tremor ran through Maggie's body. If the fire burning in the streets ever stopped, she would act on the blaze burning within. But first, they had to get through the awful destruction happening outside—and she had to figure out a way to get Elizabeth to rest.

Chapter Fourteen

April 21, 1906

IN THE WEE hours of the morning, most of those in the Gibbons' house gathered in the parlor and stared at one another from various perches. The last victim brought to them required extensive life-saving measures. His arm had been shattered by a dynamite blast and both Doctor Gibbons and Elizabeth worked on him, amputating the remaining tattered flesh and bone to save his life. He slept in Doctor Gibbons's bed after his ordeal. Jo Holtz watched over him.

Doctor Gibbons opened the front door to a knock. A lieutenant from the 22nd Infantry Division, who announced the fires around the city were under control and dynamiting operations had been called to a halt. There would be no need for them to evacuate.

After the soldier left, Doctor Gibbons relayed the information to the group and a great shout ensued. However, Doctor Gibbons cautioned any further celebration might be premature as the lieutenant informed him the shoot-to-kill order against looters was still in force, and he warned them victims of the remaining fires might need treatment. The energy in the room dissipated as fast as it arose.

Maggie watched Elizabeth as Doctor Gibbons spoke. Her head bobbed as she tried to stay awake. Maggie couldn't stand it any longer. She stood up and announced, "Only one person in this house has not gotten enough rest in the past few days and she's struggling to stay awake now, with no good reason."

She looked around the room to find everyone nodding in agreement.

"Elizabeth," Maggie called.

Elizabeth's head jerked up and she blinked rapidly, trying to keep her eyes open.

Maggie held out her hand and said, "Time for bed. Explosions should no longer wake you. The curfew is in effect, so no one should be out on the street. If I have to sit on you to keep you on your cot, I'll do it. Now let's go."

Elizabeth managed to widen her eyes at Maggie's threat. She stood, swayed, and crumpled back onto the couch.

Maggie heard someone scream Elizabeth's name. Before the

shrieking stopped, she realized she was the one making the terrible noise.

Doctor Gibbons pushed her out of the way. Voices buzzed around her as someone escorted her to a chair. Another person handed her a glass of water, but swallowing a sip proved to be difficult and she abandoned any more attempts to drink.

Time slowed. She watched as Mr. Spear passed Doctor Gibbons his stethoscope and a small, brown vial. Voices slowed, becoming so garbled, she couldn't understand anything anyone said. When she tried to get up to go to Elizabeth, someone pushed her back into the chair. Just as well, she thought, my legs are like rubber anyway.

Doctor Gibbons uncapped the vial in his hand and waved it under Elizabeth's nose. Her head shook like a cat doused with water and she revived. Time spun up to a normal tempo. She heard Doctor Gibbons ask Elizabeth if she had any pain or dizziness and heard her firm response of "no." Maggie breathed a sigh of relief.

If someone gave an order for what happened next, Maggie didn't register it. As if in a choreographed dance, Spear and Gibbons lifted Elizabeth from the couch in unison. At the same time, the other two Stanford men lifted Maggie. Her feet never touched floor until they arrived at the little storage room.

The three students stepped back and Doctor Gibbons left without a word. A few minutes later, Jo sailed into the room. She dismissed the men, informing them Doctor Gibbons attended to their surgical patient in her place.

Maggie watched as Jo helped Elizabeth lie down, marveling at how gentle she was with her. She removed her shoes and covered her with an army-issued blanket. Then, she turned her attention to Maggie.

"I heard you received quite a shock when Doctor Kellogg collapsed," Jo said.

Where was she going with this? Maggie said nothing.

Jo said, "Get up, please."

"What?"

"Get up. I'm going to make sure both of you get a good night's rest. I know Doctor Kellogg hasn't gotten a proper night's sleep since the earthquake, and I suspect you aren't far behind her."

"How?"

Jo ignored her incoherent questions. "Get up."

Maggie rose from the cot. What would come next? She looked over at Elizabeth and saw her watching Jo's movements with curiosity.

Jo walked over to Maggie's cot and pushed it against Elizabeth's. Maggie saw Elizabeth smile. Maggie furrowed her brow.

Jo turned to Maggie and said, "I've suspected for some time. Get into bed."

Maggie's heart pounded. Jo just admitted she knew they were more than friends. Should she be concerned?

"Do as I say, please."

Maggie walked over to the cot and sat down. When Jo made to take off her shoes, she pulled away and said, "I can do it."

Jo watched her and waited until she reclined on the cot. She covered her with a blanket, a twin to the one covering Elizabeth.

"When I leave this room, I'm going to put a sign on the door forbidding anyone to enter. You are both to stay in here and not get up until you've had at least a few hours of sleep. Do I make myself clear?"

Both women nodded as if they were children caught jumping on the feather bed.

As Jo turned the doorknob to leave, she turned back and said, "We are not so different, you two and I, you know. The only difference is I have not found someone special yet."

When the door closed with a soft *snick* behind Jo, Elizabeth grasped Maggie's hand and promptly fell asleep. A short time later, scratching in the hallway woke Maggie. She smiled, remembering Jo's promise to keep people out with a note on the door. She took a deep breath, relaxed, and let sleep carry her to a place of rest, still holding Elizabeth's hand.

MAGGIE STILL SLEPT beside her when Elizabeth awoke a few hours later. She slipped out of the room without a sound and found Quan Luck in the kitchen, brewing tea. She noticed he no longer wore the shirt Doctor Gibbons had lent him. Instead, he wore another worn, black tangzhuang jacket. Elizabeth wondered if he borrowed it from one of his distant cousins.

"You're back," she said. "I hope you found your cousins."

"I did. They camp at The Presidio. Some of them are talking of taking the ferry to Oakland for a fresh start."

"Will you go with them?"

"No. I don't think so. My home is here. I wish to stay. Rumors about the politicians trying to prevent us from rebuilding in our community are buzzing throughout the camp."

"Why on earth would they do that?"

"Chinatown's land is valuable. If they prevent my people from moving back, they can claim the land and sell it to the wealthy people. They will build hotels and apartments, which none of us could afford. My people lost everything in the earthquake and fire and if the politicians succeed, they will lose their future."

"How terrible. They must be stopped."

"It is another example of the way we are treated. It is why I dream of becoming a lawyer, so I can come to the aid of my community when injustices such as these arise."

Elizabeth's scowl turned to a wide grin. "I have news for you on that very subject, Quan Luck."

Maggie entered the room, interrupting the conversation. "Here you are. Why did you let me sleep?"

"You looked so peaceful. I didn't want to disturb you."

Quan Luck said, "You both finally got some sleep? I'm glad to hear it."

Both women nodded.

Elizabeth said, "I was about to tell Quan Luck about my conversation with Mr. Spear. The president from Stanford Law School is due at Camp Stanford today. Quan Luck, Mr. Spear has agreed to take you to meet him. He says there is a good possibility the president would allow you to study at the school. He says Chinese students from all over the country study there." She turned to Maggie and added, "This year, they opened the doors to women, too." Then to Quan Luck, she added, "You must go to Camp Stanford with Mr. Spear. He's already agreed. He said he will vouch for you himself as he's found you to be hardworking and thoughtful. You have made a fine impression on him."

Quan Luck's dark eyes shone with excitement. "I'll go look for him now and see if we can make arrangements." He stood up, but before he left the room to search for Spear, he said, "I returned from the Presidio by Van Ness Avenue. Many mansions and fine houses no longer exist, but those on the west side of the street between Sutter and Golden Gate are untouched by the fire. Your house is still standing, doctor, and looks to have only minor damage." His face saddened. He looked at Maggie and added, "Unlike us, you have a home to return to."

Elizabeth put her hand on Quan Luck's shoulder. "Maggie has agreed to move in with me, Quan Luck. You are welcome to come and stay as long as you like, too. I would be honored."

Tears welled up in his eyes, but he pulled himself together quickly. "Some people would be unhappy if they found I was living in your house. They expect us to keep to ourselves. They would talk. Speculate. Your reputation might be harmed."

"People are living in tents in the parks. You know this. Your own family is there. If they talk, let them. You're my friend. I won't send you roaming the city to find some piece of canvas to live under when you can easily stay in my home."

"But Mrs. Stockton might have something to say."

"You leave Mrs. Stockton to me. I doubt she would have me turn you out when you have been nothing but kind and helpful to Maggie and I. No. Don't worry about other people. You'll come and stay with us."

He bowed his head and whispered, "Thank you."

"Now, go find Mr. Spear. You mustn't lose your opportunity, then come back and tell us what happened."

Before Quan Luck left the room, he reached down onto one of the kitchen chairs and handed her a pristine, folded, white shirt, the one Doctor Gibbons loaned him, now clean and pressed.

"Please return this to Doctor Gibbons for me."

She looked to the bundle, then back at Quan Luck. "How did you…"

He smiled. "Once the son of a laundryman, always the son of a laundryman."

She didn't press him further. "I'm sure Doctor Gibbons will be pleased to have his shirt back in such wonderful condition. Thank you. Now go, before Mr. Spear leaves without you."

When Quan Luck left the room, Maggie walked up to Elizabeth and stood so close, she thought she might kiss her and she worried someone would walk in on them. Maggie had other plans, though. Instead, she whispered her thank you for Elizabeth's offer to Quan Luck. Then, she mouthed, "I love you," and turned to pour them some tea.

MAGGIE AND ELIZABETH bid Tom Spear and Quan Luck goodbye as they left for Camp Stanford. Quan Luck voiced his concern for not being appropriately dressed to meet the president and his anxiety about failing to make a good impression during this important meeting. Everyone, including Tom, assured him the president wouldn't be looking at his clothes. He would, rather, look at the cut of the man—and Tom assured Quan Luck the president would not find him lacking.

Later, Maggie found Elizabeth in the storage room, sitting at the small table they used to prepare bandages, with her head propped up in her hand, her eyelids drooping.

"You need more sleep. It's quiet. We haven't had a patient all day. Go to bed. Or better still, perhaps it's time to leave and go back to your house. You'll have a much better rest there, I'm certain."

Elizabeth yawned and said, "Mr. Taylor came by earlier. He told me the camps in the parks are filled with people in need of a doctor. Clinics are being set up to tend to them. The women of the camps could use the benefit of a woman doctor."

Maggie so wanted to shout a loud "no" to this suggestion, but she knew it would do no good. She had to figure out a way to get Elizabeth to rest. She looked so tired. Maggie was concerned she might collapse again. Then, an idea struck her.

"I'll make you a deal," Maggie said.

Elizabeth gave her a wary look. "What kind of a deal?"

"I'll accompany you to any park of your choosing to see if we can be of help, but first you must do two things."

Elizabeth raised one eyebrow.

Maggie continued. "I want us to go back to your house. When we get there, I suggest you get cleaned up and comfortable and go straight to bed and sleep. I refuse to let you go out to start working in the camps without a real rest. From what we've heard about conditions in the city, those people are going to be living in tents for a long time to come. A day or two more without the great Doctor Elizabeth Kellogg won't make them any worse off than they are now. Tomorrow we'll see how you are. If you've recovered enough, perhaps we'll go to one of the camps the next day."

Elizabeth opened her mouth, but Maggie held up her hand to silence her.

"This is not a discussion, Elizabeth. It's is an order. I won't have you jeopardizing your own health. You'll be no help to anyone if you keep this up." Her voice softened to a whisper as she added, "And you're scaring me." Tears pooled in Maggie's eyes. "I just found you. I don't want to lose you."

MAGGIE'S PLEA STUNNED Elizabeth. She didn't realize pushing herself, not only affected her, it distressed Maggie. Elizabeth's shoulders slumped. It was time to admit she needed to agree to Maggie's demands.

"I'm so sorry, Maggie. I didn't mean to cause you such worry."

Maggie said nothing. She swiped at her cheek to dry a tear.

Elizabeth felt wretched for the distress she caused. There was nothing to do, but agree. "I consent to your terms. It's time to go home."

Maggie let out a shuddered sigh. "Thank you." Tears welled up in her eyes.

Elizabeth grasped Maggie's hand. "Why are you crying? I've

said we'll go home. I promise I'll rest when we get there. I'll do as you say."

With her free hand, Maggie batted Elizabeth on her forearm. Through her tears, she said, "You dolt! I'm crying because I'm relieved. I've been so worried about you."

Elizabeth pulled Maggie to her and embraced her with all her might. "I'm sorry, Maggie. I can't say it enough. I just, well, I feel people need me."

Maggie pushed away. "What about me, Elizabeth? I need you, too. I didn't know how much until I saw you working yourself into a collapse. I was so frightened."

"I'm sorr—"

Maggie put her finger on Elizabeth's lips. "Don't say it. You don't need to apologize again. I know you're dedicated. It's part of why I love you. But you must be reasonable. You need to rest. We've got to think of something to make sure you have time to recuperate from this."

ELIZABETH DISCUSSED HER plans to return home with Doctor Gibbons. He told her he had already arranged to take their surgical patient to the hospital to complete his recovery. With the fires under control, the hospital would be safe.

"I'm glad Maggie talked some sense into you, Doctor Kellogg. She's been worried about you, you know."

"Yes, doctor. I do know. Do you need me to stay until our patient is moved?"

"No. We'll be fine. Two of the Stanford men are still here as is Miss Holtz, and Mr. Taylor will be back with an ambulance carriage, so we'll have plenty of assistance. I'll be staying at the hospital to help out there once we've settled our patient in."

"Thank you, doctor. I've enjoyed working with you."

"As have I, Doctor Kellogg. Your work has been exceptional. Perhaps when life gets back to normal, we can continue our mentoring program."

"I'd be delighted, Doctor Gibbons. Oh, and something else, if Quan Luck should return before you leave, would you ask him to come to my house?"

"I will. He's a fine young man. Mr. Spear told me of his hopes to get into Stanford. I spoke to him about it. I told him if he needed a recommendation, I'd be happy to offer one."

"I'm sure he's grateful. I hope he'll take you up on it."

His face softened as he said, "Go home, Doctor. Go home and listen to Miss Weston. She has your best interest at heart."

As Elizabeth packed up her doctor's bag, she made a mental

note to replenish her depleted supplies as soon as she got home. She and Maggie roamed the house, bidding everyone goodbye before they headed home.

AS THEY WALKED toward Elizabeth's house, the magnitude of the devastation hit them again. The skyline looking out toward the San Francisco Bay had been flattened. An occasional fragment of a building, looking like the boney hand of an enormous skeleton, grappled skyward. The smell of burnt debris drifted around them as they trudged toward home, sidestepping chunks of brick, plaster, and burned debris strewn along their route by the wind and the blasting.

When they reached their destination, they stopped. Everything on the other side of the street was flattened rubble, her neighbors' houses gone. When she turned to her own residence, Elizabeth noticed a piece of scrolled wooden decoration, which should have been wedged between a column and the roof, dangled at an odd angle. One of the upper windows had a spider-web like crack in the glass. She decided these problems would be easy to fix.

They ascended the steps to the porch. Elizabeth glanced up and down the block. An eerie scene spread out before her. A few buildings, scattered here and there, appeared untouched by the earthquake and the fire. "I wonder what prompted the Hand of Fate to spare some buildings and not others?"

Maggie didn't answer.

Market Street, once screened by structures was visible now. Trolleys could be seen running up and down the street amid the rubble. People, like tiny ants, picked through wreckage, looking for the shattered pieces of their lives. Elizabeth felt two emotions at once—gratitude for still having a home and guilt at its survival.

Maggie shook her from her reverie. "Let's go in, Elizabeth."

Elizabeth found it difficult to avert her eyes from the scene spread out before her. "There's so much to do."

Maggie pulled her toward the front door by the sleeve. "And unless you are capable of erecting a building all by yourself, you won't be doing any of it. Let's go inside. You're here to rest, remember?"

"Yes, rest." She took one more glance toward the Bay and followed Maggie into the house.

MAGGIE SAT IN the parlor, looking out the front window,

continuing to formulate her plan to make sure Elizabeth recovered from her state of exhaustion. Elizabeth slept soundly in the next room, but Maggie knew, faced with the needs of the inhabitants of San Francisco, she wouldn't continue to rest. They needed to get out of the city for a while.

Movement on the sidewalk below caught her attention. Quan Luck ascended the front steps. She had locked the front door to ensure they wouldn't be disturbed, so she ran downstairs to open it.

His face beamed when he saw her.

"Come in," she said.

Quan Luck stepped inside with a small bundled tucked under his arm and looked around. Maggie closed the door and locked it again.

"Let me show you where you will stay."

Quan Luck nodded and followed her through the examination room, his head swinging from side to side as he took it all in.

Maggie opened the door to Elizabeth's office and Quan Luck stopped at the doorway and peeked in.

"This is where you want me to sleep?"

"Yes, I'm sorry it's not a proper bedroom, but you should be comfortable enough here. The couch is quite pleasant. I've slept on it myself." She didn't know if Quan Luck would be sensitive to a reference to his small stature and the size of the couch, so she chose not to comment about it.

"Oh, I'm not worried, Miss Maggie. I'm sure it's quite comfortable. It's just that, well, this room is so…grand."

She laughed. "It's Elizabeth's office. Make yourself at home. Move things around, if you'd like. Elizabeth won't be setting foot in here, at least not if I can help it."

"How is Doctor Kellogg? She looked so tired."

"She's exhausted. I am concerned about her. I think I need to get her out of the city for her to rest and recover."

Quan Luck nodded.

"I have an idea, but I don't know if I can get her to agree. I'm going to see Mrs. Stockton. Will you stay here? Upstairs? In case she wakes up. I'm going to leave a note on her night table, letting her know you're there, so she won't be surprised to see you. If she wakes up and needs anything, you can get it for her."

He looked hesitant.

"If you don't want to do it, it's all right. I'll go and hope I'll be back before she wakes up."

"I — I don't mind. I am concerned the doctor will not want me in her living quarters."

Maggie stared at him. "Elizabeth invited you into her home to stay for as long as you like. She meant it, Quan Luck. We've given you this room, not because you are not allowed upstairs, but because we wanted you to have some privacy. We talked about it on our way here. You are most certainly allowed to go upstairs. There you'll find a kitchen where you're also allowed to make yourself some tea and to eat anything you find in the pantry. Do not hesitate. This is your home now, at least for as long as you want to stay."

He grinned. "It won't be for long. President Jordan is pleased to accept me into Stanford Law School."

"How wonderful. Oh, Quan Luck, I'm so happy for you."

"Thank you. We talked for a long time, too. President Jordan told me Mr. Spear also wrote him a letter about me. After we spoke, he told me I could come to Stanford to study."

"When do you start?"

"The school has much damage. A great deal of repair is needed. Classes are suspended until August. I will begin my classes then. He said my reason for wanting to go to Stanford is noble. He offered to help me with expenses." He beamed. "I am going to be a lawyer, Miss Maggie, and it's all thanks to you and Doctor Elizabeth."

Maggie patted him on the shoulder. "It was more Elizabeth's doing than mine. All I did was tell her about your eagerness to become a lawyer. As soon as she found out Mr. Spear and his friends were from Stanford and they studied law, she made sure he knew of your ambition and enlisted his help."

He placed his bundle on a chair and turned to her. "I am grateful to her and to you. I don't know what you are planning for Doctor Elizabeth, but if you need my help, I'll do whatever I can. It's the least I can do for her and for you."

"Truth be told, I'm not entirely certain of my plan. I do know if I don't get her out of the city for a while, she's going to work herself to death. She wants to go to the camps in the parks to help out there. I'm hoping Mrs. Stockton will be able to offer a suggestion and I know Elizabeth won't leave without Mrs. Stockton's permission. Whatever happens I'm sure I'll be able to use your help. I'm going to go up to check on Elizabeth and write her a note. Come upstairs when you're ready."

IT OVERJOYED MAGGIE to find Mrs. Stockton remained in the city and her home had not been affected by recent events. As they sat in her parlor, two young children ran down the hall, squealing with delight.

Mrs. Stockton smiled at the noise.

A few seconds later, a young woman tore after them, demanding they behave. "Children, you must be quiet. Come into the library and read your books. You mustn't disturb Mrs. Stockton. She has a guest."

Mrs. Stockton shrugged and said, "I've told Mrs. Howard the children are not a problem, but she insists they behave like adults. It's so difficult for them after being displaced from their homes and left with little to do. She's trying to entertain them in the library, but the books in there hold no interest for children. They are far too young to appreciate the contents of my library."

"It's kind of you to take them in."

"Actually, I have four families staying with me. The Howards have the youngest children, though. The others are all out at the moment, trying to see what charity they can find for us. I hear the lines are long for food, but at least relief is available and the dreaded fire is out."

"Yes. The fire came close to Elizabeth's house. Did you know?"

"I heard they set off explosions. We could hear them all the way over here. I'm glad her building survived, though I've heard other homes on Van Ness were not so lucky. I also heard you two kept quite busy at Doctor Gibbons's home attending to those who required medical attention."

"Which brings me to the reason for my visit. During the aftermath of the earthquake and the fire, Elizabeth worked tirelessly. She slept for minutes here and there. Toward the end of our stay with Doctor Gibbons, she collapsed from overwork and lack of sleep. Only then did she get a little rest, but when she awoke, she still looked exhausted.

"We finally made our way to her house, where I knew she'd rest a little better. At least it's quiet now. When I left to come here, she was already fast asleep. However, before she went to bed, she was talking about going out to the camps set up in the parks. I'm afraid she won't stop working unless I can get her to leave the city. I came here hoping you could offer a solution...and to get your permission, of course."

Mrs. Stockton studied Maggie. Did she think her too forward in coming to her with this request? Perhaps she'd be thrown out. No, Mrs. Stockton was too much of a lady. But she might be summarily dismissed.

When Mrs. Stockton finally spoke, Maggie couldn't help but register surprise.

MAGGIE LISTENED TO Mrs. Stockton's solution, her excitement building with every word.

"...We call it Skycroft. It's located in the hills of San Mateo. I haven't been there in quite some time, but I have a couple who serve as caretakers of the place. When Mr. Stockton and I would go there during the summer months, Mr. and Mrs. Candelaria always took good care of us. They take care of the place, still. The last time I was there was two years ago, but my poor old bones can't make the trip any more.

"I would like you and Doctor Kellogg to go there and stay for as long as it takes to restore your health. Yes, Miss Weston, you look like you could do with a rest, too."

"I'm fine, Mrs. Stockton. But I'm troubled about the state of Elizabeth's health. I know if we got out of the city, though, she'd be able to relax and put her concerns for people who need medical care aside. She'll be much more effective when she returns."

Feeling emboldened by Mrs. Stockton's openness, Maggie added, "As I think you know, a young Chinese man worked for me at my shop. He lost his family in the earthquake. He's a diligent young man. He's been accepted into Stanford to study law next term but for now, since he has no home, Elizabeth told him he was welcome to stay with us—I mean her—well, I mean, she asked me to stay, too."

Maggie felt the blush rise in her cheeks. She stumbled over her words as she said, "Would it be...all right...if Quan Luck also went with us to San Mateo?"

"Is he the young man who worked for Amelia Rosemont sometimes?"

Oh-oh. Maggie's confidence plummeted. If Amelia had spoken about Quan Luck, she suspected it wasn't in praise of his virtues. "He did work for her on occasion, but he hasn't done so for quite some time." She felt as if she might cry.

"A lawyer you say?"

Maggie perked up. "Yes. He has wanted it for a long time. He met with the president of Stanford Law School and was accepted today. He's a thoughtful and hard-working young man." She thought better of telling her Quan Luck's true motivation for becoming a lawyer since she wasn't sure of Mrs. Stockton's views on the subject.

"I know Mrs. Rosemont's opinions of people, especially the Chinese, are not always kind or without prejudice. If you vouch for this young man, then I'm sure he is respectable. He certainly sounds conscientious. I imagine it isn't easy to impress the President of Stanford Law School. Please invite him to go with you. I'm sure he'll be a big help to you on the way down."

"Yes, he will. He's offered to do whatever we need to help Elizabeth."

"I'll let Mr. Candelaria know you're coming. He'll meet you at the station in San Mateo. Can you be ready to leave in the morning?"

"All I have to do is convince Elizabeth."

Mrs. Stockton's gaze bore into Maggie. "Somehow, I suspect Doctor Kellogg wouldn't refuse you, Miss Weston. But just to be sure, I'll send a carriage for you to take you to the train. Perhaps you should tell your Quan Luck to have a rope ready—in case you need to tie her up." She chuckled at her own joke.

Maggie smiled at the jest. She hoped Mrs. Stockton's first suggestion, that Elizabeth would deny her nothing, was the correct one.

But why would Mrs. Stockton think such a thing? Her cheeks colored again as she realized Mrs. Stockton suspected the reason.

BY THE TIME Maggie returned home to Elizabeth's, the afternoon sky had started to darken. She walked up the stairs to Elizabeth's living quarters and found Quan Luck pacing. When he turned toward her, she knew something was wrong.

Panic filled her chest. She couldn't breathe. "What happened?"

Quan Luck looked frantic. "I couldn't stop her, Miss Maggie. I tried, but she wouldn't listen."

Maggie tried to get control of the dread. "Calm down. Tell me what happened."

"A man. A man came to the door. He was most excited. Upset. He said he needed a doctor. I tried to tell him to be quiet, he would wake up Doctor Elizabeth, but he kept yelling.

"The noise woke her up. She called to me. I told her to go back to sleep. It was nothing. The man called upstairs to her and said his wife was having difficulty. She was having a baby, but it wasn't going well.

"Doctor Elizabeth told him she'd be right down. I told her 'no,' you didn't want her to go out. The man yelled he needed help for his wife. They were living in the park. She got dressed and came downstairs with her doctor's bag. I tried to stop her, but she wouldn't listen. I'm so sorry, Miss Maggie. I have failed you."

He hung his head.

"Quan Luck, listen to me. You haven't failed me. Elizabeth is a grown woman. She's also a dedicated doctor. If I were here, under those circumstances, I doubt I could have stopped her either. A woman in need during childbirth—someone in trouble giving birth—I don't see how anyone could have stopped her. Do you know where she went?"

"Jefferson Square."

Two blocks behind them. Not far. She could be there in five minutes. But then what would she do? Drag Elizabeth home by the ear like a child while a woman in labor was left, perhaps to die? Elizabeth would never stand for it.

"Stay here in case she returns before I find her. I'm going to the park."

DEBRIS AND DARKNESS made Maggie's trek slow. Fortunately, a half-moon in a cloudless sky gave her a little illumination, but she had to be careful. It took more than twice her estimated time to reach the park. As she approached, she saw row upon row of white tents reflecting the light of the moon. Some glowed with lantern light from within, others were in darkness.

When she reached the edge of the park, two men approached her. She shrank back for a moment. Then, she mustered her courage and continued toward them. One looked like a younger version of the other, father and son, perhaps.

"Do you know where I can find the woman in labor? I'm here to help the doctor."

The older man said, "She told us you might be coming." He pointed and said, "Five rows up, eight tents in. My son, here, will show you the way."

"I'm grateful to you," she said to the older man. The younger one turned and led the way without a word. When they were a few rows away, they heard the wails. The young man cringed.

Maggie said, "I can find my way, if you'd like to go back to your father."

"No," he said, "he gave me this task. I won't leave until I see you there."

The screams turned to loud moans as they got farther into the camp. When they turned into row five, they heard the cry of a newborn.

They reached the tent and found a man standing outside the flap. "It's a boy," he said, chest puffed out. His face beamed. "Our first. Thank God the doctor came. If she hadn't, I think I may have lost them both."

As he spoke, Maggie noticed the worry lines hadn't quite smoothed out yet.

"Congratulations," Maggie said.

"Are you Miss Weston?"

"I am."

"Doctor Kellogg said you'd come. She said to go inside." Maggie nodded. She thanked her escort and entered the tent.

A lantern lit the inside of the fabric structure, giving it a golden glow. A young woman rested on a cot, her dark hair plastered against her forehead as a result of her labor. She held a tiny bundle with soft, brown fuzz sticking out at the opening of the blanket. An older woman stood by the cot, talking to her softly.

At the foot of the bed, Elizabeth knelt on the ground and washed blood from her hands with water from a shallow basin.

Maggie walked over to her and knelt beside her. She looked into Elizabeth's tired eyes. "I've come to take you home."

Elizabeth nodded. Maggie picked up the cloth lying beside the basin and handed it to Elizabeth to wipe her hands.

"I want to check on them one more time before we leave. You should come and meet this young man. He was reluctant to come into the world, but we coaxed him out. I had to turn him. He was caught up the wrong way."

Maggie mumbled under her breath. "Just like a man."

Elizabeth chuckled at the comment, but she sounded tired.

"Are they all right?" Maggie asked.

"They will be. Mother needs rest and baby needs love and his mother's milk, nothing more." She smiled, but the lines in her face told Maggie this incident had negated the rest she'd gotten earlier.

"Let's check on them so we can go home," Maggie said.

Chapter Fifteen

April 23, 1906

AFTER THE INCIDENT in the park the night before, Elizabeth was more convinced than ever she was needed there. How many women and children would die if she decided to take a holiday now?

Elizabeth resisted Maggie's suggestion they go to Skycroft in the morning. Yet Maggie had been adamant, packing a bag with Elizabeth's clothes and bundling her own meager possessions, including her camera, into a sack tied up with a string.

Elizabeth still struggled, fighting with herself against leaving, until fatigue overcame her again. She plopped down on the settee, staring into space, unable to move until Quan Luck came up the stairs. He announced Mrs. Stockton had arrived and was waiting outside. He said she wanted to talk to Elizabeth—alone. Elizabeth sighed and trekked down the stairs and went out into the street to Mrs. Stockton's waiting carriage.

Mrs. Stockton didn't waste any time. "You know why I've come?" she asked.

Elizabeth nodded.

Mrs. Stockton leaned toward her driver and said, "Kingsley, will you leave us for a few moments, please."

Kingsley secured the reigns and climbed down from his seat. He pushed a chock beneath the carriage wheel, tipped his hat toward both women, revealing a shock of white hair and sauntered down the block with his hands behind his back. Elizabeth watched him stop to talk to a man stacking wood from a collapsed house a block away.

Mrs. Stockton said, "Get in, dear. Let's not talk in the street like stable boys."

The carriage bounced once as Elizabeth climbed in and sat beside Mrs. Stockton who watched her with intensity.

Mrs. Stockton scrutinized her. "She's right, you know. You look awful."

Elizabeth raised an eyebrow. "Maggie said this?"

"Yes, but only because she's sick with worry about you. I've seen for myself, now. I have to agree."

"I've been rather busy doing the task for which you brought me here."

"I didn't bring you here to make yourself ill. How will you attend to others when you collapse? Again."

Elizabeth raised both eyebrows. "I see Maggie's been busy telling you all my business."

"Miss Weston has your best interest at heart, my dear, as do I. You'll be no good to us if you're unwell. You've been doing such marvelous work. Don't stop now."

"It's what I'm trying to do."

"I didn't mean right this minute. Yes, we need you, but not to your detriment. Maggie thinks the only way you will rest and recover is to leave the city. Looking at you, I see she's right. We care about you, doctor. If I may say so, Maggie cares for you a great deal."

Elizabeth tried to control her surprise at the declaration. Did they have any secrets from anyone in this town?

"I see I'm right. We touched on this before. It is a great gift to have someone to care deeply about you. Even if you won't take my advice, you should listen to her. Take my offer. I have a house sitting empty outside the city, in San Mateo. The caretakers live there by themselves right now and they are both caring, self-effacing people. Go there. Rest. Don't come back until your strength returns. When you are ready to return, we'll be waiting for you. There will still be plenty of work to do. Don't dismiss Miss Weston's concern. Let her take care of you for a change."

Tears welled up in Elizabeth's eyes. "I must admit, I am so tired. Thank you for your generous offer."

As if on cue, another carriage pulled up behind Mrs. Stockton's.

Without glancing back, she said, "That will be the carriage to take you to the train. Take your Maggie and her friend and go, Elizabeth. You've all earned this time. Make the most of it."

Elizabeth put her hand on Mrs. Stockton's gloved one. "You are so kind, Mrs. Stockton. I'm sorry to have brought you out of your house to insist on this in person."

Mrs. Stockton waved her words away. "Did Maggie tell you I have four displaced families living with me?"

"No, she didn't, but then, I didn't give her much of a chance."

"Well, I do—and I'm happy to do it—but an old lady who lives a quiet life alone needs a moment's peace when her home turns into a hotel of sorts. Taking this ride gave me the respite I needed. So, don't trouble yourself about me. I'm fine, my house is intact, and I'm able to help those who were less fortunate and lost their homes. I'm glad to do it, but I'm glad for this chance for a pause. It's time for you to take your own pause, too."

"I appreciate such thoughtfulness. Thank you for understanding about...everything."

Mrs. Stockton nodded. "I'll look forward to seeing you — both of you — when you return."

Elizabeth clambered down from the carriage and noticed Kingsley approaching. As she stepped toward her house, Mrs. Stockton called to her.

She turned back and Mrs. Stockton said, "Give Maggie a message for me, will you?"

"Certainly."

"Tell her she won't need the rope."

Elizabeth furrowed her brow, trying to decipher the message. As Mrs. Stockton's carriage pulled away, she shrugged and gave up trying to puzzle it out.

MAGGIE SAT NEXT to Elizabeth on the San Mateo bound train. As soon as the train left the station, Elizabeth leaned her head against the car window and closed her eyes. Maggie watched the city roll past them until they reached the outskirts and the open lands of the Peninsula.

She thought Elizabeth was asleep, so it surprised her when she asked, "Why don't you need a rope?"

"What?"

Elizabeth opened her eyes. "Mrs. Stockton said to tell you no rope would be required. What did she mean?"

Maggie chuckled. "When I went to see her, she told me I'd better make sure I had a rope. She said if you refused, as I suspect she thought you would, I'd need to tie you up to get you on the train. I'm so glad I didn't need to do it. Can you imagine the looks we'd get?"

Elizabeth giggled. "It would cause quite a stir."

"More of a stir than we did cause? Did you see how people looked at us, strange trio we make?"

"Speaking of which, where is Quan Luck?"

"He was told to go to the back of the car."

Elizabeth's face contorted in anger and she tried to stand, but Maggie put her hand on her arm and pulled her back down.

"Elizabeth, it's fine. His seat is no different from ours, except for the location. Let it be. He'll be mortified if you make a fuss. We'll be at our destination in no time. If Mr. Candelaria makes him ride with the luggage, you can give him a piece of your mind then."

Elizabeth sat back and mumbled, "It's not right."

Maggie patted her arm, saying, "Go back to sleep. We'll be

there before you know it."

They left the city in ruins behind them.

THEY WOKE WHEN the conductor came through the car announcing San Mateo as the next stop. Maggie brought Elizabeth's valise and her own small bundle down from the overhead storage rack and handed Elizabeth's to her. Elizabeth already had her ever-present doctor's bag gripped in the other hand.

Before they left San Francisco, Maggie suggested she leave it behind since she wouldn't need it for the duration. The look she got from Elizabeth told her the subject wasn't open for discussion, so Maggie said no more.

Quan Luck met them on the platform holding on to his own meager parcel. He took Elizabeth's case from her as he had so many months before when she arrived in San Francisco. This time, he didn't offer to take the doctor's bag. He knew better.

When they exited the station, a short, compact man wearing a large straw hat as a shield against the warm, spring sun approached.

With a hint of an accent, he asked, "Are you Mrs. Stockton's guests?"

Elizabeth thrust out her hand. The man took it and shook it with enthusiasm.

"I'm Doctor Kellogg, but please call me Elizabeth."

He let go of her hand.

"This is Miss Weston."

"Maggie," she said as she took his hand to receive another vigorous shake.

"And this is Quan Luck," Elizabeth continued.

In order to be sure the man understood Quan Luck wasn't a servant, Maggie added, "He's soon to be a law student at Stanford University."

The man smiled and reached out for Quan Luck, who hesitated. Maggie nodded to him, giving him encouragement to accept the man's hand. He did.

She regretted it, though, worrying Elizabeth might have to reset a dislocated shoulder when she saw how Quan Luck shook when the man greeted him with even more exuberance. Apparently, he tried to be more delicate with Elizabeth and Maggie.

When he let go, he said, "I am Luis Candelaria. I will take you to Mrs. Stockton's Skycroft." He took Maggie's bag. When he gestured toward Elizabeth's doctor's bag, she informed him she needed to keep it with her and he didn't argue.

"Please, come this way." When he pointed toward the waiting vehicle, no one moved. Maggie looked over at Quan Luck and saw his mouth formed into a tiny "o." Instead of a carriage, a shiny automobile the color of over-ripe cherries stood a few yards away.

Mr. Candelaria cocked his head at them. "It's a fine automobile, I assure you."

Maggie responded first. "I'm sure it is, Mr. Candelaria, we're just surprised."

"Why would it surprise you, and please, call me Luis. No one calls me Mr. Candelaria."

"Well, Luis, I'm surprised Mrs. Stockton would be so progressive as to own an automobile. She still rides around in a horse-drawn carriage in the city."

Luis laughed. "Oh, that old thing? She uses it because she wants to keep Kingsley employed. She won't get rid of it until he dies." Luis crossed himself before continuing. "Mrs. Stockton likes to keep up with new equipment more than you might think. At Skycroft, we have all the newest and the best. Please, let us get out of the sun." Again, he gestured toward the car.

As they approached the vehicle, Elizabeth asked, "The best equipment for what?"

"*Para las vacas*—pardon me. For the cows—and the milk."

"You mean Skycroft is a working farm? Mrs. Stockton didn't tell me," Maggie said.

"If I know Mrs. Stockton, there is much she hasn't told you. Skycroft is the largest dairy in the area. We supply milk up and down the entire Peninsula."

Maggie and Elizabeth stared at each other, wide-eyed.

Once Luis stowed the bags in the luggage compartment, he helped them into the car. "Mr. Quan Luck, you may ride with me up front. I hope you do not mind."

"I don't mind at all. I would also not mind if you dropped the 'mister.' I am simply Quan Luck." His face glowed with excitement as he added, "This is only my second automobile ride. I'm looking forward to it."

When they pulled away from the train station, they headed out toward the west. The hills, still bright green from the winter rains, looked beautiful.

Maggie took in a deep breath as they ascended the hill and felt tension leave her shoulders for the first time since the earthquake hit.

Luis and Quan Luck chattered on like old friends about the automobile in which they were riding. As they ascended another large prominence, a long, low, adobe-style house, the color of clay, came into view. Beyond the house were a few wooden outbuildings and a large barn, several trucks lined up at the side. A herd of black and white cows dotted the next hill over, many of them munching on tender green grass. In the distance, more cows roamed on another hill.

Luis shouted, "There she is. Skycroft. Is she not beautiful?" They had to agree.

For the first time since the morning of the earthquake, Maggie felt her heart filled with joy. She looked over at Elizabeth and decided she looked almost refreshed. Perhaps Mrs. Stockton was right. Skycroft was an excellent place to rejuvenate. It was already working its magic on them.

They pulled up in front of the house and a woman with a gentle face and outstretched arms greeted them as they disembarked. "*Bienvenido*. Welcome. Please come in." She spoke in more accented English than Luis did.

Luis walked over to the woman and planted a firm kiss on her cheek before turning to them and saying, "This is my lovely wife, Manuella. Two things you need to know about my beautiful wife. One, she is the best cook in all of San Mateo and the surrounding towns and, two," he lowered his voice to a growl and said, "she doesn't like anyone in her kitchen."

Maggie said, "Manuella, it's good to meet you. Thank you for letting us impose on you. We promise—" she looked at her companions and nodded, "—to stay out of your domain, and we look forward to your wonderful meals."

Manuella blushed. "Don't pay any attention to Luis. It is him I make stay out of the kitchen. He only knows how to do one thing—get in my way. If you want to come in, you come in. We have nice chats while I cook. Anytime, you come."

Maggie looked at Luis and raised an eyebrow.

He smiled and shrugged. "You go with my Manuellita. She will show you to your rooms. There you may rest from your journey. I will bring your bags."

Manuella chattered on, pointing out various places in the house as they walked through the main room on bright colored, patterned tile floors. Down a long hall, she stopped in front of an open door and turned to Quan Luck, saying, "This is your room. Please, make yourself comfortable. When you want something to eat or drink, come to my kitchen and I'll give you something."

Quan Luck poked his head into the room and said, "This is beautiful. Thank you, Miss Manuella." He stepped into the room and she led Maggie and Elizabeth down the hall to another doorway. As she walked, she said, "Mrs. Stockton says you will share a room. I told her we have plenty for everyone, but she said no. I hope you do not mind."

Maggie looked at Elizabeth, wide-eyed. Elizabeth raised her eyebrows, but said nothing.

Maggie said, "This is fine, Manuella, thank you. Mrs. Stockton was correct. We prefer it." She tried to sound as casual as possible when she spoke. She didn't know if she succeeded. Her heart was pounding with so much force she thought Manuella might be able to hear it.

Manuella gestured them into the room. Maggie took in the bed, the largest one she'd ever seen. Its frame was made, not of boards, but of thick logs, stripped of bark. The mattress was covered in a bright, colorful blanket, with a crisp-looking white sheet turned over it at the top. Large pillows graced the head of the bed. The plain terra cotta tile on the floor in this room glowed in the sun streaming through the large, open window. Gossamer curtains on either side rippled in the gentle breeze. Even though the afternoon temperature had risen on their journey from the train station, the house remained cool.

"Mrs. Stockton has told us you are here to rest, especially Doctor Elizabeth. So, you rest. I will cook. When you are ready, you will come to my kitchen." She looked at Elizabeth and said, "I will feed you good food. Food to make you strong again."

Manuella left them. A few minutes later, Luis delivered their baggage with similar instructions to rest before leaving them.

Alone in the room, Maggie went to the window and looked out to see cows grazing in the distance. Some had calves beside them.

"It's so peaceful here." She turned to find Elizabeth reclined on top of the bed covers, saw her eyelids flutter as she tried to respond to Maggie's comment.

Without another word, Maggie walked over to the tall, heavy wood door and closed it. She went to Elizabeth's side. When she started to remove her shoes, Elizabeth tried to sit up, protesting. Maggie pushed her back down.

"Now begins your real rest. Let me help you. Then, you are going to get under these covers and go to sleep. And your bag," she pointed, "is going in the cupboard." She pointed to the other side of the room where a large wardrobe stood. "You won't need it here."

Elizabeth fell back onto the bed with a loud sigh. "Yes, Maggie."

Maggie grinned as she went back to her task of helping Elizabeth out of her clothes. When she got down to her undergarments, a thrill ran through Maggie's body. She pushed the feeling aside. Elizabeth needed nothing now but to rest. Later, when she was better and had her strength back, then, it would be different.

She thought about Mrs. Stockton again and her heart pounded as she thought of her telling the Candelarias Elizabeth and she would share a room. I wonder what they thought? She'd discuss it with Elizabeth, but not now. Now Elizabeth needed to sleep.

She pulled the covers back. Elizabeth plopped into bed as if her bones had turned to jelly and could no longer support her. Maggie pulled the covers up, settling them around her. She kissed her on the temple, and left the room. Elizabeth was already asleep when Maggie closed the heavy door and walked down the hall.

AS THE SUN set behind the hills in the west, Maggie sat in Manuella's kitchen and sopped up the remains of the most delicious pork and green sauce dish she had ever tasted with a homemade tortilla. Manuella stood beside the table wearing a wide grin.

Maggie pushed the bowl away and said, "Manuella, Luis was right. This is the most wonderful food I have ever eaten. You must be the best cook around."

"I am glad you like it. Would you like some more?"

When she reached for the pot from the stove, Maggie put out her hand to stop her.

"I'd love some more; however, if I put any more into my stomach, I'll have to wake Elizabeth up to take care of my stomach ache. Not something I want to do. This is the first time since the earthquake she's been able to sleep more than two hours at a time—and it didn't happen often. Normally, she napped for fifteen or twenty minutes at a time. The rest of the time, she was on her feet attending to patients. It's why she's so exhausted."

"Dios, mio. It's terrible what happened with the earthquake. So many people no longer have homes. We heard there were hundreds killed."

"I have a feeling the politicians want us to think the number was low."

Manuella shook her head. "When we go to church on Sunday, I pray for all the people. I will pray for Doctor Elizabeth, too. Are you sure she is all right? She's been sleeping all afternoon."

"I think it's what she needs. I thought about waking her to come and eat, but I think it's more important she sleep."

"Mrs. Stockton said you were the one who would know what

was best."

Mrs. Stockton said that? She'd have to thank her for her insightfulness when she returned to San Francisco. The woman was a wonder.

Quan Luck came in and stood before Maggie. "Miss Maggie, is there anything I can do for you or Doctor Elizabeth?"

"No. Elizabeth is still sleeping. I have a feeling she'll sleep through the night. I'll be off to bed myself soon."

When he turned to Manuella, his eyes widened. "Miss Manuella, I found the library. So many books. One section is filled with law books."

"Those were Mr. Stockton's. He was a lawyer. Didn't you know?"

"No. I did not. May I read them? I would like to find out about what I may be studying when I start my term at Stanford."

"Everything in this house is for you — all of you — to use. Please help yourself to any books you would like to read."

He thanked her and bounced out of the kitchen, no doubt heading toward the library. Maggie wondered if he'd get any rest tonight.

She yawned as she said, "Let me help you clean up the kitchen. You must be tired, too."

"No. Mrs. Stockton said you needed to rest, too. She said you helped the doctor during the disaster, so you must not have gotten much rest. You go now. I put many towels in the bathroom. If you'd like, you can have a bath."

"I don't want to trouble you for a bath, Manuella."

"It's no trouble at all. All you need to do is turn on the faucet. We have hot water whenever we need it here." Manuella picked up Maggie's empty bowl and walked over to the kitchen sink. As she turned on the water, Maggie noticed for the first time there were two faucets instead of the single one she was used to in her apartment and in Elizabeth's kitchen.

"I think I'll say goodnight if you won't let me help you." She stepped over to the sink and watched the stream run into the bowl Manuella rinsed. She put out her hand and stuck it under the water. It was hot. She turned to Manuella and said, "It's heavenly."

She yawned again.

Manuella gave her a look of concern. She shut the water off, dried her hands on a towel lying on the counter and said, "Maybe you should wait until tomorrow for your bath. Mrs. Stockton would be upset with us if we let you drown."

Tears welled up in Maggie's eyes. She had no idea why. Perhaps it was Manuella's concern. Maybe it was the thoughtfulness Mrs. Stockton expressed by allowing them to come. It might be as simple as hot water from a tap. It could also be caused by exhaustion similar to Elizabeth's. It didn't matter. She knew what she needed now was to curl up next to Elizabeth and sleep.

"I think you're right. I'll take a bath tomorrow. Good night, Manuella. Thank you."

"Good night, Maggie. Sleep well."

April 25, 1906

ELIZABETH SHOVELED THE breakfast Manuella put in front of her into her mouth. Manuella and Maggie sat opposite her, following every forkful. They both sported the same delighted look and silly grin.

Maggie said, "I'm so glad your appetite has returned."

Elizabeth mumbled agreement around another bite.

"Maggie was worried about you. We all were," Manuella said.

"I can't believe I slept so long. Two days! I'm so sorry. I should have gotten up."

Manuella and Maggie shouted their objection in unison. Maggie added, "You needed every minute of sleep you got. As a matter of fact, you should go back to bed once you've finished eating. You still have dark circles under your eyes."

"Maggie, I've slept enough. I don't even remember getting up to relieve myself and drinking the broth you said Manuella insisted I drink. Right now, I feel the need to move around."

Maggie looked to Manuella for support.

Instead, the older woman said, "She may be right. Some exercise might be good for her." She wagged her finger at Elizabeth and added, "But not too much. I will be the doctor now. I think you should walk out to the porch and sit there for a little while, but not too long. Then Maggie should show you how special our bathrooms are." She winked at Maggie.

Maggie understood. A nice hot bath would do wonders for Elizabeth. She'd keep the magic of getting hot water directly from a faucet a secret until Elizabeth was ready to bathe.

They strolled across the wide front porch, arm-in-arm, taking a seat on chairs made from a smaller version of the bulky stripped logs of their bed. The early morning breeze cooled them. Maggie's hand wandered to Elizabeth's resting on the thick arm of the chair. Elizabeth smiled at her and squeezed her hand.

"How are you feeling, Maggie?"

"I'm fine. Don't forget, I'm not the one who was near collapse for days. I want to know how you're feeling."

"I feel much better, although I will admit to an underlying fatigue I still can't quite shake."

"You must keep resting. It's the only way you'll get your strength back. Well, that and eating Manuella's wonderful meals. She's an absolute magician with food."

Elizabeth laughed. Maggie's heart leaped with joy to hear her elation. For the first time in a week, she felt Elizabeth might recuperate fully.

"I don't want you to tire yourself, but I have something to show you. When I do, I think you should take advantage of it, then go to bed again for a little while."

Elizabeth gave her a guarded look. "What are you talking about?"

Maggie stood and pulled Elizabeth up. "You'll see. Come with me."

"COME HERE AND feel this," Maggie said.

Elizabeth approached the claw-foot tub. "What's so special about it? I know a bathtub is quite a luxury, but this whole house is lavish."

Before she could say another word, Maggie pulled her hand under the water cascading from the faucet.

Elizabeth pulled it away, her eyes wide. "Incredible."

"It is, isn't it? I'm going to fill this tub. I want you to get in and take a bath. I'll bring you some clean clothes. At least you have some. I'm not so fortunate. I have one dress, a few underclothes and my camera. It's all I could scoop up before the ceiling started to crumble onto my head."

Sadness filled Elizabeth as she said, "Oh, Maggie, I'm so sorry. You need to get some new clothes. Maybe Manuella—"

"I already asked her. She said Luis needs to go into town later today. I'll go with him and do some shopping. I have some money I managed to take with me when I fled. I'll be able to buy a few articles of clothing."

Maggie shut the water off. "Get in. I'll be back in a few minutes with some fresh clothes."

Elizabeth watched her go, grateful for Maggie. So many people had come into her life to make it better for her. Baltimore and her brother's bullying was a distant memory. Mrs. Stockton proved to be a paradox, but a benevolent one. The Candelarias were so open and accepting. Quan Luck was to realize his dream in a few months. It was all turning out to be so wonderful.

She left her clothes in a heap on the floor beside her. As she sank down into the water, one word came to mind—glorious.

When Maggie slipped back into the room with Elizabeth's clothing in her arms, Elizabeth noticed her fleeting look of appreciation. Steam rose from the surface of the clear water to match the expression she saw in Maggie's eyes.

Elizabeth's body responded.

Maggie set her clothes on a small stool. "I—I," she took a deep breath and started again. "Manuella says we can use those towels hanging on the rack. She said to leave the clothes you had on in here and she'll clean them for you." Maggie fiddled with an invisible string on her dress. "I told her we could take care of ourselves, but she insists it isn't a problem. She will do—"

"Maggie," Elizabeth called. "Why are you so nervous?" She picked up a bar of soap and began washing her arm. "

"I—I don't know."

Elizabeth suspected she did know.

"Hmm. This feels wonderful. You should join me." She held Maggie's gaze as she rubbed her shoulder and her neck with the creamy bar of sweet-smelling soap.

Maggie stared. Elizabeth watched her breathing become ragged.

"Wouldn't you like to come in? The water is wonderful." She switched the soap to her other hand and began stroking it across her chest and down her other arm, knowing full well what would happen if Maggie joined her.

"I—I—you're torturing me, Elizabeth. I can't stay and watch you. When you're finished with your bath, come into the bedroom, I'll tuck you in for a nap."

Her rejection stung. "I don't need another nap, Maggie. I'm fine. Please, come and join me." She held out her hand.

Elizabeth almost didn't hear Maggie's strained whisper. "We can't."

THE DISCUSSION CONTINUED after Elizabeth's bath. After more coaxing, Maggie agreed to lay beside her. She smelled so fresh and clean, it was hard to resist nuzzling against her shoulder. Elizabeth had the blankets tucked under her chin. She asked what Maggie and Quan Luck had been doing while she slept.

As Maggie lay on top of the bedding, she spoke softly. "Quan Luck is turning into a farmer, it seems. He's been out with Luis every day. If this keeps up, I'm afraid he might abandon his dream to become a lawyer and stay here with the Candelarias."

"I doubt he'll give it up. His passion for helping his people is too strong. He'll go to Stanford, don't worry," Elizabeth said.

"I hope you're right. It's taken an earthquake to get him there. I'd hate to see him sacrifice his chance at becoming a lawyer for a few cows."

"I think there are more than a few cows around here. It looks like there might be more than a hundred."

"I know." Maggie put her hands behind her head on the pillow and stared up at the ceiling. "Luis told me they have one hundred and twenty-seven of them, including four new calves, and they are expecting three more to be born soon. Quan Luck is so excited about the prospect of watching a calf being born," Maggie said.

"Luis must have people helping him. He can't manage all this by himself."

"Oh, no. He told me he has four other men to help him. They have a bunk house on the southern ridge. Luis and Manuella also have two sons who help Luis. One of them is married. Mrs. Stockton gave him a small plot of land to build his own house as a wedding present several years ago. Manuella said her other son is living in the bunkhouse with the other men while he builds a house close to his brother. She didn't say if he had married, but Mrs. Stockton gave him some land, too."

Elizabeth's voice sounded sleepy as she mused, "Mrs. Stockton is such an interesting woman. I didn't know she had another life outside of San Francisco. To think she owns this dairy and all this land. It's amazing."

"Manuella said she used to come here once a month before it became too difficult for her to travel. For a while, Luis went to San Francisco every few weeks to discuss the running of the dairy, but it would take a whole day away from the farm, so Mrs. Stockton had a telephone put in here and in her mansion. Now they discuss business at least once a week, she said."

"No wonder the Candelarias knew of so many of Mrs. Stockton's wishes for us when we arrived. I thought she sent them a telegram, but it would have been quite long."

"I asked Manuella about it. Mrs. Stockton did call and gave specific instructions. She told them all about your work and about my photography studio. Oh, and Manuella has asked me to take a family portrait. I'm going to do it one of these Sundays when the family is together. Luis told me there's a photography studio in San Mateo. I thought I might inquire about developing some photographs there. I've already taken a few of the farm and I'll have the portrait when I take it."

"That's nice...."

Maggie turned to Elizabeth, who opened one eye and said, "I'm not asleep. Tell me how you found out so much about the farm and about everything going on around here." She yawned.

Maggie knew it wouldn't be long before she fell asleep.

"You can learn a lot snapping peas with Manuella."

"Hmm...."

Maggie turned to her again. She waited. When Elizabeth said no more, she slid from the bed and left the room without making a sound.

As she walked down the hall, she took a deep breath glad Elizabeth hadn't brought up love-making. The sensitive spot between her legs throbbed. Maggie whispered into the hallway, "Stop it. She needs to rest."

Saying it didn't stop the ache. When she reached the great room, she sat on the couch and squeezed her legs together, willing her desire for Elizabeth to recede for a while longer.

April 27, 1906

LUIS POURED WINE into four glasses and set one in front of Elizabeth, Maggie and his wife. When he took his place at the head of the long oak table in the dining room, he raised his glass. "I would like to make a toast. Doctor Elizabeth, I'm glad to see you looking so well."

Elizabeth smiled, trying to hide her embarrassment at his attention.

He continued, "I pray you will continue your recovery. I don't want to see you or Maggie leave us — we love having both of you and Quan Luck here — but I hope you are back to your full strength soon." He raised his glass a little higher and said, "To your health." Maggie and Manuella joined him in raising their glasses and they each took a sip. Elizabeth lifted hers and joined them. When they placed their glasses back on the dining room table, Manuella passed a large bowl of golden-orange sweet potatoes to Maggie. She followed this with peas, rice speckled with red peppers and corn, and chicken in an aromatic green sauce. No one spoke for a while as they dug into the meal.

Luis piped up after a few mouthfuls, saying, "Manuella, you have outdone yourself again. This is the most marvelous meal you have ever cooked."

Manuella laughed and directed her comment to Maggie and Elizabeth. "He says the same thing at every meal. Each one is greater than the last. I don't know how to put up with his—how do you say?"

"Exaggerations?" Maggie offered.

"Yes." Manuella chuckled.

Elizabeth said, "At least he appreciates your hard work."

"Yes, he certainly does." Manuella looked at her husband through glistening eyes. "And I appreciate everything he does for me, too."

Luis blushed.

Elizabeth cleared her throat. As she scooped up another forkful of rice, she asked, "Where is Quan Luck this evening? Does anyone know?"

Luis said, "He went to the bunkhouse to eat with the men and play cards with them afterwards. He is becoming a good friend to them, so they invited him to join them. He's a good young man, a hard worker. For someone who has always lived in the city, he has done well during his time here."

Maggie said, "He enjoys spending time with you, Luis. He was thrilled when you let him drive the other day."

"Oh, he's been driving every day. Every day after lunch, I let him take the car to an empty pasture and he drives around with a big grin on his face. I love to see it. By the way, we invited him to go with us to my cousin's house on Sunday after church. He doesn't know it yet, but I thought I would let him drive on the road part of the way."

"Oh, goodness, he'll be thrilled."

Luis broke into a wide smile. "I know."

Elizabeth wore a frown when she asked, "The men at the bunkhouse won't corrupt him, will they Luis? Will there be drinking?"

"Oh, no. We do not allow it here. The last time someone drank more than a glass of wine, we threw him down the well. We haven't had any problems since."

Elizabeth choked on her wine.

Manuella gave her husband a stern look and said, "Don't pay attention to him. He's joking. About the well, I mean, not the drinking. Luis doesn't allow the men to drink. We know they do when they have a day off and go into town, but they never do it on the property. He is strict about it and they respect it."

"This is not my land. I am only the steward of it," Luis said. "If the men act in ways they shouldn't, they bring dishonor on Mrs. Stockton. I will not allow it. The men know this. They know if they want to work here—it is a good job to work for Mrs. Stockton—they must respect her and her property. Rule number one is no drinking. Although we do allow a little toast with wine every now and then."

Elizabeth marveled at his philosophy. Obviously, the men respected him. She hadn't interacted with them much, but what little she did, gave her the impression Luis and Manuella were exemplary in their eyes.

The conversation moved on to other topics. When they were done eating, Maggie stood up to help Manuella clear the table, but Manuella motioned for her to sit. Luis rose from his seat to help his wife. Before Manuella followed Luis into the kitchen, she said, "I made a special cake, *tres leches*, I think it might go well with your tea."

Maggie's eyes lit up. Elizabeth watched her and nodded to her host.

Manuella smiled. "You sit here and relax. We'll be back in a few minutes."

After they disappeared, Elizabeth closed the gap between her and Maggie by sliding down the length of their bench seat. When Maggie grasped Elizabeth's hand under the table, Elizabeth leaned in close and whispered, "If I don't kiss you soon, I'm going to explode."

Her remark surprised Maggie. Elizabeth had been getting stronger by the day, taking only a brief afternoon nap of late. Maggie squeezed her hand and laughed before letting go. "Be patient, my love. We're one dessert away from retiring to our room and, this time I might just let you get away with kissing me."

"At last," Elizabeth breathed.

Chapter Sixteen

April 29, 1906

TWO DAYS LATER, Quan Luck came into the great room as Elizabeth slipped a letter back into its envelope and rested it in her lap. He wore a light colored linen shirt, the sleeves rolled up to his elbows. His copper colored cheeks were highlighted with a flush, darkening them.

"Have you enjoyed being out with Luis?" Elizabeth asked.

"Oh, yes, Doctor Elizabeth. I have learned to milk the cows," his eyes opened wide as he said it. "They are such wonderful creatures. And Luis showed me how to drive the automobile. He took me to a flat pasture where he said the automobile would be safe with a new driver. He calls it his baby. He has even given it a name. He calls it Chiquita. He says a car is like a woman and needs to be treated well. Apparently, Chiquita is a woman's name. He also told me he thought I might be ready to drive on the road soon." He threw his hands out as if to embrace the entire room. "Skycroft is an amazing place."

Elizabeth laughed at his eagerness. She knew he would be ecstatic when Luis allowed him to drive later. She almost wished she could be there to see his face, but she would not. The Candelarias invited her and Maggie to accompany them, but Maggie turned them down, saying Elizabeth couldn't tolerate a whole day out. The two of them would stay home to allow Elizabeth the rest as she needed. Elizabeth suspected she was motivated more by the thought of the house being empty for hours before the group returned. Elizabeth looked forward to it, too. Now, with the letter, she had wonderful news for Maggie to add to their day together.

When Maggie entered the room, Quan Luck repeated the whole narrative again. His enthusiasm didn't wane during the second telling, nor did he leave out a single detail.

Maggie reacted the same way Elizabeth had, with a hearty laugh, but she added a hug. When she pulled away, Quan Luck looked into her eyes with tears in his own. He smiled at her, looking fragile, then turned and left the room.

"You disarm him with your warmth and tenderness, you know."

Maggie shrugged. "He's become like a little brother to me. I can't help it. When I think about his family, lost to the earthquake, and more distant relatives all moved to Oakland, I want to wrap my arms around him and comfort him."

Elizabeth held her hand out to Maggie. She grasped it tightly.

Elizabeth whispered, "And I love you for it."

When Quan Luck returned, more composed, he told them, "The Candelarias are leaving for church now. Miss Manuella says she has left you some lunch in the kitchen. They won't be back until later this evening. They said they told you they are going to visit Mr. Luis's cousin in Mayfield. I will go with them if it's all right with you. They said you were invited, but you will stay because Doctor Elizabeth needs to rest. They understand."

Maggie said, "I don't think Elizabeth is up to an all-day outing yet, but thank them for us, again. We'll stay here. You enjoy your outing with them. Wait. Are you going to church with them?"

"I told them I would not. I am Buddhist. Mr. Luis said he knew where there was a Joss temple right down the street from their church. He will show me. I'll go there to honor my father and my uncle and all of my ancestors. Then I will go to visit his cousin afterwards."

"I'm glad you'll be able to go to the temple. Afterwards, go and have a good time with the Candelaria family. I'm sure they are a lot of fun. You should have a great time."

He agreed and left the room to join Luis and Manuella. When he was gone, Elizabeth turned to Maggie and said, "And while they're gone, whatever shall we do with ourselves?" She batted her eyes.

Maggie swatted her arm. "Elizabeth Kellogg, I know what's going through your head right now and I cannot believe it. You still need to rest. Wipe those thoughts from your mind."

Elizabeth pulled her in and kissed her soundly. Maggie pushed away, concerned the others hadn't left yet, but they heard voices outside, Luis, then Manuella, and finally Quan Luck. A few minutes later, they heard the car start and listened to the rumbling ebb as they moved down the hard-packed earth road, away from the property.

Maggie pulled Elizabeth up from the chair and wrapped her arms around her. Elizabeth kissed her. Maggie's lips parted and Elizabeth entered. Their breathing roughened. When Elizabeth broke the kiss, she said, "Let's go to bed."

Maggie stepped back. "No," she said. "No bed. You aren't to exert yourself. I will allow kissing. Nothing else."

"Maggie, I assure you I will not exert myself. It won't be a problem."

Maggie stood her ground with a firm, "No."

Elizabeth stared her down. "Maggie, I'm a doctor. I know what I can and cannot do and right now, I also know what I want to do — with you. We may not get this chance again. Please, Maggie. I've missed you."

Maggie stepped closer. "I've missed you, too. You don't know how much I've missed you, but no. No more than kissing on the couch." She pointed.

Elizabeth sighed. She wondered how long it would take to coax her from her resolve?

She fell to the thick cushions and pulled Maggie down with her. As she covered Maggie's mouth with another passionate kiss, she felt her lips melt into hers.

She smiled into the kiss. Maybe it wouldn't take as long as she thought.

MAGGIE LAY ON top of the covers of their bed, her skin burning, her body aching for Elizabeth. Elizabeth had led her to their room after they kissed for a long time. When Maggie reached out and touched Elizabeth's breast, she knew it was time to leave the great room. Maggie's clothes lay strewn across the floor. Elizabeth lay disrobed to her underwear.

When Maggie lifted her head off the pillow and kissed Elizabeth on the neck, she moaned. The sound thrust Maggie into a hopeless spiral of desire. *Where is my resolve? This wasn't supposed to happen. I have to get up.*

Elizabeth's mouth moved to her nipple and the fight went out of her.

"Elizabeth." It was all she could manage.

Elizabeth looked up, removing her mouth from the object of her desire, leaving Maggie sorry she had distracted her. Maggie lifted her chest. A smile appeared across Elizabeth's face. When she dove back down and took Maggie's nipple again, her moan thrust Elizabeth's passion to new heights.

As she worked her way down Maggie's body with her kisses, Maggie moaned and arched into her mouth. When Elizabeth stroked her, Maggie exploded as rapturous waves ripped through her.

Still panting, she wrestled Elizabeth onto her back and tore at her remaining clothes. When they joined the rest of the garments on the floor, Maggie positioned herself over Elizabeth, straddling her thigh, holding herself with her arms on each side of Elizabeth's shoulders.

Elizabeth reached up and cupped Maggie's breasts. She

leaned in and moaned again. When Elizabeth ran her hands down her sides and continued moving toward her center, Maggie stopped her.

She rolled over to her side and placed a leg over Elizabeth's body. "It's close to your nap time, my love."

Elizabeth looked at her through half-closed eyelids. "I'm not tired."

"Why are your eyes half closed, then?"

"Because...I want you. I...need you. Please..."

The word broke through the wall of concern inside Maggie. She laid her body against Elizabeth's and rocked. Elizabeth's moan sent a bolt of desire through Maggie. She had to have Elizabeth. She gave her a firm kiss and moved along her body with lips and fingers until she touched her in her most intimate place and felt like Elizabeth shattered apart. Finally, she kissed the pieces back into wholeness, as Elizabeth embraced her, humming her pleasure in Maggie's ear.

THEY SLEPT FOR a while, then Maggie drew a bath for Elizabeth. When Elizabeth insisted Maggie join her, she surprised her by doing so.

As Maggie knelt in the waist-high water facing Elizabeth, she rubbed soap over her arms and shoulders and said, "I hope our...activity wasn't too much for you. I couldn't live with myself if you're fatigued now."

Elizabeth lifted her hand out of the water and placed a wet finger against Maggie's lips. "Shh. I'm fine. As a matter of fact, I couldn't be better. I feel...wonderful."

Maggie grinned as she rubbed the bar over Elizabeth's chest.

Elizabeth caught her hand and said, "As much as I'd like nothing better than to continue our earlier...activity, I think we should make every effort to be dressed and sitting in the great room, looking as if we've had a quiet, uneventful afternoon of reading and resting, don't you?"

Maggie pouted.

With one sultry look, Elizabeth felt a thrill run down her spine and she almost abandoned her concern about the other inhabitants of Skycroft returning. Fortunately, Maggie came to her senses.

The pout turned to a look of comprehension. "You're right. We need to be presentable when the Candelarias return." She bent toward Elizabeth and kissed her on the nose.

Elizabeth's sigh rang out through the small, tiled room.

A short time later, she sat re-reading the letter. When Maggie entered the room, she said, "I didn't know you received a letter. Is it from Mrs. Stockton?"

"No. It's from someone I knew back in Baltimore. She lives in Boston now."

"Oh?"

Elizabeth plunged on, noting Maggie's look of concern. "Her name is Edna Remington. She's a Pinkerton agent."

This time, Maggie's "oh" came out more as a squeak.

"Sit down, Maggie, I want to share it with you."

Maggie plopped into the chair next to Elizabeth.

"I wrote to her after we first spoke about your troubles with Harry Ryan. Between the time it took for her to complete her investigation and the complication of the letter finding its way to me here, it's taken a while to receive her answer."

Elizabeth ached for Maggie. Her face looked so strained. Best to get the information to her as fast as possible.

"The first piece of information you need to know is Harry Ryan was alive when you left him. You didn't kill him."

Maggie's shoulders relaxed. Some of the tension left her face.

"According to Edna's investigation, he recovered from what he reported to a doctor as an accidental fall in which he struck his head. After his recovery, he went on to get himself in trouble with the law for various offenses over the next several years. Along the way, he managed to talk a young woman into marrying him. It sounds like it was an unhappy marriage. His temper came through as it did with you. The neighbors reported he and his wife fought all the time and they told them he often beat her.

"Which brings us to the second thing you need to know: he'll never bother you again. You see, he is 'quite dead,' as Edna puts it. Someone else killed him, not you."

Maggie's eyes widened. "Oh, dear."

"There was some suspicion his wife may have done it, but there was never enough evidence to bring her to trial. You understand what this means, don't you, Maggie?"

"I'm free of him?"

"Yes, you are free of him."

Maggie repeated it several times as if to allow the reality of it to sink in. Her eyes glistened as she said, "I don't have to think about him anymore. I'm free of him."

Maggie's relief was palpable. She got up and went to Elizabeth's side, pulling her to her chest.

"This is the best day of my life. I found out the millstone hanging around my neck is gone—and I got to spend some...exceptional time with you. Thank you, Elizabeth."

Elizabeth smiled. "You're welcome."

They passed the rest of the afternoon and into the early evening exchanging steamy glances every now and then. Each time she made eye contact with Maggie, Elizabeth had to tamp down the desire bubbling up inside.

When the car drove up and stopped in front of the house, doors slammed, voices rang out, and Manuella's contagious laughter filled the air. Then, Quan Luck burst through the front door, face flushed, excitement filling his voice. "I've had the most exciting day," he said. "I got to drive Chiquita on a real road."

Elizabeth and Maggie gazed into each other's dancing eyes, reveling in their own afterglow.

"Wonderful," Elizabeth said, never taking her eyes off Maggie's.

SOON AFTER THE Candelarias entered the great room, another group of people came in behind them. Manuella introduced her eldest son, Carlos, who looked like a younger version of Luis, with a stocky build and barrel chest. Diego, Carlos's younger brother, favored Manuella's looks with finer features and slimmer build. Their dark hair glistened in the light of the great room as they bowed, in turn.

Carlos introduced his wife, Bianca. Diego introduced his friend, Rico. Manuella pulled Rico toward her and told them, "Although I did not give birth to him, he is like my third son." Rico beamed.

Manuella cleared her voice and said, "Maggie has graciously offered to take a portrait of our family. If you don't mind, Maggie, we would like to take you up on this. We all have our Sunday clothes on, so this is an ideal opportunity."

"Yes, of course. Let me get my camera. You understand it won't be as good as if I had my studio camera." Tears formed in her eyes as she recalled the equipment she lost. She pushed her sadness away and continued, "But it will be a beautiful portrait just the same."

She busied herself arranging the room and everyone in it. Elizabeth stood beside her as she focused the camera. Quan Luck looked on from his perch on a chair large enough to look as if it could swallow him up.

When she finished up the portrait of the entire family, Carlos asked if she would take one of Bianca and him. As Maggie set up the camera for another shot, Rico came and leaned over her shoulder, asking her questions, taking an interest in what she was doing. He placed his hand on her shoulder and laughed at something she said as she explained everything.

Elizabeth leaned against the stone fireplace on the other side of the room. She stared at Rico with tight lips and arms crossed over her chest. Her cheeks colored pink when Maggie laughed and leaned in toward Rico as he spoke.

When Maggie glanced over at her, she wondered why she stood apart from everyone, looking flushed. If she felt fatigued, Maggie should make her sit down. Perhaps all the excitement, both earlier today and now with so many people around, was too much for her and it was getting late. However, when Rico asked her another question, she turned away to answer him. When she turned back, Elizabeth had moved to a chair.

After taking several more images, she released her charges. To her surprise, Luis opened a large cupboard and pulled out two guitars, handing one to Diego. Carlos brought a base out of a closet. He handed his wife a tambourine. They began playing a vibrant tune. Manuella disappeared, returning with goblets and several bottles of wine on a tray. Perhaps they would only have one glass, but these glasses were huge.

When Manuella set her tray down, she joined the musicians, opened her mouth, and sang like a nightingale. Maggie couldn't understand the words, but it didn't matter. The beauty of her voice and the inflections in her phrasing conveyed a sultry love song. It made Maggie think of her afternoon with Elizabeth.

The music ended. An emotional silence filled the room. After a few seconds, Maggie clapped once, twice. Elizabeth joined her, picking up the tempo. So did Quan Luck and Rico.

Maggie said, "What a lovely song, Manuella. You have a beautiful voice. I'd love to know the meaning of the words. Maybe you could translate them for me sometime."

Manuella blushed and said, "Tomorrow, while we shell the peas for dinner. It's better if your hands are busy at something mundane when you hear the words."

Everyone laughed. The musicians picked up their instruments again. Manuella passed out the filled wine glasses. Maggie raised an eyebrow when Elizabeth downed hers in three gulps, but said nothing.

The party went on until well past dark. When they said goodbye to the younger Candelarias and Rico, Elizabeth said goodnight and left the room. Maggie followed her. Quan Luck and the Candelarias looked as if they'd be up for a while.

WHEN MAGGIE TURNED from closing their bedroom door, Elizabeth backed her into it. Elizabeth's fierce growl and the brutality with which she claimed her lips surprised her. When she forced her tongue into Maggie's mouth, the power of her action made her lightheaded.

At first, Maggie's breath quickened with excitement, but when Elizabeth's actions turned even more aggressive, Maggie's eyes flew open full of questions and Elizabeth saw something else—fear. Maggie's fright slammed into Elizabeth, thrusting her backward into the center of the room.

"What are you doing?" Maggie snarled. "I've never experienced you like this. It feels...wrong."

The power Elizabeth felt earlier deflated. "I—I'm so sorry, Maggie, I don't know what came over me. Please. I—I don't know what happened."

Maggie stepped toward her.

Elizabeth staggered back. How could she have treated Maggie this way? She knew the answer full well—Rico.

"Elizabeth, talk to me. What's going on?"

"It was Rico. When he came to you, fawning over you, getting too close, talking, laughing, I—I couldn't stand it. He—he wanted you, I could tell. I've never felt such rage, such jealousy. I don't know what came over me."

Maggie stared at Elizabeth. A soft rumble began in her chest. The reverberation turned to laughter, the laughter to an uproar.

Elizabeth shrank back and stumbled to the bed, sagging onto the mattress. How could Maggie humiliate her this way? Couldn't she see how distraught she was? Why was she laughing at her?

Maggie regained her composure and sat down next to Elizabeth. When she reached out for Elizabeth's hand, she shrank away.

"Elizabeth."

Elizabeth looked at her through tear-filled eyes. "How could you laugh at me like that when I'm so distraught? Do you think I'm a fool for feeling the way I do about you? About my fear of losing you to some lothario like Rico?"

"Elizabeth."

"When he put his hands on you, I wanted to kill him. Me, a doctor, sworn to uphold the sanctity of life. Now, to have you laugh at me, at my feelings for you, it's devastating."

Maggie's voice softened. "Elizabeth, listen to me."

Elizabeth looked into Maggie's eyes. Did she see concern? Was there a chance she still cared?

"First of all, I think Rico was more interested in the camera than he was of me. Second, I can't say whether he's a lothario or not, but there's one thing of which I'm certain. He only has eyes for Diego."

Elizabeth blinked several times as she tried to process the

information. "Diego?"

"Yes. Diego. Didn't you see how he looked at him with the eyes of a puppy worshipping his master? Diego has Rico's heart. Believe me, Rico has no interest in me, except, perhaps, as entertainment with my camera. He's certainly no threat to you — to us.

"And I wasn't laughing at you. I was laughing at the absurdity of Rico having an interest in me. All the while Diego played his guitar, Rico's eyes were fixed on him. I had his full measure before he came over and started talking to me about the camera."

Elizabeth still struggled to understand the information Maggie gave her, wondering if it could be true. All the anger she felt, visions of tearing Rico's arm off when he touched Maggie's shoulder. For nothing? Now she felt quite the fool. She plunged her face into her hands and wept. Between sobs, she offered her apology over and over to Maggie.

When she calmed down, Maggie got up and knelt in front of her. "Elizabeth, only one person has my heart — you. You've had it since the day you walked into my shop trying to get away from Michael-the-Maul. You will always have it. No one can take me from you, I promise."

She dropped her hands and another tear cascaded over Elizabeth's eyelid and ran down her cheek.

Maggie reached up and brushed it away with her thumb. "I'll never leave you, Elizabeth."

Elizabeth pulled her into an embrace. "And I never want you to leave. I love you, Maggie. I want us to be together for the rest of our lives. Please forgive me."

Maggie looked into Elizabeth's eyes. "There's nothing to forgive. But if you need it, then, yes, I do forgive you."

Elizabeth kissed her again. This time, Maggie settled into Elizabeth's soft lips and warm embrace willingly. This time, Maggie growled into Elizabeth's mouth and pulled her closer.

May 7, 1906

ELIZABETH AND MAGGIE climbed up into the rear seat of the shiny burgundy Buick. Quan Luck took the driver's seat. Luis stood outside the driver's side of the car.

"All you need to do is take it slow and you'll be fine. Don't forget, you must keep your eyes everywhere when you get beyond the countryside. Drivers in town are *loco*. You understand?"

"Yes, sir. *Loco.* Crazy. I will keep my eyes everywhere." Quan Luck started the engine.

Maggie looked at Elizabeth wide-eyed. Elizabeth patted her hand. "We'll be fine. Quan Luck is the least *loco* person we know."

"But he's never driven alone before."

"He's not alone. We're here."

"But we know nothing about automobiles. We haven't even been properly introduced to her—Chiquita, I mean."

Elizabeth laughed and leaned forward. She shouted over the engine's roar, "We're ready when you are, Quan Luck."

He started off slowly. Luis waved and smiled as they pulled away. By the time they were a few hundred yards from the house, Quan Luck's confidence soared and the vehicle hummed along at a more normal speed.

Maggie leaned in toward Elizabeth's ear and said, "Thank you for being willing to do this."

Elizabeth smiled. "It's what we do for friends, isn't it? Besides, I'm intrigued with Chiquita. I wonder whether I should learn to drive and get an automobile, myself."

Maggie gave her a wide-eyed look. "Can we name her Artemis?"

Elizabeth laughed. "We can name her anything you wish."

When they reached San Mateo, Quan Luck slowed again as traffic increased. He parked Chiquita with care in front of the photography shop and struck out to explore. Two Sundays prior, he noticed a Chinese shop selling sweet delicacies and he promised Manuella he would bring her some to try.

Maggie and Elizabeth entered the shop where Luis had dropped off the film to be processed a few days earlier. Maggie was excited to see the images of the earthquake aftermath she took during their time at Doctor Gibbons's house. Also on the film were some photographs she'd taken of Skycroft. She hoped to have captured the beauty and peacefulness of the place. Finally, she wanted to examine the portraits of the Candelarias and one she took of Elizabeth as she sat reading in front of the big stone fireplace in the great room.

They entered the shop and found a middle-aged man behind the counter.

"May I help you, miss?"

"Yes, I'm here to pick up some photographs Luis Candelaria left for developing. Are they ready?"

He reached under the counter and pulled out a stack tied with white string. "Right here," he said. "You got some terrific pictures of what happened in the city and your portraits of the

Candelarias are excellent, too. Are you looking for a job?"

Maggie chuckled. "No, I'm afraid not. I'll be returning to San Francisco soon."

"Luis told me you had a studio there. I'm sorry about your loss of equipment. Are you sure you don't want a job? You do fine work."

As he spoke, she untied the photographs and shuffled through them. Some looked a little underdeveloped, but they were adequate. She'd tell the Candelarias when she got her studio back up and running, she'd visit them and take the portraits again, so she could develop them herself. Then, they'd have something of better quality. The last photograph in the stack was the one of Elizabeth.

The afternoon sunlight streamed through the large windows opposite her, illuminating her face as she read. She looked beautiful. Maggie smiled and touched the photograph with a delicate finger. Elizabeth stepped toward her and examined the print. She gazed into Maggie's eyes.

"It's a beautiful photograph," Elizabeth whispered.

The man behind the counter cleared his throat. "Will there be anything else, ladies?"

Maggie blinked to clear the tears from her eyes and said, "No, nothing else. How much do I owe you?"

"Nothing. Mr. Candelaria already paid."

Maggie pursed her lips. She'd have to speak to Luis about reimbursing him. She wanted the portraits to be a thank you for the way they welcomed them and took care of them during their stay.

Elizabeth leaned in and asked, "Ready to go? Quan Luck's already outside."

Maggie nodded and they left the shop. When they got in the automobile, Maggie tied up the bundle of pictures again, leaving the one of Elizabeth on top so she could look at it again on the way back to Skycroft.

May 16, 1906

ELIZABETH SPOKE INTO the telephone receiver. "Yes, Mrs. Stockton, I'm feeling quite well. Coming to Skycroft was perfect. The Candelarias took excellent care of us. Thank you for allowing us to stay here."

She listened to Mrs. Stockton on the other end of the line.

"Yes, I'm looking forward to coming back to San Francisco

and getting back to work. I'll make sure Maggie is prepared to leave, too. We won't go anywhere until she's ready, I assure you. Quan Luck has decided to stay with the Candelarias until he begins his term at Stanford. I hope it's all right. Luis said he's happy to have him. He's been a great help."

She listened again.

"I'll let you know when we're leaving. It would be wonderful if Kingsley could pick us up at the station."

When she placed the phone back on its hook, she turned to Maggie and said, "Mrs. Stockton says they're already rebuilding. She's sent two women from Violet's mission over to the house to clean already. She's been helping them by giving them employment. She said she doesn't want us to have to overexert ourselves when we come back. As you probably heard, she'll have Kingsley waiting for us when we tell her our arrival date."

Maggie smiled at her. "You're excited, aren't you?"

"I have to say I am."

"So Violet's all right? Her building survived the fire?"

"She's fine, but her building burned. The Friends have already secured her another one further down Ninth Street, so the Mission is running again, handing out clothes and food for those who need it. People are still living in the parks. Mrs. Stockton has assured me our house is standing as straight and tall as ever, even amid the aftershocks they've experienced, so are the ones belonging to our neighbors on both sides."

"We're so lucky to have a home to go to," Maggie said.

"Yes, *our* home, Maggie. I've been thinking. I seldom use the little kitchen on the first floor and I can store supplies in the cupboards in my office, so I don't need the storeroom either. We could turn it into a darkroom and supply room for you. We might even be able to figure out a way for you to use the basement as a studio."

"I don't know, Elizabeth. What will Mrs. Stockton think about me taking over part of her house?"

"Oh, it's not her house any more. At least it won't be when we get back to the city and I sign the paperwork."

"What do you mean?"

"We came to an agreement. I'm buying the house from her. I decided I didn't want those ladies of hers thinking they could tell me what to do and who I could have in my house with me. The only way I can control it is to buy the house. I know Mrs. Stockton would never impose such dictates, but you never know if some newcomer might be a problem."

Maggie took her hands. "You did it for me, didn't you?"

Elizabeth grinned. "For both of us."

Maggie blinked back her tears. "I love you, you know."

"No one has ever made me feel the way you do, Maggie, no one. I love you, too. So what do you say? Shall we go home?"

"I think we should, doctor."

About the Author

Anna Furtado is a New England transplant living in the San Francisco Bay area. She's always loved to write, and when she discovered lesbian literature back in the days of Naiad press, she was smitten and knew exactly where her writing focus should be. She published her first book while working full time. Two more books in the series followed. After a hiatus and retirement, she's embraced her writing with gusto, telling the stories the characters in her head relate. Her books have been finalists for literary awards and Anna has been a member and supporter of the Golden Crown Literary Society since its inception. She reviews lesbian fiction for Lambda Literary Review and on her Facebook page. When not writing, Anna and her wife like to travel, exploring beautiful country-sides and historical places (along with the occasional amusement park and entertainment venue).

OTHER YELLOW ROSE PUBLICATIONS

Brenda Adcock	Soiled Dove	978-1-935053-35-4
Brenda Adcock	The Sea Hawk	978-1-935053-10-1
Brenda Adcock	The Other Mrs. Champion	978-1-935053-46-0
Brenda Adcock	Picking Up the Pieces	978-1-61929-120-1
Brenda Adcock	The Game of Denial	978-1-61929-130-0
Brenda Adcock	In the Midnight Hour	978-1-61929-188-1
Brenda Adcock	Untouchable	978-1-61929-210-9
Brenda Adcock	The Heart of the Mountain	978-1-61929-330-4
Janet Albert	Twenty-four Days	978-1-935053-16-3
Janet Albert	A Table for Two	978-1-935053-27-9
Janet Albert	Casa Parisi	978-1-61929-016-7
Georgia Beers	Thy Neighbor's Wife	1-932300-15-5
Georgia Beers	Turning the Page	978-1-932300-71-0
Lynnette Beers	Just Beyond the Shining River	978-1-61929-352-6
Carrie Carr	Destiny's Bridge	1-932300-11-2
Carrie Carr	Faith's Crossing	1-932300-12-0
Carrie Carr	Hope's Path	1-932300-40-6
Carrie Carr	Love's Journey	978-1-932300-65-9
Carrie Carr	Strength of the Heart	978-1-932300-81-9
Carrie Carr	The Way Things Should Be	978-1-932300-39-0
Carrie Carr	To Hold Forever	978-1-932300-21-5
Carrie Carr	Trust Our Tomorrows	978-1-61929-011-2
Carrie Carr	Piperton	978-1-935053-20-0
Carrie Carr	Something to Be Thankful For	1-932300-04-X
Carrie Carr	Diving Into the Turn	978-1-932300-54-3
Carrie Carr	Heart's Resolve	978-1-61929-051-8
Carrie Carr	Beyond Always	978-1-61929-160-7
Sharon G. Clark	A Majestic Affair	978-1-61929-177-5
Tonie Chacon	Struck! A Titanic Love Story	978-1-61929-226-0
Cooper and Novan	Madam President	978-1-61929-316-8
Cooper and Novan	First Lady	978-1-61929-318-2
Sky Croft	Amazonia	978-1-61929-067-9
Sky Croft	Amazonia: An Impossible Choice	978-1-61929-179-9
Sky Croft	Mountain Rescue: The Ascent	978-1-61929-099-0
Sky Croft	Mountain Rescue: On the Edge	978-1-61929-205-5
Cronin and Foster	Blue Collar Lesbian Erotica	978-1-935053-01-9
Cronin and Foster	Women in Uniform	978-1-935053-31-6
Cronin and Foster	Women in Sports	978-1-61929-278-9
Pat Cronin	Souls' Rescue	978-1-935053-30-9
Jane DiLucchio	A Change of Heart	978-1-61929-324-3
A. L. Duncan	The Gardener of Aria Manor	978-1-61929-159-1
A.L. Duncan	Secrets of Angels	978-1-61929-227-7
Verda Foster	The Gift	978-1-61929-029-7
Verda Foster	The Chosen	978-1-61929-027-3
Verda Foster	These Dreams	978-1-61929-025-9
Anna Furtado	The Heart's Desire	978-1-935053-81-1

Author	Title	ISBN
Anna Furtado	The Heart's Strength	978-1-935053-82-8
Anna Furtado	The Heart's Longing	978-1-935053-83-5
Anna Furtado	Tremble and Burn	978-1-61929-354-0
Pauline George	Jess	978-1-61929-139-3
Pauline George	199 Steps To Love	978-1-61929-213-0
Pauline George	The Actress and the Scrapyard Girl	978-1-61929-336-6
Melissa Good	Eye of the Storm	1-932300-13-9
Melissa Good	Hurricane Watch	978-1-935053-00-2
Melissa Good	Moving Target	978-1-61929-150-8
Melissa Good	Red Sky At Morning	978-1-932300-80-2
Melissa Good	Storm Surge: Book One	978-1-935053-28-6
Melissa Good	Storm Surge: Book Two	978-1-935053-39-2
Melissa Good	Stormy Waters	978-1-61929-082-2
Melissa Good	Thicker Than Water	1-932300-24-4
Melissa Good	Terrors of the High Seas	1-932300-45-7
Melissa Good	Tropical Storm	978-1-932300-60-4
Melissa Good	Tropical Convergence	978-1-935053-18-7
Melissa Good	Winds of Change Book One	978-1-61929-194-2
Melissa Good	Winds of Change Book Two	978-1-61929-232-1
Melissa Good	Southern Stars	978-1-61929-348-9
Regina A. Hanel	Love Another Day	978-1-61929-033-4
Regina A. Hanel	WhiteDragon	978-1-61929-143-0
Regina A. Hanel	A Deeper Blue	978-1-61929-258-1
Jeanine Hoffman	Lights & Sirens	978-1-61929-115-7
Jeanine Hoffman	Strength in Numbers	978-1-61929-109-6
Jeanine Hoffman	Back Swing	978-1-61929-137-9
Jennifer Jackson	It's Elementary	978-1-61929-085-3
Jennifer Jackson	It's Elementary, Too	978-1-61929-217-8
Jennifer Jackson	Memory Hunters	978-1-61929-294-9
K. E. Lane	And, Playing the Role of Herself	978-1-932300-72-7
Kate McLachlan	Christmas Crush	978-1-61929-195-9
Lynne Norris	One Promise	978-1-932300-92-5
Lynne Norris	Sanctuary	978-1-61929-248-2
Lynne Norris	Second Chances (E)	978-1-61929-172-0
Lynne Norris	The Light of Day	978-1-61929-338-0
Paula Offutt	Butch Girls Can Fix Anything	978-1-932300-74-1
Surtees and Dunne	True Colours	978-1-61929-021-1
Surtees and Dunne	Many Roads to Travel	978-1-61929-022-8
Patty Schramm	Finding Gracie's Glory	978-1-61929-238-3

Be sure to check out our other imprints,
Blue Beacon Books, Mystic Books, Quest Books,
Silver Dragon Books, Troubadour Books, and Young Adult Books.

VISIT US ONLINE AT
www.regalcrest.biz

At the Regal Crest Website You'll Find

- The latest news about forthcoming titles and new releases

- Our complete backlist of romance, mystery, thriller and adventure titles

- Information about your favorite authors

- Media tearsheets to print and take with you when you shop

- Which books are also available as eBooks.

Regal Crest print titles are available from all progressive booksellers including numerous sources online. Our distributors are Bella Distribution and Ingram.